VIOLATED

by Barbara Ker-Mann

Other titles by Barbara Ker-Mann

Yes To Success 1995

Death of a Sparrow 1991 Hazard Press/Leafgreen

POETRY

The Russian Doll 1981

Your Snow Falls in Summer 1986

VIOLATED

by Barbara Ker-Mann

HORIZON PRESS

© Barbara Ker-Mann 2002

ISBN 0 9582126 8 6

This book is copyright under the Berne Convention. All rights reserved, no reproduction without permission.

Cover artwork, design and layout by Unicorn Design Studio Ltd

Printed by Hutcheson, Bowman & Stewart, Wellington

This book is sold subject to the condition that it shall not, by way of trade or otherwise, be lent, resold, hired out, or otherwise circulated without the publisher's prior consent in any form of binding or cover other than that in which it is published.

This is a work of fiction. Names, characters, places and incidents are either the product of the author's imagination or use fictitiously. Any resemblance to actual events, organisations or persons is entirely coincidental and beyond the intent of the author or publisher.

Published by
Horizon Press
PO Box 5520
Lambton Quay
Wellington
New Zealand
Phone: 04 479 7337
Fax: 04 479 8589 or 04 233 8204
Email: chris.mundy@horizonpress.co.nz

The inks used for the printing of this book are made from vegetable oils and natural resins, are biodegradable and do not use polycyclic aromatics or volatile organic compounds. The paper is a mixture of chlorine free pulp and pre-consumer and post-consumer waste.

Dedication

Violated is dedicated to Barbara Ker-Mann's family: her late husband John Ker; their four adult children Alastair, Christine, Dorothy, and James; their partners; and her six grandchildren, with much love.

Thanks

I am grateful to Allan Hubbard and his wife, Jean, of Timaru, who have sponsored this publication. It has been good, too, to have had the advice of Alastair and Christiane Ker on matters of language.

Julian Bateson and Horizon Press have given of their time and expertise to bring the book to fruition, and I am indebted to them for their support.

The Author

Barbara Ker-Mann is a New Zealander. Her writing reflects a passion for family, music-education and ideas. She has been a teacher of English, art, and music and studied violin and music-education at UWO, London, Canada, while doing her Master's Degree from Auckland University, New Zealand.

Her thesis, *The Suzuki Violin Method*, was researched at the Talent Education Institute, Matsumoto, Japan, in 1983-84 and was supported by an International Fellowship from the American Association of University Women.

While living in Japan Barbara studied traditional Japanese art and *chigirie* and practises these arts.

Barabara now resides at Paraparaumu on the Kapiti Coast, north of Wellington, New Zealand.

PRELUDE

Prelude

Soft lighting bathed the performer, enough for just him to be the focus of the audience. The red cummerbund at his waist, and the visible tip of one wing of a red bow tie beneath his violin, relieved the black shirt and trousers and black shoes. He was small, dwarfed by the wide stage, yet looked 'right' standing there in the hug of the grand piano. The violin could be a part of him, but his bow was crossing the strings at such a pace that one felt it might fall over itself, get entangled and fly away on the notes of Bach's E Major Prelude.

The music escaped his instrument so fluidly it could have been playing itself, or coming from heaven – a gift to end the recital and celebration of Jiro Fujiwara's completion of repertoire eight of the violin course at the Fujiwara Institute in Nagoya.

The audience that filled the tiered recital hall of the institute was enthralled. It was not just that Jiro, son of Kentaro and Yuki Fujiwara was a mere eight years old, but that he was playing with insight and skill way beyond his years. Another Paganini! Yehudi Menuhin! Isaac Perlman! He must be the greatest Japanese child violinist ever. The recital was meant to be ended by the Bach, but when the piece stopped, and Jiro bowed with a flourish, the audience cried for more. '*Motto. Motto.*' The television crew at work in the recording bay prepared to go on filming.

Kentaro was proud of Jiro, but he knew that his twin brother Ichiro, his accompanist for half of the recital, was equally deserving of praise. He sent him on from the side room saying '*The Flight of the Bumble Bee* – do it again.'

Ichiro strode on to the stage, whispered to Jiro, and took his place at the piano. He wiped his hands on his trousers and looked at his twin, waiting for the sign. A tiny smile tilted the corners of Jiro's lips – the smiley face sign that was their secret code – and he lifted his bow. Zing, zing, zing. The bee kept buzzing as the children flew together in tandem. Every face in the hall was concentrated. One could sense the hidden terrors in this piece, the zing of cruelty, an irony when on the surface this was a showing-off piece – clever and fast. And when it was over, the twins stood side by side looking exactly alike, their faces round and pleasant with a childish grin. Shining black hair cut short and brushed to the left, rimless spectacles before sparkling dark eyes, long black pants and black shirts lifted by the red adornments – except that one held a violin and a bow, the other some music. The crowd stood, and from the back came chanting.

'Mendelssohn, Mendelssohn. *Moo Ichi-do.*' Kentaro was astounded, and confused. The orchestra were no longer in place. It would take too long to get them back and tuned up. He conferred with Jiro's teacher, Chiyo san, and it was decided that Ichiro must accompany him again.

The moment of contact of bow on string, the exquisite release of that first note, sent the audience into a trance. This was his *pièce de résistance*. They were under a spell.

After the light, fast fluttering of double-stopped notes calmed to become a single note melody again, reaching higher and higher, Kentaro began to get edgy. The boys could easily get carried away and break into the last movement, so as soon as the final note of the slow movement began, he walked out on to the stage with Chiyo Maki, ready to present the graduation certificate. But the boys did not budge until the full effect of the pause on the final note had reached every corner of the large auditorium. Then, the clapping started and the boys acknowledged the applause with deep and courteous bows, and Kentaro and Chiyo, feeling awkward, stepped back and clapped and smiled and nodded some. Then, with a nod to the boys, the two adults stepped forward again and Ichiro stood aside. He had already graduated and knew his place, and the crowd sat and listened. Dr Fujiwara's voice was light but strong. He congratulated Jiro as he formally did every student at his or her graduation, smiling, passing the certificate into the child's left hand, shaking with his right, and bowing slowly and respectfully in response to the child's deep bow. Then, with a sweep of his hand, and a bow toward her, he presented the teacher who had filled in for him if he was not available.

'Chiyo *sensei*', he said, while leading the applause. Chiyo Maki bowed her acknowledgement to Jiro, Kentaro and the audience. Three people walked briskly on to the stage bringing a large bunch of flowers for each of them. Then Kentaro indicated to Ichiro that he should stand with his brother and, with him, acknowledge the flowers which were being placed along the front of the stage as the audience filed past between the front row of seats and the platform. He had already instructed Jiro and Ichiro that they must keep bowing for several minutes and then, when he signalled them, they must leave the stage, no matter what.

The people had formed a queue that seemed to have no end. Kentaro nodded to the boys, and they backed away from the edge of the stage, then almost ran to the dressing room. 'Well done, Jiro and Ichiro,' he said. 'Mum is coming to take you home. Go to bed quickly, please.'

Yuki, who had sat mid-way through the hall joined them now. But before she spoke to the boys she whispered to her husband.

'You came in too soon. People were offended.' The boys were together, laughing. She gave them a bright smile and a big hug – flowers, violin, and all – but very quickly, the violin was in its case, the music and certificate in the satchel, and the three bunches of flowers laid behind the back seat of the car which was positioned at the exit door from the staff foyer. Two excited but very tired boys were buckled in and sharing laughter and embarrassment about their 'dumb father' and their mistakes, while waiting for their mother to drive them home.

'You played the chords too wide! You spread them all out, dork!' said Jiro, in a high-pitched voice, pummelling his brother.

'I was the whole orchestra,' said Ichiro. 'Remember? You're the dork!'

By the time all the flowers were placed on the stage, then cleared and placed for their final destination – some into vases at the institute, some to be taken home by Chiyo, and Kentaro, and the rest into a van to be shared with the people in the hospital next day – the boys had been bathed and were asleep in their adjacent beds.

When Kentaro looked in on the twins later, he saw that the certificate had pride of place on Jiro's dresser, and that the music satchel was lying on Ichiro's duvet beside a note for his father. He kissed them both lightly on the cheek and whispered, 'Sleep well, son.' Then he picked up the satchel and the note and carried them to the music room where, tomorrow, the music would be put on to the growing pile of known repertoire. He unfolded the note, and by the light on the wall by the piano, he read:

'Dear Dad, You said we'd get to go to Galtür to ski if we did well tonight. We'll be going won't we?'

Both boys had signed the roughly written note and drawn lots of kisses. At the very bottom of the page in tiny characters, Jiro had said, 'Dear Dad, for helping me to be a violinist – thank you. Jiro'

Part One

The space above snow gives one a reason
to believe that there can be something and
someone more

Part One
Chapter 1

Fujiwara battled to hear the sounds of the recorded music. With shaking hands he lit another cigarette and put his mind to listening. It was not called Spring Sonata for nothing. He could associate it with the delicate, rippling sounds of water in the stream near his home; could imagine the bursts of colour where snow had melted, green buds forming on the cherry trees. It was those pictures he had given his boys as he taught them to play the sonata, and because Jiro was quick to translate the pictures into liquid tones on his violin, and Ichiro, into mellifluous tones on the piano, they were now coming through the eight speakers. But Fujiwara could not hear the music. His head was consumed by that terrible night of fourteen months ago at the ski resort of Galtür in Austria.

> Outside a violent wind blew. They had no way of knowing it was more than another of the violent winds that sometimes blew through the ski resort and incapacitated everyone for a couple of days. Whatever, they were trapped. There was nowhere to go. Hang on they must – the plane would come tomorrow if at all possible and whisk them away.
>
> The three children were terrified but too tired to play games, so their parents had persuaded them they would be better off in bed. The adults had stayed on at the dinner table and talked and kept the fire going. Eventually they left the table for the comfort of the hearth and talked on. And then, just after midnight, airborne snow burst through the windows and door and exploded the walls from the inside. Everything was blacked–out, all signs of life extinguished. Kentaro was

jammed between rubble. Snow packed the cavities of his eyes and mouth. He tried to call out but could not. Yet one of his hands was free, and as he gagged on snow, he knocked on a board that crossed his forehead, and hoped that someone would hear him.

Yuki kept screaming into the wind. Almost buried, Yuki had been able to clear her mouth of snow and miraculously her arms were free. She was upright. She could hear muffled sounds, and knew that she must tread snow and free herself and go to their rescue. But when she heard the thunderous roar of an avalanche and felt the swoosh and the power of it close by, she passed out from terror as it scooped up and buried the rest of the chalet.

She did not know how much time had elapsed when help came. Rescuers poured from the army helicopter on to the site and almost tripped over her. A scream pushed out by the weight of snow against her chest, alerted a soldier to where she was. They had painstakingly dug her out and rushed her into the helicopter for warmth. She became the source of information about who had been with her, the children and where they had been. She was told to be calm, given a warm drink. They would uncover the people as quickly as possible. Time was on their side, the path of the avalanche in their favour.

Rangers and soldiers worked under lights to probe the snow and dig with their equipment to uncover people as fast as possible. Sniffer dogs were immediately put to work, and the paramedics were ready to rush survivors to the helicopter.

Trish McLeod, daughter of Dr Hamish and Mary McLeod

of Scotland, was the first to be found and brought into the helicopter. Yuki watched as paramedics freed her mouth of compacted snow. It was difficult and took too long. They worked for many minutes to apply different methods of resuscitation, but there was no response. Finally, the two paramedics stood and conferred, then looked sadly at Yuki. She fell to her knees and put her head on the chest of the young girl and sobbed.

She had lost all sense of time when, unbelievably, she heard the voices of her husband, and Mary McLeod. They had both been dragged from rubble and were mostly unscathed. But a paramedic had to break the news to Mary that Yuki had identified the body brought in, as Trish. She shrieked as if pierced with a knife, then collapsed. When she came to on a stretcher with Yuki sitting on a crate beside her, she looked surprised. Gradually her reason for being there came to her.

'Oh, Yuki! Any news of your boys, or Hamish?'

Yuki nodded sadly. 'None.'

Tears filled her eyes, and she reached about her for a tissue. As she searched her trouser pockets she looked at Yuki in distress.

'My pants are soaked! I fainted, didn't I?' Shakily, she sat up. 'Yuki, what can I do? I'm wet.'

A paramedic came to the rescue, and with Yuki's help, they gave her privacy enough to take a sponge bath and sort her clothing so that she was comfortable again and only wanted to go and see Trish.

Yuki watched as Mary looked on the face of her beautiful daughter. It was as if Trish were in her bed about to open her deep blue eyes and say, 'Just pretending. Mummy. Please tuck me in,' which is what she had said every night since until she was twelve, and even in this last year. Her usually ruddy cheeks were pale and her long auburn hair, her daddy's hair, was wet and stringy. But this was her Trish, her only daughter, only child. Mary pulled her rosary beads from a pocket and knelt to throw an arm about Trish's body. She put her face against her child's and cried softly. When, much later, she stood, and let out an enormous sigh, Yuki placed an arm about her shoulders and at the same time kept glancing toward the door. And then the moment she both wanted and dreaded occurred.

Two soldiers struggled against the wind to bring in a stretcher on which a little boy lay. 'Yes. Yes. This one's alive!' said one of the men. Kentaro and Yuki shrieked for joy in recognition of Ichiro. They patted his cheeks until he was fully awake.

Still dazed, he screamed, 'I can't see anything. My glasses. My glasses!' And until he realised that Jiro was not there, he kept screaming, 'Help me find my glasses! My glasses! I can't see!' Yuki hushed him.

'Ichiro, we'll find them, but they're still looking for Jiro. He's buried deep in the snow!'

Once he heard that, he snapped awake, and there was the heart-rending scream that comes from the desperation of losing something so personal it could be a limb or an eye. 'They'll keep digging, Ichiro,' was all his father said as he patted him and tried to comfort him, and also shield him from watching Trish being placed in a body bag.

And then, Hamish McLeod, the biggest and heaviest of all the group, was brought in on a stretcher, his face covered by a oxygen mask. Mary kissed his cheek and held his hand, and talked to him, and cried, and talked some more. Then she knelt beside his stretcher and prayed. Cried and prayed aloud, 'Dear God, not Hamish too!' The paramedic, who was monitoring his responses touched her on the shoulder.

'Your husband will soon come round. He's going to be OK.' His kindly smile persuaded her and she wept quietly, but shook with the terror she felt at the prospect of telling him their news.

After an hour, when Kentaro and Yuki knew that it would be a miracle if Jiro were still alive, two soldiers carried him into the plane on a stretcher. The faces of the men – ghost-like and sad beneath head lamps – told them that the child was dead. They fell upon the stretcher and saw for themselves that he had been cruelly disfigured, almost certainly crushed by the upper bunk as he lay sleeping. He was frozen stiff. Blood lay congealed across his broken nose and splintered cheek bones. Eyes wet with snow stared at them, unknowing. They shrieked and covered their faces. Then enveloped Ichiro and each other with their arms, and cried bitterly.

Yuki asked that when Jiro was placed in a body bag, his face be left free. She bathed and stroked it and kissed it and smoothed the icy hair with a towel. Ichiro stamped around the plane beating his face with his hands and yelling, 'Don't do that. Don't do that. He's not dead! Make him get up.'

Kentaro did his best to comfort Ichiro by hugging and stroking him until he sank into a seat, curled up, and remained motionless. He was so quiet that his parents began to worry that they had lost two sons, their twins, their precious little musicians who were uncannily merged in partnership as they performed on violin and piano. They sat holding hands as the rest of the personnel and their two amazing dogs piled into the helicopter, the door was closed and tested and a decision made to leave.

Kentaro lit another cigarette and sobbed with each exhalation. It was more than he could bear to remember the disfigured, expressionless face and stiff, cold fingers. Apart from the recordings, the sound of Jiro's playing was silenced for ever. He wished that he himself had died. The child was only eight years old, but he was all his father ever wanted. A son who played the violin with miraculous dexterity and feeling, a superior violinist in every way. He had outdone every other child Fujiwara had ever taught. And if pressed to reveal his innermost thoughts, Fujiwara would have admitted that Jiro would have become a much greater musician than himself, given but a few more years.

The recording ended. He stubbed out his cigarette and left the institute, locked the door as he went to get his bicycle, and cycled home to bed. The road was clear. Stars twinkled in the moonlit sky. At this hour of the morning time stood still. The commercial district through which he rode was closed up. An occasional light showed in a small window above a shop, perhaps a sick child was being bathed with a damp cloth, or an elderly person who could not sleep was binding up a bundle of hand-stitched baby clothes. Tomorrow, as early as the shop-owners dared, the doors would be opened, shutters released and awnings lifted. If the shop was chilly, the kerosene stove would be lit. Then the fruit and the hardware, the clothes and the jewelry stalls would be hauled on to the pavement. Kentaro turned into the small park to take the winding path over the wooden bridge. There was something gentle in the atmosphere, a spirit talking to the earth-bound bulbs, encouraging them to take a peek at daylight for themselves and see that it would be OK to break through the soil. Very soon it would be cherry blossom time and everyone would be happy; would picnic by the avenue and celebrate beneath the dazzling pink and white blossom.

The thought of spring was too much for Fujiwara. Another spring without his complete family? He could not face it. As he turned into his road, the sameness of the two small moonlit houses with their steep roofs, and their latticed wrought iron fences adjacent to the footpath, starkly reminded him of something Hamish Mcleod had said in Galtür: 'Japanese people like to copy don't they? Cloning is a very Japanese concept. Could Jiro's twin be cloned? The child had done nothing to deserve the terrible fate that had befallen him. They would have a good case for cloning.' Why, yes! It felt like an inspiration.

With his bike in the porch beside Yuki's and Ichiro's, at the front entrance to his home, he slipped from his shoes into his slippers and crept upstairs. Hamish McLeod said he had been in the team that cloned Dolly and hinted at cloning humans, so why not start with him. If he could not do it maybe he would be able to suggest an embryologist who could, and would create a child for them. Give him the genes to play the violin like Perlman or Paganini. Like Jiro. The world would benefit by the beauty of his playing. Before he went to wash himself, he took a look at Ichiro on his futon. The child was restless, tossing and turning all the time. He moved the boy's glasses to where he could not break them with his flaying arms, spoke quieting words to him, hummed the theme of the sonata he had tried to hear above the din in his head. A smile crossed the boy's face and he lay still. Kentaro stroked the silky black hair and felt the warmth from the boy's body. You have suffered too much young fellow, he thought, and he pulled the cover back up to his chin. You are no longer yourself. Perhaps you feel as if you are half yourself! Sleep well, my son.

Part One
Chapter 2

There was to be another summer camp at Banff in the Rockies.

'We'll have loads of fun, Tom,' his dad said. 'We'll sleep in a chalet – just you and me together, with a few others.' This was all a new experience for Tom and his dad. The thought of going to violin classes and sitting through concerts was daunting. Especially when a gondola was close to where they were camped. They could be taking rides up and down the mountain all day.

Like most children aged five, Tom was bubbling with personality and quite certain he knew what he wanted, even to the way his fair forelock was slicked back. He was sure that the violin was too hard for him. He had given it a go back home but he was not enjoying it all that much. He believed that he should emulate his school teacher and play the guitar and sing. His dad wanted him to keep learning though, and now that they were setting up camp he supposed he would have to. His dad was patient in showing him new things. But there was still the sadness in his eyes that he had after his mother had said goodbye and gone to live with Hardy, the ugliest man he had ever seen. Tom had lots of time to think about things as they travelled by train from Calgary to Banff. He reckoned his dad's eyes looked like the valleys, a stony blue, sometimes misty. It did not make him feel any better that his dad was still sad.

All the teachers for the summer camp were called to stand at the front of the hall after they had eaten supper. Tom could not help but notice the boyish likeness between his school teacher and a woman called Donna Beastly, or something, who was introduced as 'The teacher who has studied at the Fujiwara Institute in Japan, and is soon to be teaching the method in Toronto.' Tom wondered why it was necessary to say that. It was not said of any of the others. They were all lumped together as Americans. So what? Tom thought. I have just come all the way from Dorchester, Ontario. That's the other side of Canada, a long, long way. No one said anything about that.

When the groups were called out, Tom only just stopped thinking about America and Japan to hear his name, Tom Blackwell.

'Dad, why did they say my name?' He was almost wetting himself with excitement. His dad whispered,

'You're in the Bears group with Miss Beasley.' Tom giggled.

'I thought they'd said beastly.'

His dad winked at him and Tom noticed his eyes looked happy and bright blue. That made him feel good for a minute. He would do his best if his dad would go on looking happy.

A lively-looking group of parents and children were already chatting like old friends, and tuning up instruments, when Tom and his dad rushed into the teaching room. They had taken a bit too long over their rostered chore of making sure that all camp scraps were put into one of the large, heavy rubbish bins, where scavenging bears could not reach them.

Looking out of the enormous window, and exclaiming at the view of lofty Mt Rundle, were two loud women. One of them reckoned she was a descendant of an Indian who sat at the foot of the mountain at the feet of the Reverend Tyrell Rundle, who preached to his tribe and any explorers who would listen. Tom stood between them listening and looking. It was rough and rocky way up there, but snow was plastered all over the peaks and hollows and made them shine. He liked that. His dad thought he was too engrossed by the view, and encouraged him to join the people who were focused on the class, then teased him as he took a lot of time polishing his small violin and checking closely for resin dust.

'Now fix your bow, please. Miss Beasley is standing in rest position, waiting.'

Tom saw that all six other children were in a line across the room and in front of her. He hurried to stand there too.

'Please bring me your violin to tune.' The teacher smiled. Tom listened as each of his strings locked into hers. 'This one was easy,' she said, handing it back, and Tom returned to the line.

'My name is Donna Beasley and I'd like you to call me Donna. Will you tell me what you want me to call you?' She looked along the row and nodded to Tom, standing at the end.

'Thomas.'

A smile crossed Tom's father's face and Donna gave him a knowing look.

'Thomas, OK.'

A discussion took place as to the pros and cons of calling their group by the name of Bears. Donna didn't want to foist it on the children, but most liked the idea. Except for Renée who wanted to know if they were grizzly or black and insisted that bears could not run down hill and she could. Then there was Tim who ran to his mother and buried his face in her lap.

'Oh, sorry. Is there a problem?' Donna asked.

Tim's mother made a face as much as to say – yes, but! Donna went over to her. The woman explained that Tim's aunt was a naturalist up in the Yukon, and she and a mate had been mauled by a grizzly.

'Oh, how terrible! Poor woman! What happened. Is she OK?'

Yes. But she was a long time recovering.'

'And her mate?'

'His skin was torn right off!' Tim answered.

Donna returned to the front of the room and played a few velvety notes on the D and G strings, swallowed hard, and smiled, then put her violin into rest position again and centred her eyes on each child, taking time for the child to copy her position. Tim came racing back.

'I think we should be Black Bears,' he said loudly.

Tom glanced at his dad. His eyes were deep blue. He wriggled with happiness. The ice was broken.

'Let's get playing our violins then, Black Bears.'

As Donna crossed to the staff room after the lesson, she glanced up the valley and said a silent prayer that there'd not be an avalanche this summer like the one in Austria that took Fujiwara's son last February. It was too sad to think about. A large bearded figure came from the chalet to her left.

'Hi, there, Peter. One cello class behind you – how was it?' she said. From his expression she thought that he would say it was bad. He smiled at her. The strain vanished.

'They're great kids. How were yours?'

'We got off to a bit of a bad start over being Bears, but then it was pretty cool. They play in tune, those wee kids, but I spent too long on some things. I didn't give each child their fair share of time.'

'Difficult, isn't it!'

Donna had not been as close to Peter as now. She decided he, like her, would be about thirty.

'Especially when your maestro has been Kentaro Fujiwara for ten months. He gave every lesson according to need, not time. Parents can't see that. A lesson is the time a kid needs, no more, no less!'

'Oh my God.' Peter laughed from his belly, an older, salted-down laugh. 'Not here. That won't work here. Fair is keeping to time. You'll have to do better! Donna, isn't it?' He pulled a face and said, 'How about a coffee?'

She knew she had blushed right to the top of her head, or so it felt. That's the worst of having a blond number two cut and fair skin, she thought.

'Thanks, I'm feeling a bit fussed about keeping to time.'

'You'll do OK.' She took a step up to join him and they entered the building together.

The rest of the summer camp was wonderful for Tom. He liked the new shoulder pad his teacher supplied, and the short lessons. When it came to the final goodbyes, Tom and his dad were sad, and decided to ask Donna if she could fit Tom into her timetable.

'Well, yes, but it's a long way from Dorchester to Toronto.'

'Not at all. It would be cool if it meant that Tom could make some decent progress. A couple of hours and we can be there.'

'And his present violin teacher?'

'I'll tell her straight that Tom made more progress in a five day camp than he did all semester.'

'But, Warren, remember he's had lots of input and stimulus.'

'Please, Donna. Please.' Tom jumped up and down.

'Call me when you've settled on a time that suits you and we'll work something out.'

Donna took one last look at the room where she had taught the group, one last look up the valley from the picture window at the mist that had settled around the top of the mountain, and the strong, icy slopes. She wished she had time to take the gondola ride and then wondered if she would be invited to teach there again.

Peter had saved her a seat on the rocky mountaineer train after putting his cello into the luggage compartment.

'Thanks,' she said, as she settled in to the aisle seat. 'Do you always travel with your hard case?'

'Yes, I use the canvas one between home and work but that's all. You're the lucky one. A violin fits so easily in these racks above us.' Donna glanced out the window at the now deserted chalets and sighed. There was still a few minutes of sitting and waiting for the whistle to blow. Time to look up the valley. The hollow feeling returned as if the news of the tragedy was yesterday. She tried to concentrate on Peter, whose closeness made her feel secure, but decided that now was a good time to prepare her camera to catch any elk or a white-tail deer if she was lucky.

She pulled out her tray and placed her Nikon at the ready.

She watched children from the camp doing a last minute spurt to reach the steps of the train. Most looked overburdened by their pack, musical instrument, shoulder bag, and a plastic bag bursting with odds and ends, and probably souvenirs. Parents followed looking calmer but also rather overloaded. She thought of how different each of her class were. Silently she hoped never to see Renée again, but it seemed inevitable that a bad penny turned up somewhere unexpected. The child I won't see ever again, she thought with sadness, is Jiro Fujiwara. She closed her eyes to relax a bit and let her memory take a hold of the beautiful view from the Banff Centre which was hidden now by trees but which she knew well. It made her feel strong. She opened her eyes at the sound of the whistle and the movement of the train. I must not go to sleep, she thought, especially when it's such a great day to photograph Three Sisters, the most amazing trio of nun-like pinnacles one could imagine, even to their hands clasped in prayer. On the way up they had been hidden by heavy cloud. She glanced at Peter who was deep in thought.

After a few minutes, he came out of his reverie.

'Good, eh?' he said.

'I don't know what's pre-occupied you, but I know what a depressing influence mountains have on me, these days. Why is it that one of the most brilliant of this world's children had to die so young?'

'What? Where?'

'I was thinking about Jiro, the Fujiwara twin who died. The mountains set me off. You didn't hear about this?' He looked puzzled. 'You know who I mean when I talk about Kentaro Fujiwara don't you?'

'Oh, sure. I've got a lot of time for his books. First class. But for the rest, no!'

'Last February in Austria, Switzerland and Italy, they had avalanche after avalanche pile down on to skiers, chalets, hotels, the lot. The Fujiwaras and their twin boys – you must know their recordings. Child prodigies a bit like the Menhuins, except these are two boys we're talking about, and a lot younger, who made CDs and stuff. They were in Galtür for a skiing holiday. Ichiro, the pianist, was rescued by paramedics, but Jiro was hopelessly buried – crushed by what must have been the upper bunk. They didn't find him for quite a while.'

'Sounds like the worst kind of tragedy, even without a prodigy.'

'Meaning?'

'Well, you know. Twins are so close, part of each other.'

'These boys were, they were identical. Apart from knowing that Jiro played the violin and Ichiro the piano, I couldn't tell them apart. They even had similar glasses.'

'So you knew them well?'

Donna had, in fact, been to study with Fujiwara more than once. She was very familiar with his way of doing things, and when he was to be absent, she was asked to fill in for him in teaching the children. Jiro had been both an enigma and a delight. In amongst the advanced players, he looked even smaller than he really was. Whenever she told people about the little guy, they inevitably challenged her on questions about his playing of the slow movement of the Mendelssohn, or the Beethoven, or any other soulful piece that demanded maturity and feeling. Peter asked the same questions. Her response was rehearsed.

'That's just it, Peter. He did. He honestly did have this amazing maturity. It was quite incredible, and tear-jerking I have to admit.'

'But his instrument! Small instruments don't do it!'

'Jiro had long limbs and had this beautiful three-quarter violin, hand-made in Cremona, a truly beautiful instrument.'

Peter was looking incredulous. 'Sounds too good to be

true.'

'That's why it's so uncanny. Was he really too good to live?'

Peter made a face. His forehead puckered.

'Is that a question you and I have a right to ask, Donna? No-one can be too good to live, for goodness sake.'

'Yuki told me that it took a long while until Ichiro began to play the piano again. Poor little kid blames himself that Jiro was crushed by the bunk he had slept on.'

'Oh, dear. Poor little boy.'

'It was more than luck that they found Ichiro alive! There was no way they could have saved Jiro. He must have been crushed within moments of the avalanche, if not the explosion.'

'Explosion?'

'Yes, the powdered snow that was forced into the chalet compacted and blew the walls apart! Ghastly beyond belief!' Donna then turned away and changed the mood saying, 'I'm on the look-out for bears and elk. Yell, if you see either.'

The rocky terrain held everyone's attention for some time as they kept on the look out.

'There, look! Three elk! Aren't they beautiful?' There was a surge of children to the window, as Donna pointed her camera and clicked. And there were shouts of 'I see them!' and 'Where? Where?' Satisfied or disappointed, everyone returned to their places, and Donna rested her camera again, and turned to Peter.

'What's happening for you, this year?'

'That's the big decision I'm facing. I've been invited to teach cello at the Music and Arts Academy, fondly called MAAC, in London, Ontario. I've only shopped there, never stayed overnight and am trying to make up my mind.'

'Well now! I hope you do. It's a neat place!' Teaching at the university in London had been part of Donna's life before Japan. She gave workshops there. She thought of Western Ontario's incredible number of students training to be teachers, and the enthusiastic staff. It will not be too different at the conservatoire in Toronto, she thought. And, maybe she would get back to Banff again with a chance to take the Gondola again, throw a few snowballs and drink in that cool clear air. Nothing could beat the Banff experience. 'Three Sisters. There they are!' She grabbed her camera and took several pictures with an elbow balanced on Peter's knee. 'Got them.'

'Ouch!' he said, good-naturedly.

'Sorry, but you kept me steady! Thanks.'

They became quiet again, each with their own thoughts. Peter had much to challenge him now that he had to decide if he would apply for the position on the outskirts of the city. He had heard strange stories about the previous teacher, CT Morensky, who had earned a reputation for favouring some students. That had cost him the numbers that made for a viable studio. No doubt more would be revealed over time, but if nothing else, he would be required to build up the department.

Donna too had things on her mind. She was returning to Brandon University for a couple of weeks before heading off to teach at the Royal Conservatorium in Toronto. They wanted her for her knowledge of the Fujiwara method, and she looked forward to that. But shifting, and finding suitable accommodation, was a huge challenge. She had already collected an enormous amount of junk, especially antique china pieces, all rather delicate and difficult to pack. She had lost a Toby jug that was an heirloom last time she moved. That took her ages to recover from because it had been her mother's. It felt like the break with her mother was made final by the loss.

Peter picked up the brochure from the pocket of the seat. If Donna was going to stay lost in thought, he might as well read the notes on the rail route: 'Three Sisters, up beyond the town of Canmore, were first named in 1883 as Three Nuns and later given the protestant designation of Sisters. And nearer the railway, Canmore, the town named after the Scottish king, Malcolm Canmore.' What was a Scottish king doing here, Peter pondered, glad to have a chance to put his mind to something other than himself. He read on, encountering history, and falling asleep on the train.

Part One
Chapter 3

Dr McLeod, now embryologist at New Biotec Centre Como, took the afternoon off to be with his wife. He wanted to surprise her, and would not have told her ahead because of the possible disappointment if he could not leave the Biotec Lab. After climbing the steps to the apartment and sneaking in at the front door, he peeked into the bedroom and found her at prayer. He waited five minutes before making noises.

She emerged from the bedroom looking surprised.

'This is nice Hamish! How come? I was feeling homesick.'

'Just come to look in on you!'

She hugged him tight, smooching her face through his beard. Then, holding her at arms length he said, 'You homesick for tiny little blink your eye and it's gone Kirkliston?'

She pulled him through to the sitting room, laughing.

'I love it. You know that. Its prettiness, the way its streets wend about, the lush countryside close enough to walk to.' From her dreamy expression, he knew that she longed for home. 'Then there's Queensferry South. I love that part of Scotland. It's in my bones. I was praying that Jeannie or Janice would visit.'

'Jeannie?'

'Yes, I've written to Jeannie and invited her to come and stay. She'd love it here. We taught together in Kirkliston and sometimes we'd whip out to Hawes Inn for a drink together after school. She was my best mate, and she's a part-timer now and could take a break.'

'I hope she says yes, then. So you weren't frightened to find me here at this time of day?'

'Not frightened, just startled!'

He laughed and put an arm around her shoulder.

She said, 'The only thing that frightens me is that the church hasn't given its blessing to cloning. It means I spend a lot of time on my knees asking God to bless our child and forgive us!'

'Mary. I knew that could worry you. Surely, it's just between you, me, and God, and not the church! We've never been that committed have we?'

'I like to think God is bigger and wiser than the Pope! Love you, I do. So tell me, truly, why you're here. Have they sacked you?'

'I want to make sure that you're OK about our baby, apart from the religious aspect.'

'Shouldn't I be?'

He sat on the couch and pulled her down beside him.

'A cloned child is different. I'm proud of what we've achieved. Not just because of history – but I'm terribly excited to have another child. I cannot let anything happen to you.'

'I'm not as young as I was fourteen years ago when I had Trish, is that it?'

'Partly. So I'm home to be with you, lassie. They can manage without me for one afternoon.'

'Does that mean that we can go out, stay in, go to bed, go driving?'

'Anything and all of those if you want.'

'Can I make you a coffee, then? I need one.'

'Let me make it while you think of what you'd like to do most of all.'

She watched her husband in his unaccustomed role. Thought him handsome with his auburn hair and beard. Melted at his soulful eyes that were oval in appearance. Knew him to be strong. Had wanted to have lots of children by him, but had managed only one – baptised as Patricia, but everyone had called her Trish. Many had teased them for choosing an Irish name.

'She's Patricia, and that's that,' Mary had said. 'I happen to have lost a good friend called Patricia, and if our wee lass is one bit as nice, that will do me.' When she was born, Hamish had agreed that it suited her. She made a big to-do about everything! Cried her heart out, and kept them guessing as to why.

'Aye, she's as contrary as the Irish, I'll have you know!' Hamish retorted, with great pride.

'Shall we drink our coffee in the atrium, then? It's the warmest place just now, Hamish.' Since moving to Italy from Scotland three months ago, Mary had not sought another teaching job. Now that she was pregnant she was relieved not to have one. Whenever she was not out there getting to know the unique town of Como, she often sat at home alone, tatting and reading history, or simply listening to her favourite celtic songs and watching the boats on the lake.

'You being home is such a nice change, Hamish. I'm lonely on my own, and more often than not I'm only just managing to keep my food down. Can't even read history, my favourite,' she laughed.

'So, what is it now, then?' He picked up a book and opened it at the bookmark. 'Och! Margaret and Malcolm of Canmore. Eleventh century stuff. I should have known.'

'Margaret is such an inspiration to me.'

'Religious!'

'Very, but also generous and giving, and a good mother.' Mary shrugged as if she recognised something of Margaret in herself, but did not want to boast of it. 'It keeps me in touch with my origins! Remember how we enjoyed Queensferry South? I felt a tangible link with Margaret there.'

'So having time to read is all right, then?'

'Yes, it's brilliant, except when I'm feeling sick like now.'

'What? Even after lunch?'

'Yes, even after lunch, and always after breakfast. If ever there's a long three months it has to be the first three of a pregnancy. I'll be glad when I'm through with this one, I will.'

'Mary,' he said, having sipped some coffee. 'Do you feel any different knowing the baby is cloned?'

She thought a minute then, looking sad.

'If you mean from the physical point of view, absolutely not. But in my head, yes. Yes, very different.'

'Can you tell if it's because I cloned the baby from Trish's tissue? Or because the egg was fertilised by artificial means? Can you help me to understand what I've done?'

'Sometimes when I'm vomiting, I wish that I'd miscarry. But that passes. If you weren't so loving I'd feel really different. Somehow cheap, I think...'

He looked at her in a strange way. As if peering down a microscope, narrowing his eyes to get a focused view of her thoughts.

Mary had had plenty of time to think about issues relating to cloning. She had even started imagining a whole class of cloned children who had been given impossibly bright intelligence so that they became depressed because she, their teacher, could not meet their demands. She decided that the worst of all scenarios would be to have a class of look-alike children, say three groups of ten who resembled all nine others in their group. She would be completely muddled. As if that was not daunting enough, she began to worry about the possibility of their having one parent and finding out that in fact all her class had a mother, only. Or a father, only!

'Cheap?' he asked.

'Yes. As if I had bought a baby along with my usual Christmas mail order of soaps and bubble bath! Something like that.'

'Oh, poor Mary. It sounds too easy, I agree!'

'Well, as I said, if you weren't so loving, I'd feel like that. But I don't, truly I don't. She's our baby. And, I believe God is in control no matter what.' She looked at him with fondness as she patted her stomach. 'How about we choose a name for her?'

'What a lovely idea. Any suggestions?'

'I have thought about calling her Margaret for obvious reasons. It would get rid of this cheap feeling, I think. Or the name of a beautiful flower such as Lily or Rose.'

'Rose would be my choice. Yeah, let's call her Rose. Maybe Rose Margaret McLeod!'

Mary laughed, looked radiant. 'Rose Margaret she is, then.' They hugged, then Mary said, 'How do you feel, about having a cloned daughter?'

'On the professional level, very very clever. I hope that this baby – Rose – will be perfect. But there's something I'd like to tell you now. It's that I've had a request from a couple of men who want to pay me to do private research in human cloning.'

'Private? But you're employed by New Biotec Centre!'

'Yes. But I'm encouraged by the Centre to do private research. In fact they want me to, but more in creating organs for transplants.' He had her attention, he must finish. 'These fellows want to pay me to develop my skills, then clone the two of them. When I've perfected my technique, that is.' He coloured up a bit. Her reply did not help.

'But won't that be impossible? For money, something that's still illegal?' Her coffee mug was barely touched. She looked down at it as if not seeing what was there, waiting for his answer.

'Lassie, drink your coffee. Let me explain.' He drained his mug and put it on the table. His eyes were shining. She wanted to match his excitement.

'The money is only part of it. It's that I'm being given the incentive to make progress, make history. We have proved that I can do it. I'm confident I'm on to something really momentous! OK, I'm forcing the hand of history somewhat, but I bet you there's many an embryologist doing exactly what I'm doing.'

Mary sighed. She drank the rest of her coffee and Hamish reached to take the mug. Then she tossed her head and smiled.

'So, it's your job. I shouldn't start fussing myself sick about you, I've got enough to worry about.' She rested her hand on her stomach. 'So, you've said yes, or are you still deciding?'

'I needed to talk to you first. But I want to do it.'

'Just one thing.' The teacher in her prevailed.

'Will you actually do the experiments at the Centre?'

'Yes. In the lab. It's my lab, my research. There's time and space allotted. It's just the extra payment and the goals that are the add-ons so to speak! I want to keep them confidential – that is, my methods and some of the experiments. It's wonderful. On the one hand the little monkeys and the mice, and on the other, human embryos. It's what I've dreamed about! As soon as I have results to publish, I can front-up to the board and say "We can do it, we can put this Centre on the map!" By the time I get around to cloning the men concerned, it'll most probably be common and legal, anyway.'

'So, you'll tell the world about our baby?'

'If she's perfect, I'll want to tell the world. Yes, you and I are making history. I feel convinced of that.'

'You look like the cat that's licked up all the cream. We're not quite there, yet.' She was serious again. 'So that's your answer as a professional. I want to know how you feel on the inside. On the human level.'

'As if a professional isn't human,' he said, laughing. 'OK, so as the child's father, I feel as excited as the first time. Very happy, lassie. And proud of my wife.'

'One thing does trouble me. The thought that we might try to turn our daughter into another Trish. You know, good at skiing and all.'

'No! I'll tell you what, we'll only take her skiing if she asks us to.'

'But what about us? We liked to ski, and just might, again except that I'm not so keen since the avalanches. You?'

'Oh, I'll never go near that ski field again. Never.'

As Hamish drove to and from New Biotec Centre, he frequently remembered Galtür and wondered if they could have done things differently. Been more aware of what the mountains were telling them.

Austria, and in particular, Galtür, where the eminent geneticist and his family skied whenever they could, had not had an avalanche problem for years. Even though Italy and Switzerland had terrible things happen in their mountains and ski resorts, no-one suspected it would happen in Galtür. The McLeods joined the other three thousand people who were just as keen as they were to make the most of their holidays.

For the first few days it was fun, as much fun as it had always been. They were glad they had come. There were eight year old twin boys who skied like champions, and their parents were more than keen to have Trish McLeod take them in hand, and give them the chance to do even better. At night, the families and the two others who shared their chalet, chatted around the dinner table.

Roaring winds hit Galtür spasmodically, and occasional avalanches that resounded like thunderclaps – very close by. People were advised to stay indoors. The roads to and from the village were closed. The children, especially the twins, thought it was very exciting. They would not have to return to school for ages. Full of energy, they spent their time in noisy indoor games that they had brought with them or made up on the spot with the other children in their chalet. Then, when calm prevailed, they would bundle themselves up in snow suits, woolly caps and boots, and struggle about in the fresh snow to build snowmen and throw snowballs at one another.

But, seemingly overnight, winds became violent gales. Nobody was allowed to venture out. Nerves were tested.

People who had special health reasons why they must leave the ski resort were flown out with a degree of risk both to themselves and the helicopter pilot. Even though Dr Fujiwara wanted to get back to his music institute in

Nagoya, it was not considered important enough to take risks over. So the family did what most other families were doing and stayed indoors, waiting anxiously for the winds to die down. They tuned their radios in for news, and very occasionally caught a word or two. Stories filtered through to them of havoc caused by avalanche blasts at the edge of the village. Cars were upturned and buried, chalets were smashed, people were trapped. The Austrian Army was seconded to help. Their regimented presence brought conflicting impressions to those who watched them.

No one knew how many people had died. But one survivor, Henry, rescued by an Austrian soldier, was escorted to their chalet. Everyone wanted to ask him questions, but he was so shaken and cold, that hot food and a change of clothing were what he needed.

Yuki had taken him in hand, feeding him a thick vegetable soup. She offered him bagels and fruits-of-the-forest jams with green tea. She chatted quietly, hoping to keep him from becoming too morose, and once he'd finished eating said, 'Would you like something more?'

'No, thanks. That was great.' He looked stunned, but insisted on going out again. He had had two friends with him and he was determined to go and search with the soldiers. Hamish overheard what he was saying to Yuki, and intervened.

'Henry, sit at the fire for a little while and get warm before you go out there again.'

Henry glanced at the blazing fire, and because his teeth were chattering again, said, 'Thanks.'

He began to tell his story to the families about him, seemingly glad to talk. The four boys stopped their game at the table, and crept to the hearth, pretending not to be there.

'They're two of the best ...' Henry stopped.

'Were you together when it happened?'

'Yes! We were skiing in a line quite close shouting at one another, and then there was a roar like a thousand steam engines all hissing at once and belting toward us. The snow compounded to become a wall which reached the sky. We were small and helpless. Tiny ants. I was buried.' He shook his right hand as if trying to get rid of the memory. 'I raised this hand as high above me as I could,' and he mimed what he recalled doing. 'I spat snow and used this hand to form an igloo around my nose and mouth, but my eyes were already jammed by snow. I pretended to ski and I stayed alive, but thought, I will die. I will die. And then, a miracle. I felt a probe against my gloved hand and held on. Someone? Is that someone? I'm not sure for a few minutes and then I sense that the snow is thinning away and not just my hand but my arm is free, then the rest of me. I can't believe my luck. I'm frozen sick. Stunned as well.

'Barely able to stand, I threw myself at my rescuer and laughed and cried and hugged him and two others who had helped. The two of them kept probing and moving on, but he hugged me back. "We've got to get the hell out of it." He yelled, to get me going. I was punch drunk. Suddenly I thought, Colette! Annetje! I kept shouting, and the soldier, he kept yelling.

"They'll find them – if they were near you, those guys will find them all right. We have to get you out of this." It was impossible to talk. My eyes were strange, he was right. He kept pushing at me to move.'

Henry looked at the innocent faces of the boys. The firelight danced in their black hair, their cheeks glowed red. For a moment he was held by their sameness.

'You two identical?'

'Worst luck!' Jiro said, and then, in a good-natured rebuke, Ichiro biffed Jiro in the ribs, and they wriggled a bit. But this was an enthralling story for them and they were waiting for the rest of it.

'When we got into a bit of a sheltered spot, I asked about my two companions. He humoured me, assured me that his mates would find them. Told me there's a whole army of soldiers up there.' He looked at his watch. 'It's nearly two hours ago now, isn't it?' His voice was loud, and shaking, 'I should help look for them. They were buried too, I know it.' He covered his face with his hands and cried again. The young boys cried. And everyone waited in sympathetic silence, passing tissues around to be used then thrown upon the fire.

When a soldier came to their chalet to check on them all, they could not stop Henry going out with him. Hamish had given him a big hug and said, 'Courage, Henry.'

And it was on that night that the worst event of all occurred.

'Let's not think about Galtür and skiing, then!' Hamish picked up the tray, and took Mary's mug from her and said, 'I'll put these away, and you'll say what you'd like to do next.'

When he returned from taking the tray to the kitchen, she said, 'Let's just meander along the lake road, find some little café and talk. I so much want you to talk to me, before you completely lose your brogue! It's your brogue I married you for!' she laughed.

'And I'm doing my best to speak proper, like you!' Hamish retorted.

'Don't talk nonsense! But, talking of the future, what I'd really like to do is to spend a night or two at Riva Del Garda.'

'You're joking!'

'I'm serious. Even just one night! It's magic. Remember? We live so near to Garda, now. Please, Hamish.'

'One thing at a time. Ready to go driving now?'

'Not until you give me a yes.'

He reached down and kissed her nose. 'For you, my darling, yes.'

Part One
Chapter 4

Fujiwara struggled to teach the little girl whose grandma had brought her to the Institute for lessons. He managed to get her name right, but one look at her posture and he said to the grandmother, 'Dr Meads, you must observe my students and how they hold their instrument and their bow. I do not enjoy doing remedial work on a child who plays so badly.'

'I paid for lessons with you and I won't go back to Chicago without them.' The woman looked adamant. Her mouth was down at the corners, and Fujiwara wished she would disappear. He was not used to such impudence.

The child began to weep quietly against her grandmother's arm.

'It's all right, Sandy, it's going to be all right,' the elderly woman whispered, her mouth settling into a straight line. To the *sensei*, she said, 'We have both worked hard to get here. Please help us.'

'I will ask one of my students to take Sandy. She will do all right.' He got up from his chair by the window and faced Dr Meads.

'*Gomen nasai*. Very sorry. I cannot teach any more today. I am not well. Please see Miss Miyazawa at the desk.'

Dr Meads picked up the child's violin case and helped Sandy pack her instrument away.

'Fujiwara *sensei* is not like his usual self, Sandy. He is still sad after what happened to Jiro. It is not you at fault, it is his. But we are here now so we must go and see who will teach you.'

Fujiwara told his secretary that he and Mrs Fujiwara would be away for some time.

'You will re-schedule all the lessons and tell the students that I am not well. I need to rest.' Fujiwara arrived home in the middle of the morning and his wife was alarmed.

'Kentaro, what is wrong? You are ill?'

'Yes, I am ill. I looked at this little girl that Dr Meads had brought from Chicago and could only see Jiro. He was so perfect. This little girl was terrible! I cannot stand to see such dreadful posture! Hear such terrible tone! Yuki, we must talk.' And talk he did, about having a clone of Ichiro created for them.

Yuki was still haunted by what she thought had been a nightmare, only to recall that the idea had been planted back in Galtür. She could not help but remember the conversation. It was as clear and chilling as the ice crystals that bombarded the chalet on that last night in the ski resort.

> The children went to bed after they had eaten supper. Henry left to search for his friends. The families knew that it would only be, if the helicopter could land again next day, that they would be leaving the resort as hoped. The wind howled and pounced, and as the adults sat on at the dinner table, everyone was trying to hold on to the structure of their lives lest the mighty forces that raged outside envelop and devour them. She felt a bit embarrassed that Kentaro talked loudly about the method he had evolved for teaching their children music from the age of three. He drank too much, and boasted while pounding the wooden table, declaring that, no matter what child was brought to his Institute, musical genes or not, he could teach him or her to play like a genius!
>
> But she let him rave on. After all, sitting listening to the wind would have been terrifying. And she could see that the imposing Dr Hamish McLeod and his warmly affectionate wife Mary, listened keenly, excited that Kentaro had come to this conclusion after much research and trial. She watched Hamish nod and pour

more wine, loved to hear him speak, but missed the odd word because it was Scottish not English!

'We'd agree, wouldna we, Mary. Just think o' Trish and how she's become a wee champion at skiing. And why? I'd wager that it's because you and I have brought her to the slopes since she was two years old.' He sat back and played with his beard a minute and then his eyes lifted from their sombre, thoughtful expression to a knowing brightness.

'Is it just that? Or is it mostly because it's in her genes. We've always been skiers. Right, Mary? So listen to this. Part of my plan for the distant future is to create animals with different preferences and degrees of intelligence, then apply that to humans. The rhesus monkeys are perfect for that. Already, reports from Washington are encouraging. They have the animals arranging groups of abstract elements such as circles in ascending numerical order, and are testing the nature versus nurture theory by playing different styles of music to expectant monkeys.'

Everyone laughed loudly at the idea.

'I can see them!' Mary said. 'A new-born rhesus nodding and smiling in recognition to the *Carnival of the Animals*! '

Kentaro went along with the joke 'Or shedding little tears to *Don't Cry for me Argentina*. He lapsed into Japanese. '*Hai. Hai. Subarashii*. Hamish, I'm sorry. Yes. Wonderful! And I'll be very interested to hear the results! I do concede that a child develops faster if there is music already in the family.'

She remembered now how suddenly the wind dropped. Each of them noticed it and shrugged or smiled nervously but said nothing in tacit agreement of their terror. Predictably it was Mary who brought them into the train of thought again.

'You'll be quite well-known for your method in Japan, are you, Kentaro?' she asked.

'Yes and no. I've followed in the footsteps of one who has become great, but my method is different.' He helped himself to a last cracker and talked as he piled it with pâté. 'This whole notion of fame! I've thought a lot about it.' He sliced some cheese and laid it on the cracker and looked at them with a boyish vigour for his subject. 'For example, if a person climbs to the top of a mountain, should the person or the mountain be revered?'

Hamish took a drink and said, 'Go on, man. This is good.'

'In my country, where Buddhism is the dominant religion, the higher the elevation the greater the holiness of the deity!'

'Just think back to the mileage that Britain extracted out of Edmund Hillary's achievement,' said Yuki. 'You'll have read about it too – on the night before the coronation of Elizabeth II, the news reached Britain, that Hillary and Sherpa Tensing had climbed Everest so they claimed colonial glory!'

'For me, it's simple,' said Mary. 'The creator God gets the glory every time! That's why I like coming here. I get a sense of myself, of humility. Just take the beauty, the stillness – well, when there isn't a wind! The white loveliness of it all, it gives me a sense of humility to take back into the classroom. Makes me love my children the more when they need me. That kind of thing.'

'She's a praying lass, is Mary.' Hamish's deep chuckle not only expressed his respect for her strong religious beliefs, but conveyed the depth of comfort he found in his wife's strength. You could tell from the way he talked and touched his wife, that he even the loved the roundness of her, the way she looked, the soft tenderness in her expression.

'But why don't we continue this at the fire?' he asked.

Kentaro was up like a shot to put on a couple of logs and get the wood flaming wildly. He loved the open fire, so different from the *kotatsu* under the table at home.

Yuki had been happy to gravitate to where the fire was, and pulled up a comfortable chair to be as near the hearth as she dared. Her legs were nowhere as long as Hamish McLeod's, but she followed his stance and stretched them out while Mary re-arranged and offered cushions and they all looked to the fire for warmth. Then, when everyone was settled, Hamish was right back into conversation without a moment's delay.

'You may not believe it, but I struggle with the same question in genetic engineering. It's like that when success comes along – you know, a new embryo or even a new-born mouse – where does the credit lie?'

'More to the point, who laps up all the praise? Come on, now, Hamish? Who loves to tell me what he has done?' Mary was smiling and looking to him for his answer. He grinned and stroked his auburn beard and looked proud, in spite of himself.

'I guess, I have to admit, I like a wee bit of the credit for myself.'

'I can't bear to think what you'll be like when you've got to the big stuff.'

'You mean cloning of humans?' All eyes turned on him, pierced his conscience. Yuki could sense that he wished he hadn't said that. He hit his knee and said, 'Och, whatever comes up. You know, there are endless possibilities.' He turned the comment around. 'Japanese like to copy, don't they? Cloning is a very Japanese concept. Am I right?'

'Historically, yes, we've been copiers,' said Yuki. 'But we are also highly creative. You will have been obsessed about copying since Dolly, eh? Clever, but questionable, don't you think? Just you wait and see. They will be patenting the production of proteins in milk, and one or two pharmaceutical companies will dominate the market. Just one more commercial venture out of something too awesome to think about.'

'Strange you should say that Yuki. I'm moving away from Dolly country to northern Italy. There's the New Biotech Centre for GE research at Como. A different scene, different life for me. And my girls!'

Mary yawned, noisily patting her open mouth.

'And guess who's doing all the packing? Except that Trish won't let me touch her stuff!' Everyone laughed.

'You'll be tired all right,' Kentaro said meaningfully. 'When I set up my Institute in Nagoya …' He was off again.

It was what Hamish had said about cloning people. Human babies! She knew now that it was not a nightmare at all. Kentaro had seen the possibilities and he was not going to let go. Now, back from work, he was on to it again.

'We have to find an embryologist who will clone a son for us. I will not teach again until it is done.'

She pushed Hamish out of her mind.

'But, Kentaro. I don't think that anyone will do it. No one in the world has said they would even if they could. UNESCO and the Bill of Human Rights, I read an article …

It said something like it would be inhuman! Undignified! There was outrage after the Dolly ...'

'So it might seem, but we know better than that. Once Dolly was cloned, any number of embryologists wanted to be the first to clone a person. Remember Hamish McLeod? That's human nature! All ethics go out the window when one can see the possibility of something yet not done.'

'Oh, Kentaro, you are sick in your head.'

He moved swiftly to slap her face. 'You are the sick one. If you cannot see the possibility of Jiro coming back to us. You are the one who needs help.' His voice followed her as she ran to the tap to dampen a cloth to hold against her cheek. She was humiliated, and sat on a chair with her head bowed. Silent tears racked her body. He walked to put a hand on her head. She pulled back to escape him, but he did not let go.

'I am sorry, Yuki. I should not have done that, but can't you see the possibility of Jiro returning is real? It can be done.'

Yuki didn't know which way to turn. Her mind was in a whirl.

'You want to clone from Ichiro!'

'And why not? He need never know!'

'You mean you will steal cells from him and he'll never know?'

'That's right. Except it's not stealing. And it will be done professionally.'

'It wouldn't be Jiro. It can never be Jiro. He's dead. Remember, his smashed face and frozen body. The report said he'd been killed by falling debris; killed outright, remember?'

'Be quiet! Yuki.' He shrieked. 'I only remember his graduation concert and all the acclaim. That is what I remember! Jiro, the child genius!'

'You are living in your imagination. You will suffer for tampering with the unknown.'

'Yuki, we are going away. We are going to find a scientist who is willing to give us a son. No one can stop us now. My heart is set on it and you will soon see the sense in it.' He turned and went to his office and Yuki knew, in that moment, that she had no choice but to go away with him. She started to think of what to tell Ichiro who would be expected to play a vital part, yet must not be told the truth. There was a certain consolation in his coming away with them. But the deception? She didn't like it one bit. She had a fondness for Ichiro whom only she knew had been her favourite son, her first-born by two minutes. And Jiro? Well, everyone loved Jiro.

Dr Meads stood waiting at the office for an answer to her question – Who will teach my grand-daughter? She had been asked to sit on the bench and had whispered to Sandy, 'We have no choice but to wait here.'

After ten minutes, a young woman appeared.

'I will teach Sandy, Dr Meads.' She smiled down at the little girl. 'Hello. Sandy, I will show you my room. Please come.'

They followed the quick, light steps of the Japanese woman who looked as if she might be about eighteen, her skin was so fresh, her face, oval, and firm.

'Quick,' Dr Meads said to Sandy. 'She looks nice.' Sandy hunched up her shoulders as much as to say, you promised I'd learn from Dr Fujiwara, but she hurried, nevertheless.

Once in the room which overlooked the small bridge that led to the park, Sandy felt better. She had had such a good time in the park yesterday, throwing leaves off that bridge and running to the other side to see them floating away.

'I like that park.' Chiyo the teacher, said, 'It's beautiful at the moment. I saw a crocus peeping above the soil yesterday. Spring is here, Sandy. And, today, you are like a spring bulb – just beginning to flower! Can you show me how well you can play?'

Kentaro came out of his office saying, 'We can fly to Milan tomorrow, Yuki. I'm going to ring the school and ask that Ichiro comes home now.' He stood before her, and put his hands on her shoulders as if to say, I am in charge of this. 'Don't tell anyone anything. I will say I am not well and Ichiro is needed at home.'

'All right, but why Milan?'

'It's best that you know nothing just yet.'

Yuki did not need to ask. She knew all right! But she would see Mary again, and that would be good. She thought of things she would need before flying out and told Kentaro she would be home as soon as Ichiro. With shoes on, and her snow jacket, she prepared to be hit by a chilly wind when she opened the door. That's straight off the Alps, she thought.

Itte kimasu,' she called and '*Itte raisshai,*' came the reply. She rolled her bike down the step and as she cycled to fetch a few things from the shop before Ichiro came home, she thought – Kentaro is mad!

She had read articles in science magazines. She knew that some geneticists were working behind the scenes to develop the technologies, even to the idea of manipulating sperm! She knew of the fears that everyone, including the scientists had of cloning children, like the possibility that a few generations down the track, weaknesses and deformities might emerge. She could not agree with Kentaro that it was the right thing to do. Not until greater advances had been made, if ever. She arrived at the drug store feeling sick at the thought. Inside the shop, she put on a brave face, replenished the supplies she needed, and then returned home at the same moment as Ichiro.

'What's wrong with Dad?'

Did she have to start lying to him?

'He didn't explain much to me. But he'll tell you, maybe.'

'I hope he won't die!'

'Of course not, Ichiro. That's a silly idea. Who put that into your head?'

'Well, the kids in my class reckoned he would.'

'That's children. Is it so unusual for a boy to be taken from class?' she turned to say as she took her bike up the steps.

'Diasuke said that when he was called home it was because his mother had died.'

'No, your dad will be better soon.' She took off her shoes and placed them beside the others.

Part One
Chapter 5

Peter had asked to meet the present members of staff of the Music and Arts Academy before making a final decision as to whether or not he would accept the position of cello teacher. The job carried a big salary, but it would mean an upheaval for his partner who had set up a physiotherapy practice in Toronto, and Peter had to be sure that a move was an advantage to both of them.

Carrying his cello case, he climbed the two flights of stairs to the room where he had been invited to go, and knocked. The dark-haired Spaniard, Miguel Garcia, answered the door, his violin in his hand as if he wanted to keep playing.

'Good, you've brought your cello, I see.' He shook Peter's free hand warmly.

'It's sure good to meet you. The others will be here in a minute. We thought that the best way for you to visit with us was to play some Schubert together. That way, we all get to have our say! Find a chair that suits you.' He then put his violin in its case and took the double bass from its stand in the corner of the room, and began to tune it.

Without moving to get a chair, Peter said 'It's a great idea. You're versatile, I see.' He looked around him. The room was large by studio standards. If Peter had not known before that Miguel was a fine painter he would have guessed it now. Brilliant depictions of ships plying the St Lawrence River carried one's eye away from the untidy desk, and on the wall behind the piano there was a painting of Niagara Falls from the American side, no mistake, and two smaller paintings of buildings in Spain. Peter chose a chair, put his heavy case in the unoccupied corner of the room, and removed his cello and bow.

Andreas, a tall, well-built student, with a pony tail of wavy black hair, was resining his bow. Peter nodded to him.

'So you're looking well, Andreas.'

'Yes, thanks, I'm well.'

'So, of course you two know each other. Andreas often talks about his six months with the Toronto Symphony.'

Miguel perched on a stool. Andreas played an A, reached to the piano to check it, did a little fine-tuning, and gave Peter the A again as an invitation to tune his cello.

'Jude's the pianist, and Jim violist,' Miguel said. 'They've been rehearsing, so they'll be here in a moment. I hope so, anyway.' Peter nodded, and played some Bach to get his fingers going. In the middle of a bourrée, his bow tip caught in a string. He stopped and laughed.

'I reckon I got to thinking about the last cello teacher here, Miguel. I've heard that there was some kind of tragedy. Can you fill me in?' He hung his bow from the music stand which Andreas had placed in front of him, and let the cello rest against his shoulder as he challenged him to answer. Andreas scraped his chair on the floor and Peter watched him with concern at his expression as he began to play his violin *sotto voce*. He would have asked him to shut up, except that he was the visitor now. Miguel did not seem to mind.

'You've heard that he was murdered, then,' Miguel said softly.

Peter nodded. At that moment, a quick knock on the door heralded the arrival of the others, and Jim and Jude burst in full of energy after what had to have been a successful rehearsal.

'That went well. I can see that from your faces!' Miguel said, laughing. 'Now, Jude and Jim meet Peter.' Jim put his viola case on the floor, and as soon as Jude had finished giving Peter a warm handshake, he said, 'It's good to meet you, Peter. Welcome to the team.'

'It's not a *fait accompli*,' Peter chortled. 'But I'm happy to meet you guys like this.' The goodwill that came from them all, and the casual way they dressed, suggested a very relaxed atmosphere in the music academy. He could hack this kind of approach.

Jude began to read the music that Miguel had placed on the piano.

'OK, so we're playing the Schubert?' She checked that all the string players were ready, and sounded the A. Each one took it up and were soon poised to go, eyes on Andreas.

Peter knew *The Trout* well. It was a favourite of his so he revelled in it and was relaxed enough to assess the playing of the others as they went on through the movements.

Andreas was playing well, the others were brilliant. Peter wondered why Andreas had been asked to play, when surely there were other violinists who were stronger.

The final bars were played with aplomb. With bows still suspended, and Jude with her hands above the keyboard, they all expressed their satisfaction.

'Good one,' cried Miguel. Peter had most certainly come through with flying colours but that was exactly what was expected and was not remarked on.

'We make a good sound, I believe,' Jim said. 'No mean cello you've got there, Peter. Have you got a stack of pieces for solo cello?'

'All the usual, and a few unusual ones, too. There's a neat solo, quite a recent composition.' He played the opening eight bars, and the others nodded in the realisation that it was a challenging piece in the way it rippled in and out of the top register. Peter laughed at his own efforts, he had been trying to impress them.

'Spirals. Exquisite!' Miguel said. 'Keep at it, and it'll be one of your star pieces. So we can go visit in the staff room now. How about it? Leave your things here, Peter. I'll lock up.'

Andreas left, and Miguel concentrated on the newcomer.

'Peter! I'm sorry we included Andreas. He's not the best at chamber music – you know that, I'm sure, but he's been acting a bit strange lately and we all feel a kind of concern for him. Keep him on his toes to help him through!'

'Yes. I saw his cheek twitch. Never seen him like that before. It was when I mentioned Carlos. Anything to do with his death? CT they called him, didn't they? That must have happened soon after Andreas came to study here.'

'Excuse me, Peter,' Judy said, 'but I must go. I hope we see a lot more of you!'

'Agreed,' added Jim. 'And look here, Peter, if you want to know what I think, I'm convinced you're the man for the job. We'll have great times together, and staff performances here are very important.' He lowered his voice and made out to whisper, 'Let sleeping dogs lie. CT's gone and that's that.' He pulled back, and shook Peter's hand saying, 'Good one, Peter. See you soon, I hope.' And Judy and Jim left the room together.

Part One
Chapter 6

Once Ichiro was tucked into bed in the Milan hotel, Kentaro and Yuki were alone. They sipped wine, and enjoyed the comfort of the enormous armchairs in their suite. Yuki thought Kentaro more relaxed than she had seen him for a long time. His buoyancy had returned, making his dark eyes sparkle, his cheeks, glow. His movements were swift. He spoke enthusiastically.

'Yuki, my pet, I have very good news to share now that no-one can hear us. You will recall what I said about getting a clone of Ichiro. Well Hamish McLeod is here. You remember him don't you?'

'Hamish McLeod. Of course! How can I ever forget that man? It was such a tragedy for all of us! Trish was so beautiful.'

'And she had to be one of the liveliest kids I've known.' He got up and began to switch on different lights until he found two that dimmed to faint, and left them on.

Yuki watched him flitting quickly about, and sensed that he was about to break the hard news. It was going to help not to see her expression too well.

'More wine, Yuki?'

'No thanks.' He sat down again.

'So, why Hamish?

'OK. So I followed up on what he'd said. He's well settled in the Biotech Research Centre. I want to ask him if he can clone us a son.'

'At Como? So why are we in Milan?'

'It's about an hour to Como. Tomorrow we go to the hotel there. Just a short run to the outskirts of the town.'

'Is it easy to find?'

'Of course. The car will be delivered at eight tomorrow and I have a map in Japanese.'

'And you think Hamish might be wicked enough to do what you want, do you?' Her voice was thin, her words, slurred. Wine always did this to her. But for the subject of their conversation, she would be dancing around the room, gliding with the white cormorants of her blue kimono, weaving between the table and bar, and luring her husband into bed by slipping the kimono off a shoulder, and looking back at him with that come hither look at which she was so good.

'I shall ask him if he will do it,' he said. 'Tomorrow.'

It was all becoming too real, too serious, for Yuki. She felt scared that a cloned child might be born deformed. She had read of the possibility of three ears, six fingers on each hand, and worst of all, two heads. Why should she be one of the guinea pigs for an inexperienced geneticist? That she might not want to carry a cloned child had barely registered with Kentaro. But he was like that – tenacious in the extreme. She had watched him develop his own method of teaching, standing for hours with a violin in his hand, then seated at his computer, writing up all his ideas and teaching precepts. He did not want to copy any other teacher, he was not into plagiarism, he had to think through every little thing he ever learned as a teacher in the school system, and apply a perfect model for his own way of developing technique. It was only after running a pilot programme for a year of lessons for ten young children that he admitted that he was pleased with his experiment and would open the Fujiwara Institute.

Yuki wanted to tell him that she was repulsed by the notion of cloning. He would blame the wine that she was enjoying. Call her notion nonsense. Yet she had good grounds for concern. She had become very heavy and ungainly carrying twins, and worst of all, her blood pressure became seriously high.

'Kentaro, remember how sick I was …?' He would not even hear her out.

'Yuki, we're talking about one baby, just think of it as Jiro!'

'You're talking now as if it were a thing. It, it, it! I find that abhorrent. You say to think of it as another Jiro. No! He's dead. Dead!' She flicked her kimono sleeve across her face and ran to kneel at the bed. She wept. And only a muffled sob broke the silence.

Kentaro waited until her body stopped shaking, then left his chair to lift her on to the bed. He threw off his clothes, put her beneath the covers, and gently opened her kimono and stroked her naked body, still warm from bathing.

'I love you, Yuki. Love you.' She saw him reach for a condom.

'No. I hate those things. If you love me you'll do what you've always done.' She turned away from him and he stretched out beside her and stroked her body, nibbling an ear and whispering, 'My pet. You are so beautiful. I have to use a rubber.'

In one movement Yuki was off the bed and looking down on him. Her black hair was dishevelled and her eyes wild with anger and hurt.

'You have to use that stupid thing because you want a cloned child. Not one conceived in love. No, no, no!' She turned swiftly and ran toward the next room. 'I'm not sleeping with you.'

He saw her in the light of the second room as she moved to prepare the bed for herself. He watched a pillow, then another, fly across the room to the dresser. Then she brushed past his bed to get her toilet bag, ignoring him. Yet he had always liked her when she was wild. She was especially attractive to him in her lingerie and he admired her shapely figure, beautiful if a little short, in a long red satin nightie. He could see the movement of her breasts, and her bottom, well developed from bike-riding and aerobics, and was overwhelmingly desirous. If they were not here for such a significant reason, for which he needed her full co-operation, he would have grabbed her right then.

It was late the next morning. Kentaro checked his watch.

They had made good time in getting to Como and easily found the central hotel where they had booked to stay. Ichiro wanted to take a boat ride on the lake, and Yuki said they would go and find out what was available. Kentaro was then free to go off alone. He found the New Biotec Centre without any problems, and took from his pocket the pass that would get him through the gate to take him into the main compound. He was confident he had found the right entrance because of what Hamish had told him.

'There is a fir tree with a mountain in the background to your right as you approach the gate. Look for that.'

Hamish greeted Kentaro enthusiastically. They had one thing in common, the death of a child. Sadness hung heavy in their limbs, their hug was prolonged by unshed tears. Hamish spoke first.

'I didn't expect I would see you again, Kentaro. Is Yuki here with you?'

'Not here. She and Ichiro are in Como, and hoping to go out on the lake. We stayed last night in Milan. Maybe you will join us for dinner this evening. You can meet her again. We'd like to see your wife, too.'

'Mary and I often talk at lunchtime. I'll check it with her then. Thank you, anyway. So what brings you to Italy and me? Please sit down.' Hamish sat at his desk. His eyes looked particularly large in his long, bearded face. For a moment, Kentaro could only think of the dominating picture of Dolly that was just behind Hamish's head. Under any other circumstances he would have joked about it.

'Before I tell you why I've come I want to ask for complete confidentiality.'

'Well, of course. That is, unless you have an earthquake warning that you know about!' He smiled, roguishly. Kentaro smiled, too, then put his hands together to calm himself, and cleared his throat again.

'You have successfully cloned sheep and you were going to be researching nature versus nurture. How's it going?'

'No conclusions yet, but going well all the same.'

'I'll be very interested in your results. But now, let me tell you why we've come.' He gave a little bow. 'We want you to clone us a child.' Hamish blinked, bit his bottom lip and studied his desk without responding. Then he looked intently at Kentaro.

'This is your way of dealing with your son's death?'

'Yes, Jiro was a very remarkable child. A great little violinist. His recital was played on national television while we were skiing in Galtür – I've never had that kind of recognition before. And I still haven't seen all the mail – thousands of letters since he died! I've had to ask my secretary to deal with them.'

'So the little fellow tasted fame, eh! Kentaro, are you sure you don't need more time on this? Do you know what you're asking?'

'Yes, I know. As for time, it's been six dreadful months. I need to know that we are doing all we can – there's Ichiro to start with. He's lost half of himself, and while I know and Yuki knows we cannot give him back his twin, we need a major distraction. All of us do.'

Hamish walked about, fingering his beard. Then he paused and looked down at Kentaro. 'Is it not possible for you to have another child?'

'We seem not to be able to have a child for some reason or other. It simply hasn't happened.' Kentaro looked flustered and hesitant.

Hamish could see it was not a line of questioning that was likely to get very far.

'You see cloning as the way ahead, then?'

'You did infer that cloning a human was on your agenda so why not a child for us?'

'I blustered rather, I must say. In terms of strong arguments against cloning, ethics and the law, it's not really accepted, you know. By the way, does Yuki want this too?' He mellowed a little. 'Is she all right? We had so much trauma to recover from – Yuki, maybe, most of all.'

Kentaro thought for a moment in silence. Hamish recognised the pain that caused the anguish in his eyes. He carried it within himself, and glanced at the photo of his daughter skiing, her long auburn hair falling loose over the iridescent clothing which covered her agile body, determination in every muscle. A striking picture. He would do almost anything to have her back. Kentaro cleared his throat, and Hamish gave him his attention.

'Yuki will come round, I know. But ethics aside, legislation aside, would you do it? The world needs the heart-rending sound of a violin. It is the very stuff of life. Jiro is a great loss, not just to our family but to the world.'

'I could clone from Ichiro? Is that what you want?'

'Yes. From Ichiro.'

'Even if I could clone a child, I cannot assure you that he will play the violin well, or even at all.'

'That is not an argument in this case.' He was irritated. 'I believe I said this to you that time we talked. I can get any child to play the violin. It is a matter of environment and nurture. My method proves that time and time again! Ichiro plays the piano because we nurtured him to play it. Jiro was a violinist because we put a violin in his hands when he was two-and-a-half. I was his model. He learned to play because we inspired him to play, regardless of genes!'

'I think you must let me ponder on your request. I'll talk with both you and Yuki at this time tomorrow, perhaps. At lunchtime I will leave a message at the hotel for you? So please give me the details of where you are staying.'

'I have the information on this card. Copy from here.'

Hamish spent a moment writing, then looked earnestly at Kentaro who was now standing.

'I make no promises at all. In fact, I might just as well say, that my first reaction is no way. Never! You must understand that I am in the employ of the Biotec Centre and no way would it be currently sanctioned here – yet. It would be a private and highly confidential matter.' He looked thoughtful, and bent a little to speak more quietly. 'I'll think about it. Tomorrow is a new day. And tomorrow I may see things differently.' He stood. And he felt the difference in their heights less acutely than when they had hugged, for then Kentaro seemed bowed down with grief. Now he stood erect.

Kentaro made a point he felt could make a difference.

'I am willing to pay a substantial amount, of course.'

Hamish shook his head. 'If we do it – not substantial. A moderate fee, only.' They shook hands.

'I'm keen to see Yuki again. A brave woman, she is that.'

Within moments, Hamish was in Bill's office asking his receptionist to buzz him when Bill was free. While he went back to his own office, Hamish was torn by a mixture of guilt, confusion and incredible happiness. Bill was his confidant who had encouraged Mary and him to use the cells that Hamish had taken from his daughter's body as it lay in the morgue, and clone themselves a child.

'Why shouldn't your lives be enhanced by your genius for cloning? And, if you didn't have this in mind, Hamish, then why did you take some DNA at all? You said it nearly killed you doing it!'

Mary had agreed – but not at first.

'Hamish, no! That would be like a doctor treating his own family. It's just not done!' she said, emphatically. But over the course of the following month, she thought and she prayed, and one night as they cuddled in bed, she said softly, 'Hamish, it's not the same. Bill's not family, and I can't think of a good reason why not. I'd so love to have a baby daughter again.' And so it had happened, and because it had occurred so easily, Hamish was ready to believe with Mary's view that it had been God's will.

The receptionist's bleeping him caused Hamish to jump but he was relieved that Bill did not keep him waiting for long.

'Bill, listen to this! You'll remember the Fujiwaras?'

'Of course. You have told me so much about them.'

'Well, Kentaro has just asked me to clone them a son.'

Bill sat back in his chair, feeling stunned at the coincidence. 'You mean he's been here? Your news got around? Japan's a long way from Italy!'

Hamish perched on the padded arm of a large chair, and looked down on the small man at his desk.

'Not at all'

Bill's eyes showed a flare of interest. 'And, he knows nothing about your cloning Trish?'

'Nothing! I haven't told him. Neither shall I at this point. You see, and you know as well as I do, this is between us. A private matter. The embarrassing thing for me is that I cannot tell them I took cells from their dead son as well as my own daughter.'

'Why not?'

'The idea is theirs. I will go through the motions, take their lead and get some of Ichiro's cells, too. I can use the cells of both boys for some very interesting studies on twins.'

'And this will be part of your private research?'

'That's it. Paid for, in the main, by our two Italian friends.'

'You'll tell Roberto and Gianfranco?'

'Of course, of course. In time, and only what's necessary for them to know. And that's the best part because we can justify their funding. Whatever else, though,' he looked more serious, 'we must maintain the Fujiwara's confidentiality.' Bill stood up and poured himself a water. He held up the polystyrene cup. 'You, too?'

'No, thanks. Let's refer to them as something else. How about Raif? Will that do?'

Bill laughed. 'It'll do! And, when do I get to meet this Raif?'

Hamish ran his hand through his beard and puckered his mouth.

'We've had one chat. Give me a day or two. We've got a bit of work to do on the wife, she's not so keen as her husband.'

'Oh, I see. I see.'

Part One
Chapter 7

Canada was in the throes of a very hot summer. As she walked from her apartment in Charles St. to Bloor St. and the Royal Conservatorium, Donna could believe that she would have been cooler in a long skirt rather than the mini she was wearing. She wished she had caught a bus. She thought of running, but then decided to hail a cab and arrive to teach feeling cool and ready rather than sizzled and irritable. The violin class demanded enough of her patience as it was.

She arrived some fifteen minutes early so she checked her diary to make certain she knew her time-table. A quiver of excitement ran through her when she saw the name Thomas Blackwell at the four o'clock time. She thought of young Tom, and how he was so keen to keep learning from her after summer camp. Toronto children were already on her waiting list, but she had given preference to Thomas because ... well, and what were her motives? She thought about it, then had to admit that she had felt quite attracted to his father. Better put that thought out of my mind. The reason had to be one that focused on the needs of the child. He certainly needs me, she thought. If he had stayed with his other teacher, his posture would have caused him all kinds of problems. Maybe arthritis in his neck or back or both. No, Thomas needed her help.

She moved past his name to the next one. It was a Renée, but not the problem-mother one. She sighed. And then at five o'clock she had a lad of seventeen. A wonderful player and a great teenager to take last on any day. His hour-long lesson would be sheer joy, especially as he was majoring in Paganini.

'Hi, there, Thomas. Hello, Warren. How've you been? All ready to start? Why not put your case here under the window, Thomas. And Warren, why not put your jacket here on this rack and take this seat?

She had spoken so quickly that the responses came like delayed reaction. She sat down and watched Warren Blackwell adjust his tee shirt so that the words, "write small for the planet" became clear as it flattened. He smiled at Donna, a smile that said don't mind this old slow coach here, and bent to help Tom with his bow.

'No worries. Warren, why don't you sit down and let Thomas do all the setting up for himself?' She twiddled with the rings in her right earlobe and Warren remembered that he had made a mental note to be extra helpful when she did that. He sat down and said, 'So how's life?'

'Fine, thanks.'

'Thomas, I'm ready for you.'

After the lesson, Donna said, 'Warren, I'd like to see your notes to make certain you've understood me OK. Thomas, here's your sticker. Now the notebook, Warren.'

'Do I have to?' He was embarrassed.

'Sure. You have to teach Thomas all week so it's important to have it right.' He didn't want her to fidget with her ear all through next week's lesson, so he handed it over, and stood close as she read the first page. She could smell his sweat. God, he has travelled all the way in the heat. Or is he that excited? The writing was very small. She smiled, and her hand went up to her ear. She had deciphered the finely written words, "Nice legs. Enjoying myself. Practise strong tone near bridge; rainbow arched fingers."

'There you are, Warren.' She avoided his eyes.

'You'll improve. Incidentally, what's your work?' She reached into a box and brought out a card. 'I forgot to get you to fill this out. Why not sit here and fill the gaps? By the way, my pupils often overlap and you're welcome to stay on and listen to Renée's lesson.' She talked too fast again but had caught, and acknowledged, his answer, 'Freelance journo', as she carried on. 'We encourage the observation of others' lessons.'

'Not the summer camp Renée, I hope?'

Donna smiled and looked directly at him. They shared a memory, distasteful though it was.

'No, this one is quite charming.'

Part One
Chapter 8

Since Mary had insisted that they entertain the couple from Japan at their favourite hotel overlooking Lake Como, Hamish conveyed this invitation to Kentaro and Yuki and they graciously accepted.

As they ascended in the glass lift, Yuki wished that Ichiro had been there to enjoy the view and the fun. He was not pleased to be left alone in the central hotel. She asked for a snack to be brought to him at 9 p.m., and reassured him.

'You'll be all right. You can play computer games – but not more than an hour and a half, OK? Then why don't you email your friends? But perhaps not. Not until you've got a bandaged finger to show them. And listen carefully Ichiro, when you tell your friends that a doctor scraped your finger for DNA, please tell them that he's a friend from Galtür and wanted to learn why you are so good at the piano. We decided not to tell anyone where we were going so only say we went back to Galtür to see about a memorial. Tell your journal about Italy instead. Got that?'

'Course! I want them to know about the memorial. But why not Italy?'

'Sometimes families like to have secret holiday places. That's all. OK? Good boy. I'm sorry to be going out tonight, Ichiro. Don't just wait for us. Read your book and go to sleep.'

'No. I'll play more games, and you won't be here to stop me. And, Mum, can I buy lots of presents to take back to my friends?'

'Of course. Shall we do that in the departure lounge? They have lots of video games and such things there.'

'Good thinking.' She kissed him on the cheek. 'You do what you want, then. But go to sleep when you're tired. We've got a booking to go up the lake tomorrow, remember.

You and dad and I. We'll all go.'

As the lift arrived, Mary and Hamish leapt up from the easy chairs to greet Kentaro and Yuki who stepped into the spacious foyer. Yuki looked particularly trim in this place with the high, ornate ceiling, and the wide staircase rising out of it.

'Yuki, how good to see you again.' There were tears in the eyes of both couples as they met in this way. The terrible loss both families had suffered almost a year ago came rushing back to them. The beautiful Trish, strong and radiant, conquering the slopes, and young Jiro in Austria to enjoy skiing and playing with his friends. It took Mary and Yuki time to recover their poise. They could only hold each other and pat the other's shoulder, as if comforting a child.

Hamish excused himself and went to the adjacent bar. He ordered champagne for three, and iced water for Mary, then suggested they sit in the glassed area adjacent to the lift where the backdrop of the lake and mountains would have a relaxing effect. He arranged the cane chairs so that the visitors would get the best view.

'Maybe you can see why Mary suggested coming here,' he said.

'It's magic,' Yuki said before she sat down. 'The moon over the lake and the mountains. Yes, it is beautiful. It's very nice to be here with you.'

'I'm very happy that you can be here; and want to be,' he added, hoping that he was not pushing it too far.

The table to which they were taken, was on the glassed-in balcony. Mary invited Yuki to sit beside her so that they could share the amazing view. The moon was beckoning them.

Yuki spoke in an undertone to Mary.

'This is an intimate place. And what a breath-taking sight.'

'I love it. And it's the perfect place to talk things out.'

'How does this suit you?' Hamish said to Kentaro.

'It is very good. A lovely place. Thank you.'

The waiter smiled, and gave each one a menu covered in red suede. Hamish looked at the grouping, not the menu, and decided it would be easier to talk to Kentaro if they shared a corner of the table.

'Mary, my pet. I so much want to pick Kentaro's brains about his famous method of teaching, would you mind if we changed places?'

'What a nuisance, you are.' It was said with a good-natured smile. Hamish beamed with love for his wife as they changed places. Mary sat down, leant towards Yuki.

'Anything's a wee bother at the moment,' she confided. 'Eating included. As a matter of fact, I've longed to eat here a third time, but being pregnant is something else again.'

Yuki's eyes lit up with pleasure.

'Oh, so congratulations. How far on?'

'Seven weeks, and we're hoping for a wee girl, we are. Can't wait till she comes.' Hamish had stopped telling Kentaro how the rest of his day had gone, and caught up with Mary in the pause. He gave her a knowing look, and a wink. Yuki marvelled at how well they had recovered from Trish's death.

The bar attendant thrust a wine list before Hamish, who had given him the nod.

'Yuki. A drink?'

'Iced water. But no, on second thoughts, spicy tomato juice. Is that all right?'

'Certainly. Mary, iced water for sure. And, Kentaro, how about we start with a full-bodied wine?'

Mary said, 'I'm glad to tell you about the baby I'm expecting because it's my reason for what I eat and drink tonight. I'm usually the first to the wine bottle. Remember those lovely dinners we had when we arrived at Galtür?'

'Yes, thank you. It is hard for me to remember now. I have become obsessed by sadness. Yes, I can remember the laughter we shared at night over dinner, at least. We were four, and you three ...'

Hamish saw his moment to find out what Yuki thought about Mary's pregnancy as a prelude to introducing the more delicate subject later, except that the waiter had returned to take their orders and collect the menus.

Yuki had made up her mind. Giggling a little as she read it, she said, 'I'd like the *pâté de fore veau au brandy avec crouton*, then *coquilles St.Jacques aux truffes noires, grazie.*'

The waiter made a mental note and his eyes then alighted on Mary.

'*Soupe d'oignon et medaillon de veau.*' She, at least, said it with appropriate fluency.

'*Caroltes à la crème?*' The waiter looked at each woman, and both smiled a yes.

'Kentaro, what's your choice?' Hamish looked directly at Kentaro and said, 'Anything you like.'

'The soup. The scallops with potatoes and carrots, no cream. Thank you.' Hamish was still deep in consideration. He cocked his head as if to clinch his decision, and as he handed back his menu, he asked for the risotto *avec saucisses et aubergine, pommes et carottes. Avec crème.*' He chortled softly.

'Tut, tut,' Mary said, with a wink at her husband. The waiter bowed respectfully and left.

'He's a sweetie, that man,' Mary said. 'Tonight he's really into the bowing thing out of deference for our guests.' Everyone laughed, then Hamish got his question in.

'So what do you think of our news, eh?' He looked at Yuki.

'Oh, it's wonderful. So long as Mary is happy, why should I disapprove?'

'The daddy has to be happy, too,' he laughed.

'Well, judging by your broad smile you certainly are! Am I right?'

'Quite right. I'm over the moon, you know. Over the moon.'

Suddenly Mary was agitated. Looked pale.

'Hamish, I forgot to ask for small helpings.'

'Don't worry, lass. You may like, what was it – veal – so much, you'll want more.' He gave her a nod, and turned to Kentaro.

'So Ichiro will have grown somewhat. How is he?'

Kentaro bent his head a moment, then looked up, moved his head as if to say "Well", but no words came, so Yuki said brightly, 'He's fine. Today we made arrangements to take the ferry to Gargnano. We've heard it's a charming place. Ichiro wants to get a ride on a yacht there. He's mad on the idea.'

'Good, good,' Kentaro nodded. He was only just coping with the bitter-sweet experience of being with these friends once again. For two successive years at the Galtür resort each evening had been spent preparing a meal, and eating together in an atmosphere charged by energy. He kept seeing the happy faces of Jiro and Ichiro. They loved to tease the playful and clever Trish, and the dinner parties were the happiest of times. It seemed impossible to relax even the smallest bit now as he tried to conceal his feelings. He drank the wine then blurted out, 'If only Ichiro wasn't in bed, he'd have been able to take the piano instead of that tipsy fellow!'

They all turned to look at the pianist in the next room and laughed a little at how he seemed to play on automatic with his eyes shut and his body swaying.

'He's swung around like that all night. Maybe he isn't tipsy at all,' Hamish said, laughing as he watched the man making circles with his torso. 'That must be good exercise.'

'I saw him stand and gulp down a drink he took from the bar steward's tray,' Mary said. 'He took yet another, after the next medley. I think they know him here!' They laughed with her and Yuki was glad she had saved the moment for Kentaro. And now, their meal served, they ate and chatted mostly about their various Italian experiences, or in Mary's case pecked and pretended, but talked a lot. It was she who had had to do the shopping and try to make herself understood. It was she who needed to ask directions and find the galleries and tourist attractions.

'There's been many a time when I've sat for an hour in *Piazza Cavour,* you know? Across from where you board the boats! Just to let the world go by. Catch my breath! Watch people. And the ferries. But if you don't want to be chatted up, then you daren't stay more than ten minutes.' She laughed. 'I've learned to act dumb! The first time I sat there I was propositioned three times in half an hour!'

'You didn't tell me about that, lass!' Hamish sent a wink her way, but looked at her plate and puckered his lips as if to say, "Can you eat a bit more, lass?"

'That's a very winding road back to Como!' Kentaro said. 'You're brave tackling that. How do you cope?'

'Just fine. I never go directly after breakfast, though!' she laughed at the awful thought. 'My car's got to know the road. But it's the narrow streets that get to me! The first time was bedlam, trying to remember which side of the one way street I had to duck into.'

As they studied the dessert list, Mary suddenly dropped her menu on to her cutlery and knocked over her glass, made a face, and hurried to the ladies' room. Hamish looked as if he would run after her, but as he mopped the water, he signalled for the waiter.

'I can't follow my wife. They won't let me in there. Poor Mary.'

'I'll go,' Yuki said. 'Order the gateau for me, please, Kentaro.'

'The down-side of a pregnancy,' he said to Kentaro. 'It's a big ask, this request of yours. And you say Yuki doesn't share your enthusiasm?'

'No. But that's not yet. And,' he grimaced, 'Mary's distress will bring her last pregnancy back all too vividly.'

'Oh, yes. I'm sorry. But, what I want to say to you while they're gone is, if I say yes and it gets around, I'm not sure that my board will accept it.'

'They won't hear it from us. For certain.'

'But it's not as simple as that, is it? Who's to say I wouldn't be found out? Someone will have noticed that you've visited me in Italy.'

'Perhaps we have another good reason for visiting you, and this country. Why don't we establish a memorial fund for Trish and Jiro – and all the other children who died in Galtür? We'll get lists of their names and addresses and set it up. You and I.'

'Yes, I'll be happy to do that.' Hamish smiled broadly. 'A very good idea.'

Meanwhile, in the rest room, Mary lent over a hand basin and splashed her face with cold water every few moments.

'Thank you for coming to me, Yuki. To be honest with you, I hoped you would.' She glanced around. 'I'll tell you why, but please just double-check that no one is in either of those loos.'

'There's no-one at all.'

'Hamish told me why you're here. I'm sorry, but he felt he had to, and that you are a bit unhappy with the idea.'

'I most certainly am. I hope that Hamish can talk Kentaro out of it.'

'Go on, Yuki, I'm listening.'

'Well, seeing you and Hamish so happy makes me envious. We've tried for another baby but it hasn't happened.'

'Right, before anyone else…' The door opened and a woman came in, glanced at them, raised her eyebrows as if she guessed that something was wrong, and closed herself in a loo.

'Italy! Ah, yes, as we were saying, everything is so much more colourful than in Japan.'

'What? Buildings? You can't mean the shop interiors, they are so pretty.'

Eventually the woman emerged, washed her hands quickly at the second basin, and let them dry under a blast of hot air.

'You're right,' Yuki said. 'I've just thought of the way we

package everything. We do it, as you say, exquisitely. Don't we?' The door slammed. They giggled.

'Now that we're alone again, here's what I must tell you. But first, will you keep my secret? Even from Kentaro? If the baby arrives healthy, then Hamish will tell all, but in the meantime –?'

'Yes, I promise,' Yuki whispered. The subterfuge had begun.

'Hamish cloned our baby.'

'Oh. Rearry?' Yuki looked embarrassed. 'Really?' she carefully self-corrected.

Mary reached out to touch her arm, and smiled. 'He took a cell from Trish's breast, created an embryo and after Bill, the gynaecologist who works with him, had successfully implanted it, he made love so often I thought we were back on our honeymoon.' There was a knock on the door, and the receptionist looked in.

'Dr McLeod asks if his wife is OK.'

'Oh, yes, please tell him we'll be back at the table in a jiffy. Thanks.'

'You mean after the avalanche?' asked Yuki.

'Yes! At Christmas. A present for both of us. We'd better go. No word of this, now. But just one last thing, it all really is OK from the woman's point of view. So long as she and her husband both really want it,' she added.

'But why won't Hamish be open with us?'

Mary looked scared by her own revelation.

'Yuki, please! It has something to do with the law. Something to do with ethics and his commitment to the Biotech Centre, all that kind of thing. And,' she smiled, and looked relaxed again, 'a lot to do with pride. Don't worry. When our baby arrives and is seen to be a healthy, normal child, he'll tell the world!'

'I see. I can understand. You have my word. And, thanks for telling me. It's already helped me see it may be OK, after all.'

Hamish stood up as soon as Mary came through the doors to the balcony. He came toward her.

'You all right Mary?'

'Perfectly,' she said, and she knew that what he meant was, you haven't lost it, have you? As she walked back to the table, she recalled how he had shared that fear with her. That she might lose the baby was his only fear. The cloning had been dead easy, it must not go wrong now. Often, and at times like this, she knew he remembered Milan where they had all been taken eventually, and the hospital morgue where they were compelled to identify the bodies once more.

The Fujiwaras had identified Jiro and had left with Ichiro for the hotel. There, in the eerie silence, Hamish asked Mary to let him be alone with the frozen body of his daughter. 'Just a few minutes, Mary,' he pleaded, and he told her later it was the most awesome and terrifying moment he had lived.

> His heart raced as he stood looking down on her beautiful face. Her soggy hair was tucked inside a green cap. The young woman, who only hours before had smiled and laughed with him about things like the way he combed his beard before skiing. The girl who had demonstrated her power to out-distance him on the slopes. His sight was blurred by tears. He wiped his eyes and kissed her cheeks, then whispered, 'Oh, my darling Trish, forgive me.' He knew he was stepping outside the boundaries of decency. 'But I have no choice! It's now or never.' He unrolled the small insulated lab pack from an inner pocket of his jacket and went into clinical mode to deal with the frozen tissue as if it had been from the udder of the sheep.
>
> Then he turned to Jiro's body, looked at the distorted little face and wanted to scream with rage. He thought he only wanted to say goodbye, but as if in a trance, he unrolled the pack again, took a layer of skin from the

child's arm, snipped a lock of hair, placed them in his cylinders quickly jotting name and time on the labels, and left to join Mary in the waiting room. The waiting had been difficult for Mary. She ran to hug him, and hold him until they both felt steady enough to leave together.

Then, when he began to plan a baby cloned from Trish, the story emerged. She did not know whether to laugh or cry. Gradually, she came to see that it could be marvellous for both of them.

And, better than with the famous sheep, fertilisation had taken from the first go. Hamish kept on about this with Mary. 'With Dolly, it had been over 200 attempts!' If only it were all legitimate! He would be famous already. As it was, no one knew much about him for he had only been a helper to Wilmut's chief lab technician's assistant. What did that make him? Certainly not part of the main team, and certainly not famous.

Part One
Chapter 9

Warren Blackwell worked late in the basement of his Dorchester home. It was his way of being a freelance journalist, and parent to Tom. When he was most tense, Warren paced around his room taking the route that avoided his tripping over stacks of newspapers, magazines, satchels, photographic gear and the waste basket. Right now he was idly browsing, looking through his scrapbook of cuttings. There were reports of drug-dealings and photographs associated with the Welland canal, too many to go through tonight. Besides, he needed more information. Then there was a set of photographs which he had just had developed – those taken in Story Book Gardens on an outing with Tom. A student, round eighteen years old was playing a violin, and had an open case at his feet. Tom had stood still to listen, saying, 'Hey, Dad. He can play!'

He thumbed through the pages back to the murder scandal of eight months ago. There were reports and photos, too many to go through again, but there were one or two that held him. One was of the straw man, the original one that smelt of fresh straw and attracted children to sit on his knee and talk to him. For a month it had brought thousands of children to see this Mr Strawman, as he became known. Tom had been one of those children, and Warren had used two cassettes of film, mostly of Tom either on the straw man's knee or his playing about in old McDonald's farm, at the castle, and even at the door of the chapel.

Tom loved the place, and once the story was out, Warren was pleased not to have taken Tom to the gardens on the day when the scandal broke.

Mr Strawman's smell had been so faint at first that the warden decided it was the composted garden behind him, and he found a new place for him to recline. But when every child who went near the creature tore away calling, 'It stinks! Mummy, it stinks!' the warden had no choice but to remove it to his garden shed and undress it to see what had happened, if anything, to the cloth body. That was when it was discovered that the murdered cello teacher at MAAC was the body.

The question as to where the cloth original of the straw man was hidden was what nagged Warren, even now that the murderer was incarcerated somewhere in the Czech Republic. OK, so detectives hunted high and low for clues, divers went under the water in the river, and door to door searches were made. But finally it was concluded that the murderer had sent it out of the country. Czech Republic police had the job of hunting it down. But who knows? Did they really bother?

Warren looked at the more recent photographs – studies of a young man busking near the new Mr Strawman. Warren had used his zoom lens to close in on the violinist. He was playing with an open case at his feet. Tom had stood still to listen to the music, and said, 'Listen to him, quick.' Warren had taken time to change his lens and wait for the right moment. The results were brilliantly detailed. The sunlight had just been right. Now he studied the handsome face of the violinist, eyes closed and a smile at his lips as he let his bow bounce its way through the *Flight of the Bumble Bee.*

Warren studied the photographs again, unsure of their particular importance. The student's skill was obvious. But it was the ease with which he coped, in spite of a sometimes wandering audience, which was so impressive! It was as if his bow shuddered its way through the music without the hint of effort on the player's part.

'It's definitely a bee. Watch you don't get stung!' Warren had said, with a wink at Tom.

'Silly!' Tom laughed at him from his bright blue eyes.

Because Warren knew of the scandal around the first of the straw bodies, the photos fascinated the journalist in him!

He still had questions without answers and that might have satisfied the police but not Warren. Why would a teenage violinist busk in Springbank? Was there some sentimental attachment to the straw body – even the pristine new one with the quaintest of denim clothes and a happy face? There was something appealing about the idea. He would do his best to find out. Somehow! He would try and find out who he was. Take the photos to MAAC and ask at the desk if they knew him. If they did not, then Western might.

The woman at MAAC reception was smartly dressed in a dark blue jacket. Her long hair was tied back. After looking at the photograph, she said to Warren,

'I'm sorry, but we don't divulge information about students.'

'Where will I find the violin professor, then?' After all, he just wanted to help the guy.

The woman looked doubtful, but said, 'I'll page him.'

Miguel's pager beeped as he was running through a scale with a student. He was annoyed. He told the student to keep playing as he replied to the office. His voice reflected his irritation. He was brisk.

'So tell this Warren Blackwell that I cannot see him until Friday at 6 o'clock. Here. Thanks.' Nicola turned to Warren.

'Sorry, but the Director will not be free until Friday evening at six.'

'Bother, I shan't be around, I'm sorry.'

'Are you police?'

'A reporter,' Warren said.

'Perhaps your only chance to find out anything about the guy is either to watch out for him as a busker. Or call on Miguel during the week on the hour, when he has a five minute break between lessons. If you time it right, you'll be able to speak to him, at least briefly. Maybe.'

'Thanks,' he muttered. And Tom demanded his attention, 'Dad, when are we getting to the park?'

'Now. Right now. Let's go.'

Part One
Chapter 10

Hamish was ready for Kentaro and Yuki at ten when they arrived to talk. He looked happier than at the first interview.

'I have some good news,' he said, as he shook their hands and showed them to the chairs facing his desk.

'Oh, so what is the good news, Hamish?' Kentaro was eager, but Yuki, reticent.

'I had a timely word with Bill, the gynaecologist who shares this lab with us. He's doing research into diseases of the womb. Quite by chance he said that if I ever apply my knowledge to the human embryo, he wants to be the first to know. I asked him a leading question. You mean that if today I decide that that's where I'm at, you'll support me? He said, "Right to the birth and after, if necessary." That's my good news,' said Hamish, beaming. 'Right here we have assured support, even before we ask.'

'That is very good, very good.' Kentaro was happy

Yuki knew that Hamish was lying. He had this support already. He's making up a story to impress Kentaro and me. She felt lonely and cold.

Grey walls, a straight-backed chair, combined with male enthusiasm for artificial fertilisation, plus a sense of deceit, and you have the scenario for depression. This was not the place for creating a new human being. Children should be born out of a loving experience. In Mary's company, she almost believed that she could be happy being pregnant again. But that was last night.

Hamish sensed her discomfort. He talked directly to her to help her re-connect with him. 'Yuki, I've been thinking very hard about what it means to a woman to carry a cloned child.'

Yuki connected all right. 'How can you possibly know what it is like? I am the one who would have to carry a clone.

Not you. Not Kentaro. You have no idea.'

Hamish coloured up, stroked his hairy chin. 'Of course you're right. I'm sorry.' That was a turning point for Yuki.

'I'm sorry, too,' she said. 'Please explain what is involved. I'm here now so please, we don't want to waste more of your time.'

Hamish opened a book with diagrams of the process of fertilisation of an egg by artificial means. They followed his explanation. 'Here, look at this, the egg, stripped of its nucleus. Then a different nucleus, a selected cell, is inserted into the egg.' His finger pointed to the appropriate image.' Now, in order to jump-start the fusion, an electric current tricks the egg into behaving like a fertilised egg. And there begins the child we want.' He snapped the book shut. 'Astonishingly easy, isn't it?'

Kentaro agreed, nodded several times and smiled at Yuki. Hamish was wound up. He continued with loud enthusiasm which continued to upset Yuki.

'We are at the crossroads of human achievement. Just last March after we returned to Scotland, a friend in California emailed me about his magnificent achievement. He and his colleagues have developed a way of treating genetic diseases before the birth of an affected baby by altering the genes *in utero*. He believes that over the next five to ten years we'll have the know-how to construct a baby from scratch, exactly to a prescription dictated by the parent's wishes.' Hamish laughed as he said, 'Yes, there'll be mail-order births.' He turned to Yuki. 'Seriously, Yuki, it's better than that. I believe we can already get the child we want. With your help, we can create a new Jiro, a violinist that will bring the world to its knees in admiration.'

'It's all so cold-blooded.' Yuki snapped. She wiped her eyes and blinked to stop her tears.

'Come on, pet, you asked Hamish to tell us,' Kentaro said, as he offered her a tissue.

'Can I make some tea?' suggested Hamish. 'This is all very

exciting, I mean new,' he corrected, as he recalled Mary telling him not to get carried away.

'Thank you.' Yuki said.

Hamish moved quickly as he strode away and was soon back with tea. They quietly sipped their drinks.

'So now, do you feel ready to talk about what I need from you all if we go ahead?'

Yuki felt a little warmer, if nothing else. 'Yes, I'm ready.' She turned to Kentaro and said, 'I don't mean that I'm saying yes to all this, but I do need to know everything so that I can make an informed choice.'

'I understand,' he said. 'One further question, Hamish. Are you sure that we have to wait for gene manipulation?'

'Meaning?'

Kentaro glanced at Yuki, and leaned forward a little.

'The one deficiency in both Jiro and Ichiro is their poor eyesight.'

Hamish grimaced, pursed his lips and said, 'Oh, that I could say yes! In a few months we may be able to say yes to that. As I said, soon we'll produce designer children. But for the moment I'm sorry, the best I can say is – a cloned son yes, but how his eyesight will be I cannot be certain.'

'So what would you want us to do?'

'You, Yuki, would let us take an egg at the time of ovulation. Your body temperature will give us the clue there. As well, as Kentaro and I discussed earlier, Ichiro's finger tissue would give us the cell, the genes. The fusion is done here as I've described, and shortly after fertilisation takes place, we will implant it into your womb.'

As Hamish engaged Yuki's attention, Kentaro was suddenly, inexplicably jealous. He wanted to say – 'And how do you think I feel? Useless? Impotent? Alone? Oh, yes. All of those.' But he held his peace, reminding himself that they were talking about re-creating Jiro. Jiro who should have lived to bring the world to their knees at the beauty of his playing. Playing from the little one's pure heart.

'What can we tell Ichiro?' Yuki looked to both men for a reply.

Hamish was about to speak, but so was Kentaro. 'Go ahead, Kentaro.'

'Quite simply, that I want to know how the tissue of a remarkable young pianist looks under the microscope.'

'But he'll get a sore finger!' cried Yuki.

'Come, come, only for a few days. He is already sorry for himself. This will give him a reason for not playing the piano that we can see. He'll like that.'

Hamish laughed quietly. 'I can see that you have a good understanding of your boy. We'll leave it at that.' They stood up, and then Hamish reached to his table and picked up a list of names which he handed to Kentaro.

'I almost forgot. These are the children who died in Galtür. You might like to make a start on tracking down their families and get their reactions about a memorial.' He looked down at Yuki. 'Tomorrow, I'll get Bill, the gynaecologist, to phone and make a time for a talk on how to gauge the right time for your procedure. It has been a great pleasure to see you here today.'

Yuki gave a slight bow but did not speak as she walked past him and out the door.

Mary was setting the table for supper when Hamish came in looking as pleased as he ever did.

'Looks like you've had a good day, Hamish.' She hugged him, and they danced a step together, whirling a little, and laughing.

'I pretended that Bill had just offered to help me!'

'Oh, you mean Yuki and Kentaro?' She looked serious now.

'Hey, it's all OK. I just avoided telling them about us, that's all.'

'And that Bill and you have been in this together for two months now. I see. Honest deceit.' Mary blushed with guilt.

'You are embarrassed? Och, Mary, I love you to bits. I just

cannot afford for it to get about that I've cloned a wee girlie for us. After all, people might think I'm past having bed games or something.'

'Come here, Hamish.' She put a hand on either side of his cheeks and said, 'I could tell them otherwise. Couldn't I?'

Part One
Chapter 11

Donna re-read the email letter from Peter to make certain she had got it all. He had had a month at MAAC and was enjoying it very much. One of the things that he especially liked was that there were classes in music education as well as performance lessons and chamber music. 'How I revel in playing cello with my new colleagues!' But he really needed some more information on Fujiwara's teaching method from her. Would she come and stay in London for a weekend or would she prefer him to come to her? He would not mind revisiting his old city haunts. "I feel sad at times", he wrote, "but of course there may not be the time for sight-seeing."

Strange he did not mention his partner. What's her name, for goodness sake? She had read it in the summer camp notes. Ah, yes. Celia. Well, why had he not mentioned Celia? She emailed him back. "I teach until seven on Friday. First, they've got all the answers at the Royal Conservatorium on Bloor. If that won't do you, of course, I'd love to see you. Will Celia come too? I'd like to meet her. We can talk while she visits old haunts. She is probably just as sad as you are."

Sure enough, the answer came. "Thanks, I'll be on your doorstep at 7.30. Celia and I decided to split. I'm embarrassed to say it hasn't affected me all that much. Perhaps I'll react later when all the excitement of moving and taking up a new job evaporates. See you Friday."

Donna mused, 'That puts paid to my bright idea that Warren will stay on through Renée's lesson, and the Paganini. And just maybe have coffee afterwards! So Peter, I'll have to make up a bed for you. Cheeky that. How could he be sure that I would have a place for him to sleep?' In her stomach she felt butterflies, and in the soles of her feet, excitement. 'This is all too much. I thought I had fallen for Warren, and now I am getting orgasmic over Peter. But I assumed he had a partner, didn't I? So, where can Peter sleep? I will leave it open for now.' She checked that there would be a couple of dry towels for him.

Late on Friday, late afternoon, there was a knock on Peter's studio door.

'Come in,' he called.

Andreas entered, carrying his violin case.

'Is it all right? I came to congratulate you on getting the position. I had heard there were five who were short-listed.'

'Thanks. Nice to see you. Sit down for a bit. I've got an hour before I teach again, but on the other hand I need a break. So let's agree on twenty minutes.'

They sat. Peter on the piano stool, which he swivelled to face Andreas, who was on one of the hard chairs used for cello playing.

'So do you miss the Toronto Symphony?' Peter said.

'Toronto Symphony? Yes and no. I hadn't made any friends there so I didn't have that to hold me. Besides, I wanted to learn from Miguel, he's such a great teacher.'

'Yes, I think that was wise. At your age – nineteen aren't you? – you're best to keep mastering the advanced stuff while you're in good shape. What do you reckon?'

Peter felt uncomfortable with the difference he saw in Andreas. He had a twitch in his cheek and eye. He didn't have that when he played in the symphony. Or so he thought. Maybe his glasses hid it from where he was seated.

'So, you've made friends here, then?'

'I've lost my best one,' he blurted out, then looked abashed.

'You mean you've lost a new friend?'

'That's right.' Andreas suddenly glanced at his watch. 'I've just remembered my landlady said she wanted to have supper early. Better go.' He stood up. 'Glad you're here, Peter.'

Peter opened the door. 'Thanks for coming. Ciao'. Andreas

threw back a 'Ciao' and ran down the corridor.

Nice of him to come. But what has happened to the lad? He is not like I remember him.

When it came to closing the studio up for the weekend, Peter was no longer thinking about Andreas. He made a short detour to his flat where he stuffed a sleeping bag and jacket into his pack which already held his books, toilet gear and shorts, and put them on to the back seat of his old Ford. The moment he hit the 401 to Toronto, he was listening to Elgar's cello concerto, and thinking of Donna.

Come to think of it, I know very little about Donna. But her Brahms at summer camp! I can still hear her big violin tone. It was dramatic. What energy she brought to her playing. All those kids sitting at her feet, spellbound. I must ask what the secret is.

Donna was curled up on her settee, and Peter sat on a lazyboy chair with the footrest under his feet. He was holding one of the toby jugs which she had put in his hands to stop him asking questions like – are they heavy? any trade marks?

'There.' she had said. 'Get to know this fellow – one of my favourites.' He was looking pleased with himself, could have been holding a warm cup of coffee after walking in snow. She thought he might start to have a conversation with Tobias himself. Both were tired.

'My Friday is the most demanding day when it comes to different kinds of lessons,' she said. 'First thing, I have a class that is so laid back you wouldn't believe it. And then I end the day with individual lessons, some from out of town. Oh, you'll remember Tom.'

'Who?' Peter was genuinely puzzled. 'I mean, there are Toms all over the country. Which Tom?' He held the jug out for her, then stood up, saying, 'No, I'll put it back. Same place?'

'Thanks. The summer camp Tom.'

'Now I'm with you. That little kid whose father had thick hair tied at the nape. Hippie character. He was great. The reason why I remember that small kid better than most is that his dad got him to ask me what was good about being able to play now that I'm grown up.' He started to laugh at the memory of this serious little boy listening to Peter's solemn answer. Donna was delighted at the thought of young Tom – who wanted to be called Thomas – asking such a question. She got up, and wriggled her skirt into place.

'It's time for a break from music talk. Let's have a nightcap and work out where you're going to sleep.' Donna sipped her drink slowly, and tried to work out how to address the situation. Peter came to the rescue.

'I've got my sleeping bag. Why don't I sleep on the settee?'

'Are you sure? It's actually not very comfortable.'

'Donna, I am so tired that I could sleep on the floor.' She laughed, relieved that it was no big deal.

Part One
Chapter 12

'Why does Dr McLeod want a scraping from my finger?'

'I thought we'd explained that more than once, Ichiro.'

In his hand, Ichiro held a tiny play-station. He neither wanted to stop playing, nor did he want to have his finger scraped for cells!

'I've never heard of anything like this. None of my friends have had cells taken for research!'

It was seven-thirty in the morning, and the lake was misty. The day promised to be unpleasant and difficult, and Yuki wished that Kentaro would come back from his early walk. Ichiro had refused to walk with him saying, 'I go biking when I want to get exercise. I miss my bike,' and he angrily threw his play-station on to his bed, and stamped around the room glaring through his glasses at his mother, the way he knew he could annoy her.

'Stop doing that, Ichiro. Stop it at once.'

He stopped and stood like a statue with a long face, and that annoyed her too. If she had been at home she would have left him alone, but she did not feel like walking through the enormous hotel just to find a place to escape her son. She needed exercise and began her aerobics routine which would have to compensate for her not being able to cycle or go to her weekly class.

'OK, sulk if you must. Your father can talk to you when he comes in. But I'll tell you now, you aren't getting out of this.'

She lay down on her back on the thick carpet where she had placed a towel, her feet stretched up beyond her shoulders, and ignored her child. Ten minutes later Kentaro burst through the door.

'It's chilly out there,' he said. Then he took stock of the situation. Yuki had put on her Walkman with headphones and swayed and stretched to the music she was hearing. She did not even see him. Ichiro was lying face-down on his bed, also with headphones on as he concentrated on a game as well as listening to music. Kentaro hoped it was classical, not rock. What concerned Kentaro was that there was a feeling of truce in the air, which meant that something had happened between his wife and son. He decided to take a shower and warm himself up, then they could breakfast together.

He returned from his relaxing shower, and after waiting a few minutes, drew Ichiro's attention away from his walkman by sitting on his bed.

'You smell nice and clean, Dad,' Ichiro said, taking off his earphones.

'What have you and Mum have been arguing about?' asked Kentaro.

'My finger! That Dr McLeod wants to take my finger off!'

'He only wants a tiny bit of DNA – you should be proud.'

'I don't like Dr McLeod.'

'You don't know him well.'

'I do so. He's a cry-baby!'

Kentaro was taken aback. 'Cry-baby?'

'I didn't cry like a baby but he did. He sobbed and sobbed and I was embarrassed.' Kentaro patted Ichiro's leg which was stretched out on the bed.

'Of course Dr McLeod cried, he was desperately sad. His beautiful daughter had been killed. It had happened so quickly we were all in shock.'

'He only lost a daughter. I lost me. Me!' Ichiro whirled over, sobbing into his pillow and pounding the bed with his feet. Kentaro rested a hand on his thigh for a few minutes but there was no stopping Ichiro. He went to get Yuki who had tactfully disappeared when he and Ichiro began to talk. He decided to have her paged, and after her name had been called four times, Yuki burst into the room.

'What's wrong?' She looked at Kentaro's face, and panic

seized her. 'Where? What's happened?' she screamed.

'Calm down, Yuki. It's Ichiro. He's crying into his pillow for Jiro.'

'Oh, is that all.' She was relieved. She heard her named paged again. 'Tell reception to stop calling my name!' She went through to Ichiro, and after looking down on him, said to Kentaro, 'How long as he been like this for?'

'About fifteen minutes.'

'Oh, poor boy. I'll sit with him and talk a bit.'

She sat on the bed.

'Ichiro, I know you're sad.' There was a moment's lull after a deep sob. 'Ichiro, I do love you, you know.'

Suddenly the child sat up and rubbed his eyes, and threw himself on to his mother.

'I want Jiro to come back. He was me. I was him. I can't live without him!' His warm wet face was against her breast. She hugged him even closer and kissed him. 'There, there, you have been too brave. I see it now.'

Kentaro came to the bedroom door and said enthusiastically, 'What say we go to breakfast? I liked the look of those sausages they had there yesterday. Let's see if they have them today. Come on.'

There was everything imaginable on the long table covered in a starched white cloth which overhung it to the floor. The chef had catered for every style of eating from a fruit-only diet of pineapples and mangoes to an Irish breakfast of creamed potatoes, sausages, eggs, tomatoes and well, just everything. There was toast and cereals and fruit juices, coffee and water. No-one need go without.

'I'm sticking to soup and fish,' said Yuki with a smile at Kentaro, whose plate already had four sausages on it. Ichiro was helping himself to porridge, and the parents smiled when they saw him pouring cream over the top.

'He's feeling better, thank goodness,' Yuki confided. Two women were pushing to get nearer the food.

'Kentaro, we're in the way here. You finish getting your

breakfast, then we can talk.'

'Of course. *Sumimasen*.'

Yuki stood apart from the table watching her family, while Kentaro helped himself to a generous serving. He then joined Yuki, and waited for Ichiro to make up his mind as to which juice to have with the toast and jam he had collected.

'Tell you what,' Kentaro said. 'We'll get Hamish to wait and not take Ichiro's DNA until just before you have your egg removed. By then he'll have had some good times. We can spoil him a bit. Lots of computer games – whatever he wants.'

'We're going to have about two weeks at the very least. Hamish is banking on everything working the first time. He seems to know his stuff.

'Then, the next big moment will be ten days after the fusion is performed,' he added.

Ichiro came up to them. 'Can I choose which table?'

'Of course.'

Part One
Chapter 13

After impressing Miguel that he was a genuine enquirer, Warren Blackwell learned that the busker was Andreas Bonnheimer, a graduate student in the fourth year programme at MAAC. He also managed to find a way to get a look at him in person. He would attend a lunch-hour recital by Miguel's advanced students. As he made his way to the office, he wondered how the receptionist would treat him today.

'Miguel suggested I attend today's lunch-hour recital and could get an entry ticket from you.' She was all smiles as she gave him the ticket, and he wondered if he might have misjudged her a little on the first encounter. 'Thank you, er...'

'Nicola' she prompted.

The recital hall sloped to the stage and, already, it was almost filled, largely by students.

Warren found a seat between two groups of youths, right in the middle of a row, at about the centre of the seating area. The lights dimmed almost immediately, and the recital was opened with the unaccompanied Prelude in E from Sonata No VI by Bach, played by Andreas Bonnheimer. Yes, the programme named the violinist as Andreas Bonnheimer. And there was no mistaking it – the lone figure on stage was the person in the photograph, identified as Andreas.

Warren hoped that in time, Tom would have the poise that this handsome young man was showing. He was unhurried, appeared to be at home on the stage. He took out a soft cloth and placed it on the piano lid, tuned his violin, turned fully round to face the audience, and after a moment closed his eyes and played the prelude with ease. The look on his face was of quiet satisfaction, almost an absence of emotion.

Warren still wanted to meet Andreas and ask him to be Tom's minder from time to time. He resolved to go forward to the front seats where the performers sat after they had played, and congratulate Andreas on his fine performance.

The rest of the hour dragged for Warren, so intent was he on meeting him. In the meantime, he kept one eye on the stage, and one on Andreas who was now in the first seat of the front row. What a head of hair. His own hair was easy to cope with, straight and long and tied back. Andreas though, had a curly mop to deal with, dark and wayward.

Miguel, as teacher-performer, ended the recital. He strode on, his rather short legs stepping with confidence. A dark-eyed smile won his audience. He bowed deeply, then announced his solo. The moment he began *Zigeunerweisen* the students' restrained excitement rippled through the hall. When the last notes sounded, the air burst in thunderous rapture. Warren stood along with everyone else and wished that Tom had been with him.

The clapping and shouting lasted a long time, then stopped abruptly. The lights came on and Warren went against the flow trying to get to Andreas. It was impossible. He was impelled to leave the hall with everyone else. There would have to be another way of meeting him. No one was hanging around today for sure, and as he reached the hallway he saw a pair of recognisably long legs taking two steps at a time up the stairs, as if the person they belonged to had a deadline to meet. He would have to call him, that is if Nicola did not stand in his way. His good imagination put words into her mouth: 'I'm sorry, but I cannot call a student to the phone for you.' He could always write a note.

For a few days Warren needed to focus on a story that was urgent – the sad and mysterious drowning of an elderly man in the Dorchester Mill pond. He worked at his computer, checking that his photographs were accurately labelled, until he was able to send the completed story down the line. Tom would be bounding off the bus any minute. That meant a short walk to meet him at the corner, a snack, then violin practice. It was the time of the day he enjoyed most. Being with Tom. It was his love for his son, and his pleasure in doing things with him, that had made it obvious, at the time of the break up of his marriage, that it was Warren who should keep the boy in his care. He did not know what he would have done if Bonny had not agreed. Even now, all these months after she had walked out with Hank, he would wake in the night in a sweat from a nightmare that he was left alone. Entirely bereft.

'Hi, there, Tom.' He waved to catch Tom's attention as he stepped to the sidewalk on his side of the road. Tom ran to hug his dad.

'You won't believe me, dad, but we got bussed to London. We went to a concert in the Fanshaw Road High school. I think that busker was there. He played real cool music.'

Warren stopped, and laughed as he thought of the story that was evolving.

'Dad, keep walking. I do think it was him. He had the same curly mop and skin kind of jacket. Like the Indian one, all fringed.'

'And do you know what his name is?'

'Yes. Er …' His dad helped him out. 'Andreas Bonnheimer?'

'That's it. Dad, can I see that photo again?'

They stopped a moment and Warren took the photograph from his wallet.

'This him?'

'Yep! Him all right.'

'We'll put it on our notice board, shall we?'

Tom enjoyed the short walk, especially with his dad. When they were not talking, he liked looking at the houses with basement windows just peeping above the ground. He was glad they had a basement in their house. It felt secretive to be below the earth like a mole. That's where his dad kept all his favourite things like special photos of his mum.

But he would not practise his violin down there. Not until he could play like Andreas who could make siren noises and sounds like a ghost breathing.

'Dad, Andreas showed us kids how to play two strings at once. Then he played on three. And, oh, wow, he got playing a dance that made all four strings sound at once. Andreas called it magic! He really played two strings together, then the next two, but he went so fast that all of the strings sounded at once.'

'He's a beaut player, I agree. I heard him play today, too!'

'Were you there?'

'No. At MAAC.'

They had reached their gate. Tom had kept the best bit for now.

'Hold my bag, please, dad. I've got something to show you.' He delved into his bag and brought out a photocopied programme. 'Look, I got Andreas's signature.'

Warren looked in amazement. Jealousy was what he was feeling.

'How come you got him to sign your programme?'

They had reached their steps and his dad opened the door. Tom threw himself ahead of Warren and puffed out his chest.

'I was the youngest boy there to be learning the violin. That's how I got it.'

'Lucky fellow. Well, then, you have something special to show Donna. We'd best practise hard to catch up to Andreas.'

Tom was already off down to the basement. 'I want to see all those photos of him first, Dad.'

Part One
Chapter 14

'Peter, do you always look so bleary-eyed in the morning?' Donna was looking down on him, his eyes only just showing above his sleeping bag.

'You're teasing me. Didn't you go to sleep? You've got yesterday's clothes on.' His voice was thick.

'And now you're teasing me. I haven't actually. I wasn't wearing these old jeans yesterday! It's nine-twenty, and I thought we were going to work hard all day.' She turned away saying, 'The bathroom's free.'

She smiled to herself as she heard the shower running in the bathroom, and collected up glasses of fruit juice and bowls of muesli. At the table she paused, thinking – will he want toast? When he came out he was dressed in a fresh tee shirt and shorts. His beard looked combed.

'Do you want toast?'

'No thanks, I don't want toast.' He surveyed the table. 'I would like coffee though.'

'OK. I'll brew up coffee, enough to see us through the morning.'

Donna collected several books and a satchel bursting with notes, put them on the floor at one end of the settee, and sat down.

'How about you sit here with me and we talk Fujiwara method until we're saturated? Then, I suggest we do a movie. You don't really want to sight-see do you?'

He spoke softly now that he was close beside her, 'So long as I can have your company, no I don't.'

'Good. So where to start?'

'Can I choose?'

'Certainly.'

'Tell me about Japan. How did you survive such a different culture for a year?'

'Let me get it straight, first. I hadn't just got back from Japan for summer camp. I'd been back for six months and finished my dissertation in that time. A lot has happened since I was there.'

'So my curiosity remains. What was it like?'

'Wonderful. Brilliant. Well, some of it was. Sadly, last time – I'd been there two years ago – it became hell.'

'Good God, why?'

'Best forgotten.'

Donna put down the book she had in her hand, emptied her coffee mug and sat for a moment. Then she tucked her knees under her and faced Peter, whose legs were in her space. He reached an arm across the settee behind her and lightly touched a shoulder.

'Have you ever been falsely accused, Peter?'

'Mm. Once when the mother of my three gung-ho friends wouldn't believe me when I said I didn't let her tyre down.' He smiled at the memory.

'Well, that's all I'm going to say: I was falsely accused. It made me sick for a while but I'm over it now.'

'OK. But just tell me that the Fujiwaras are still your good friends.'

'For ever, I'd say.'

'So that's all that matters isn't it?'

'That's important. Yes.'

Part One
Chapter 15

Kentaro and Yuki had been relieved that Ichiro experienced some light-hearted moments with Hamish when, eventually, he went to his session with the eminent Dr McLeod. Not only did he like the kind of spacecraft capsule he and Hamish entered to ensure sterile surroundings, but also he got to like the big fellow with the ginger beard because they laughed about how right his fingers were for 'tinkling the ivories'! Hamish had joked with him saying that he reckoned a little pruning would make his finger even more shapely and able to go even faster than before! All the teasing was such a distraction that the taking of cells hardly hurt at all. In fact it didn't hurt, but he wanted to believe it did and came away with the bandage he so badly wanted.

'Tell you what,' Hamish had said, 'Just before you leave for home I'll fix you up with a fresh plaster which you can show to your friends. How about that?'

And so now, the day before flying from Milan, the Fujiwara family kept their final appointment at the laboratory. Yuki felt very nervous about going through the implantation process. She told Ichiro that she had met an old friend in the medical library. She said she would visit her while he and his dad kept their appointment to see Hamish and have his bandage exchanged for a plaster, then take a tour around the Biotec Laboratory as a bonus.

Ichiro did not mind. He would be seeing Hamish who was now his friend. So, at the entrance to the lab, Yuki went one way and the men the other. Outside Hamish's office Kentaro said 'I'll be in the waiting room. Off you go.'

Hamish was quick to answer to Ichiro's knock.

'Hello. You're looking healthy. You've been sailing a lot, I think.'

'Oh, yes. We've been on the water most days. My bandage

came off, but I've come for the plaster.'

'Good laddie. That's what we agreed. You know the routine. Into the capsule ready for take-off. So you've had good fun in Italy, then?'

'Much more fun than Austria. *Galtür wa, dame deshita*!'

Hamish knew what he meant by the crack in his voice, the fire in his eyes. He shared his hurt.

'You know, young man, you and I will always have bad feelings about snow and Galtür. But you and I, we're going to cope, aren't we?' He prepared to place the plaster on the smooth, unblemished finger which the little boy offered him. First he dabbed it with disinfectant, then dried it in a soft blast of hot air.

'Now it can be covered up for a few days.' He turned the plaster back on itself, making it fit the slim little finger. 'Looks neat, don't you think? Your friends will be very impressed.'

'Hamish, do you think I'm clever?'

'You are, Ichiro. Very clever.'

'What will you learn from my DNA?'

'All kinds of things. What makes you clever. The colour of your eyes.'

'But we know they're black-green!'

'Yes, but it is fun for someone like me to identify the gene that makes them black-green! Best of all, our computer will show us the pattern of your genes. From that pattern, we will see what makes a person into a great pianist such as you.'

'Can you send me a picture of that pattern when you get it?'

'I think we just might, part of it anyway.' He was smiling. They were both smiling. 'Come on. Your dad is waiting.'

The tour through the laboratory was fun. All the people they talked to, and especially the student picked to guide them, seemed to take the round-faced boy wearing spectacles very seriously. Ichiro caught on quickly, thought of all the questions he possibly could, and listened carefully to the answers. The best part of all came when he was able to look through a telescope at human cells. They plucked out a hair from his head, and one from his father's, and spent a lot of time laughing and talking about which had the most marvellous colours. They agreed that they would each believe it was their own!

When the family sat in the Malpensa departure lounge waiting to board the Japanese Airline flight to Narita, Ichiro reckoned his finger was still sore.

'I'll have to wear this plaster when I go back to school, won't I, Mum? Hamish said I have to.'

'Well, then. You must!'

He turned to his father, 'And I won't have to practise the piano, will I Dad?'

'No. Not until your finger is quite better.'

Now that the real reason for going to Italy was known and behind him, Ichiro was feeling a lot happier than when he was called home from school and told his dad was not well. It had been like a bombshell that they were going overseas. He thought his dad could have seen a doctor at home. He had his own suspicions as to where they would be going. 'We'll feel sad all over again if we go near Austria,' he had said. His mother had just smiled.

'No! Tell me. Are we going to Galtür?'

'No, no. Not to Galtür. To northern Italy, for a lovely holiday. We'll meet up with some of the people we met at Galtür, but that will be nice, won't it?'

'No. They'll want to talk about my dead brother. I don't want them to.'

He felt really honoured that a real life scientist had wanted to test his genes because he was such a clever pianist. This was the best day of the holiday by far! Going home to tell his friends.

Once aboard, and with their luggage stowed above them safely, they sat three across in the middle rows of the plane.

Ichiro was between his parents. Kentaro and Yuki exchanged glances as he started to talk straight away about the tragedy.

'Mum. Why did Jiro die and not me?'

'No-one can say why Jiro died, Ichiro. So it's not as if one of you had to die. It was just a terrible accident.' Yuki was finding it hard to talk this way, especially as the people were filing along the aisles chatting and heaving luggage about. Kentaro came to her rescue and kept his voice as low as possible.

'We'll never know why it happened. In all, eleven children died, you know that don't you?'

'Yes, and you've got all their names, haven't you?'

'Yes. Their families all think like we do, that building a memorial will be a good idea.'

'Dad, I feel proud that you and Mum thought of that.'

'Thank you. And you enjoyed going sailing with Marika, Rudi, and Pattie's families, didn't you? That turned out really well for all of us. We've had a good holiday, haven't we?'

'It's been cool, Dad.'

'Can you see now that we're not the only ones to feel sad?'

'Yes, I can see. Oh, dad, it's so awful.' He looked very forlorn and small between his parents. Kentaro reached across his back and put a strong hand around his shoulder. 'Ichiro, it's very hard for you losing a twin. You were such good mates. You've been very brave.'

Ichiro could not hold back his tears. His dad strengthened his grasp on the small shoulder as it shook with silent sobbing. A flight attendant came by to check that their trays were up and their luggage stowed, and gave the Fujiwaras a little extra attention.

'Is your seat-belt comfortable, Madam? Sir? What about Ichiro?' She even knew his name. The parents nodded their appreciation, and she moved along the aisle.

Kentaro lightly rested his head on his son's, and when the sobbing lessened he whispered, 'I love you, Ichiro.' They stayed like that, giving each other strength until Ichiro said,

'When will my finger be better?'

'Hamish said quite soon. You might just be able to play the piano a tiny bit when you get over jet lag.' He smiled into the child's searching eyes.

Ichiro's smile was so full of trust that the parents went spinning back into the sore places of their hearts, the child they had lost, their recent ordeal, the deceit. The conversation, which the parents had when the light was out on their last night before returning home, had been full of doubt.

'Will the baby be all right?' Yuki had panic in her voice.

'I don't know, Yuki. But so far, it's gone brilliantly. Hamish confessed he'd thought he would never get the cells and your eggs minus their nuclei to fuse at the first attempt. But two did. I'll never forget his voice!'

'What if I have two babies?'

'Well, it's possible, but unlikely. We'll have to be satisfied with one, most probably.'

'And I don't want to go through that again.'

'Of course you don't.'

'Those strong lights, the doctor's face. In Nagoya it was so much nicer.'

'You told me they put a curtain between you and the doctor at our clinic.'

'Yes, they did! I can't see you now because it's dark. It was like that; I could hear but not see.' She started to giggle, and he caught the intensity of her feelings. Turning on to his side, he held her, and her giggles turned to tears of anguish for all they had been through. When she finished crying, she felt his sobs and his pain.

'Poor Kentaro,' she said. 'It has been hard for you, too.' She moved her hands across him. The tears ceased, and he pulled down her nightie to kiss her breasts. The force of their love overtook them so that they each made the other come again and again. But he would not enter her. As they lay on in the darkness, Kentaro asked, 'What was it Bill said?' Yuki laughed. 'You remember. He was so matter of fact, wasn't he?' Kentaro laughed a bit, and tried to imitate the deep voice of the portly gynaecologist, as Yuki had repeated it to him. 'No sex until we know for sure you're pregnant, Mrs Fujiwara. Otherwise we'll always be in doubt that it is the clone.'

'I suppose he's right. And, my darling, we've obeyed his instructions to the letter. So far. As soon as I miss a period, I'll tell you, and then we can, well you know …'

'Know what?' His laughter shook him so much that at first she thought he was crying again. Then she laughed too.

'I'm going to shower. Why don't you have one with me?' she said, playfully.

'A cold one? No fear. But put the light on so I can see you.'

'Watch my wobbly bottom, you mean.'

He reached out a hand to her. 'Yuki, come here. Only tell me when you're certain, when you've had the pregnancy test. Promise?'

'Promise.'

Now, three across and homeward bound, they are happy.

PART TWO

There are people spaces
on either side of a child
places
for two people.
Sometimes a child reaches out
and there is no one
to hold on to.
She does not know where to place her hand.

Your Snow Falls in Summer, Barbara Mann, Puriri Press, Auckland 1989

PART TWO
CHAPTER 1

The filled school hall was unusually quiet. On the stage, the grand piano stood open, the lid, raised. A little to the right of it was a large *ikebana* arrangement of pink and white *sakura* in a highly polished black vase, illuminated by a faint light. The boys and girls from Ichiro's class sat in the front seats feeling a special connection with their classmate. They hoped he would be all right, knew how he had gone cold on the piano when he lost his twin and stopped playing for a while. The principal knew the full story and hoped that by Ichiro's performance today, he would gain some of the confidence he had lost. He stepped, smiling, onto the stage and walked to where the reading desk normally stood.

'Today is a very special day. Ichiro Fujiwara, a fourth year student here, is going to play the piano for us again.' He led the clapping as he directed his voice to the side of the stage saying, 'Come on to the stage, please, Ichiro.' Ichiro came from the wings and stood close to the principal.

'Ichiro, we've missed your performances greatly, and we know that you are courageous in playing today. We look forward to hearing your solo, very much. We're proud to know you, and happy that we have you in our school.'

It had been decided that today the principal would relieve Ichiro of having to speak so, addressing the junior girls and boys who packed the hall, he announced, 'Ichiro Fujiwara plays Mozart's Rondo in D.'

Ichiro placed his left hand on the piano and bowed. Suddenly, led by the children in the front rows, all the children stood and clapped very loudly until the principal put his hand up, palm facing the children.

'That's enough,' he said. 'Keep some for later.'

The children, including Ichiro, saw the funny side of that. Ichiro smiled through his tears, but then had to wipe his eyes and glasses. Seated, and becoming composed by controlling his breath, he waited a moment, the audience waited, and he began.

By the end of the school day, Ichiro had been showered with kind comments from class-mates and teachers, and he felt OK about himself and playing for an audience again. But he was mad that his best friend, Hideo, could not cycle home with him like he usually did. They had spent lunchtime talking about the arrangement he had with his mother to put his *jitensha* in the back of their family wagon, and go shopping after school. He just had to meet her and go buy some clothes to attend a family wedding.

'Sorry,' Hideo said. 'My Mum says I have to get a new shirt, and pants, and shoes or I can't go to the wedding.' He smiled, then and added, 'Hey, she's getting me a new bow as well.'

'That's good news. You'll start getting decent cello tone, then!' Ichiro grinned, then went back to being petulant. 'But couldn't you bike home? And meet your mother there?'

'She said we need every minute for shopping.' Hideo knew why Ichiro was tetchy about going home alone. He missed his brother terribly. They had always been together, even did the same crazy tricks on their bikes. Since Jiro's death, Hideo had been encouraged by his mother to bike with Ichiro, even on the days he hurried home because of his cello lesson, to fill the space, if not the gap that his brother left. He could at least stop other kids from taunting Ichiro about losing his twin, which is what some of the boys did if given half a chance.

At the bike stand, Ichiro looked about him as he mounted his bicycle, and straight away got the feeling that three boys from a class other than his, were starting off with him and were going to keep close. He toyed with the idea of going back into the school and waiting until everyone had gone, then remembered the words of the principal – you are courageous – and he did not want to let the principal down! He pushed off and tried not to stay with the boys, by wending in and out amongst cars, and on and off the footpath more recklessly than usual. But he could not lose them. He began to feel panic and fear, and then, when they came close enough to taunt him, they shouted, 'You're a half-wit now. You've only got half a brain! Boo hoo.'

For a while he could pretend to ignore them, but his glasses became so clouded by tears of anger and self-pity, that he was compelled to stop and wipe them. The boys called back, 'Big sook!' and went their way. For the rest of the trip home he felt shaky in his arms and legs, angry that Jiro had deserted him!

The house was full of shadows cast by the moon. Yuki was determined to stay up until Kentaro came back from the institute. She turned on the soft light in the stand behind her chair, and sat in the reclined position with her feet up. Taking up the top piece of origami paper from the pile on the table beside her, she deftly folded the shape she intended. The completed crane pleased her. She smiled and put it in the box she had made, also by folding paper. By the time the baby arrives, I will have folded one thousand! She reached behind her to turn off the light, then closed her eyes.

Yuki knew well the origin of that story about Sadako, the little girl wanting to make a thousand cranes to bring fulfilment of her wish to live, and felt she had something in common with the little girl. Suffering from leukaemia, and carrying a clone, were quite different experiences, yet both were imbued with the fear of the unknown, were clouded by a not-knowing. She sat there thinking about that, and other quite alarming things which came from the shadows of her mind. She remembered the bomb. The wickedness of it. She remembered the story of the scientist who wished that he had not been a party to it because it was too dreadful in its consequences. She thought of cloning, and how serious a thing it was for her to be carrying the first, no the second, cloned child. Remembering Mary made her smile for a moment. She felt like the pilot of the Enola Gay, the person in charge of the thing carried – sadistically named Little Boy. Her heart was heavy.

What if this child is like the bomb? Wild and destructive! Her little boy could be a terrible monster with no soul. And she would carry the stigma into old age. Feel violated until she died. All her dreams of happiness would be polluted by this event. The world, if it got to know about her monster son would hate her. Sign petitions against cloning of more human beings, demand execution for those who dared to play God. I will try not to think of my son as 'Little Boy' but it will be hard. There is so little known about cloning of humans. She must continue to read anything and everything on the subject, not hide from it.

And then, when the moonlight fell on her, she thought with a mix of happiness and bitterness about Ichiro. Today had been both marvellous and unhappy for him. He had come inside after biking home and burst into tears shouting, 'Jiro's mean as mean!'

Yuki talked to him, gave him an afternoon snack of bean cakes and milk, and learned the full story.

'Jiro didn't leave you,' she said. 'He was taken from you. There's a big difference. And those horrid boys. Do you think I should tell the teacher?'

'No! No! And anyway, Hideo will come with me tomorrow.'

Yuki was relieved that when bed-time came, Ichiro seemed happy again. She heard more about his performance, and could see that he loved playing for people again. He had re-connected with his inner self, the self that found true expression through music.

His piano playing was considered by his teacher to be imbued with a new depth of feeling. He showed maturity beyond his age. And what was more, he had become insatiable for repertoire. He was now a genius beyond their expectations.

Yuki's eyes were heavy. Soon she was asleep, and her dreams were happy ones. When Kentaro came in, he saw the light at the chair and was alarmed. And then he looked at Yuki's expression and guessed that she had good news for him. He must wake her. She would want that.

'I had the test today, and the doctor said that I'm pregnant for sure, and due on November the sixteenth.'

'November the sixteenth? Why that's marvellous, Yuki.' He was almost dancing, which happened when he was elated. 'I'll fix my schedule and we will welcome our little son with joy and celebration. He raised an imaginary glass and said, '*Kampai! Kampai*! I drink to you! I love you! You are wonderful.'

'It's early days.' She put her feet to the floor. 'But look, I'm making a thousand cranes for our child.'

'You mean for you. Or even us. Don't be afraid that your dream, our dream, will not come true. You've made a great start. We will get our son, and he will be perfect.'

'Well, I'm making the cranes, nevertheless,' she said. 'Come with me to put the first one at the shrine. That's where it belongs.'

They went quietly through to the small room where they had a pedestal on which stood the shrine for Jiro. The only other pieces of furniture in the room were the grand piano, piano stool, music cabinet, and a chair. A night light illuminated the shrine. The smell of freshly offered spring flowers was strong. Above them on the wall, the young face with the clear, honest eyes behind frameless glasses looked from the large photograph as if to say, now I am going to play Mozart. He loved Mozart more than any other composer and he was as childishly eager to play Mozart as other children would be to play a video game. Carefully, Yuki placed the crane at the shrine and sounded the gong. They held hands, and closed their eyes for a moment, then turned and left the room. Back in the living room, Kentaro said, 'The cranes are a wonderful idea, my pet.'

She laughed, and said, 'I think so too.' Sharing the news with her husband had cheered her up. She would have been such a disappointment to him if she had not been pregnant. I'm happy. On course. 'We'll have to tell Hamish soon, won't we?'

'Right now. We'll tell him now. I don't care what time it is. He said to use his second number any time, and to use the words "journey" and "begun", and tell him some up to date news of the memorial fund so that if anyone hears the conversation they will not guess about the baby. But before I do anything else, I want to kiss you. I am so proud of you.'

She giggled as they moved toward each other, and he bent to kiss her. And within her husband she sensed a change. He was very gentle. Already she felt special, and happy. They kissed again and again, and long, his tongue searching her moist mouth. Suddenly she pulled away from him and ran up the stairs to the bed.

Naked, she slipped under the duvet and waited. When Kentaro bounded up the stairs, her heart raced within her.

'Hamish is over the moon. He sent his love to you which also means he's astonished at how well you've adjusted to the whole thing. I could tell he was bursting with pride but dare not give himself away.' He stripped off and slipped in beside her. 'Oh, I am so pleased that we shall have another son.'

Yuki touched her husband's groin and he put a hand down to clasp her fingers in his. 'Yuki, I love you and want you, but I'm so much in awe that I cannot make love to you. No, I've decided, not until we have our child.'

'Oh, no!' Yuki cried out. 'All that time. That's cruel. I didn't expect this. I hate you for this. Hate you!' Her shouted words vibrated the screens of the bedroom.

Shouting back, Kentaro said, 'Yuki. Listen to me. It's not my fault. I don't want you to be disappointed after doing so well. All you went through in Italy!' He became moody, quieter. 'We can't run the risks. You might abort. Mightn't you?'

'If you're going to shun me for nine months then fuck you, Kentaro!' she yelled.

She remembered Mary's words "It reminded me of our honey-moon!" and she was jealous! But she also remembered that Hamish's one fear was that Mary might lose their child. Yuki reached for her nightie and pulled it to cover her. She felt afraid. But she did not want to lose her son, in spite of all her negative thoughts. 'I don't know what to think, Kentaro.'

As she was dozing off, she remembered Ichiro's unhappiness.

'I forgot to say that Ichiro's recital was brilliant, but after school he was followed and taunted by some kids on bikes. They called him half-wit and other nasty things to do with Jiro's death.'

Kentaro pushed himself up on his elbows. 'Oh, no! Poor boy. I'll speak to the principal tomorrow. That's terrible.'

Yuki was too exhausted to say, no, Ichiro does not want that. She went to sleep with tears on her cheeks, and he with his arm about her, his other hand cupped lightly around her crotch.

When Kentaro had called Hamish, he was reading, and the moment his phone started to ring, he snatched it from his pocket.

'Hello.' He spoke quietly. Mary was asleep, their apartment small. But the news was so good, that after phoning Bill who was the only colleague he could share the news with, he made a cup of tea and woke Mary.

'Wake up. I have some tea for you.' Since this was the way they began every day she awoke easily. 'Mary, here my darling, drink your tea.' He had her attention. 'Yuki's pregnant!'

'What?'

'Yuki Fujiwara.'

'Oh, really? They've just rung or something? So it is the middle of the night! Hamish, that is such great news.' She sipped from her cup and put it down.

'Come here, my clever husband. You are absolutely amazing.' She kissed him on the lips. 'You are so clever. What is it, now? Two women pregnant by you inside of four months!'

'Hey, now. Don't be putting it like that. Because of me might be better.'

Mary thought of how she had become even closer since the cloning of Trish.

'I'm happy for them.'

Hamish perched on the bed beside her and she noticed that his mood had altered. She knew why when she heard what he had to say.

'Mary, I want to tell you something that no one else knows!' His voice was subdued. He needed to confess. She watched him, feeling nervous.

'In Galtür, when Jiro lay there in the morgue, I cut some hairs from his wee head, and scraped a wee bit of skin from his arm, and kept them safe.'

'Are you saying that you cloned their baby using the dead twin's cell and not Ichiro's.'

'Yes, that's what I did.'

'Hamish. How could you?'

'I hardly know but I remember feeling driven, compelled, maybe mad. In all my work and thinking, and even in moments like that, I'm obsessed by cloning. Didn't want to miss any chances. I guess it's a bit like being a photographer like our friend Jamie. Remember Jamie?'

'I couldn't forget Jamie!'

'Yes, well, he took photos wherever he went didn't he, just for the record? "Just in case," he'd say. No real reason except his obsession with images. It's the way of seeing – for him and for me.'

'So, you'll tell the parents?' He stood up suddenly.

'No. I don't need to tell them, not now, anyway. They're happy. Let them enjoy the pregnancy – I'll tell them when it matters.'

Mary sighed. She hated being woken up in the middle of the night and only wanted to get back to sleep.

'It's your decision and not an easy one, I can see that. And now, how about coming to bed. It would help me get back to sleep.'

But he had a lot of thinking to do. He needed time, and it could not wait. The historical implications were enormous, but there were personal issues to sort out too. He felt scared to death because cloning was still illegal, and even though Mary kept telling him that other geneticists would be cloning humans, he still felt guilty. He had been stretched enough, just reassuring her that the birth would be fine. And what if the baby was a crier like Trish had been? How would they cope with that?

Part Two
Chapter 2

While Ichiro played Schumann at his home in Nagoya late in the evening, Tom, almost three years younger, put away his violin in Dorchester, Ontario, and looked longingly from his window. He wanted to join the squirrels and play in the garden instead of going to school. He thought the trees beautiful now that they were getting their colours.

'Tom, it's almost time for the bus!'

Tom swung down off the window seat and snatched up the school pack that he had carefully filled with all the things he liked to take when he was going to spend the night with his mother. His dad commented on the amount of stuff in his bag but he swore there was nothing more than usual. And yes, his coat was there just in case it rained tomorrow.

'OK.' Warren checked that he had left nothing on in the kitchen, set the alarm and locked the front door after them. He looked down on his young son knowing that even one night without him would be too long! Yet, he believed the time would fly with Andreas to talk to.

As Tom clambered on to the yellow bus, Warren called, 'Wait at the school gate this afternoon.'

'Yes,' he yelled back, and waved out the window.

Andreas was fed up with playing the Sarasate. He put his violin under his arm and Miguel saw that his cheek twitched badly.

'There's that one bar that sticks me every time. I'll never get it right.'

'Here, now. I suggest practising it like this.' Miguel played the bar slowly, with the bow on the string. Then he played it *spiccato*, as if it were simple.

'You mean, I should be able to rip through it like that. I don't think so. I'm packing it in.' Andreas said.

It was a frequent occurrence that senior students became disappointed in themselves, even to the point of throwing it all away. But the wise teacher knew that it was burn-out in most cases. Andreas was no exception. He took the cloth from his violin again and used the silk to remove the resin from the table of his instrument.

'You can't help. No-one can help.' He wrapped his violin again, replaced it in the case, and briefly looked at his teacher. 'No one can bring CT back. Or can they?' At that, he moved quickly to the door, and left.

Miguel then saw that the note he was to give to Andreas was still on his desk. He picked up his phone.

'Nicola, intercept Andreas who's just left here, and give him a message please. Can you find him and tell him that a Warren Blackwell is picking him up at the main entrance at four today.'

After dropping Tom off at Jane Street, Warren headed down Hamilton Road to the music and arts academy to pick up Andreas. He had just pulled in near the music building when the men saw each other. Warren waved to Andreas. He smiled and joined Warren at the car.

'I'm Warren Blackwell. How are you, Andreas?' he said, shaking his hand.

'Oh, a lot fed up with practising, actually. And you?'

'Really glad that you're willing to hear my request.'

Andreas opened the passenger door, not sure what was meant, but Warren was evidently trusted by Miguel, and he liked the guy so far. He needed a change. He had begun to feel that if he did not get a break he would die. Warren relieved him of his violin and put it in the back seat.

'I can't believe I'm being whisked away out of that music factory for an evening.'

The car pulled away, and Warren found Andreas easy to talk to. He learned that he took on busking for the sake of the money, but then enjoyed it so much he did it often. By the time they had reached Warren's place in Dorchester, Andreas had revealed a little of his background – a German father and a Canadian mother. MAAC seemed as good as any academy, especially now that Miguel Garcia was the professor of violin. He was a technical wizard and had the demonstrative enthusiasm for the instrument which was inspiring and infectious.

The house was empty without Tom, so much so that Warren wondered why he felt the need to get to know Andreas alone. After all, the relationship between Andreas and Tom would be the crucial point in whether a child-minding arrangement occurred. He offered tea or coffee. While he was brewing coffee, Andreas allowed his eyes to wander about at the furniture, the pictures on the wall and notice board where he saw, on closer inspection, a picture of himself. 'Hey, this is me!'

'That's right.' called back Warren.

He wondered at the preponderance of black and white photos of a little boy, one as large as he had ever seen. The image was quite magical, the photographer had made the very most of the elegance of the instrument. The mousey-haired boy who was playing it had such intense focus on his strings. Suddenly it twigged! He had signed the boy's programme at the Fanshaw concert.

'Warren,' he shouted excitedly. 'That little boy with the mischievous twinkle and slicked back hair, I met him the other day at the school's concert. A really neat little guy. He's Tom isn't he?'

Mugs of coffee in his hands, Warren beamed. 'Yep. It's Tom. Here, take this.' He sat down again on the rich tapestry cushion, and crossed his legs. There was pride in his voice. 'The youngest violinist there.'

'He was so proud to get my autograph. I thought he'd never stop grinning.' He sipped. 'Good coffee. Well, so you're Tom's dad? Amazing! Where is he?'

Warren spent a few minutes telling Andreas about his situation and said that he was totally devoted to Tom, but because of his work as a freelance photographer and writer, he often worked odd hours.

He told him how they discovered this marvellous teacher at the Banff camp and how he was really hooked on the method she used. However, it did mean racing off to Toronto every Friday afternoon. He was fortunate that Tom practised, especially since before the camp it had been push, push, push.

'Did you enjoy your childhood and learning the violin, Andreas?' He realised this was a touchy question when Andreas answered it by giving the distinct impression that he had hated practising while trying to read the music as well. He had believed that reading books at school was enough reading to do in any one day when he was a child. It had been at the age of eleven, the time when he was playing Mozart concertos, that he suddenly took off. He craved to play.

'I got hooked. They couldn't stop me practising.'

'And now you're fed up?' Andreas looked tired all of a sudden. His cheek twitched.

Warren felt surprised that he was so obviously tired, and suggested he make supper.

'Oh, great! Yep, that'll be good.' He stood up, and Warren was relieved that he looked alert. Andreas stretched and yawned.

'Excuse me,' he said. 'I'd like to walk in your garden if that's OK. Fall excites me. Brings poetry and yearnings of all kinds back into my head again. I'll be happy out there. Please give me an idea of the time you'll be ready for me.'

'OK. Around twenty minutes. Tell me though, do you like Italian?'

'I sure do.'

Andreas walked out into the garden enclosed by large maples and a stone wall. Whereas at noon the colours would have been bright red and orange, now at dusk they are dull. Some damp at his feet. The hushed mood is evocative. The persona that arrives arm-in-arm with fall each and every year is a consistent guest, bright, warm and always its breath is ominous.

As a small boy, Andreas was almost wholly rebellious of practising his violin, yet there was a little part of him that told him that the sounds he made carried outside his house to touch the leaves of trees, join with the breeze, and spiral into the sunset. At times, such as now, he found he was reconnecting with those sounds – they have travelled the airwaves around Europe only to land, all these years later, at his feet in this garden. Deep within him he feels the stirring of happiness.

Part Two
Chapter 3

Hamish worked feverishly to get away for the weekend. Mary's pleas for a day or two at Riva Del Garda had goaded him into agreement. The look of excitement and the hugs and laughter had made him glad that he had not only promised time away, but had booked a room at Hotel Sole, overlooking the lake.

The other members of staff had left at the usual time of four-thirty. He made his usual check of the lab – everything at the right temperature; everything in its place. He had arranged for his colleague, Muriana, and two of her team, to check on the animals and embryos. That was the best he could do.

He drove home as fast as he dare, but the traffic on the winding and narrow road was restricting. It was Friday, and everyone was heading home or going to their holiday homes along Lake Como. At last, he pulled into his garage and walked up the internal steps. Then in the hallway, he smiled at the sight of the one packed suitcase standing ready. Mary heard him, and ran to hug him.

'I'm so excited, I can barely tell you.'

'And I can guess – you've cooked pasta and it's ready and waiting.'

'Right.'

It was dark when they drew up at the brick paved entrance to Hotel Sole in Riva Del Garda but the foyer was brightly lit. The figure behind the reception desk moved and the doors swung open. They were expected, and the figure they had glimpsed from their car materialised as a small, balding man who beamed at them, and beckoned a footman to help with luggage. Once they had booked in, they were led to the elevator, and it was with a proud flourish that the hotel manager opened the door and switched on the lights to their room, inviting them to enter. He had done as Hamish expected and on the small side table near the patio had placed a silver platter arranged with chunks of fruit, cheeses, and finely sliced meats. There was a carafe of fruit juice and a bottle of chardonnay. Hamish turned to thank him, and put a note into his hand, but the beaming manager said, 'No. No. This is our privilege, Dr McLeod. Is there anything more you require?'

'I think that is all for now, thank you, sir.'

Hamish joined Mary on the balcony, and in the hushed stillness they stayed silent, enjoying the scene. Illuminated lamps near the wharf shimmering in the water below, the black incline of the cliffs to the right where a tiny light showed itself in an aura of mystery and there, away up at an impossible height, another light shaped like a minute statue on Bastione.

Below them, their attention was caught by a strolling couple, their profiles outlined by a light from the bar below. There was a laugh and a skipped step, answered by a deep voice of indeterminate accent. Then the two figures merged, and passed into the night. Mary and Hamish turned to one another as if to continue what had been started by the couple below, and kissed for a long time.

After making love on the first of the three-quarter beds, they each pulled one of the heavy drapes across and laughed.

'Should have done this first,' said Hamish. 'Let's have the feast that charming gentleman left for us. Shall we?'

Mary answered with a smile, and pulled the table nearer the bed. They sat close on the turned back sheets drinking their wine and fruit juice, and eating the meal with relish.

'I had no idea I was this hungry,' Mary laughed, folding the last slice of ham and taking a black olive in her other fingers. 'But after this, I'm done.'

Hamish picked up a serviette and said, 'Let's keep those bits of cheese and grapes, and tomorrow we can buy panini and a drink and take a lunch with us on our bike ride.'

'Good idea, and while we're into details, let's have a look at the map and decide on our route.'

With her finger outlining the way she suggested, he followed as she traced along the familiar cycle track – Viale Carducci, Via Boschetto, then into Via S. Alessandro to eat lunch in the churchyard. 'No matter what time it is, that's where I have to eat lunch for old time's sake,' she said.

'Fine by me.'

'So which of us will go ahead?' Mary was standing with a leg on each side of the bicycle she had chosen from the selection of hotel-owned bikes. Hamish was about to mount another.

'Go ahead, lassie. Set your own pace.' As she set off, she turned and laughed, 'Pace!'

It was a matter of giving way to those who strolled in a leisurely manner and straddled the pavement between the cafè tables and chairs, and the lake. At times, they almost stood still, moving the handlebars just enough to keep them upright. But at the turn of the parade along the canal with its tethered boats, and contemporary sculptures on the opposite bank, there were bunches of people sauntering about in holiday mood. They were obliged to walk, and wheel their bikes side by side. Wide gardens of tulip bulbs showed green leaves above the soil.

'Remember these three years ago?' Hamish asked.

'How could I forget? Unabashed red and brilliant yellow.'

Before mounting their bikes again, they stopped to buy bottled water and panini. Hamish fell behind again and let Mary set the pace as they took the cycle tracks and meandered up the valley, ever mindful of the backdrop of mountains. It was as if each one had thoughts too private to share to ride side by side, even though they met hardly another person on the way.

The day was perfect, clear and crisp, the familiar landscape reassuring.

When Mary stopped at the churchyard, she was feeling a bit shaky and put an elbow on a handlebar to rest her head in her hand for a minute. He pulled up beside her as she lifted her head again and was surprised by her pallor.

'You're pale, Mary. Is this too much for you, lassie?'

'I don't know. I was all right till I stopped. Maybe. Let's sit down on the shaded seat under the spire and then I'm sure I'll be OK. I probably got too hot without noticing.'

Hamish unpacked the lunch and suggested she go first, as he laid out the cheese pieces and grapes on the napkin. She drank from her water bottle.

'I feel better all ready,' she said, as she broke open her panina and started to fill it. 'It's still there, you know.' She laughed a little then took a bite.

'What are you talking about?'

'You know how we used to laugh at the way that church kept reappearing?'

'At every bend of the road? Yeah! I noticed that again. Kind of mesmerizes you.'

Mary held up a grape. 'Open,' she said, and he took it into his mouth, then pretended to bite her finger. Snap.

'Ouch, ouch,' she cried, pretending to pull and pull some more. Her eyes were full of merriment and love for him. She wiped her finger along her knee. Suddenly, a darkened expression appeared in her eyes.

'Hamish. What if I were to lose this baby?'

'No lass. We cannot have such talk.' He looked credulous. 'You mean, you might?'

'I only thought of that just now. I love you so much, Hamish … so much want this baby. But, well I did get a bit of a fright.'

'You mean when you stopped biking?'

'Yes.' She sighed. 'I had thought we'd go on to the lake edge but maybe we'd better go back to the hotel. Do you mind?'

'Och, no! But we won't hurry back.' He pulled her to be closer to him. 'Just you take a rest. We've got all the time in the world.'

She laughed quietly. 'You mean we can stay here till Christmas?'

He squeezed her shoulder and chuckled.

'Hamish!' It was a scream, not a call.

He froze, stopping dead with his towel on his groin which he had been drying.

He knew in his heart what it was that Mary was telling him. In one movement he ran back to the bathroom and swept her off her feet to carry her to the bed where he laid her down gently.

'You're bleeding, aren't you?'

'Yes. But just a wee bit.'

He pulled on his clothes and said at the same time, 'Don't move, lassie. Here,' he grabbed a dry towel, rolled it up, and placed it under her knees then covered her with the duvet. He kissed her on the lips, gently, tenderly.

'Don't move at all,' he whispered close to her face, and stroked her cheek. 'I'll get help, I will. We're going to keep this baby, we are lass.' He rang reception. She heard him say, 'We need a doctor at once. My wife may have a miscarriage. Yes, now, at once.'

'Hamish, please give me my rosary,' she said as soon as he put down the receiver.

The beaming and rotund *dottore* wore his stethoscope like a medal. His nostrils visibly inhaled, as if the air were freshly spring-cleaned, and deflated with a spread of pride and confidence. When he said, '*Buongiorno. Come sta*?' The change in Mary's mood was palpable. She smiled into his eyes, whispering 'I'm OK, OK.' He spoke gently to her, listening to the child's heart-beat, taking her blood pressure, and pressing ever so gently on her abdomen. He almost crooned as he told her she would keep the baby.

Aside to Hamish, in a mix of English and Italian, with much waving of his arms, he revealed his deep concern that she would have to get to a hospital. But the roads had too many corners and were rough in places! Como hospital, where there was a helipad, would be the best, but the helicopter was on a call to Lago Maggiore where there had been a boat accident, and it would be about an hour before it came. But there was no choice. Helicopter it had to be. They must wait. He would sedate Mary after giving her an injection which should stop the bleeding, and save the baby whose heart rate was a little on the fast side, but would reduce as Mary rested.

'*Grazie tanto,*' Hamish repeated several times, nodding and watching Mary as the doctor talked. Once the injection had been administered, Mary dozed off, and the room became terrifyingly still. This was day-time, siesta time, but he would not be able to rest. Not for a minute. The doctor had departed for some reason which was not clear to Hamish, but he knew from the number of times he had said, '*Mi pardoni,*' and '*Aspetti,*' that he would probably be back quite soon. There was no choice but to wait.

Yet, when all the implications of being helicoptered out from Riva Del Garda hit him, Hamish hastily packed their bag, and picked up the small back-pack which had held their lunch. He put their toiletry bags into it, then rang through to reception to find someone to drive his car back to Como, as well as arranging to make the necessary payments for the hotel room. Once all that was done, the radio filled the time, or had he dozed? Whichever it was, Hamish caught the whirring of the helicopter as it purred above the lake and headed straight for the town square outside the hotel. He watched from the patio, but within moments, the doctor was back to master-mind the transfer of the patient to the paramedics. Mary was gently placed on a stretcher and whisked to the waiting machine. He glanced about the room in a mixture of emotions then bounded down the stairs to catch a ride. He and their small amount of luggage were given space enough, and he sighed with relief that they were on their way. He looked askance at the pallor of his wife's usually ruddy cheeks, and marvelled that she was asleep in spite of the juddering and noise of the helicopter. It lifted them away from the gathered crowd of holiday-makers, above the walkways, shops and colourful street stalls and jetty, away from the prayerful guardianship of Bastione. He found himself uttering the words that Mary prayed as she responded to the doctor's injection, 'Mother Mary, please save us in this hour of our need.'

Part Two
Chapter 4

It was arranged that Warren and Tom would watch Andreas busking. If it was fine, he would be at Springbank, and if wet at K-Mart on Highbury. At twelve Warren and Tom set out for the park.

'I'm so happy that it's a good day, Dad. I didn't want to go to K-Mart.'

They walked quickly, hand-in-hand, along the path that led eventually to the drawbridge and the make-believe castle. The weather forecast had left them in no doubt that Andreas would be there. On their left along the riverbank, dozens of people were taking a look at the boats moored at the brand new jetty. This was a day for taking rides on the river. Children ran every which way. Tom and his dad had to leave the path to avoid them, and crossed through the car park to the castle entrance. At first they thought that Andreas must have found a new spot to play in because they could not hear his violin, but as they got near to the Jolly Miller, they heard it. Standing in the shade of an enormous maple, Andreas stood playing with his eyes shut. Warren recognised the piece as the popular and sentimental *Meditation* by Thias. At his feet were several families. Some people were diving in and out of cane baskets and chilly bins, to get little parcels of food and cans of drink to enjoy along with the music.

'I want to get nearer,' Tom whispered. 'We can't see how much money he's got.'

'After he plays his last piece. We'll put money in as well.'
They joined in the clapping while Andreas acknowledged the applause with a broad smile. He spotted Tom.

'Hi there Tom, what would you like me to finish with?'

'The bumble bee piece,' he flashed back. This made Andreas smile and announce *The Flight of the Bumble Bee*. Ziiing! The piece went like lightning, and when it was over, most of the children clamoured to speak to Andreas, and throw down a coin at the same time.

Tom and Warren waited for the last one to wander off, and Tom said, 'You've got heaps of money in your case.'

'Hey, that's none of your business. And you can put this in too,' his dad chided.

'I should have the proverbial hat, but my case does the trick.' Andreas said. He wiped a cloth over his forehead and said, 'I've worked hard for that money today. Let's put it in this bag. Tom, can you help me?'

Tom watched his new idol clean and wrap his violin while crouching down.

'You like that violin, don't you?'

'Oh, yes. It's my best friend, Tom.'

'Can I be your second best?'

Andreas zipped up his case, and looked into the eager face of the young boy. He tweaked Tom's already rosy cheek, and said, 'I think you just can. Come on, we're off to your place now and you can show me your violin.'

'Will you teach me some of those tricks you showed us at Fanshaw?'

'Sure. As long as you don't take all of your lesson time by showing them to Donna.'

Warren thought rather guiltily of his own frivolities in relation to Donna. Rather a misuse of lesson time.

Andreas was taking a close look at a book on Niagara when Warren got back to the living room.

'Neat kid, that Tom.'

'Enjoyed your tricks,' he said.

Before he left, it was arranged that Andreas would mind Tom one evening soon, when Warren would be in Toronto. Andreas liked the idea of staying overnight. He had not had a break from his lodgings since he began at MAAC four years ago.

The first thing that Tom felt he had to tell Donna when he

arrived for his next lesson was that a real violinist was coming to their place on Sunday.

'My goodness. Where did you find a real one, Tom?'

'Dad and I took him home from Springbank Park.'

Donna caught her breath, and looked questioningly at Warren. He gave a quirky smile then said, 'Tom, how about you get your violin out.' He looked at Donna. 'We've worked hard this week, and Tom is playing much better.'

After the lesson, Warren said, 'You haven't looked at my notebook recently.'

She laughed. 'I can tell from the way Tom plays that your notes are good. No need to look.'

'Please do. I was a bit puzzled today. You know, on that tone study.'

Donna read his notes, tipping the book to catch the light as the writing was so small. She had almost finished when she read the note meant for her eyes only. 'I'd like to take you out some time. Tell me if you'll come, and when.'

Donna felt herself blush, and took the pen from around her neck, and wrote, 'I'm spoken for. Sorry.'

He read the answer and wrote down, 'I'm persistent!'

Donna smiled and thought, what the heck. Peter's too involved with work to have an affair that satisfies me.

'OK. Call me,' she scribbled.

She didn't have to wait long for her phone to ring. As soon as she threw her jacket on to its hook inside the door to her apartment, the phone rang and her pulse raced. Goodness, he is home already. But it was not Warren.

'I'm aching to see you, honey.'

'Peter, it's been forever. How soon can you get here?'

'I'm on the outskirts of Toronto now. See you soon. Is that OK?'

'Sure is.'

She fingered her ear. What am I going to do about this? Play one off against the other? I have half a mind to. Yep, I can string two along and see which comes up with the highest stakes!

No sooner than she stepped from the shower and put on her bathrobe, than her doorbell buzzed, and she went to the wall panel.

'Who is it?'

'Peter.' She activated the lock for the front door. When he reached her, she laughed and said, 'Hello Peter. God, it's been too long.' The look of him, a strong face, brown eyes that constantly seemed to catch the light, eyebrows that lifted toward the temple, hair receding from the front, brown beard with obvious grey. She loved the look of him. And the smell of him. As they kissed, she peeled away his jacket and his shirt and said in muffled tones, 'All go?'

'All go.'

Pulling him to the bedroom, she pulled back the covers, pushed him on to the bed and lay beside him, her robe undone.

'Go as far as you want,' he said, slipping out of his jeans. He was ready very quickly for the whole concerto.

'I'm playing soloist, tonight,' she said. 'You did last time.' She lifted herself to be on top of him, and her orgasms threw her whole body into explosive rhythms. They made noisy, erotic love.

Exhausted, she was tucked in against his hip, playing with the soft black hair of his chest. 'That was wild.'

'You're one amazing woman, you know that?'

'I want to do all this again later, but let's go cook some supper. I'm hungry. I barely have time to eat on Friday.'

'Me, too. I'll take a shower.'

'Come on. We'll shower together.'

As he dried himself, Peter hummed. Donna prolonged drying herself to listen to the rich and evocative sound, then put on her kimono-style wrap-around.

'*Sakura, sakura*' – she mouthed the words as Peter hummed them, and was back in Nagoya, smelling the smells of spring, and nodding to her friends who parade in their kimonos.

> The day doesn't belong to her as it does to the people of Japan. Her eyes are the eyes of a Canadian, her heart the heart of a North American woman. She is clumsy by comparison. She stops to witness the tea ceremony being performed, and wishes that she could appreciate it from her host's point of view. In her home she has a room designed as the place to share the ceremony with her family, with Donna and with all her many guests from around the world. She takes every part of it seriously, dresses in her kimono, with all its detail of folding and tying. And on her knees, circled by people, she performs the ceremony with grace and ease. The bowl is turned and appreciated, the drink shared.

'I was remembering what Japan is like at cherry blossom time, and got to thinking about the tea ceremony. Your humming reminded me.'

'Did you like the taste of the tea?'

'I'm afraid not. I felt badly about that. The tea ceremony was very important to my host. But, that tune? How come it's in your head now?'

Peter told Donna about the cello classes he had held that day, and that he used that favourite folk song of Fujiwara's to teach tone development. The students had readily picked it up, and if the truth be known, he was sure they would all be singing it tonight, too. It was the strong melody line which suited the rich possibilities of the cello, and he was now enamoured by the idea of using such a simple song in place of other dull exercises he had been using for years. Dull stuff which left one with nothing to sing, or sing about! Cherry blossom conjured up delicate and ephemeral mind pictures, a feeling of nostalgia associated with spring. And, what is more, it tapped the poignancy of his favourite instrument.

Part Two
Chapter 5

His glasses were misted over, but he had heard the music so many times, Ichiro knew it well. He liked to play it with his eyes closed, anyway. The *Moonlight Sonata* was to him a piece to be rippled through when a mood was on you. Right now, he was in a mood. He could not identify the feeling but he knew it had something to do with Jiro's death. He was on to the second page and suddenly stopped. He removed his glasses and put them on top of the piano and leaned his face into the keys in a boom of discordant sounds, then lashed out at his thighs.

'Jiro, why did you leave me? I hate you for going away.' He did not need his glasses to see Jiro's face. He could see things that far away. Jiro appeared to pucker his lips. 'And well you might. You're a stupid dork for dying. I can't play the stuff I want to.' He played a little of Monti's *Czardas*. 'See? It makes no sense without your part. Jiro. Come back at once.' He put his glasses back on, and stormed noisily out of the room to the foyer. 'I'm going for a ride,' he called to his mother. She registered, but was doing her exercises to music. He would be all right.

He used the phone before he left the house and asked Hideo to meet him outside the fruit shop.

'Yep. I will, but just for twenty minutes, OK?'

'*Diajōbu!*' Ichiro was glad that he had a friend who lived so near.

At the evening meal, Kentaro said to Ichiro, as usual, 'You've done your practice, then?'

'Course,' Ichiro snapped.

'I beg your pardon?'

Ichiro put down his chopsticks and looked keenly at his father.

'I love playing the piano but I can't play the pieces I like best.'

'And which ones are those?' he asked with noodles balanced for slurping.

'The ones for violin and piano.'

Kentaro drew up his many noodles. 'Jiro, yes. You miss playing with him, of course.'

'Shall we get Hideo to play his cello with you?' Yuki said.

'No! I want only Jiro. He made me feel good. Hideo is too clumsy.'

They ate in silence until all were finished.

'I'm sorry, Yuki but I have to go out,' Kentaro said. Ichiro watched his mother gulping her tears. She didn't like his father going out. Why did he go?

'If you must,' she said from the sink with her back to him.

Yuki sat at the *kotatsu* in the living room. It was not yet winter but she felt chilly after vomiting her meal yet again. She was lonely too, but spurred on by the cranes. They had become her companions of the evening once Ichiro was in bed. But it was no fun for Yuki being alone night after night with no one to talk to. Cranes or no cranes.

She had an uneasy feeling; thought that the house was not at peace. She put down her square of blue paper and went to see if Ichiro had called her. He was restless, she could see that. She knelt beside him and stayed a little. Out of the quiet came his voice in a whisper.

'Mum, did a part of me die when Jiro left?'

'Darling, I thought you were asleep.'

'I can't sleep tonight, Mum, I can only think of that night.'

'You mean the avalanches, don't you?'

'Yes. Jiro and I, we were not scared. We told each other that there were the two of us, and we made each other strong as two people. We'd been talking about that when I must have fallen asleep, and he went to the toilet. And that's when the avalanche ploughed into our chalet. We didn't know it would do that, did we?'

'No, we thought it was all over, my darling. All over.'

'So Mum, did part of me die with Jiro?'

'No. Even twins have their own spirit, their own soul.'

'So I still have my soul?'

'Yes, you do. Can you sleep now? It's late.' She stood up.

'Mum, just one last thing. I think Jiro isn't really dead.'

'Why?'

'It's a feeling. It's like we still talk to each other.'

'How?'

'I go to his shrine every day even before you and daddy are up, and we talk. Mostly about how to play great music. I know he helps me.'

'Oh, that is so beautiful. But you must sleep now. Night-night, my darling.'

Before returning to the living room, Yuki spent some moments in front of the shrine, with her head bowed, then she looked intently at the photo. Jiro, are you all right? She touched the cheeks of the child, and felt a chill run through her. Jiro, are we looking after your spirit well enough? Her heart cried within her. She fingered the black ribbon which adorned the photograph frame and lifted it from a drooping position, up a little, to look perkier. Her efforts made her smile, and she whispered, 'Sleep well, my little one', and returned to the *kotatsu* where the kerosene still burned. She counted those in the box. There were twenty-three, and she laughed aloud. Oh, there are so many to reach one thousand. Perhaps I am being stupid. And then she thought of the people she must share her joyful news with. As soon as I am three months on I'll tell all my family and friends, and they can help me.

Invigorated by the thought that she would get help, she worked quickly to make five cranes before she decided that Kentaro was not coming home in time to say goodnight. She must get herself to bed. Alone again. She knew that Kentaro would be with his geisha. She knew too, that there was nothing she could do about it. He has needs. But I should say to him that I have been told from none other than Hamish's wife that it is all right to make love while carrying a cloned foetus. It is absolutely no different carrying a clone from carrying one's own baby. She smiled wryly as she thought – it is just as awful. Morning sickness, evening sickness, it is no different. And she had promised Mary, and anyway, Kentaro is not Hamish, and I am not Mary. Besides, I do not want anything to go wrong for me now. I would feel such a failure.

She packed away the cranes and decided that tomorrow she would make a second box. She had put two more cranes into the first box, and thereafter thirty in each new box. Goodness, what a line-up of boxes that would mean. I wonder where little Sadako kept the cranes she made? Did she string them up? I think she did. And nearly made one thousand, too. What a brave little girl. I must be brave too.

The bedroom was one of Yuki's favourite rooms. From the window, she could see over the tops of houses, to the far distant hills. Her eye carried her imagination over to the snowy tops of the Alps as she remembered them in her childhood in Matsumoto. Her dad would take them on the road which meandered up the lower slopes to see the autumn colours that were as beautiful as any in the world. For a while Yuki stood with her eyes closed, remembering. She could feel the tang of mountain air on her skin. Imagined herself at a lookout above a ravine, and marvelled at the colours all about her, below and up the slopes to the sky. Always, the slowness of the journey made them especially meaningful. She remembered the times that they asked their dad if they were actually moving. It was a way they had of joking together, in an otherwise stressfully prolonged journey, nose to tail.

Yes, she must encourage Kentaro to do that journey with Ichiro and the new baby – carry on the tradition. Then they could teach their youngest to ski on the Alps in the winter.

They did not have to go to Europe! They needed to get beyond Jiro's death and be happy again. She was smiling as she dropped to sleep. And she appeared to be smiling when Kentaro crept into bed at two in the morning, tired out and tipsy.

Part Two
Chapter 6

The notebook was put to much use at the end of Tom's next lesson. Without even asking her to check it, Warren thrust it under her nose, and told Tom to hurry up and get his coat on. This time, Donna answered him directly.

'I'll expect you on Thursday evening, then. You've got my address. Seven o'clock.' She said it all in an undertone, but as soon as they got outside, Tom said, 'Could Andreas come and stay on Thursday, Dad?'

'Oh, so what makes you think I won't be home?'

'Dummy! You're going to Donna's.'

So Warren called Andreas. 'Sure, Thursday night it is.'

As soon as he got off the phone, Andreas began to shake.

'Oh, God, I thought I was over this.' He took his violin from his case that he then left open on his bed, and he played double stopped notes very slowly, to try and get himself together. He could feel his cheek twitching, and that did not help. He stopped playing to splash his face with cold water, and began to play again, a slow scale in thirds. Gradually, very gradually, he got himself together, but as he put his violin in the case to take a rest, he silently addressed his dead father.

Mein Gott, you have a lot to answer for!

Tom was beside himself with happiness that Andreas had said yes. He practised especially well, and he and his dad improved his bowing. He would get Andreas to help him too, and they would play Spring Song patterns together. He was liking the violin more and more and he decided to call his violin Andy, not quite Andreas because that would muddle everything up, but after Andreas nevertheless. He gave his violin a kiss, and then shrugged his shoulders and laughed. He had never kissed anyone but his parents. And sometimes he thought he did not need to do that so much any more, he was seven after all.

On Thursday, Donna could not eat. The day had been too exhausting. She had had twelve pupils all working in the fifth and sixth books. They were great kids, but demanding. As she stretched out on her bed, she wished she had not said Thursday to Warren. But she had, and in an hour he would be here. They had not talked details so she began to think about the time it took for him to travel to Toronto from Dorchester and was quite sure that he would want supper when he arrived. The idea of cooking for him was too much so she planned to suggest eating out.

He kissed her when he arrived, a light, affectionate kiss which signalled the beginning of something more. After chatting about this and that, and without dwelling on the fact that she felt exhausted, they decided to eat at a Greek restaurant on Dunforth Street. They went down the stairs and kissed again before closing the street door behind them. Undecided as to the best restaurant, they cruised up and down Dunforth, where the street signs are in English and Greek, to see which restaurant looked least crowded, then came back to the largest one which Donna said was the friendliest anyway. Once they had parked they walked back to the main street.

'Nice atmosphere here. Always popular!' said Donna.

They chose to sit indoors where the background music was audible but not too loud. 'I like it. Sixties stuff, makes a change!'

'And the street's too busy for comfort out there tonight'

The moment they were seated, a good-looking Greek in white shirt, black tie and black trousers greeted them. 'Hot day!' he exclaimed with a grin as he handed an open wine list to each.

'Yes', said Donna, 'So could we have a carafe of iced water to start with?'

'Sure, I'll get that now.'

'I'm having their vegetarian *moussaka*. I love it.'

'That's easy. I'm tossing up between the *seftalia loukaniko combo* and the *sanakopita*. And which wine, Donna?'

'Oh, the red. Naousa.'

Warren took a look at the wine list, and gulped at the high prices. When the waiter returned, the knot in his tie had been loosened. He looked happy, in his element. 'I'm run off my feet tonight,' he teased, spinning the silver tray above his head and clicking his heels to the music!

Warren and Donna laughed with him. 'Busy, but you like it this way?'

'Not so busy. You should see us sometimes. Those blue chairs out there, we've got more we can bring out and spread across the pavement. So have you decided what to eat?'

They gave their order and while they waited, Warren looked up.

'God! Who's insides are those? That's not how you pay here, is it?'

Donna laughed behind her hand, repelled by the thought. 'It's unabashed modern architecture. Tell me what you're writing for goodness sake. It'll beat galvanised piping any day.'

'Oh, I don't know so much. But since you ask, this week it's been all that exciting local stuff like the opening of a new outdoor pool, the Lion's Senior Club demonstration of line dancing, the Home and Garden show at the Arena. Hot stuff, eh?'

'But the stuff small towns are made of, and don't forget it, my journalist friend! Dorchester is leaping into the big time. I hear there's whole new sub-divisions.'

'And you have heard right.'

The waiter returned with two lighted candles. 'You missed out. Have these,' he said. Then he soon returned again with their steaming food and salads. 'So here we are.' Donna pulled her elbows off the table and inhaled deeply as the *moussaka* was placed before her. 'Wonderful,' she said.

The smoke from the freshly lit candles drifted upward,

and the flames settled down, content to cast shadows here and there. At the same time they each added considerably to the ambience of the Greek restaurant by exuding a perfume which Donna swore was jasmine, and Warren, pine forest.

'So you're knowledgeable about such things? How come?'

Listening to Warren talking about his ex-wife's passion for aromas, whether from candles or burners, Donna learnt something about his past relationship. He was still hurting from the fact that she had left him, but grateful beyond belief that he had custody of Tom. Aromatherapy had meant little to him, or so he thought, yet because associations with what had been their first home were strong, he found his mood change when someone sprinkled an oil around or lit an incense stick. For a while they ate and drank without talking, just hearing the babble around them. They sat back and watched other diners. Dark heads, olive skin, and laughter-filled eyes which flashed signals to their friends. Unmistakably Greek. Their fingers tapped, and bodies swayed that little bit to the voice of the balalaika relayed through the speakers. Warren smiled and said, 'Hey, thanks for bringing me here.'

'Things are warming up, eh?'

'It looks like family, doesn't it.'

'With us the odd ones out!'

After a few moments of simply enjoying the ambience and drinking as if they had hours of this ahead of them, Donna asked, 'Who's staying with Tom?'

'Andreas.' He noted Donna's frown. 'Did I do or say something I shouldn't have?'

'You know he's gay, don't you?' Warren thought for a minute to avoid jumping to wrong conclusions.

'No. I didn't know. Does that upset you?'

'It's not me I'm worried about, for God's sake.'

'Hey, Donna.'

The waiter came back to take their plates and offer them the dessert menu.

'No thanks, not tonight.' She looked at Warren. 'You?'
'No thanks.'
'Coffee, madam? Sir?'

Warren hesitated. The waiter noticed the sudden change in atmosphere. He tried a joke. 'Non-fat!' He raised his eyebrows.

Donna answered for them. 'Could you bring the bill, please?'

'Where were we? Oh, yes, Andreas.'

'It's all rather sordid somehow. I don't really know much, but at the time of CT's death there was a rumour that things were not what they seemed on the surface.'

'Good God, Donna, spell it out.'

She fidgeted with her earrings and then said, 'It was rumoured that he and another gay friend, Joachim, who was found guilty of murder, were vying for CT's affections, and that Andreas was favoured simply because he was here.'

'And so the story unfolds! Donna, I have to get home to Tom. I can't stay tonight knowing that I have good reasons for being at home. I'm dreadfully sorry, but I have to see for myself that Tom's safe. That's my first priority, but I want to get Andreas to talk some more too. He's either denying or hiding stuff.'

Warren attended to the payment of the bill and left a hefty tip on the plate. 'Let's go.'

Back out on the street, they talked as they hurried back to the car.

'You're determined to find out what it is?'

'Oh, yes.'

And in the car, Donna could see that it was no use trying to jolly him along, he was hell bent on getting out of Toronto and back to Dorchester. Once inside Donna's front door, Warren gave her a quick kiss, and ran down the steps to his car.

'Drive safely' called Donna, thinking, Damn! What a fizz!

Pulling into his garage was the best and worst moment of the past two and a bit hours for Warren. He had set cruise control at 100 and was relieved to arrive safely. He felt both angry and frightened. If that blasted violinist has raped my son, I'll kill him. By God I will. He locked the car, and went to the house through the internal access. Suddenly, yelling seemed inappropriate. The house was still. Maybe Andreas was already in bed. He put down his jacket, took off his shoes, and crept to Tom's room. The child was sound asleep.

'Hi.' The voice came from the bean sack on the floor, and Andreas said, 'I must have gone to sleep crooning to Tom.' He stood up and stretched and said, 'What's the time? Aren't you supposed to be gone till morning?'

Warren felt awkward, but none the less glad to be home.

'I didn't feel well at the restaurant so told Donna I'd be best off at home if I was in for something, and well, come and tell me how you've got on anyway.'

A sleepy looking Andreas followed him to the living room and sat heavily in the bean sack there. Warren said, 'I'm having a herb tea. What would you like?'

'Sounds good. Yes, thanks.'

As Andreas talked about the way he and Tom had passed the evening, Warren felt increasingly embarrassed, annoyed with Donna and with himself. When he suggested that Andreas might have found Tom a problem, Andreas had hunched his shoulders a little as if to say, should there have been a problem? He had read at least six stories before Tom admitted to being tired. Then he had pulled Andreas down to him, and given him a smacker on th⸺ li⸺ and said, 'That's because I love you.' That's when ⸺⸺ ⸺⸺ flopped back into the bean sack, and after crooning for a bit, had gone to sleep.

'He kissed you?'

'Yes. Hey, I didn't mind. Don't for goodness sake say anything to him. He said it was to be a secret.' Andreas was smiling. 'On the other hand, I'm telling you because I don't think secrets are all that good sometimes.' He drank his tea quickly. 'That was what I needed. Any more in the pot?'

The wind had been taken out of Warren's sails. He wanted to laugh, more at himself than at Andreas or Tom. Or should he cry? Can he really trust this guy?

He made two fresh cups of lemon and ginger tea and they settled for a chat. Warren knew they had a lot to discuss, and Andreas could guess what was coming, at least some of it.

'Andreas, I want to come clean. Donna told me tonight that you're gay. Is that true?'

'Yes, but I have no problem with that, do you?'

'Only with one or two things.'

Andreas caught his ponytail and sent it back over his shoulder. He's not going to proposition me is he?

'One or two. Go ahead, I guess.'

'Well, for one. If you are going to be Tom's friend, then I need to be sure that you don't go for little boys, to put it bluntly.' Andreas's cheek twitched and Warren saw it and felt embarrassed.

'OK, so perhaps you can tell, God, I don't know. But it seems like some of you journos have X-ray eyes or something.' He was angry. 'You get hunches and edge your way, and find out things that no-one else even wants to know. You make me nervous you really do. So if I tell you I was molested by my father and that that's why I hated my first years as a child violinist, that he would both punish and reward me with the same filthy medicine, you'll jump to conclusions. But I hated him and I hated the violin. So there you have it. And now you probably won't trust me with Tom because you think that history will repeat itself.' He kicked the floor and shouted, 'But you're wrong. I have to struggle inside myself, afraid that I might do something bad, but I don't and won't. I can tell you now. I'd kill myself rather then hurt Tom. Not the way my father hurt me.' He put his head between his knees and he cried. Warren sat until he had finished crying – a long time. Then he said, 'Thanks for telling me, Andreas. You've had a rotten time of it. And yes, I am very sorry.'

'Sorry, about what?'

'Well, I suddenly felt I didn't know you when Donna told me you were gay. I lost my nerve.'

'What else did this Donna say?'

'That there was some kind of liaison between you and CT.'

'Oh, she did, did she? For goodness sake. I've never cried like that about dad and me. In fact, the only other person who knew was CT. But I tell you now, CT was a great guy. I'm sad he's gone. Very sad.'

Part Two
Chapter 7

Yuki's friends were very happy with the idea of getting together to make cranes. Especially as it was in celebration of a baby on the way. Tomorrow was the day, but today the whole house had to be cleaned. Yuki's mother had been told the momentous news and was excited at having a new grandchild after a gap of nearly nine years. She had come by train from Matsumoto, a two-and-a-half hour trip, and she had brought only her bundle of nightclothes, an easy amount to handle. As she undid the knot in the scarf around her clothes, Yuki knelt beside her at the bed. A few golden leaves and some berries fell out, and she watched as her mother placed these with tenderness on the duvet then ran her twisted hand over the stark white cranes on the vivid blue silken fabric with the greatest care, folding it into a square. Then, after the dear woman who had taught her to be neat and tidy in all she did, placed her nightclothes at the head end of the bed, their eyes met.

'There, now, I'm ready to help you clean your lovely house, Yuki.' Then she remembered. 'Oh, no, I must visit the *butsudan*, pray for our darling Jiro once again. Will you come with me?' She picked up the berries and leaves.

'Of course.'

At the shrine, the elderly woman's eyes streamed with tears as she placed her autumn tokens. Then on the cushions before it, she knelt and fingered the prayer beads as she prayed. Yuki knelt beside her and waited, remembering the fondness the grandparent had for her violinist grandson. 'Play to me. Play to me,' she always said, the moment the violin was placed on the table in her lounge. She reckoned Jiro's sound was best when he played in her house. She opened her doors wide saying, 'I think your grandfather's spirit sings with you here!'

Yuki chided her, but the old woman would not listen! She just smiled her wicked smile, and Yuki knew only too well that she knew her neighbours would hear her little one play. They always talked about the sound that carried into their homes, and spread joy like the wind blows the leaves 'without needing to be swept up afterwards,' her closest neighbour always added with a laugh, while waving her straw broom above the strewn ground.

They swept, dusted and polished everything from the stairway at the front entrance to the back rooms. All the while, as they worked together, they chatted on about the children. At times it seemed as if the mother had forgotten that Jiro was dead, she spoke as if he were still playing his violin, or chasing her with the broom. She vividly recalled the funny and the happy memories, and Yuki laughed with her, and they felt refreshed rather than tired by all the work they did. The elderly woman insisted on fussing around Yuki a little and ordered her to sit in her reclining chair while she cooked a meal of tempura. 'A chance to make a couple more cranes,' she said.

Yuki agreed, delighted that her mother was so enthusiastic about the cranes. 'One thousand?' she had said. 'We will make one thousand and one.' Yuki hugged her tight for such a great response.

'I'm glad I have dresses here in your cupboard,' the older woman said, appearing in the kitchen in her red dress, an hour before the friends were to come.

'You look really lovely in that dress, mother. I'm glad you chose that one today!' Yuki took her hands out of dish water and dried them. She gave her mother a hug.

'You don't really mind wearing western dress, do you?'

'When I'm here, I quite enjoy it, I feel young and pretty.' She did a little pirouette and Yuki caught her by the arm in time to steady her. They laughed and hugged, and felt good about being together in a happy mood.

The house was imbued with incense. It shook with the sobbing of the crowd that filled every space. The mood was one of unutterable sadness. The Buddhist priest stood waiting, and all those that could see the enormous photo of Jiro, focused on the bright young face. His *obaachan* was close by Ichiro, their black kimonos their outward expression of deep grief. And they were not alone in wearing black, all but one New Zealand friend, wore black. She was in deep blue.

'Yes, this red dress will be good for a long time yet. Now give me something to do.'

'How about making sure that nine cups are ready beside the teapot. Apart from that, I need to make the table ready with origami paper just in case they don't bring their own. We'll get all the chairs around the table, but don't you do anything that's too much for you, Mother.'

'Now look who's talking! It's you we need to fuss around. I've had my babies!'

When the front doorbell buzzed, all was ready. Yuki welcomed her friends and they hugged her and showered her with gifts which *Okaasan* whisked away, along with the cookies brought, to the living room. Full of chatter and laughter, they slipped out of shoes into the house slippers they brought, then took up a place at the large table. This is such fun! All were saying it, not in words, but in their laughter and enthusiasm.

'What do you reckon? Can we each make four or five cranes?' one woman ventured. 'How about ten or twelve?' another said in challenge, and laughing, they settled to work with flying fingers, chatting all the while, boasting about their babies, and moaning about their husbands. It was only after they had had tea and eaten the cookies that they reminisced about their university days, and the five years they had shared doing business studies. Noriko lamented that none of them was able to work full-time at the career they had trained for because of children. 'Except, Myoko and I do work from home now. 'But, as for leaving the house to work in the city office, we are all as bad as each other. Stuck! Confined! Imprisoned!'

'I'm simply not having more children,' Kyoku said. 'One is horrible enough and I'm applying for a job next year. If Daisuke doesn't like it, I'll leave him.'

'Leave your husband?'

'Yes. I have Daisuke as my husband and I have a son, Diasuke Junior. I will take him, run away in the middle of the night while Daisuke is snoring it off.' She said it with drama writ large all over her expressive face. And they all laughed knowing that she had always been the one who was best able to encapsulate their worst feelings and say it for them! They also knew that next year she would say the same thing again, that she was a squash champion and in fact, led quite a happy life. Before they left the house, they all promised to get together and celebrate two months after the baby arrived.

When they had gone, and the house was restored to order, Yuki and her mother set out to take a bath together in the public bath house. Once inside, they stripped off, placed their clothes in a basket, took up a rolled towel and went into the next room. Through the steam from the bath, appeared small clusters of women, chatting and laughing and lolling about. Yuki whispered, 'There's still room for us. Here, you take this stool, and I'll do your back first.' With a cloth and soap, she lathered and rinsed her mother's back, taking the utmost care of the wrinkled skin at her elbows. She lifted the unclasped hair that now fell to her shoulders, and carefully lathered and rinsed her neck. She loved to linger in those places, thinking – these are the signs of maturity, wisdom and hard work. The signs of love.

When it was her turn to be lathered, Yuki worked on her toes and lower body while her mother soaped and rinsed her back. 'Got to take care of you two,' she whispered, and they laughed at having intimate knowledge of each other, stepped hand in hand to the pool, and lowered themselves into the steaming water, into the company of the neighbourhood of women.

The house was still again except for the gentle snoring of the old woman. Yuki took up some paper and began on a crane, determined to wait for Kentaro. The day had been wonderfully productive in the number of cranes the women had made. An average of ten each and all vowed to go on making them. But the day had brought something else with it. Three months gone, and just like last time, she stopped feeling ill and was strong and ready for any challenge. Oh, how she craved for Kentaro's love-making. It made her tearful and angry that he should be so abstemious toward her just because he was over-awed. A child should be conceived in love. Loved – even in the womb. She believed that with every fibre of her being, yet there she was, mother to a cloned embryo. All done with clinical precision and calculation. Was she still a woman? Or some kind of clinical host? A robot? A zombie? She did not know how to describe her situation. Science bamboozled her. Oh, how I hope that we do not have to pay for this.

Part Two
Chapter 8

Sparrows caught his eye outside the window where his nose was pressed. They have puffed up chests, looking expectant. The sun-tipped leaves of gold fall to join the frosted earth. They spill from the tree, like crumbs from a boy's hand, suddenly scattered about.

Tom left the house to join Andreas who was standing outside in the frosty air. He saw tears in Andreas's eyes and put a hand into the larger hand of his friend. A black squirrel, tail as bushy as they come, leapt from the tree to the grass, fled across it, stopped and sat on its haunches, looking about and listening. The only new sound was the laughter of the friends. The squirrel went on its way.

When Tom was asleep, Warren and Andreas had time to talk. Yet another lunch hour recital was behind him, exam programmes had been adjudicated.

'How did your performance recital go, Andreas?' Warren asked, as he sipped tea, and reclined against his corn-patterned cushion.

'Really well according to the panel, most of whom you know. Miguel, Peter the cellist who replaced CT, and Danielle Springer from the RCM.'

'OK. But how do you think you played?'

'Well. Yep, my best yet. Even *Zigeunerweisen*. Although it was a bit of a race with the piano at times.'

'It must be fiendishly difficult to control.' Andreas appeared disinterested. There was something else on his mind.

'Warren, can I get CT's story off my chest?'

Warren was working towards that. 'Why not? I'm ready.'

Andreas' voice quivered with emotion as he recalled how impressed he was that CT – 'the cellist of the century' – asked him to play duos with him. The Brahms Trio had been the final compliment. At first he had felt flattered, quite apart from wanting to learn as much as possible by playing with the chamber music tutor. Miguel had encouraged him knowing well his need to upgrade his skills. He drained his cup. 'I'd kill for another tea. Shall I get it?'

'No. I'm ready for one, too. Half a moment.'

'So, on with the story.' Warren was glad to see that the tick had vanished, at least for now, as Andreas continued. 'To cut a long story short, CT started to invite me to his place after any of our music events, even those with six of us. It was always me he asked, and always with a kind of undertone as he was lifting up his cello or some such movement, when our faces were close. It seems painfully obvious when I think about it now.'

'I guess so.'

'Well, he had this luxurious apartment. Settees and loads of cushions scattered all around.' He laughed and raised his eyebrows as he patted the one he was sitting on, and glanced at Warren's and two others not in use, and continued, 'And there were lights that dimmed, and a small bar which he had ready access to. He'd put on some soft, evocative music and invite me to relax. Always wanted me to relax. He plied me with drinks, turned the dimmer switches even lower, and sat down beside me.'

It was CT's insistence on calling him darling that irritated and alerted him. It hit him smack on the jaw. He's gay! Then when CT asked him if he was gay he'd stuttered and stumbled about not knowing what to answer. He told him that he'd been so abused by his father that any sexual feeling he was supposed to have was numbed. Certainly, he had no words to express anything.

'CT made it his business to arouse me. It was all very subtle and gentle, and I began to lose my frozen state without reacting against it. I was dazed by the drink he'd plied me with, and well, like you will have guessed, we became lovers. He convinced me I was gay and that it was me that he loved above all others. He even wanted me to live with him. I believe I would have, if Joachim hadn't turned up.'

'I don't mean to interrupt,' Warren said. 'But where does the straw man and playing in the park come into all this?'

Andreas manoeuvred his cushion a bit to face Warren a little more squarely. He sat up and hugged his knees.

'At first, I was just fascinated that at the castle gate in the children's area of the park there was this kind of scarecrow. I called him Mr Strawman when the children came to hear me busking and we'd kind of include him in my concerts for the fun of it. Children were allowed to touch him, even carry him about, so long as they were supervised, and sometimes they'd sit him on the grass with them and pretend that he threw money into my case by holding his arm and letting some money fly.' His face began to twitch.

A child's voice, Tom's voice, called, 'Daddy, daddy.'

'Coming, Tom,' Warren called. 'Sorry, Andreas. I'll have to go sit with Tom. This sort of thing doesn't happen often,' he said, setting out for Tom's room. 'But he is hard to settle when it does. See you in the morning. Sleep well.'

Andreas took a long, warm shower, but found it hard to sleep. Stretched along the wide bed, memories took over.

> CT stands at the side of the bed, a glass of wine in his hand; Andreas feels that he is taunting him, moving about, pausing every now and then to pirouette a little, and blow him a kiss. Andreas is bewitched. The man is beautiful. His limbs longer than his body suggests; his face, swarthy, his chest hair black and thick as loose carpet weave.
>
> He has music playing, and as the tempo increases, so does the volume.

For a moment Andreas was disoriented. He sat up in bed and rubbed his face with his hands and sighed away the memories. Turning his pillow over and pummelling it a little he switched on his bed light, lay down on his other side and read for a while but was soon asleep.

Warren saw that Andreas had not turned out his light so he looked in to tell him that Tom dropped off quite quickly. Andreas, though, was asleep. Warren picked up the book and turned off the light. He went to the basement to write. He decided that he would use the material that Andreas let him tape about his childhood, fill in the rest from his observations of Andreas's wonderful playing and concerts and the biographical bits he had read. Tomorrow he would ask Andreas to play for him while he took a close up shot. A good portrait of him and his instrument. That would enhance the article and keep him in the good books of *Music Review*. They would pay him well. He did not have the heart to do anything now to hurt Andreas. He was telling him the true and sordid story that would not ever be told in *Music Review*, however much they paid him. But getting to sleep became a problem for him. What if Andreas was involved in CT's death? He would find out all too soon. And about that he was deeply disturbed.

Peter had finished adjudicating student recitals and cruised along the streets of Toronto heading for Donna's place. He saw dozens of people were out with their rakes, brooms and blowers, dealing with the piles of leaves shed by the trees. It was a sight which brought with it a promise of snow and Christmas lights. Peter felt a touch of excitement that spilled over into anticipation of two nights with Donna. She had said it plainly: 'I've been invited to play the Tchaikovsky with the Toronto Symphony and have to practise like crazy. But, yes I need a break too. No teaching at the moment so I'm quite free of that. Do come.'

He pulled into the curb outside the house she shared with three others and took his bag from the back of the van. He ran up the three steps and pressed the button. It lit up. Her voice said, 'Hi there.'

'Hi! Peter.'

'Come on up.' The door opened and he ran up to the second floor and found her door ajar,' and she called, 'Come in.'

He had just put his stuff behind the settee when she came in saying, *'Voila!* How do I look?'

For a moment he said nothing. Half her head of hair, now only a centimetre long, was purple, the other half yellow. On her body she wore only black. Tight fit from top to trouser.

'Mm,' he said. 'Is this hip?' He wished he had not said that. She looked marvellous. Quite marvellous.

'Oh you stunning creature. I think you look wonderful. Come here.'

'Your fault. I miss you so much I keep changing my image to entertain me until you come again.'

They kissed. And when they got their breath again, he said, 'I'm sorry. I'm wrapped up in teaching and get exhausted. And I get more and more irritable with my students, and totally unable to socialise. But anyway, you said you were flat stick on the Tchaikovsky.'

'I have to take breaks from that, too. I make for the bathroom mirror between movements and fantasise!' They laughed together. 'Come and tell me all about your teaching.'

'That will send you off to dye your hair orange and red! Let me just say that I'm making good use of your notes on Fujiwara's method. Preparing for next semester. They're good. I can actually read your writing, well, mostly that is.' It was said with that deep chortle and she made a face at him.

'Now, how do you feel about a bed-game?' he asked.

'I've just got myself dressed, positively squeezed myself into this get-up, and now you want me to take it all off. Oh, poor me.'

'Tell you what. I'll help you.'

'Oh, you are so kind.' And then she ran into her room, calling, 'Catch me if you can.'

And in order that she might tantalise him, again, once

they were naked, she rolled off the bed, and scampered around the apartment calling, 'Catch me, catch me.' He followed, in good spirits, just avoiding catching her, until she stood on the sheepskin rug to find her breath, and then he grabbed her and kissed her until her knees gave way. She lay down and they made love on the rug.

'I love you,' he whispered in the breaks. Finally, she said, 'And I love you, Romeo. I've waited on my balcony for too long, hearing your voice, but being hustled inside by my maid, the dragon.'

'Oh, Juliet, thou art so fine a maiden.'

'Curtain's down now, darling Peter.'

Over pancakes dripping with maple syrup, they managed the odd comment, then had to catch the maple syrup before it hit the rug. Donna told Peter about the email she had received from Yuki Fujiwara and her joy at the prospect of a new baby. Their other great news was that Ichiro was playing the piano again.

The phone interrupted. Donna coloured up slightly, and when she heard Warren's voice, she said, 'Hold on,' which had to do for both Peter, whom she was looking at, and Warren. She carried the handpiece to the bedroom and closed the door. The explanation of entertaining friends to dinner did not feel convincing, and she sensed that Warren did not believe her. She asked about Tom and Andreas, and Warren gave her a rather dismissive reply which suggested to her that he was already not convinced about everything she said. Yet he still wanted to see her.

'How about mid-week Wednesday, here, at six?' she said. 'See you.'

When she returned to him, Peter looked down in the mouth as he said, 'Someone else in the queue?'

'Yes, if you must know, there is.' She hadn't realised how hurt she was that Peter came to see her so spasmodically. She felt it now. 'And don't ask me any more questions. We're going to have coffee and act like two civilised people, and take in a movie or something. Sort out our emotions, and then come home to bed. How's that?'

'And am I back on the couch?'

She rubbed noses with him and said, 'Most definitely not.'

He is running the risk of loving.

Each working day is filled with a diet of music. He teaches it. Plays it. It is no light thing to be training young minds to appreciate subtle nuances in the works of many and varied composers. It extends him. It tires him. His zest for life is spent until that time when he wakes from sleep and can begin again.

It is one thing to begin again where he left off yesterday – tackle the next phrase in the score. But to begin again in loving another woman, that is like taking up a new score by a little known composer. He has already passionately loved, and, lost. It is not so long ago in time that he cannot help but remember her all too vividly, see her in the now, feel and smell her.

He knew her every mood, her fears, her hopes, her charms, her beauty. He knew her patterns of sleep and temper; the strength of her tea, her whims, her longings. And what is even more wonderful, she knew him. Every part of him. His skin. His hair. The sharpness of his nails, the contours of his lips, his teeth, his eyes, his ears. She knew the map of his body, the uplands and lowlands of his soul. She cried at the power of his cello. Loved him. Accepted him.

Yet now, they are like two transplanted trees growing in different forests. Reaching for fresh air, a place for their roots. And they have lost the opportunity to shed their leaves to one another.

Could he make a commitment to any one else? Or

would he be a failed Romeo, never able to get his lines correct, and end the play with any semblance of dignity? He felt that he had already lost the script.

Donna was still asleep. Peter put his feet on the floor, and stayed with his head in his hands for a minute. He had a head on him that demanded painkillers. Where would he find them? But more important was that, through the fog, he could see a little light. He showered and dressed, and looked about for a note-pad.

"Dear Donna," he wrote. "I am running away before I get any closer. Please forgive me. The problem is not you, it's me. I feel compelled to talk with my ex, Celia, here in Toronto. I am driven to find her again. I'm very sorry, dearest Donna. Peter." He put the note beside the coffee pot and crept out and down the stairs.

Part Two
Chapter 9

Yuki took the steaming rice from the cooker, filled three bowls, and into a small dish she put a spoon of rice. She set three places at the western-style table, and put on the coffee percolator, nudging the packets of biscuits and dried fruits she had not yet put away, to make a space. A ray of early morning sun fell on her, adding an aura of light to her ebony hair which she had had cut into a stylish bun just yesterday. When Kentaro joined her, she said, 'I'm very fat, Kentaro. Look at me!' She lifted her loose floral blouse to show him that the baby's growth had justified these new clothes, especially the designer jeans for maternity wear. He came close and placed his hand on the bulge in her tummy.

'Growing fast, little fellow. Keep it up.' he said. He was freshly shaved and smelt wonderful. Yuki had woken in a good mood and was pleased to see that Kentaro was his buoyant self. He looked into her eyes. With tenderness, he said, 'I'm so proud of you, pet. So proud. And happy. These days my teaching goes really well. I do not lose patience with anyone. It is like a tonic for me.'

'I'm glad for you. Please come and put the rice before the shrine.' They went through the hallway to the *ten-titami* room. Ichiro was rippling through the *Minute Waltz* by Chopin. He was used to his mother coming to give a little of the first rice of the day to Jiro's spirit, but not his father. He stopped playing, and joined his parents. This was special that his dad should be there with his mother. Would he be late for work today?

Yuki placed the small dish at the shrine. Ichiro was invited to sound the gong as she lit an incense stick, and all of them, together, were silent a minute. Then Yuki whispered to Kentaro, 'We should tell him now.' Kentaro's face lit up and he nodded assent.

'Please come into the kitchen now,' Yuki said to Ichiro. 'We have some news for you. After we've eaten.'

They had finished their rice served with fish, and put down their chopsticks feeling satisfied and excited. Ichiro was impatient, and his parents were anxious to find out what his reaction would be.

As Yuki poured the coffee, and a glass of choco-milk for Ichiro, Kentaro said, 'That was a good strong sound you were getting in the Grieg, earlier this morning. Keep it up. Now, your mother and I want you to know that next November you will have a baby brother. Or sister,' he added, self-consciously.

Ichiro felt awkward. He looked from his father to his mother and back to his father.

'It seems a long time away,' said Yuki. 'But the baby is growing fast in my tummy. We needed to tell you.'

'I can't imagine having a baby in the house. And I don't know what to say. Mum, what should I say?'

'Nothing, sweetheart. Nothing. Just make a space in your heart for another family member in November, that's all.'

'Can I finish my practice now?'

'Have your milk then, yes off you go. And remember, tonight you are to look after yourself till dad gets home. I'm going to *Obaachan*'s and will be back tomorrow by the time you get back from school.'

Ichiro went, not to the piano, but to the shrine to talk to Jiro.

'What about that! My parents are getting a baby. What do you think, Jiro? Will it be a boy? Do they want a boy? Dad said boy first then added girl.' Jiro's presence was strong. Ichiro could hear the sound of his tuning up. 'It'll be ages before any baby can play the violin. I'll be gone by then. Won't I?' Ichiro listened a minute. He could hear distant sounds of his mother's exercise music. He felt cut off from her. His father was at work. He felt distant from him. He looked at his right hand; he looked at his left. There were empty spaces. 'Jiro, I need you!' he shrieked.

The car stood ready in the driveway; Kentaro had checked it over for the long journey on which Yuki was about to start. It was the annual pilgrimage which she took with her mother to place flowers on the family grave in Matsumoto. She hurried to leave the house clean and tidy. Then she picked a bouquet of chrysanthemums, the last of the autumn flowering, put a damp cloth around their stems and placed them across a scarf, two corners of which she knotted, and put them with her small bag on to the back seat of the car. 'Time to go.' She looked in on Ichiro, and had to repeat herself, so absorbed was he. 'I can give you a ride now. Just for a change. Please come,' she said, close to his ear.

'No. Because I meet Hideo!'

'OK, but I want to close the house up now.'

'So ask Hideo's mother if I can go to their place first, please.'

'Right, then, and maybe play there after school for a bit?'

'Sure. I'll take my accompaniments for his cello pieces.'

'If you want.'

After seeing Ichiro off on his bike, and closing up the house, she drove away thinking of how Jiro would have reacted to the news of a baby. He would have come round the table like a shot and hugged her and said, 'Good, good, good. I'll play him to sleep, and when he's big I'll show him how to play the violin. And he can ride my bike. I'm so happy, Mummy.' It was as if Jiro had the heart, and that it was big enough for both of them. Oh, how she missed his cuddles.

With her eyes on the road, but glancing every few moments at the countryside which she knew so well, she did not need to trouble herself by changes, for there were none. The only differences that they experienced here were the natural changes that each season brought, the ambience that was stage-managed by the mighty sun and the natural processes of birth and death. She thought of how good it was to have a shrine at home where the ashes stayed in the tiny urn, and how splendid it was that the large bones of the deceased lay buried in the grave. As time went on and the seasons came and went, the bones would become part of the soil, a thought that helped Yuki to cope with the death of one so alive, so precious.

A half-hour from Matsumoto, she turned up the temperature of the car, the chill from the early alpine snow had reached her, and she felt sad. But she tried to cheer herself. Out of all this something new will come. The child within her stirred, and she laid a hand on her stomach, momentarily, one hand on the wheel.

Her mother was waiting for her. She opened her door the moment Yuki stepped up to it.

'Come in, my darling. You must be very tired.' To Yuki, who replaced her outdoor shoes so quickly she barely hesitated, her mother looked rather frail, dressed in what was now a favourite and old kimono. Yuki hugged her carefully, tenderly, not wanting to crush her. *Okaasan*. Would she be here for the baby?

As they drank the healthy green tea, which her mother had been heating on the gas stove at the kitchen table, Yuki shook herself, and told her mother that she needed to be cheered up.

'Mother, please help me not to be sad. I felt my baby stir. We've told Ichiro. And I'm happy that I am so well. But it is nearly winter, and today I feel snow at the end of my broom, not leaves.'

'I have an idea. We will go to the cemetery, then to the park and the castle; take a walk together. I've got bread to feed to the ducks.'

Yuki smiled to herself. It was like being four years old again. 'I'd like that!'

At the grave, the old lady cried as she put her flowers at Jiro's headstone. Yuki also. She took the deep red and gold chrysanthemums one by one from her scarf, and cried as she re-arranged them, watered them with her tears. Her mother spent the time in polishing up the other family headstones, weeping a little for lost family. Remembering her husband with clarity.

'Mother, we needed to cry. It will help us to laugh later.'

Back in the car, Yuki said with a smile, 'It's been great making this visit with you again. Thank you for coming with me. Now for the castle, eh? Can't leave without seeing that garden, the moat, the swans. You've got the bread that we can throw to the ducks, haven't you?'

'Yes. And I'll climb to the top of old *karuso-jo* today!' The old lady's eyes twinkled wickedly at the thought of the old castle. Both knew that the old wooden stairway was not the place for either of them now.

Yuki laughed merrily. She recalled the times that they had all gone to the top, the games they had played. It had been such ridiculous fun making their footsteps echo inside the cavernous and ghostly castle. And spine-chilling to go hide and seek, and make out they had got lost. And then, just about out of steam, they would try and outdo everyone else and be first to the top.

There was no suppressing the old woman. 'And when you peep out, I'll take a photo of you, just for evidence.' They laughed, and the rest of the day was set to be good fun.

When it was late afternoon, they drove back toward the family home. Even though she knew that the streets would come alive in the evening with many floats, and people would line the footpaths, she did not feel up to it. The shinto festival had always been one that her family attended. They especially enjoyed weaving in and out of the stalls in the grounds of Shihashira Shrine, buying small trinkets, eating *sushi* and listening to the bells that boomed lustily into the night. But she must get her mother home, as well as herself, then tomorrow there was the long drive back again. Kentaro had given her one night off, but Ichiro needed her to be there for him after school tomorrow to see to his homework. If they were lucky, they would hear the bells from her mother's kitchen.

She drove along the main street, and slowed as they passed the Suzuki institute where Kentaro had studied, but secretly began to develop his own method of teaching. 'Look at that, Mum. Three bonneted and bent elderly women sweeping up the last of the leaves in Lilac Park. They're making way for winter snow. It's a pretty sight. I have to admire those old ladies.'

Her mother laughed. 'Someone's got to do it.'

Part Two
Chapter 10

Still dressed in a knee-length tee for the night, Donna read the note and yelled. 'Peter, you bastard. You mean, ugly bastard.'

She picked up the phone, and left him her message: 'Peter, get your act together. You're shit! I'm pissed off. How dare you leave my house without saying a thank you, or goodbye. I hope I never see you again.'

Then she took up her violin and played the Tchaikovsky concerto with more power and dexterity than she knew she had in her.

Even then, it was still only mid-morning. She sat down on her settee and thought about the effect Peter's note had had on her, and what she might do now. The awfulness of being alone when she had been so aroused prompted her to phone Warren.

'Hello. So things have changed here. I'll come clean. You know how I said that I had people here? Well, it was only one guy. Now he's walked out, gone running back to his ex. I feel pissed off! I was going to practise, but I've just played the concerto through like the devil himself! I don't feel like going back over it! Can we spend time together?'

'Whew! Donna you're in top gear. Yes, I could come now but a hot story has come down, and I want to do some work – in Toronto, as it happens. And of course there's Tom, but I guess he could go to his mother. I'll phone you back. Right?'

She paced about doing all the unnecessary titivating that she felt obliged to do when she knew a visitor was coming. Then she caught sight of herself in the mirror and said, 'Stink. My hair's ghastly. She went closer to the mirror. It's my face. I'm white with anger and shock.' She filled the next half-hour bringing her hair back to its usual red tint and, having got her hair right, she worked down her body, dressing and changing, and dressing again, only to end up with a lime green tee, and the baggy jeans with the pockets down the leg that she had had for a couple of years.

Even though she'd filled a hell of a long time getting herself right, Warren hadn't called. Hadn't called, bother him. But then he did, and she knocked the hand piece off its button and cut off the phone. She replaced it, and it rang again a few moments later.

'Hello. It's Warren. What happened there?'

'I'm sorry, I'm kind of flighty today. Can you come?'

'Yes. But I'll be bringing my notebook and camera, just in case.'

'Oh, well! I'll carry your tripod.'

'You're on.'

When he arrived, Donna had just got to her place after taking a fast walk. He gave her a quick kiss, opened the trunk, and handed her his camera bag. He carried the rest of his gear, and when they were together in her living room she said, 'So what might be hot news? Tell me.'

'Toronto scientists have outdone the Koreans who claimed to have cloned a human foetus.'

'Didn't know about the Koreans. Tell me. No, wait. I'll get coffee, and you can begin at the beginning.' She was just about to reach for the percolator then went back to him. 'I didn't say how pleased I am to see you.'

He was standing in the middle of the room deep in thought and said, 'Sorry. No, me too. This story has grabbed me.' He put his arms around her and hugged. She responded to his kiss,' then pulled away, laughing. The coffee had percolated and she had steaming mugs in no time. 'So the Koreans? What's this got to do with them?' She sat beside him on the settee.

'Back in December a story broke that Korean scientists claimed to have taken steps towards cloning a human being. Very provocative stuff. But they had taken note of what the Scots scientists had done to produce Dolly the sheep, and applied it to a human cell and ovum. They reckoned they aborted it when the fertilised egg became a foetus. That provoked the scientists and law-makers of the world. They were sceptical and condemning.'

'Whew! Heavy stuff. And what's the Toronto story?'

'They've denied it, but it's been leaked that they have actually cloned a mouse with a gene which prevents Alzheimer's and are heading towards applying it to a human. I'm not sure where to begin, but there's no time to lose.'

He invited her to come along, carry a camera, and play the part. She acquiesced. 'Right then, I'll get my jacket.'

'And here's the camera.'

Warren parked the car in the parking lot adjacent to the Biogenetics Unit just beyond the university. 'Here we go to find a Keith Robertson. Please bring the camera and look like you mean business. I presume you know how to take pictures?'

'What, with a fancy camera like yours just has to be? No way.'

He laughed. 'I'll make it easy for you, I'll actually fling the thing about my neck right now.' They stood at the car, organising his equipment, then set out at a fast pace to follow the signs to the laboratory where Warren was told he could find Dr Robertson.

'Nervous?' Donna said with a sideways glance at him.

'Excited as always when on to something as big as this that hasn't broken yet.'

'How did you find out, then?'

He turned to her, sharp chin stuck out. 'Friends at court.'

'I see.'

They walked in silence up steps and into a maze of corridors until they reached the lab where Dr Keith Robertson was the name on the door. Warren sneaked a sheepish smile at Donna, and knocked briskly. A short man in a white coat answered the door.

'Hello?' The camera was at his chin height. His tone was immediately suspicious.

'Yes, what is it?'

'Dr Robertson, Warren Blackwell, journalist. My card.' Warren held the card between his camera and the man's eyes. 'You are conducting experiments with mice, I understand. I'd like to write a story for *Science Boom*, a new magazine.' The scientist studied the card, looked up at Warren and the woman with him then said, 'Come on in.'

They moved to the inside of the lab where a row of adjustable chairs stood along a bench taken up by computer monitors from one end to the other. All computers were on. Two white-coated staff members sat chasing data, and totally ignored their presence, but from the range of screen savers – lounging lizards, floating seahorses, and clouds in motion – one might get an impression of inactivity. Dr Robertson stopped them before they reached the men, and Warren introduced Donna to him. 'My assistant, Ms Richards.'

'How do you do,' he said. 'Why don't you two sit here a moment, then we'll go through to where the mice are.' He wheeled over a swivel chair and perched on it. He was now eye to eye with them, and they felt a lot more able to communicate. 'So where shall I begin?'

Warren took out his dictaphone and said, 'Do you mind?'

'Not at all.' In fact, he looked pleased. Behind his tired expression was considerable pride. Warren marvelled how the man's thick eyebrows seemed to be less evident now that they were seated. His eyes were bright, and very blue.

'You work in a team, I believe.'

'Yes, I head that team.'

'And now let me get this right. Your aim is to find a gene that will combat Alzheimer's in humans, is that so? Or a way of deleting the gene that produces it?'

'That's right. We believe that predisposition for the disease can be detected at birth and can also be prevented by the alteration of the gene pattern soon after conception.'

'Let me get this straight. You can alter a gene pattern in a foetus?'

'Yes, the brain cells of a foetus.'

'Very, very skilled stuff.' He looked at the face of the professor and detected a slight flush of pink. 'I'd like to take a photo now. The light is just right,' and before he could object, the camera had recorded several images of the smiling Dr Robertson. 'So can we see the mice now?'

'Oh, certainly, come this way.'

He led them to an inner lab. They passed through an area which reminded them of the old school lab, yet was anything but. It had a state-of-the-art look – an intricate array of test tubes, microscopes, displays of graphics, jars and glassed shapes of all sizes and colours, neon signs and labelling, various clocks and gauges. Plus a large computerised area of flashing stuff that Warren had no immediate words to describe. After a considerable amount of unlocking of doors and pressing of security numbers, they entered a chamber where the temperature was controlled and soft music, played.

'This is a very pleasant place,' Warren commented, laughing politely, and taking a few photographs of mice in cages set in rows on shelves. The mice carried on being mice, oblivious of the flashes.

The scientist stopped at a particularly large cage.

'This is the one which is going to make the headlines.'

Warren was ready. 'What, you're breeding it with the Alzheimer's gene, then altering it?' The tape was whirring.

'That's right.'

'You must be really proud of your achievements so far. Gene manipulation for the sake of good health, eh! Next, you'll be keen to do it by cloning. One step then to cloning a human?'

Dr Robertson was taken aback. Didn't answer. They were moving along the counter too quickly. He turned in haste as they approached the door marked Certified Staff and Warren turned his gulp into a smile and said, 'Thanks, Dr Robertson. Very interesting!' while wondering if the sign indicated that their staff, gone mad, were kept beyond that door. He could not hear any screaming, but of course, it could be padded!

'We'll leave it there, if you will, please.' He led the pair towards the door, did the security routine very speedily, then took them back through the maze of laboratory equipment, and past the computers, where a third person had joined the night shift. Warren stopped short of the exit.

'Dr Robertson, why not make this huge leap for mankind?'

'Well, that's what I say. This most certainly will – ,' he corrected himself, 'could be the biggest embryology success in the history of mankind. It will be a matter of good timing.'

'You mean getting it out into the media before any other human cloning.'

It was clear that he felt he'd said too much. 'I can't say anything more.'

'Let's put it like this then, Dr Robertson. How many steps away are you from cloning a person?'

'I'm not prepared to say. Can we leave this, please? I must ask you and Ms Richards to leave.'

'Just one more thing.' He looked down at the man, whose bushy eyebrows appeared to hide his thoughts as well as his eyes. 'If you do clone a person, can you let me have the story before any other?'

The man lifted his head, smiled broadly, and said, 'I've got your card. I'll give you a call. I expect you, in the meantime, to treat this with the utmost discretion, and the strictest confidentiality when that is called for.' He nodded towards the recorder. 'Don't misconstrue my words.'

'You have my promise. Good day, sir.'

They raced along corridors and down the steps. 'So near, and yet so far.'

'But you've got a story, haven't you?'

'I have. But better not mention the certified staff sign. Could be a can of – body parts!' Their laughter only just subsided when their gear was packed away and they were ready to drive off.

Part Two
Chapter 11

Hamish rushed across the road to the office he rented whenever he required a private meeting, to arrange the five chairs necessary for the quarterly conference with his fund providers. It seemed inevitable that the two lab assistants, Bertha and Muriana, involved in both his Biotech and private research, would occupy their chairs in silence unless requested to speak. They had confessed to him that the financial linchpins of the private enterprise intimidated them.

He arranged the five chairs in a semi-circle well back from his desk knowing that Bill, the gynaecologist, would sit between his assistants and the two Italians. Finally he sat and waited, leaning into his desk. He looked, Mary had told him at early breakfast, rather dishevelled, hair and beard longer than he liked to keep them. He had not slept much this last week and when he had, his dreams had been of pipettes and lab dishes, bits of foetus, frozen cells and duplicated images. Mice ran everywhere, monkeys watched with silent and knowing stares. Now in spite of how he looked or felt, he had to report on behalf of his team to his sponsors. But news of the two growing babies? He was not ready to tell them yet. If Giano and Roberto knew that he had leaped into cloning humans, they would pressure him into cloning them without delay!

As he heard voices and footsteps, he stood to greet them. Although he had never seen Giano without his heavy black glasses, Hamish knew that his appearance was probably improved by them. Roberto flicked his dark glasses off as soon as he entered the building and seemed to have no problem with his friend keeping his on. They were an odd pair – Giano, squat with broad shoulders from which his arms flung about whenever he wanted to make a point, and Roberto, with sharper features and finer movements, and almost as tall as he was. Bill looked as flustered as always with his white coat unbuttoned, and his stethoscope dangling. But the women! Well, he had been working with them, so was not surprised by Muriana's elegant appearance and made-up face, and Bertha's over generous bosom that preceded her. He understood the coolness of their greetings toward the two men, and invited them all to sit.

When ready, he looked to each of the five people in a sweep of his eyes and with a smile said, 'I'll get straight to the point. In our research on human cloning, the good news is that we're getting excellent success rates by splitting the embryos, as outlined at our last meeting.'

Roberto looked confused. '*Dottore*, are we talking humans or monkeys?'

'I'm referring to the rhesus macacque, the very beautiful little monkey with the brightest of eyes. I want to reinforce the invitation I gave last time. Do come by and see them sometime.'

'Why not humans? Thought that's what this is all about.' Gianfranco looked glum.

Hamish looked directly at him. 'Och, Gianfranco. Right now we're doing the necessary preliminaries; the more skill we develop with these rhesus embryos, the more easily we'll clone humans. We have the human twin's cells to work on as soon as we're ready, so keep that in mind. And Bill is collecting and freezing a store of human eggs, so very soon we'll be slipping one or two experiments through.' He cut his right hand with his left as he said, 'We want to be totally sure of the process by working with non-human primates first. Make any sense?'

'Sure, *Dottore*, it makes sense,' Giano spoke roughly. 'We want our job to be perfection so we're not pushing. But why don't you take some of our skin cells now and freeze them?'

'Could do. But I'll be around and you'll be around for a while. We have a choice here. I could take them whenever you like, or wait till we're all set to go.' He felt that now was the time to reinforce his major concern. He moved from his chair to stand against the front of his desk, and bent a little towards the men. 'Giano and Roberto, there is one crucial issue we have to increase our knowledge of before we clone from adults such as yourselves.' He made sure he had the full attention of both men. 'We think, from the signs of faster than normal aging in Dolly, that cloning from adults may cause the child born to age more quickly than if we were to use a split foetus that would normally grow to become one baby. You can see why our research is crucial to future success for you and clones of you.'

Roberto nodded. 'Sure, *Dottore*, I can see what you're getting at.' Giano looked more uncertain. His scars coloured somewhat, making what one could see of his expression, appear angry. Roberto wanted to be certain, however, that all was being done that could be done.

'This is out of Biotech time. Right? After hours, so to speak, but because you have the rhesus whatevers to care for and monitor and all that, both your jobs will be a bit mixed up won't they?'

Hamish liked Roberto's curiosity and knew it to be perfectly justified.

'Each day, Muriana, with her team of five, has oversight of the private research made possible by your generous funding, until I can give it my full attention, and that usually happens around three-thirty in the afternoon. It just means I work longer hours and do what amounts to a day-and-a half's work, six days a week.'

Roberto conferred with Giano who waved his arms about while Roberto remained calm. Giano spoke for them both.

'*Dottore*, we're satisfied you're doing all you can.'

Then Roberto said, 'I'll drop by after three-thirty one day and, yeah, I'll think about your taking my cells before they grow any older, but I don't want mine mixed up with someone else's.' He chuckled, and Hamish laughed, and reassured him.

'Never happens.' He perched on his table and crossed his legs.

'So,' Giano said, 'Tell us what you're doing in Biotech time, *Dottore*.'

'In Biotech hours it's stem transfer; developing the art, shall we say, of creating body parts from specific tissue. Growing them. We are mighty pleased with our results so far. We've had a mouse grow two human ears at one time.'

Giano grimaced. 'Oh, man! Don't tell me any more or I'll throw up.'

Roberto glanced at his companion with a look that said cool it, man, and addressed his question to Hamish.

'Talking about splitting embryos, *Dottore*, is that like making twins?'

'Yes. And we can make triplets too.'

Giano smiled. 'Now you're talking! I want three of me.'

Hamish laughed, and Giano almost did, but it was important to him.

'Three it has to be,' said Giano, 'and if they grow up quick, well all the better I'd say!' He flicked his chin in an assertive gesture.

'Whichever way we go, I could split an embryo into four!'

'No, sir! Three. There's something special, holy, about three. Been brought up on that.' He crossed his heart rather ostentatiously.

'You're right! But you know the saying?'

'What? Three's a crowd?'

'Yeah! that one.'

'Oh, you can believe that if you want, but we're the one's that have the dosh. You might as well remember that *Dottore* McLeod.'

'Perhaps I'll have four little clones of me!' Roberto was playing along, and grinning broadly as if the idea had strong appeal.

'What do you think, Bertha? Could we manage a four-way

split of Roberto?'

She pushed her heavy glasses back up her nose and smiled affably. 'Four sounds perfect to me, Hamish.'

He laughed, and went round the back of his desk. 'They could be implanted two at a time, and spaced some time apart.'

'You mean – begin growing two babies say next year, then two more from frozen bits say in 2004?' Roberto was sorting it.

'It will be possible.'

'My God, man. This is awesome!'

'It is. OK. Is that it, then?'

'That's enough for me to get my ugly head around,' said Giano. 'I'm out a here, *Dottore*. You can have the big time.' He jutted out his chin to his friend, and Roberto said, '*Grazie, Dottore. Ciao.*' And they went out together.

As soon as the door closed, Bill wanted to agitate to get the Japanese mother and baby back in his care, right here in Italy.

'I want to deliver this baby. You and I must be the first to view this wonder child. Must!' He leaned back in his chair, his rotund belly filling the space of his open coat, and his hands folded across it.

Bertha spoke up now, 'Bill, I can understand your point of view, but why not leave them to have their child in their familiar surroundings.'

'Why is it that you're always on the side of expediency? I'll think it over. Yes, I will. So tell us how you see the Biotech programme.'

'We've an order from a clinic in Honolulu for as much bone marrow as we can produce, and we're beating the rest of the world in that, and in stem research – at least, as far as we can tell.'

Sitting at his desk, he opened the latest copy of *Science Boom* and said, 'Now that the two guys have gone, take a look at this.' They gathered round him. Bill took in the headline and sub-heading: "Cloned Child Soon? Dr Keith Robertson of the Biogenetics Unit Toronto hints at human cloning."

'Then why the hell didn't you show this to the Mafia?'

'For goodness sake, Bill, Don't call them that!'

'But that's what they are Hamish. Mafia. And since we're on the subject, we – all of us – are in their employ. That makes us one with them!'

'Look,' Hamish reacted, 'If we weren't in this together it couldn't happen.' He leaned over his desk and said very guardedly, 'Just for my peace of mind Bill, if nothing else, do not ever refer to them again as Mafia.' He looked at Muriana and Bertha and said, 'Forget this conversation ever took place. Please.'

Bill laughed and said, 'I didn't mean to upset you, Hamish. Yes, let's just forget that one. But, tuck it away for future reference.' He read the lead paragraph aloud: "Dr Robertson has achieved the production of mice with the Alzheimer's gene. He is keen to alter the gene pattern of a child just conceived and growing in the womb, to eliminate that gene, if inherited. He is not prepared to say how many steps away from cloning a human person free of Alzheimer's he is, but the writer suspects he is very close." He whipped off his glasses, wiped his forehead and eyes, and replaced them. 'If you show this to Roberto, he'll kill to get our news out first. My God, Hamish, we cannot have Dr Robertson stealing our thunder. Look, why don't we issue a preliminary release?' He put up his hand as if to stay the slung arrow, and said, 'Just a release, no names of parents.'

'As you know, we have not told our sponsors yet but ...' Hamish hesitated. The idea had some appeal. His expression relaxed. 'When I think of it I promised Raif to keep his name confidential, but the fact that we have cloned two babies is another matter. Quite separate.' He was smiling. Visions of fame filled his mind. 'Yes. We must think carefully about timing. Och, Bill. That's it. Timing. We could well beat Keith

Robertson. If the article is right, a clone is only in his mind as yet.'

'Yes, but that may mean sooner rather than later, if that writer ... what's his name?' He checked the article. 'Oh, yes, Warren Blackwell. If what he says has half a grain of truth in it. And of course, that article will have been taken up by all the media.'

'It's on the internet. Hugh, our faithful watch-dog, pointed it out just before we came over. My thoughts are exactly as you expressed them, Bill.'

'Thanks, Muriana. But I must say this. There is one thing that Dr Robertson has over us here, and that's the medical reason for the clone.'

Hamish knew he was right.

Part Two
Chapter 12

'No. No. No.' Yuki kept repeating the answer she had given to Kentaro, who had conveyed it to Hamish, as she used the straw broom to sweep away the light fall of snow on the path which led from their back door to the road. She was quite affronted by the idea that her son would be born in Italy. How could she tell Hamish, in the stupid code language that Kentaro used with him, that tradition was very important to her. She so looked forward to being with her mother for that month before the birth. And after the birth, another month at least. She thought, *Okaasan* is so wise! Babies make her happy. No. No. I will not go to Italy for the birth. She hurried indoors, laughing as the snowflakes fell on her head and arms. Look at that. Winter is here for the second time.

Kentaro made a point of being home early in order to catch Yuki before her bed-time. As she folded a crane, she heard him slipping out of his shoes, and called, '*Okaeri nasai.*'

'*Tadaima*', he repeated, opening and closing the *shoji* quickly. He smiled at her stretched out in the reclining chair.

'Just look at you. Cranes all over your bulge. You must be just about there.'

'It's not just me. *Okaasan* has made at least two hundred. And my friends, too many to count. But going by the boxes we've filled, it has to be about eight hundred with this one! Soon, we will start counting down.' She stopped to put the cranes that walked all over her into the box beside her. 'They're good company!' she laughed. She swivelled her legs around so that she faced him, square on. 'How has your day been?'

He pulled a chair up beside her. 'Good. I guess the highlight was when little Sandy Meads played for me. She used to play so very badly! Remember, I told you that her grandmother brought her for lessons and I walked out on her that day when I wanted to think only of getting a new child.'

'Yes, I remember all right. I felt for them because you are usually so careful not to let a child know he or she has played badly. You are such a wonderful teacher.'

'Well, we'll see if that applies when our wee man arrives. Sometimes I feel very nervous that I won't be able to teach him the violin. Very nervous.'

'Don't be. We can have him taught by one of your teachers!'

'But I'm his father.'

'And you'll inspire him. You know how you trust your teachers for the hard graft!' She laughed. 'Why, you are the finest model a child could ever wish to have. You will play to him, just as you did Jiro. Of course he will be a violinist!' She stood up and said, 'Would you like some tea? I'll make it.'

Seated opposite one another at the table, they sipped their tea. Kentaro surprised Yuki by saying, 'I agree with you that the baby should be born in Matsumoto. Your mother is keeping young at the thought of looking after you both. Only a Japanese person could see it our way. Every culture has its tradition. I like our way. It gives the father a lot of support since he has to go on working.'

Yuki looked a little sad. 'But I want you there at the time.'

'Oh, yes. I'll be as near as they'll let me. Don't worry about that. But it's before and after. I like to know that you're safe and that there's another person to help with the baby.'

Yuki reached across the table to touch his hand.

'I'm happy, then.' She smiled, but Kentaro saw that she was thinking about something that amused her.

'What are you thinking? Tell me.' He gently squeezed her hand.

'I was wondering how you say that in code to Hamish.'

'That isn't easy,' he laughed merrily. 'But I can pretend not to understand him, you know! How about we go up to bed now. Talk a little there. Maybe even think of a name.'

He let her leave the living area before him, then switched out the lights behind them. She led the way up the stairs.

'It was snowing when I biked home. Do you know what I think we must do?'

'What?' she said, into the darkness, his hand remaining on her tummy.

'I think that only Ichiro and I should go to the dedication of the memorial.'

Yuki was disappointed, but thought it preferable not to travel at this time. She did not want to re-live the stress of going to a commemoration of those children and young adults buried under the avalanches. Neither did she want the baby to be stressed. The worst scenario of all would be to go into early labour in Italy. She took up Kentaro's idea of asking her mother if she would like company for a week.

Hamish caught Bill before he entered his office to start his day's work. 'I have something to tell you.'

'Come on in.'

Slapping his colleague's desk, Hamish said. 'There's no way the Fujiwaras will come here for the birth. No way.'

Bill flared up. 'Who the hell does Fujiwara think he is?'

'I believe he thinks he is the child's father. No question. He is head of the family, and that must stand.'

Bill looked as if he had turned up the trump card. 'He is not the father, you know.'

'Och, my God, Bill. Don't say that too loud. Of course he's not the father, but I'm not out to break the news.'

They reflected together on who already knew, and Hamish defended his staff against the proposition that one of them might leak it. But worst of all was Bill's suggestion that it could easily slip Mary's tongue.

Hamish turned away in anger. 'How dare you suggest such a thing!'

Part Two
Chapter 13

Warren had permission to take Tom out of school to attend the lunch-hour recital that Andreas was giving. It was to be at the home in Dorchester of the music critic, William Poote.

'Hi. Dad. Are we in time?' he asked, as he buckled himself in and brushed snow off his sleeves.

There was sufficient time, but the recital was in a part of town that Warren did not know so well. Tom looked from the window and exclaimed at the large houses, long drives and statues at gates. While Tom looked with astonishment, Warren filled him in on what he should expect. Tom was happy to learn that Donna would be there. They drove on through the sub-division looking out for Valley View.

'It's not far now,' said Warren, turning at the sign. 'We're to find the house bordering the cornfield down here on the left.

'Wow! What a ginormous place!' exclaimed Tom. 'And look at the lights near the front door.'

'And the light stands along this stately drive-way,' said Warren, pulling in behind the last car which he recognised as Donna's. 'They're brass. Or look like it,' he said, as he locked up the car.

At the front door, they were greeted by the critic himself. 'Come on in. You're just in time. Snow jackets this way please. There are two hooks on the left.' Warren and Tom slipped out of their shoes and put on the slippers they had brought.

Donna had kept two chairs beside her and they smiled their greeting and sat ready for Andreas to play. He was already standing beside the piano. Jude made her entrance and sounded an occasional A, and at the same time earmarked the first few pages she was to play from. The people who filled the large room gave them their full attention.

Warren marvelled at the calm that always descended over Andreas when he played. Right through a range of excerpts of violin sonatas from Corelli to Prokofiev, he maintained a serene composure. Quite a feat. Not once did he show signs of the twitch.

'Impressive playing,' he said to Donna. 'What did you think of that, Tom?'

'I'm going to play like that, soon,' he said. Warren and Donna smiled over his head, their eyes communicating something else.

'I must say hello to Andreas then fly back home. I rehearse with the orchestra tomorrow and want to be ready,' said Donna, picking up her satchel from the floor and going over to speak to Jude and Andreas who were already surrounded by eager fans. Eventually, it was her turn. 'I'm Donna Beauchamp,' she said. 'Congratulations, that was a great recital. Your Prokofiev was spine tingling.' She smiled at Andreas, then Jude.

'Thanks.' Andreas smiled. 'So you're Donna. I'm coming to the Tchaikovsky on Friday.'

'Great. I hope we get it together by then! I must fly back now and get stuck in again!'

Donna had a quick word with Warren while Tom was quizzing Andreas and getting him to sign his programme. 'How did your article go?'

'Oh, it set the cat among the pigeons – the scientific ones anyway! I think Dr Robertson's taste of fame will prompt him into phoning me quite soon.' He grinned. In hushed tones he confided again his conviction that the geneticist was hiding something. Donna could not have agreed more. But there were more pressing matters. They arranged to meet in the dressing room after Donna's Tchaikovsky, and since she wanted it so much, Warren promised to arrange for Andreas to accompany Tom home on the shuttlebus – Robert Q bus – so that he could go back to her home with her.

'Great. See you then.'

Donna went her way, so Warren waited with Tom for Andreas to take him back to his place. Tom eagerly carried the music satchel and said, 'I wish I could come home with you now.'

'Oh, no. It's back to school, for you.' They put on their jackets and shoes and went to the car.

'This has to be the last of the snow,' Warren said, as he cleaned his windscreen. 'God, it's cold!' Everyone in, he shut his door and turned on the heat. 'You'll be glad that went so well,' he said to Andreas.

'It was OK. The audience was attentive and Jude's marvellous to play with. She kind of carries you along.'

'Yeah. I know what you mean.'

'I do too,' said Tom. 'She was real loud in the last one.'

Part Two
Chapter 14

They had good seats. Upstairs, in the centre block. The Toronto Symphony was starting to tune as they arrived.

'Dad,' whispered Tom as the lights dimmed, 'Will Donna be able to see us?'

'No, we're hidden in the shadows. Besides, she'll be – '

'Sh...' a voice cautioned.

'Here's Donna.' Tom wanted to tell everyone that the soloist was his violin teacher.

'Sh...' said the voice again, so Tom looked at his dad and pouted. She's looking very with it, thought Warren. He liked her striking use of colour layered over colour in flimsy fabrics, giving a shot green and gold effect. Stunning with her red hair. Her face showed no sign of nervousness, and the hair of her bow was steady as she tuned her instrument. He relaxed into his seat, and smiled down at his son who looked a little lost, but bubbling. His hair had been thoroughly well slicked into place for this stupendous event. Warren glanced at Andreas and caught the look of approval.

When Donna's solo violin melody sang out through the hall, then seduced the orchestra into joining it, tears ran down Warren's cheeks. He edged closer to Tom and reached for his hand. The small hand squeezed hard and the squeeze did not go away. Oh the pain of the poignant melodies, and how they dropped into the G string as if they poured their collective sonority into that one string. And the sparkle of the high notes, they tore at his heart when reinforced by the orchestra's harmonic figures! They set him afire for the violinist herself. My, Donna, you're something again.

When Tom's silent question arrived at the squeeze, Warren whispered, 'She's playing two strings at once.' The slow movement was sonorous, and their now entwined fingers lurched into a private dance which stopped and started suddenly in response to the energy of the music.

When the audience rose to their feet to acknowledge the superb performance, Warren whisked Tom into his arms so that he could see the stage better. Three different people walked on to give Donna a bouquet of flowers. Her right arm clutched a whole garden of colours. And it's winter! Before Donna responded to the audience with a third bow, she looked around the hall, and her eyes seemed to envelop Warren and Tom for one moment. Tom waved, and her smile was like an answer. 'She saw me, Dad. Donna smiled at me.' Warren let him slip down his body towards the floor and he said, 'I believe she did. Let's go.'

Andreas caught up with them. 'I was spell-bound. You were, I could tell.'

'Oh, you can say that again. We're off to see her now. Coming?'

'Yes, and I won't stay for the rest of the concert. I'll take Tom home as soon as we've seen her. The next bus is in twenty minutes, if you can get us to it.'

'Sure.'

'I'll be back for you.' Warren said to Donna. He kissed her hand in a gallant gesture, and the people who crowded into the dressing room smiled, and made sure that Tom was not lost amongst them.

Andreas ushered Tom on to the bus before him, telling him where to sit. 'The middle row is best; you have the window seat.' He followed him in but soon had to squeeze over a bit as the small bus filled up. They waved to Warren as the Robert Q bus pulled away, and settled into the journey with broad smiles on their faces as if the memory of the evening spent in admiration of Donna's playing held them enraptured.

Warren stayed in the background waiting for Donna to receive all the people who had to claim her friendship, had to get her autograph, or wanted to be close to the soloist for a few words. As the crowd thinned, he could see that she was wanting to get free, and he wondered how to help.

'Excuse me, but shall I put your flowers in the car?'

'Pardon me! Yes. Good idea, Warren', she said, over the head of a woman who insisted on telling her that she played the Tchaikovsky with the Vienna Philharmonic when she was Donna's age. Donna picked up her violin and jacket thinking she could leave. 'That is wonderful. What a lovely memory. I'm sorry, but my ride is waiting for me. Goodnight.'

Once returned to her apartment, and away from the lights and the public eye, Donna was set to relax, but Warren insisted he take a couple of photos of her while she looked so special. Donna agreed, but not until he had kissed her.

He let his camera slide back into the bag, reached to switch off the lamp and gathered her into his arms. The concerto had opened his heart to new sensations, taken him orbiting to such heights that touching her had new dimensions. The kiss sealed them in and gave them permanence, and an urgency that was barely controllable.

'Oh, wow! You are so lovely, Donna. I can hardly believe that this is us. The you that's just played that mighty concerto – solo performer backed by a great orchestra – and me. Me!'

She laughed and turned the light back on. 'This is me, all right. And I wouldn't want to be anywhere else right now. Come on, let's get the photo session over and done with.'

'Just as you say.'

'No, as you asked! Come on, tell me how you want me to pose.'

He picked up his camera. 'Right. Play that opening phrase, right here under this light.'

She took up her violin and played, and his skin shivered at the sensuous sound. It was a problem to hold his camera steady and he was only able to do it by pressing his elbows into the walls of his chest. 'Right. Good one. Now full length.

That gown's exquisite. Sit on the arm of the settee please, and rest your violin on one knee. He grabbed one of the bouquets, and tucked it into the fold of the settee so that it added complementary pinks and mauves to the picture. Perfect. Great, that's done.' He turned off his camera and packed it away. Donna replaced her violin and bow, and ran to her bedroom calling, 'Time to let my hair down. I'm changing. You, too? Come on. Use my room.'

Warren whipped off his tie, and took two steps toward her. At that moment his mobile phone rang. He almost turned it off, but thought it could be Dr Robertson or Andreas. Cannot ignore either.

'Warren speaking.'

'Robertson here. Get to the Petrie Maternity Annex, now.'

'But…'

'Or miss the biggest story!'

'I'll be there.' He picked up his camera, yelled out, 'Donna, I have to go. Sorry.' And flew out of the door almost tripping over himself and hoping he had yelled loudly enough.

Donna emerged from the shower, grabbed a towel, and heard the door slam. 'Not two bastards in a row. Oh, no! Warren, you creep.' Then, while drying herself she noticed the abandoned tie, and thought he's had to go some where really urgently. Oh, God. Why did it have to be now?

The traffic was fairly light, so Warren drove like a maniac, and it was only when he heard a siren that he collected himself, and just drove at the limit, swerving tightly on the corners as hard as he dared. He parked illegally, and dashed into the maternity annex and made for the desk. A receptionist stood with her back to him, chatting to a nurse. 'Pardon me. But …'

She had turned. 'Can I help you?'

'Yes, Dr Robertson. Where shall I go?'

She looked bewildered. The nurse had overheard him and said something to the woman and she then smiled and said,

'Maynard, room four.'

'Come with me, sir,' the nurse said. As she moved quickly along beside him, she said, 'Now that we're out of her earshot, I can tell you that Dr Robertson asked me to look out for you.' She smiled a knowing smile, while Warren thought, you know more than I do. Then it struck him that maybe she did not know the truth at all. He did not ask. And he still did not know what on earth he was there for.

Dr Robertson noticed him through the crack of the door and joined him. He beckoned him to follow to an office. Once the door was closed he said, 'Now, here's the big one. Get ready and I'll talk.' He lit a cigarette apologetically, 'I need this tonight.'

Warren's dictaphone was ready. Robertson's voice activated it as he said, 'The child just born will make a revolutionary contribution to society.' He inhaled deeply, then continued through the exhaled smoke, 'She's free of the Alzheimer's gene that we removed as we cloned. A first. A world first.' He smiled at Warren, 'You wanted it. Now it's over to you.'

'Photos. Can I get photos of the baby?'

'Yes. Of course. With me!'

'Of course. First though, you said she. It's a girl? Weight? Healthy? People will want to know.'

Dr Robertson led the way to room four and knocked quietly.

'Come in.' He and Warren entered. A young man stood beside the bed holding the bundle. Its small face was visible in the midst of the wrap, the eyes were wide open, and Warren marvelled at the depth of knowing in the eyes. The man looked nervous and tired.

'Meet Warren, the journalist I told you about. He'll get some photos and the story will be on the wire tonight. Jianne and Don.'

The young woman managed a tired smile from her pillows. Then she sat up as if with something urgent on her mind.

'Warren, please make a plea on my behalf. Dr Robertson has done wonders for our baby, but I still have the Alzheimer's gene. Get those scientists to find a cure for me before it takes a hold.' She flopped back on to her pillow, and Warren took a step closer to her, smiled, and congratulated them both. Then he asked if he might take photos and while they said yes, it was on the condition that the baby was held by Dr Robertson and that they and their names remained unknown.

'That's right. Even my doctor doesn't know. The nurses, too. They think it's Don's.'

Warren glanced at the young man. He could not see his face. 'Right, no names except Dr Robertson.'

'Don,' the mother said. 'Hand the baby to Dr Robertson, please.'

He carefully placed the bundle into the older man's arms then undid the shawl so that the tiny hands were free. The baby immediately put one to her temple, fingers slightly splayed, as if to aid deep thought.

Warren moved to centre the man and baby in his lens, and took a succession of pictures.

Suddenly the door opened and the nurse said, 'Time's up.' Then she said to the mother, 'You're lucky to have a photographer in the family, aren't you?'

She simply smiled. Then to the visitors, she said, 'Goodnight.'

Warren said to the fast-walking scientist, 'The staff will spill the beans, won't they? As soon as we hit the papers?'

'Never,' Dr Robertson whispered. 'They're under oath. They'll maybe tell their grandchildren that they were present at the birth of the first …'

They were nearing reception. 'I don't want to be seen.'

Warren made a point of saying 'Goodnight' loudly, as the older man sidled past, very hurriedly.

He caught him up. 'What about her?'

'She won't talk. None of them will.'

The men chatted before parting at Warren's car. Dr Robertson looked up at him.

'Get it right, now. Emphasise the medical breakthrough for Alzheimer's sufferers. And give credit to my team.' He reached in his pocket and scribbled two names.

'Thanks. I've got that. This camera is digital. I'll have these pics on the internet in half an hour. Tomorrow this will be front page news.' They shook hands.

'Be prepared for the onslaught, Dr Robertson. I'd change my home phone number if I were you.'

As soon as Warren was back in his car, he dialled the news agency Reuters to ask for front-page coverage, and then rang Donna's number. A sleepy voice said, 'Donna.'

'Darling, I'm so sorry. But I've got the story of the century. Will you have me back? I'd like a bit of comfort as I send the news down the wire.'

'What, you've got your laptop? Did you take photos?'

'Yep. I'll be at your place in a few minutes, I'm already into Bloor Street.'

'Fine. I'll have the coffee ready.'

Part Two
Chapter 15

Hamish sat stunned. The headline at the top of his monitor was plain enough, but it was the medical reason for cloning which irked him.

'Bertha, take a look.'

She dropped her heavy bosom over his keyboard to focus through her thick lenses on the small print: "Alzheimer's Gene Removed in Cloning of Girl. A World First." 'Oh my goodness, my goodness.' Her richly German accent grated through the word, Alzheimer's. And she said it three times. 'Unbelievable, eh?'

'Of course it's believable, Bertha. It's just that no cloned human has been reported before. I don't care now about my Mary's child being made news. I'm pipped, but at least we'll come a good second.' He had a sense of urgency. 'I'm glad now that I told my board last night. Bertha, wasn't it incredible! They were full of congratulations, but didn't seem in the least surprised.'

Bertha's complacent smile told the full story.

'You mean ... och, well, I'm glad they knew. It's paved the way for what will be next; sets my mind at rest. And the big question now is how will the world react?' He gathered up the print-out and said, 'I'll show this to Bill.'

He entered Bill's office after getting a 'Come in' to his brisk knock.

'Bill. Good morning. And you've seen the news?'

Bill was watching his monitor, and pressing keys. 'I was about to email this around the labs,' he said. 'We've been beaten by a few days.' Standing looking on was someone Hamish had not seen before. Bill swivelled round and stood up.

'Terri, I'm sorry. Hamish, I want you to meet my new colleague, Terri de Medici. Hamish, Terri.'

Hamish blinked from tiredness more than anything. He felt disoriented. A fine-boned, tall, very dark and stunningly gorgeous woman in a doctor's coat was a sight he could barely cope with right now. He put out a hand to take hers, and smiled as he said, 'Pleased to meet you,' but he was soon engrossed by his thoughts about Dr Robertson and his astonishing news.

'Why oh why couldn't Mary have been early?'

'Hang on. Let me send this, and then I'll talk.' He brought up his mailing list, and sent the letter and attachments. 'Incredible photos. There.' His large, bulging eyes were filled with humour. 'There is one good thing about this – we know we're not the only ones cloning humans!' He stood up to talk to Hamish. 'There's nothing we can do. So it had to be Keith Robertson. And from what we read, the baby is perfect.'

'Robertson got it right. Trust him. But I am a wee bit sore, you know.'

'Look at it like this, we'll be first on purely humanitarian grounds. No disease carrying genes programmed out in our case. A little girl born out of love.'

'But you can't put it like that, Bill. That infers that she was conceived in the usual way. Sure, we are in love. We love each other, we loved our Trish, and we love this baby. Och, we love the child all right!'

'Well now. Why don't you go home and tell Mary the news. But stay with her. She's maybe three days away. Baby's head's almost engaged. All the signs. The moment she's in labour, I want to know.'

'Right. Of course I'll get home. I'll let you know the minute anything happens. And you've got Plan A ready to go?'

'Indeed. The world will get the news the moment I call my secretary.'

There was bleeping from Hamish's breast pocket. And at the same time Bill's pager bleeped. Their voices were synchronised as they said, 'Mary?'

Her voice was faint. 'I'm already in the ambulance, Hamish.'

'Mary!'

'Dr McLeod, come straight to the birthing suite. Please.' It was the paramedic. 'Your wife is into the second stage and it's going to be a quick birth by all the signs.'

He heard the beginnings of a pain-filled groan which was abruptly cut off.

After a fast ride with the siren sounding, Mary was relieved to be told, 'We're there. We're at the birthing centre, Mrs McLeod. You all right, love?'

'Ooh,' was all she could manage as a third stage contraction overwhelmed her.

The ambulance door opened and two nurses appeared. 'All right, take her in.' She was wheeled into the labour unit so fast, Mary closed her eyes to the flying walls and people about her, and did her best to hold back the mounting contraction. Suddenly they were stopped in the birthing room and the nurse who had run along beside the trolley said, 'Relax and push hard there, Mary. Good, good. There we are! Oh, splendid work, Mary.' She held a child up by the feet, 'You have a daughter. A perfect child!' Sunshine filled the room, flooded Mary's heart. Within moments, the face that looked down at her above a mask was Bill's. His eyes were smiling.

'Very good, Mary. Congratulations.'

'Where's Hamish?' Mary ignored Bill and spoke to the nurse who placed the wrapped baby into her arms, and she peeked into the blanket. In that moment, she connected with two bright eyes looking straight at her. 'Hello, hello,' Mary whispered as she pushed back a lock of bloodied hair. 'You're beautiful. Your daddy is coming.'

Hamish had been shown straight to the labour room and was all fingers and thumbs trying to deal with a coat and mask which had been thrust at him with the words, 'You have a daughter, Dr McLeod.' He heard a baby's cry. Bill turned to him and said, 'A girl, a beautiful girl, Hamish.'

He took it all in at a glance – Mary looking amazingly relaxed. In her arms the precious bundle, the cloned daughter that he had created and she had carried and Mary had already become acquainted with. He felt intense pride and jealousy. Bill had beaten him there. Mary looked up and said, 'She's absolutely sweet, Hamish!' He took a peek into the opened bundle and then put his head into the pillow supporting Mary's head and wept. Occasional words reached Mary's ear. 'Wonderful. Mary, my darling. We've done it. And look at that hair!'

Mary's chuckle brought him round.

He slipped down his mask and kissed her on her cheeks, on her lips. 'Now let me take a look at our wee Rose,' he said, thrilled at being able to use the name for real.

'Hamish, you didn't get here,' she whispered into the bundle as she handed it to him.

'Och, Mary, I'm sorry, very sorry,' he said, softly, while looking in awe at his child. He opened the covers enough to reveal her tiny hands, and put one against his cheek and he smiled and sighed. 'She's all I hoped for! Fine hands. Can we see her feet too?' He laid her gently in Mary's arms and she assisted him in undoing the wrap enough to reveal the tiny feet, complete with a neat pink wrinkle at the ankle. They laughed together in that moment of inner satisfaction that parents alone can appreciate.

Within a few minutes of the birth, Bill's secretary had gone to work on plan A, and within minutes, the news had been flashed around the world:

"Italy Wins Cloning Stakes –

Child Cloned for Humanitarian Reasons"

As he left the hospital half an hour later, Hamish was bombarded by the media. He stood on the steps of the Vitali Birthing Unit to answer questions, be photographed and filmed. He was overjoyed. At this moment of which he had dreamed, he felt brash, confident and peacock-proud. He stressed that this child was the first cloned child which had nothing to do with gene manipulation. Rose was begun for loving, humanitarian reasons.

'She is a love child in the best senses of the word.' He laid it on. 'Yes. Yes. It was relatively easy. No. I am the father. Yes, of course I had a team of helpers.'

On two questions he was silent: 'Have you any other babies on the way?' and 'What other types of cloning are you doing?' He did not want to detract from the main story, and certainly was not going to let anybody else steal his moment. Not even the Raifs. Besides, the Biotech Centre had more than enough research to keep it busy. No need to solicit orders.

'Are you saying, Dr McLeod, that gene replacement done for medical reasons is not humanitarian?' A young woman thrust her microphone at him for a reply. He had to say something.

'I'm saying that the motivation was different. Very different!' He felt beads of sweat gathering on his forehead and top lip. He was suddenly afraid. Afraid that he could not really justify taking cells from Trish, let alone Jiro. He could not keep going out here on this debate. Not now! He gave a smile, waved, and beat his way to his car which was parked just six metres away. Photographers caught his every moment.

Italia News splashed it on the front page in the largest possible print, and two photographs filled the remaining space. There was a photograph of mother and baby taken one hour after the birth, and one of Hamish looking straight at the camera with pride evident in his stance, and smile. "Biotech Centre Has Done It! Baby Girl Cloned for Humanitarian Reasons." This time the family names were published. Gifts of flowers, cards, baby clothes and toys, and messages of congratulation flooded into both the Vitali Birthing Unit and the Centre.

The one photographer who'd been permitted to take a mother and baby picture sold it around the world. Others did their best to gain entry to the ward, and there was an angry outburst from staff when they learned all too late that a woman had visited Mary under false pretences and taken a photograph before anyone realised what had happened. The picture was unbecoming. Whereas the official photograph showed a radiant mother with her equally lovely, bright-eyed daughter Rose, who already had thick, dark copper-coloured hair, this one showed a tired and sad looking mother who seemed to have lost touch with the baby beside her. The worst of it was that it found its way into many publications as well as on to the internet, and a foolish nurse showed it to Mary. She cried her heart out. She was angry and hurt.

Hamish returned to see Mary late in the afternoon armed with a sample of gifts and cards, and was beside himself with disappointment. Mary had no interest in all the joyous messages, flowers and news stories. She just wanted to sleep. 'Of course you must sleep, my darling,' he said, with a last peek at the sleeping baby in the cot beside her bed, and thought – she's exhausted. He kissed her lightly as she lay with her eyes closed, and walked noiselessly away. At the work-station he spoke to the receptionist.

'Take good care of my wife. I'm angry that she saw the terrible picture of her. Why the hell did that stupid nurse show her? *Italia News* was perfect! That's the one to enjoy!'

The receptionist smiled and nodded. 'We apologise, *Dottore* McLeod. Yes, we will look after your wife.'

As he walked sorrowfully away from the unit, now deserted by media, he thought she must never see the scurrilous messages! He had felt sick to the stomach when he read them, but they would kill her. "Traitor", "Liar", "Devil's advocate", "God Almighty," were only some of the names he had been called. All hurt him equally badly. But then, he had run that very risk.

'Och, Mary, we have our wee lassie and she's perfect,' he said on the phone early on the second day. She sounded rested, and he must blot out all of the down side of what he had done. The only thing that mattered now was that he must take good care of his Mary and Rose. It made him feel young again. His team was full of admiration, and Hamish was ecstatic about his achievement. But the message that encouraged him most was from the Academia of Humanists. "Well done. A magnificent achievement. Many lives will be improved, both now, and in the future. Congratulations to you both."

At the Biotec Centre, the champagne flowed. And in spite of Hamish's previous misgivings about the board, nothing but positively overwhelming messages of congratulations came from them within minutes of his news being out. 'This will put New Biotec Centre on the world map,' the Centre Manager said, shaking his hand. His words resounded through every laboratory and office, behind doors that were all too soon to be locked out of desperation to keep out the media, and the madmen. Hamish had been happy to leave Mary in the care of the unit. His lab work had reached a peak of success and he had now to consider the latest request – or was it a demand – from Gianfranco. The suave but disfigured Italian had visited him as soon as he could, following the birth, and confronted him with an egotistical wish.

'You are a genius, Hamish. Now, you have proved you can do it, it is time to do the next thing and clone from an adult! Me. Three times! His voice became like a loop tape – three times, three times, three times …'

Hamish felt sick. He did not like the man but it had always been part of the deal.

'I cannot answer that today, Gianfranco. My head and heart are in a spin. I've interviewed the world, been photographed and filmed by the world. And we still have to deal with international repercussions.'

Hamish found a few minutes in the evening to return to Mary's bedside and, this time, was alarmed to find her very upset.

'Hamish, I hate this place. Rose has cried all day and they've put her into Coventry. I must go home.'

'But who will look to you?'

'A nurse. Get me a nurse, Hamish. Please.'

'Just give it one or two more days, lassie. You'll be stronger then. Please, just two more days and I'll be able to organise a nurse. Of course I will.' He kissed her tenderly. 'I wish I could stay but I am so tired I'm almost asleep on my feet.'

She smiled weakly and closed her eyes, and he left without stopping off at the nursery, to catch up on some sleep himself.

In the morning before daylight, he was woken by the phone.

'Hamish, I'm going to Scotland. I want to go to Scotland. Rose is crying all the time. I need my friends, Jeannie, and Janice. And I'm scared.' She burst into tears, and cried so hard and so long that Hamish could not get through to her. Eventually a nurse spoke into the phone. 'Dr McLeod, is that you?'

'What is going on? My wife sounds ill.'

'She will be if you don't let her get to her friends and family, Dr McLeod. Please come at once.'

Hamish got dressed and went straight to Mary who was holding her crying baby, patting her, and putting her to her breast, but the child would not feed, and would not be pacified. 'Och, my darling,' he said, trying to understand the awful change in his wife. Her usually placid and rosy face was white and distraught. 'Why isn't there a nurse looking after the wee one?'

'Because I'm the one with the breast milk. Hamish, she won't even drink from me.'

Mary was shrieking.

Hamish held out his arms. 'Shall I take her?'

Mary handed the writhing baby to her daddy, and he wrapped her tightly, saying, 'There, there, Rose.' And he put her against his shoulder and paced about. She quietened and Hamish and Mary smiled at each other with relief, but then a nurse came in and took the baby from Hamish and said, 'Sleep time.' She tucked her firmly into the cot and another nurse wheeled her away to the nursery while the first nurse rushed away to get an injection to make Mary sleep. With a nod of dismissal to Hamish, she injected the limp arm that lay across the bedclothes.

'What was that? What are they doing?' Mary cried, half sitting, half lying, before her head retreated to the pillow again. She was asleep almost at once so Hamish went home puzzled and disappointed, and rang his sister in Scotland just to talk to someone in the family.

'I feel worried sick, Janice. If only you could be here. We both need family I believe!'

Janice replied that if it could help she'd look after Mary and the baby at her home. 'I'm just not able to come to Italy right now.'

'Och, well, I guess we'll manage. Thanks.'

It was after he had made the call that he found flowers lying on his doorstep. "With love and good cheer to the three of you, K and Y Raif", the message read. He wished he had been able to share them with Mary tonight.

The next day, Mary barely acknowledged the flowers, and was keener than before to get out of the place, and go to Scotland. 'Help me, Hamish. I need to go back home to Kirkliston!'

After a conference with the staff, and a long talk with Mary, Hamish agreed to let her go back to Kirkliston on day five.

The farewell at Malpensa airport was harrowing. It hurt him that Mary was so cheerful about getting away from Italy and him.

'I'm doing what's right. You'll see.' Rose was in a nurse's care, silent for once, but he hardly got a look in.

'Mary, lass, it's all too quick. I'm at a loss to know what to do next.' He was tearful. 'We're both exhausted,' he muttered.

'Janice'll be able to help me. I need her help. And you can come and see us soon and we'll have Rose Margaret baptized in the little church on the hill as soon as you get there.' He was not answering, just fighting the tears. 'Please be brave. I'll be back before you can count your toes, love.'

'Och, just look to yourself and get strong again.' The doctor in the unit had described Mary's condition as post-natal depression. 'Give into her, Dr McLeod. Do exactly what she wants and she'll come through this.'

'And my wee daughter? How is she?'

'Oh, she's bonny, but a crier is that one. She would tire any mother out.'

Hamish only just restrained himself from saying, 'She's just the same as Trish which is what I dreaded!'

Bill became angry once he found out. 'You didn't tell me what was happening.'

'No. And I hardly knew myself, Bill. But you know how it is in the unit! You're at their mercy!'

'I called in on day three and Mary was asleep. If she'd been awake I'd have talked to her about going home with a nurse. She'd have been in my care then.'

Hamish recalled Mary's wish that she did not want to visit Bill after the birth. 'Well, she's chosen to be in Scotland and that's the way it is. Sorry, Bill.' And he slammed out of the room where he had hoped to find some solace after seeing off his wife and daughter at the airport.

Part Two
Chapter 16

'It's becoming monotonous!' Warren said to Donna when he called her one evening.

'Two cloned children, and both perfect according to reports. I missed out on the second story but the first one was worth its weight in gold.'

'You mean for you, I'm sure. Tell me, what are the international responses?'

Warren boasted that Dr Robertson had so much confidence in him that he had made a habit of sending him stuff before it got out. More than that, he shared many of the tributes, letters, and requests that had come his way as a result of his elimination of the Alzheimer's gene. The news had spread like wildfire around the world.

'Sounds overwhelming to me.' She laughed. 'After the Tchaikovsky I got dozens of calls and messages – all complimentary I must add – so I had a taste of what fame is like. But I haven't received requests for dozens of performances. Just one.'

'Oh, tell me.'

'The New York Philharmonic!' Her voice revealed her pride but she still wanted to think it through as the engagement would be next spring when all her pupils took their exams, and there was graduation as well. Not a good time for practising a monumental work. The Beethoven, especially. 'Teachers shouldn't be soloists.'

'Well, maybe. But you are already.'

'I'll see. But tell me about the second cloning.'

He told her about Hamish McLeod who had been involved in the cloning of Dolly, and how he was carving out a career at Como, Northern Italy, at the New Biotec Centre, leading a team doing research into human cloning. The wire had said, he confided, that the Roslin Institute was not into cloning humans but the Italians were mad keen. 'And he's cloned a child for himself!'

'Is this good or bad? I don't like it myself!'

'Well, they reckon it's all in the name of humanitarianism. The McLeod girl, Trish, aged thirteen, was a champion skier, and was killed by an avalanche in Austria last February.'

'So they cloned her? Oh, my God. You don't think the Fujiwaras are expecting a clone also?'

'What makes you think they might be?'

'The same avalanche catastrophe. You remember? Hang on! I didn't tell you, did I? It was Peter.'

'Hey, where does this all lead?'

'Oh, nothing. I'm way off-track I guess. But one of the Fujiwara twins was killed in the same incident, and now the parents are expecting. Quite soon, actually. Just a coincidence.'

'But wait. What if you're right?'

Donna went hot and cold and pleaded with Warren not to offend her friends by quizzing them or Dr McLeod or anyone else. Warren reassured her and talked, instead, about Tom and how, on the morning following the Tchaikovsky performance, Andreas had taught him to play the Strauss Waltz in C Major as a duet. It was his turn to swell with pride as he claimed that he got it in one evening!'

That was Donna's cue for reinforcing the precepts of the Fujiwara method and, in lighter vein, they laughed together as they reminisced about the frustrations of getting involved with a client against one's better judgment. And that led to Donna's refusing to go as far as staying at his place one weekend lest Tom got upset about it.

'Just don't push it, Warren. But do come here soon and please, please turn off your mobile. And don't bring your camera. Right?'

'Right. Promise. Goodnight, then. Until Tom's lesson.'

'I know! Bring Andreas to play the Strauss with Tom for me, and then put the two on the Robert Q bus – it'll take them right to your door, won't it? You stay on. What about it?'

'Yep. If I can, I will. Sounds a great idea to me.'

No sooner was Warren off the phone than Andreas came to his door. 'May I come in?'

'Sure, I was about to make some tea. Good timing.'

Andreas took off his shoes and jacket and Warren said, 'I've just got off the phone with Donna. I told her about the waltz and she wants to hear it.'

'Well, it's something again. Tom amazes me! He learns so quickly!'

They walked through to the living room.

'It's warmer tonight than I can remember a January night being for some years,' Warren said. 'Are you warm enough – I've got it on 18 degrees?'

'Sure. May I sit here?'

Warren noted the twitch, the need to talk. 'Anywhere you like – I'll get another cup.'

Andreas's pain had surfaced. It would be kind to let him talk.

'Go ahead,' he said, as Andreas devoured the tea at an alarming speed then put down his cup.

Andreas eased his body deep into the bean-sack. 'CT was more than kind. As I said, he always manipulated things so that we could be alone. He was determined to keep me for himself. Asked me to live with him. In fact, offered to keep me, pay my fees, treat me like a partner. I wanted to keep my freedom. OK I thought I loved him, but there was something that made me feel unhappy. I couldn't put my finger on it until one night just before we were to go to Niagara together for a weekend, this guy called Joachim turned up.' He got up and went to the kitchen. 'Hang on.'

Warren heard him pour a glass of water. He returned, drinking, and finished the glass. He looked into Warren's eyes intently, sadly.

'Ever felt a chill go through you like you'd swallowed an

iceberg?'

Warren resisted joking. 'Once. Maybe.'

'Well, this Joachim had been CT's lover for some years back in Czechoslovakia. But since CT left to come and teach at MAAC, he had worked really hard to make the trip to Canada. He came to the door thinking to give his lover a welcome surprise. "I'm here, darling Carl," he said, pushing his way in. CT tried to get him to go into the kitchen as a way of avoiding me. "No," he said. "Let's play our little game, darling. Let's have music and dance like old times." Then he saw me. Oh, wow! Was he livid? And no doubt embarrassed.'

'You mean that CT had no idea that Joachim was coming?'

'He had some idea, actually, but hadn't been certain of the date. Joachim had insisted on doing this surprise thing.' His cheek twitched even as he laughed. 'He was quite a toy boy, you could say. CT had told me about him and his silly games and that he'd tired of them. Yet he couldn't shake him off. He was the kind of guy who wouldn't take no for an answer. "I'm sorry, Joachim," CT said very loudly, as if to penetrate his brain, "but I hoped that you wouldn't come. We agreed not to see each other again. Don't you remember?" It was interesting for me to see this side of CT. And it was rather flattering to know that he loved me, not Joachim.'

'So when did the friction begin?'

'Oh, right away. Joachim looked at me, then at CT and said, "So this is your new lover boy? Isn't he a little on the young side for you Carl, darling?" He tried to belittle me. "You always said you appreciated my experience!" I was very surprised at what happened next. He looked wild, disoriented and, quite frankly, ill. He looked at CT hard-eyed and said, "You've lost any attraction for me, Carl. Yes," he said, "I would like to leave. Show me where to call a cab, will you?" CT and I were taken aback. He left almost as swiftly as he'd arrived.'

'But with a plan already in his mind, I gather?'

'Oh, yes. He contacted me after the weekend and asked if we could talk.'

'When Joachim was with me, he seemed more together somehow. Less silly. And as we were talking about CT, the man himself phoned me to tell me it was over between us.' His cheek twitched unmercifully. 'I was so shocked I couldn't speak. Joachim was sympathetic. He said, "Do you not know his reputation?"

'I was too shocked to make any comment. He got me a drink of tea and revived me a bit; was quite kind, really. He persisted about CT's reputation though. "We knew Carl as a man of straw back home. He led us so far, then dumped us. Always for a younger fellow. Always."'

'So why had he come all this way to see him?'

'Aha. There's the rub. He said that he was bringing a message from all the young men he'd dumped.'

Warren looked askance. He must keep Andreas talking.

Part Two
Chapter 17

Fujiwara was going to conduct the orchestra. It was usually a student who did it, but for this first performance of his son with orchestra, he wanted to do it himself. There had been plenty of student performances over the years in which the institute had been functioning, but a ten-year-old playing the Grieg concerto, that was special. He had invited his best students to come to four weeks of rehearsals. This morning, Ichiro would practise with them. A scattering of students sat in the body of the hall and up in the balcony.

The child came on to the stage looking bright-eyed and tidy in his dark navy uniform. His father smiled and indicated a chair. He was going over a few of the challenging bars at the end of the first movement, it would take another few minutes.

Then the moment of preparedness came. 'For those of you who don't know my son, this is Ichiro.' Ichiro stood and bowed.

'We're all set. Come and take your place, Ichiro. The young performer almost ran to take the piano stool, sat down and fixed its height, rubbed his hands together and on his pant legs, and looked up at his dad. Fujiwara raised his baton, waited for calm before doing a quick up-beat, then nodded to the soloist.

The piano lid was fully open and Ichiro handled the keys with fluency and considerable power. As the movement progressed and the tone of the players matched the drama of the music, Ichiro managed a sonorous sound but at times Fujiwara reined in the orchestra, just enough to allow the soloist to be heard continually throughout the large hall. When lyricism was the mood, a hush overcame the players and the students who had come to listen, but it was those singing passages which Fujiwara wanted most of all to be perfect, and he stopped and started the orchestra and soloist until he attained the appropriate lyricism. When the rehearsal ended an hour-and-a-half later, the students in the body of the hall stood and cheered.

Ichiro hopped off the stool and acknowledged their applause with a deep bow. The orchestra stamped their applause, their instruments still in their hands. He turned and bowed to them. His dad shook his hand and whispered to him, 'Good, Ichiro. Very good. You must return to school now.'

Ichiro cycled off to school, and when his mother greeted him at home at the end of the day, he said, 'The Grieg was fun, Mum. I liked playing with those guys.'

'Oh, very good. I knew you could do it. So do you think you can play it on Saturday night?'

'Of course. But waiting is difficult.'

Yuki was making a crane, and had stayed seated in the reclining chair. 'Ichiro, can you get us both a drink, please?'

'Yes, Mum. Are you all right?'

'Yes. But tired, very tired. I'll be glad to just stay here.'

Ichiro went to his mother and hugged her. 'Mum, I love you. Will I like this baby, do you think? He or she makes you so tired.'

'Of course. We'll all forget about my being tired when he or she is here. You make some tea now and I'll feel better.'

As he lit the gas ring and made the tea, Yuki watched her son through the opened screen and wondered how like him the little boy would be. Would he have the same bright eyes and short but agile fingers? Soon, she thought, I will know. We will know. In her head she had begun to call the baby Hiro, the name both she and Kentaro liked. She wondered at the news of Mary's daughter that had been headlined everywhere, and was glad it was Mary and not herself. I could not take such publicity on top of having a baby. And she got to thinking – it will not be long now. I must get to Mum's place perhaps tomorrow.

'Ichiro, I've just finished making the last of the thousand cranes. We'll celebrate. Please bring those bean cakes. They're my favourite.'

'Good one, Mum. Coming.'

Ichiro took delight in waiting on his mother. Happiness was written all over his shining face as he carried in the lacquered tray. She felt proud and happy and smiled inwardly at how he had brought the best cups and small teapot with the *sakura* pattern on them, and the red and black lacquer dish for the bean cakes.

He poured her tea and passed it to her before fixing his own. 'Where will you put the cranes?'

'I was going to ask you that.'

He sipped some tea and then suddenly his eyes lit with inspiration. 'I know. At Jiro's shrine.'

Yuki stopped drinking and looked intently into her boy's eyes. 'Of course. It's a wonderful idea. Can you think how to arrange them?'

'I'll work on it, Mum.'

'Excellent. Do you know, I think the baby will come soon. It isn't quite due, but I have a feeling that it will be early.'

'Is that why you're tired?'

'Yes, the baby is getting ready to come. I shall have to go over to *Obaachan*'s place very soon.'

Suddenly it dawned on Ichiro that his mother may not be able to attend his concert. 'But, Mum! The Grieg! I want you there!' He got up from the chair he had brought close to his mother and he snatched the crane that was on her stomach and tore it up. 'Don't have that naughty baby! Not yet! And don't make the last crane until after my concert.' He ran from the room, and his mother heard him begin the Grieg concerto with pounding anger. She rested her hand on the baby and wept quietly. But as the mood of Ichiro's anger changed to match the soft lyricism of the music, she felt calmer too.

When Kentaro came home, Yuki was back in her reclining chair after preparing and eating the evening meal with

Ichiro, and had fallen asleep. Seeing the light on, he went to her and softly whispered, 'Yuki, pet.'

She readily awoke. 'Kentaro talk to me please. Bring your chair.'

'What is it?' he said, as he sat down.

She told him about what Ichiro had said, and done, and then with tears in her voice she pleaded with him not to tell Hamish when the child arrives.

'I couldn't bear to go through the trauma that Mary must be going through. I don't want anyone to know we had this baby cloned. Nobody!'

Kentaro thought for a minute. 'I understand. I too felt repulsed at the news and how it was splurged over everything. Mary should never have been seen in the hospital. She looked terribly tired, didn't she? Depressed, I thought. I don't wish that on you. But Hamish promised it would be kept anonymous. No names will be broadcast. Isn't that enough?'

Yuki swung her legs around. 'No, it's not enough. I don't want Hamish to know either, and especially that Bill.' Her face coloured up. 'Please just don't tell them when Hiro is born. Don't.'

'Hang on. You don't even want Hamish to know that the baby is born, how the birth went, or anything at all about the birth?'

'No. Think about it. If we phone Hamish, he will tell Bill for certain. Then he will call the media and it will be out. But what's worse, they will trace the calls! It's so easily done. Hamish was stupid to promise anonymity. Stupid, and probably not telling us everything. Didn't you think he looked so smug on the steps of the Institute? Stupid but puffed up and as proud as a peacock. No, I won't let you tell him!'

Kentaro puckered his lips, sighed, and looked at his wife with a touch of admiration.

'Well, maybe you're right. Especially now that we've seen how Ichiro can turn on the baby. I had no idea that he carried so much anger inside of him. That makes it doubly important that we keep quiet. Play the birth down a bit. You're a wise woman, Yuki.' He stood and hugged his wife and she gently bit his ear and they giggled a little together. 'I'm going to get you to your mother's tomorrow. And I'll tell Ichiro we will have a video made especially for you. I'll sort the young man out. And let me tell you now – his playing today almost knocked me off my podium. He's a great kid. He'll be OK.'

'And you won't tell Hamish? But you will see him when you go to the dedication of the memorial sculpture?'

They were in total agreement that he would tell whatever seemed appropriate, such as that Yuki was overdue, but had the dates wrong or something. Kentaro would make it clear to staff at his Institute that they were to give information to no one. That comforted Yuki. She tidied up the papers, and put them away.

'I'll make the last crane on Saturday night about nine. By then, Ichiro will have played and Hiro can come.'

They went to the stairs and tried to go up side-by-side. 'I'm too big.' She laughed at him and at herself. He stepped down. 'We might not be able to climb the stairs together, but give me a few weeks and I'll race you to the top, Kentaro Fujiwara!'

Part Three

Diminutive Song Sparrow
partner of the sunrise
taps on my windowpane
to call me
from vain dreaming
a self-defined task
to alert me
to each new morning
warning
that there is but one today

Part Three
Chapter 1

Yuki took three-year-old Hiro to room seven at the Institute for his weekly lesson. She felt proud of him now that he had been promoted to playing a real violin instead of the tissue box and ruler model. As participating parent, she was required to learn, too. Be ahead of her son at first. Her own full size instrument had been specially made for her at the Suzuki factory in Nagoya, and she loved playing it. Already she had advanced to playing a Japanese folk song. As well, she had done all the things that Chiyo, her teacher, had asked her to do. She had faithfully played the music which Kentaro's recording studio had dubbed on to a mini disc, and practised bow games and violin games with Hiro. He was eager to learn, and already seemed to know so much!

She had laughed with Kentaro over breakfast just this morning. 'I never had to do this for Jiro because you took him over. If I had, I might have been playing concertos by now.'

Kentaro laughed, too. 'I can't let you get better than I am, pet. That would never do.' Kentaro was buoyant, his old self now that he had a little son. But it had not been an easy road and it pained him to remember.

Hamish had visited them in Japan. When Yuki opened the door to him, she did not recognise this tall thin man with a trimmed beard and cool manner. Yet, there was this accent, the way he said her name and of course, when he said his name. She was so embarrassed.

'Hamish, of course. You are welcome. Please come in.'

Six months had passed since Hiro's birth, and she had regained her strength.

'You look very well, Yuki.'

'I am, thank you. Very well.'

Hamish knew that it would have been courteous to let

them know he was coming but he was not going to risk being turned down. 'A lot has happened since I saw you', he said, slipping on the footwear he was being offered. 'But, first, tell me about your wee son.' He was on shaky ground, assuming the boy had been safely born. He was relieved to hear Yuki say, 'He's a great little chap.' A baby's cry from a room some distance away brought light to his doleful eyes. He stood still for a moment and looked enquiringly at Yuki. She was standing on the floor of the house and he had not yet mounted the step from the foyer. Pity welled up in her. She could tell from his appearance that he was miserable. 'Here. I'll take your coat.' He gave it over, gladly, and looked more comfortable in his blue sweatshirt and brown trousers. 'Yes, that's our baby Hiro. You must see him. Come with me.'

She turned to him and smiled. 'He is beautiful. Perfect.'

As he followed Yuki to a bedroom at the back of the house, he said. 'And Kentaro? Is he well? And what about that lovely boy, Ichiro. His finger?'

'Both very well, thank you. That is if you ignore the nightmares and taunting that poor Ichiro endures!' She was now whispering. The crying had stopped and she was not going to wake Hiro – not for Hamish, not for anyone. 'Take a peek.'

Hamish stood looking down on the small face showing above the covers. He was mesmerised. Yuki waited a minute or two, then coughed softly, but he did not move. Suddenly he turned to Yuki. His eyes were fiery and, at the same time sad. Tears ran down his cheeks. He dabbed at his eyes with a tissue. She beckoned to him to leave the room and he followed her along the hall to the living room.

'I'll make you some tea,' she said, 'Then we can talk.' Together, they exchanged their present slippers for others neatly lined up at the *shoji* screen.

As she made the tea she said, 'Kentaro will want to see you now that you are here. I'll call him to come home. Please wait.' Twenty minutes later Kentaro burst into the room and walked to Hamish, who rose from his chair to greet him.

'Hamish. I should have guessed that you would come.'

Kentaro sensed bad news, and invited their guest to sit again. Yuki served tea, then sat to share tea with them and hear why Hamish had come. But Hamish had some catching up to do himself.

'Before I tell you my news, please tell me about the birth.' He had addressed Yuki. She smiled. 'Easy and quick at the Matsumoto birthing centre. No complications. Then when I got back home to Kentaro and Ichiro it was as if Hiro knew his routine already.' She leaned a little nearer to Hamish and said, 'It's like he's been here before!'

'Oh, yes! That's mothers' talk,' laughed Kentaro. 'And he'll be out of naps soon. And walking and running way ahead of time!'

The ice had been broken, and Hamish did all he could to stop himself trembling. He stirred sugar into a second cup of tea, plagued by thought that he alone knew the reason why this child was unreasonably advanced for his age, and that the whole scenario being played out in his very presence was proof of yet another of his theories – that if you clone from a child, you get a child. Clone from an adult, and you get an adult. All he could say was, 'I want to say I'm glad you didn't get in touch.'

Kentaro and Yuki exchanged glances that expressed disbelief.

'Yes,' Hamish continued, 'it's been a terrible time for my Institute. Especially for me. After little Rose, our baby girl, was born it was as if something powerful and menacing – another avalanche – had been let loose. I received death threats and developed paranoia about that. But saddest of all, Mary became extremely ill. It was worse than the usual postnatal depression. Clinically, it's termed puerperal psychosis. It was not diagnosed until she got to Scotland. At the hospital in Italy, she couldn't stand to hear the baby cry. The wee thing cried all night, and Mary began to think she was crying in the daytime, too. In fact, she began to call the child

Trish and expected her to talk to her. Its true, the baby was just like Trish had been at the same age.'

Hamish looked about him as if wanting some support. He was finding this difficult, and Yuki and Kentaro held on, nodding a little to keep him talking. 'Mary was deluded and I didn't realise. So I let her return to Scotland thinking that that would cure her. Janice, my sister, rang sometimes and sounded desperate. Finally she rang to say that the doctor had admitted Mary to hospital because she said strange things. Things like, "I can't take it, sir. Where did this baby come from? I hate babies. I can't bear it. I'm too busy being Queen."'

He knew then that it was an acute illness, and had requested permission to administer ECT.

Yuki's memory of Mary in the women's room at the restaurant was such a picture of joy that she could not believe what Hamish was saying. Yet, the international news pictures after the birth were of a very different Mary. She was fighting the tears as she took in what Hamish was saying. He sat clasping and unclasping his hands. He had not told the whole story yet, and was summoning the courage to continue. He cleared his throat and blew his nose then said, 'I should have gone to her then. But I believe now I was out of my mind.' Tears dripped to his lap without touching his cheeks. 'I should have gone to Mary then, but I didn't. I told myself that she wouldn't recognise me, and I should go maybe after another week. If I'd gone when she asked me, she might be here today. I never saw her again alive. It was only after she was pulled from the firth and lay silent as stone in the funeral parlour, that I saw her.'

Yuki and Kentaro sat in total silence until Yuki rushed out of the room. The men heard her weeping. Kentaro knew that she was at Jiro's shrine, and would be there some time. Softly, he said to Hamish, 'I'm very sorry, Hamish. Very sorry.' Hamish's bowed head lifted in acknowledgement, then fell on to his chest again. He buried his head in his hands.

After the funeral in the Queensferry Parish Church, he had gone alone to the place where Mary had last stood. He asked the cab driver to wait.

'My wife's funeral was today. She drowned here.'

'I say now, that was bad.'

'Aye it was bad.'

A chilly wind blew into his face from off the grey water. Mist hung around the boats. What he had been told was that Mary had walked into the icy-cold water. He was at that place now. She had drowned almost at once because of heart failure. So well she might have, but he knew why she walked in there. He knew that she was ill, needed to escape the crying baby, needed to escape her illusions that this was Trish all over again. The doctors had known that her depression was not postnatal depression but puerperal psychosis. That's what they said. She had this terrible affliction. Yet they had told him that they thought she was much better. Their treatment had worked. She had stopped seeing herself as Queen Margaret! Even laughed when the doctor told her. Yes, she was much improved. Had been discharged. And the baby? Janice and she had to make a schedule so that they each got four hours sleep before caring for the crying child again. Oh, what a difficult baby. And so like Trish at the same tender age.

The water lapped six steps away from his feet. He hugged himself to find warmth. Mary, Mary, if only you were here now. Rose is a great little girl. Her own person. Trish was not so sweet. But Mary my love, I cloned her for you as much as myself. Och, Mary. We were so happy. The price has been too high. I need you. You keep returning. A homing pigeon. I cannot live like this, Mary.

We have to say goodbye.

The cabby felt concerned. Sat on the horn. Hamish stopped sobbing and snivelling and stood to his full height, straightened his coat lapels, and breathed in the chilly air. He strode to the cab. 'I'm ever so sorry, sir. You've waited a long time.'

'I was worried about you, sir.' He started the engine once Hamish was seated beside him.

Yuki and Hiro were expected for their lesson. Yuki knocked before entering the studio. On going in, they took their seats at the back of the room. Chiyo gave them a smile and continued teaching. She was hearing the little girl her poem to round off her lesson, and said the first line of one of Hiro's favourites *'saekaeru/ima sakura saku …'* and Hiro, in a voice which was much louder than the girl's said *'wasurijimo'*. The teacher and the other two parents and children sitting watching the lesson laughed. The mother of the little girl was not so sure. She whispered to her daughter something that no one could hear. The child bowed as the teacher asked her to place her violin in her case. Then she gave the girl a big hug and said, 'You did very well, today, Temoku.'

Yuki spoke crossly to Hiro. 'It wasn't your turn, Hiro. You must only answer when it is you that's being asked.' She turned to his teacher. 'I'm sorry,' she said, loudly, and she and Hiro took their violins from their cases and went forward for their lesson.

Part Three
Chapter 2

Warren asked the leading question.

'You used to call CT a man of straw?'

'We did. And you might have guessed that's why I went busking near that quaint figure in the park. For a while I liked the name, the association. You see I didn't believe Joachim's story of how he led young guys up the garden path. Not even after he dropped me. Sounds stupid even to my ears now. But I believed he'd come back to me, love me again. When I played near that straw man I was, if you like, wooing him.' His face twitched terribly and Andreas saw the tea cup shaking in his hand.'

'So?'

'Well, Joachim went away for a while, and then one night he reappeared. He looked evil. Demented you might say. He asked me if I believed him yet, and since CT had continued to spurn me, I felt more and more wounded. Yes, I believed Joachim and said so.'

Andreas put down his cup, now empty, and put his head into his knees and sobbed. Since he had been tearful once before, Warren was less dismayed than he might have been. He made more tea and refilled both cups. When he had done this, Andreas sniffed, blew his nose and said, 'Thanks.' He drank the second cup straight off.

'Do you know that I didn't even stop Joachim doing what he said he was going to do?'

He looked directly at Warren, his face still. But his eyes belied disgust for himself.

'I didn't turn a hair when he said he was going to – deal to him.

'You knew?'

'I knew of the threat but didn't believe he intended to murder him. We joked! I suggested he replace the body of the straw man in Springbank Park, with CT. We laughed our heads off it was so absurd!'

'Andreas, do you realise that you were partner in the crime? You could – maybe should – have been taken to trial just as Joachim. Do you know that?' Warren paced about anxious to know now what to do. If he did not tell someone, he too could be accused of complicity. Oh my God. What do I do? He sat down again.

'Andreas, listen carefully. Who was the detective on the case?'

'That's where the complicity lies! That bastard! When they had caught Joachim and held him in prison, he asked to see me. We had five minutes with bars between us. He told me that he'd paid him to be quiet about the details. Said he had the backing of ten young gays back in the Czech Republic, and they would give evidence at his trial there.'

'But there is one thing I don't understand.'

'And what is that?'

'Why was Joachim the one to do it?'

Andreas was composed again. Warren watched him for signs of strain. He didn't move for quite some time. Warren waited.

'Joachim had AIDS. He was the only one who hadn't practised safe sex. He was likely to die. And incidentally, so was CT, except that somehow he was stronger and in remission.'

Warren was feeling rung out. He had had a big day and was tired. But this, this was like falling from a boat under the Niagara Falls. The force was uncontrollable within him. It overtook all boundaries of stories that he had called "Hot, Breaking News". They paled into insignificance. Here was a revelation that, at minimum, was a millstone about his neck, at maximum, was as explosive as a bomb blast. There was not just the murder, there was the whole problem of HIV. Could he bear to ask the question that was on his lips? He took a deep breath and said, 'Andreas, have you got AIDS?'

Andreas looked calm. White but calm.

'No! Absolutely not. I'm all right. I'm well, safe. Yes. CT kept me safe, thank *Gott!* Safe.'

Warren was silent, trying to make some sense of the whole sordid saga. He knew that he was not going to do anything about this. Here was a young man of high ability with his life ahead of him. He was not going to do anything to spoil that. If the law had not found the answers, well too bad. CT was dead. Maybe Joachim too, by now. No-one could verify Andreas' story.

Andreas stood up and said, 'Thanks, Warren. I'll call a cab. You've helped me, you have. I know that when I wake tomorrow, I shall feel like a new person. But that park, it still gets to me when I play there. Tainted a good thing, actually. I used to love it.' He was smiling. Looked beautiful. Tired but whole. He turned to speak to Warren after calling the car. 'One silly little thing and my confession is over. The original straw man's body, well it's now stuffing the settee in my apartment. Too bad you won't get a chance to sit on it sometime and find out how uncomfortable it is.'

Warren laughed. As Andreas stood by the open door, he hugged him and said, 'I'll have to say this, Andreas, but I'm really glad you're going to Berlin. Just don't lumber me with your couch!'

Andreas didn't ask why. The reason was obvious. 'I know I've put a lot on your shoulders. But believe me, I didn't think Joachim would really carry out the threat. I guess you could say I played Devil's advocate.'

Warren nodded with puckered lips, as if to bring the whole thing to a conclusion. 'Sleep well.' And then he added, 'I'll listen for new vigour in your playing at the wedding,' and smiled, warmly. 'I know Tom can barely wait.'

Andreas smiled too. 'You most certainly will,' he said with enthusiasm. *'Ciao'*. The door closed behind him. He paused to take a long look at the tree-lined avenue, breathed the fresh air deeply into his lungs, and flew down the steps to the waiting cab.

Part Three
Chapter 3

Donna woke early on Saturday morning because she was hearing a song sparrow pecking at her window. She marvelled that on each of the three mornings she had been staying with her aunt and uncle on their estate at Keswick Ridge, she had heard the same sounds – the pecking and fluttering, then the song. It was as if she had a new friend.

She went to the window and looked out. The bird had disappeared, but the May sun caught the spokes of an old cart wheel, trapped the branches and leaves of the maples, and sent patterns of light and shadow to dance across the yard. It was seven o'clock, and she knew that her aunt would not yet be up. On the other hand, Uncle JJ would be out in the garden digging over the soil. She would dress and join him.

When she got as far as the hallway door he was taking off his boots, so she said, 'Let me make the tea, Uncle JJ. I'll have mine with you today instead of in bed, for once!'

They sat either side of the small table from where Donna could look out on the acres of young Christmas trees. Uncle JJ stirred his two spoons of sugar and took a gulp of tea.

'So he's a nice guy, this Warren of yours, is he now?'

Donna blushed a little. 'I think so. I've known him for five years, in fact we've had this on-going affair for four, and he insists it's time I moved in with him. I insist on being married first. It's not just him. He has a son of ten, and I want to do things properly for his sake.'

'That's my girl. There's not many as think like that nowadays.' He smiled, and Donna marvelled at how his skinny face radiated sunshine. She smiled at him.

'Well, I want to include Tom in the wedding, and make him feel part of the marriage. His mother doesn't live far away actually, so I don't want to give him a reason for running back to her. But I didn't say, did I, that I've been Tom's violin teacher since he was six and he's called me Donna – always.' She laughed. 'When I first met Tom we were at a summer camp at Banff. He was quite a lad. Asked me to call him Thomas. Very proper, he was!'

'More tea?' said her uncle after chuckling about the young lad. 'There's more in the pot.'

'No thanks.'

'So the wedding's real soon?'

'Very soon. I leave here on Tuesday, and the wedding is next Saturday.' She looked at her eighty-five year old uncle and said, 'Too bad you and Aunty Beth can't be there. You're my nearest and dearest now.'

'Oh, we're too old for gallivanting. And there's always jobs to do. The garden takes all my energy now.'

'When you sell up, perhaps you could stay with us for a change of air.'

His thin, weathered face lit up and she marveled again how much it reflected a sense of fun and adventure.

'Good idea, I reckon. But when we'll sell up I can't imagine!'

Donna smiled. In her heart she knew it was very unlikely. Christmas trees had been his life. Nurturing an unbroken succession of trees, selling the seven-year-old ones trimmed and ready to grace some family's lounge room at Christmas, and planting replacements – it was never ending. And so it would go on.

'Whatever happens, Uncle JJ, I shall always be grateful for this break. And all the other holidays I've had here. You and aunty have always been marvellous to me.'

His face looked a little sad. Bony. 'You've been the nearest we've had to a daughter. We've loved you like you have been.'

She felt tearful as the old man spoke his heart. He was usually very restrained. But with Aunty Beth being so bothered by arthritis, he was feeling more sentimental, and probably lonely too. At one time she was always up with the lark and out-of-doors working beside him.

In the quietness of the moment, Donna noticed that the old clock ticked loudly. She loved that clock. 'Uncle JJ, please tell me the story behind your old clock.'

Suddenly his face lit up, and he told the story he loved to tell, no matter that Donna already knew it.

'It was in the late 1800s, it was, and owned by my father the coal-miner. You knew him, didn't you?'

'Only because photos remind me. I was so very young when he was alive.'

'Well, then, the story goes that there were massive mines full of coal that only the locals of Canmore knew about. They dug it out at Pine Pass just for themselves.' He laughed, and his eyes sparkled at the wickedness of it. 'Mind you, if it had been me, I'd have been tight-lipped too. Such hard times those, and coal gave them a life.' He walked over to the clock, and Donna got up too. 'Look here, you can see how black it is, especially from the bottom up, it fades a bit up here.' He placed his hand over the curved panel that adorned the top. 'That's all because this clock sat on the mantle shelf above the coal-burning stove for over forty years. We've never done more than dust it over. It's such a bit of history, it is.'

Donna marveled at a clock being so black and shiny and exclaimed to her uncle about it. It kept perfect time, she had been assured, and never seen it wrong herself.

'And the secret mine? It eventually got out that it was there, didn't it?'

The old man laughed and laughed. It was a memory full of his father's bragging about how long it was before the government took it over, and yarns and serendipity about how they blew the mine apart. 'They grabbed the lot!'

Donna gave her uncle a kiss on the cheek. 'Thanks, Uncle JJ. It's been good to hear that tale again. I'm going to practise my violin now. Catch you later.'

'And it's time I was back in my garden, too,' he said. 'The

song sparrow called me back a good half hour ago, and here I've been yarning on,' he laughed, as he went to put on his boots.

Later in the day, her aunt was up, and wanting to take a walk around the property.

'Donna, leave that violin alone for a bit and come and walk through the maple grove, why don't you?' She said it with an air of one who had worked so hard on the land that this was her music, her concerto. She needed to take centre stage for a bit.

'Sure. I'd love to.' Donna placed her violin and bow in their case, and put it on top of the piano which her aunt insisted, should not be strewn with sheet music.

'So what was that you were practising?' Her aunt was already in her outdoor shoes and a jacket and was watching Donna get into hers.

'Oh, from the Paganini *Twenty-Four Variations* – number five, that one.'

'I liked it. Will you pass me my stick – there by the door – good, thank you. Now we're ready.'

They walked slowly along the wide driveway past the vegetable garden and the large shed where special machinery was housed. 'See that vat, just there? Well JJ is making berry jams and compotes and has a lovely little home industry going.'

'Do you help him?'

'No, he has a lad come in the season, just for that. We've been eating that jam for lunch. That's it. Good, isn't it?'

'I thought it was better than the bought stuff. Yes, it's wonderful.'

They passed the berry garden and entered the grove. Aunty Beth's eyes scanned the ground both under her feet and out, beyond the grove. She saw everything. Every tiny flower, every change in a leaf. She knew her score like the best conductor. Suddenly she stopped. 'See, this flower almost hidden,' she said. 'It is blood root. It stays close to the earth.' Her ears alerted her to a sound. She stood erect and looked beyond the trees, again. Quietly she said, 'Look, the mother fox.'

Donna saw the sleek chestnut body, every limb alert to sounds and sights, ears standing sharply tall. 'Oh, look at that!' Behind the mother fox, scampered two young foxes. 'So that's why she's on guard.'

'I see them every year in the same place.'

'What a lovely sight. Look, they're frolicking.' They watched them, smiles on their faces, entranced, not wanting to disturb them.

Aunty Beth took Donna's arm and guided her around some trees on their left. 'I want to ask you about your man. Is he handsome?'

Donna laughed, partly because she knew that her aunt had an ulterior motive for taking her walking, and partly because she knew that her aunty believed that one should marry well.

'Oh, I think so. He is, well a gentle person. Yes, he's a bit taller than me, has mousy coloured hair that he ties back, and I like the way he carries himself. He's rather self-opinionated, but in the right way. He's a journalist and photographer, and he needs his confidence to get the hot stories. Sometimes has to barge right in. You know. Nose out the hidden truth. Get that one and only best photo. All very pushy, really.'

Her aunt laughed. 'And quite profitable I hope.' That was a straight-forward comment but Donna knew she was fishing.

She held firmly to Donna's arm, and now stopped close to a maple. 'See this tree? See how the bark is healed after the tapping? Marvellous isn't it. We'll have maple syrup on ice-cream for supper, we will. You can't leave here without eating some of last season's. It was wonderfully sweet. But come on, tell me about this man of yours.'

'Remember when that Toronto scientist cloned a child that

had the Alzheimer's gene removed?'

'Oh, yes. Sure I do. I felt happy for Alzheimer's sufferers. Splendid achievement. Wish they could do it for arthritics.'

Donna stroked the old lady's bent fingers. She teased her aunt. 'I'll get Warren to suggest it to Keith Robertson. But seriously, Warren broke that story, and he's in the scientist's inner sanctum now. Follows him all around the place when he gives talks and so on. Warren gets his notes ahead of lectures. Robertson won't let anyone else have them. He's made big money, has Warren, from that one association.'

'Oh, I'm pleased to hear it. He'll look after you, then?'

Donna laughed. 'Of course he will. But I'm my own person too. In fact, Warren is going to move to London – Ontario, that is – so that I can teach at MAAC. I've got a job there. It's a wonderful opportunity. I have specialist knowledge in relaxed string playing. That's my favourite kind of teaching. Remedial work. But ordinary violin teaching as well. It's a good job.'

They were back on the gravel driveway again. Her aunt's arm was heavy on Donna's, and she puffed a little but she chatted on.

'I know what you mean about journalists. They're judge and jury as well as detective. I've seen it happen. Here in our community. Especially on the tele.'

'Aren't they ever!' Donna agreed, eyes full of knowing.

Her aunt stopped at the door to put back her stick. She removed her outdoor clothes. 'You said that Warren trails the scientist. Who looks after his wee boy?'

'Not too wee. He's ten. And Warren's had a very good arrangement. A young violinist is doing his doctorate and stays overnight, sometimes for nights on end now. He looks after Tom. They're great mates.'

The screen door swung back as soon as unlocked, and Donna held the heavy maple door for her aunt. 'Andreas is just about finished his degree, so that means he'll take a job somewhere. Maybe back in Europe, I guess. Then I'll be looking after Tom quite a bit.'

Aunty Beth patted her arm as Donna closed the door after them. 'You now. Don't leave having your babies until too late like we did!'

'Oh, Aunt. Is that why?'

She laughed, and pulled at Donna's sleeve. She took her to a corner of the lounge where a wooden stand held a large earthen pot. 'See this plant?'

Donna looked at the leathery leaves and said, 'Yes, I see it.'

'Well,' said Aunty Beth, 'this plant is like me. It hasn't flowered yet! And we've had it for forty years or more!'

'And you keep it?'

'Oh, yes. One day it will flower! Its time will come, you'll see.'

Donna smiled to herself. What will we see?

Part Three
Chapter 4

The day Hamish had met Terri, his wife of four months, was the day he was full of the news about Robertson's cloned child. He was feeling miffed at the internationally acclaimed event which put him in second place, at best. But as time went on, he found support in this new gynaecologist who had joined Bill's team, and began to go to her for advice. She revived his enthusiasm for cloning, and was willing to implant foetuses, take some risks in the name of genetic engineering. Had even supported his making of three healthy babies for the detestable Gianfranco, attended the births and baptisms of the children and along with Hamish, had cut the cake at their first birthday. But best of all she adored Rose.

'You know Hamish, Rose is special. I feel privileged to have a daughter cloned by you. Your superb skill, your brain, they made Rose what she is. She's a great kid. I never feel that she is soon to be four, but fourteen! I adore her company.'

For Hamish, the turning point for him after all the sadness and the torment he had endured, had been his trip to Japan. Talking to Yuki and Kentaro had sorted out a lot of stuff that had been unresolved. Seeing them in their home and confirming the birth of a strong, healthy baby, had been a tonic. The Fujiwaras were so self-assured, that he had decided against enlightening them about using Jiro's DNA, not Ichiro's. Not just yet, anyway. And he had not cared that news of his second cloning was not broadcast. He could not have survived another barrage of poisonous letters just then. Not even with the acclaim.

He noted the time as he prepared to check the latest batch of embryos and call Terri to implant them, if ready. He was almost trembling with excitement as he entered the heat-controlled lab. He always had these feelings of nervous excitement, even though it seemed so ordinary now that his success rate had sky-rocketed. The successful cloning of Gianfranco three times over, had done wonders not only for him and the team but for Gianfranco. For some private reason, Roberto had re-considered his request and wanted to wait, so it had been Giano's goading which had given him a goal to live for after Mary had died. It had carried him from despair to success. From then on, and especially when he had Rose back from staying with her aunt in Scotland, he began to live again. And now that he had a new wife, he was feeling like a re-invented man. After checking the embryos, he paged Terri. 'It's all go, Terri. Within the hour, if you can. I'll send them over now.'

'That's good. Yes. I'll bring in the women. Get things ready.'

Now that the embryos were on their way, Hamish walked along the extended glassed-in corridors that brought the colourful outdoor gardens into view. It made the walk to the new complex – where he expected he would find the industrious Bertha – a delight. He rather coveted her modern laboratory and large staff, but was assured that without his research into cloning none of this expansion would have happened. He suspected she would be working adjacent to the inner chambers, so walked quickly past the banks of mice and piglets, saying the odd 'Hello' to staff, to where there was a faint whiff of rhesus monkeys, and there she was talking to the white-coated Muriana. He overheard Bertha say, 'We've done it!' as she threw her arms into the air and swung her large body around. Muriana was laughing. Then as the pirouette ended in a hug, Hamish moved in close and whispered, 'What have you done?'

Bertha had not noticed him. She jumped. 'Oh, *mein Gott!* Hamish we have succeeded. Let me tell you. Come, sit in my office. This deserves a celebration.'

'I'm not joining you,' Muriana said. 'I'm off to write it up for Hugh. Time to get it on to the net.

Seated at a small round table together, Bertha served coffee and talked at the same time. 'It's nothing you don't already know, but until we saw it with our eyes – that the skin cell from our little Alpha the rhesus had begun to grow into a liver – which is what I'm saying is happening in the chambers this very minute, until then we didn't know it would work. But it has worked. Hamish, it's too good to be true. *Ja, ja, ja.* A liver from a skin cell?'

'If you can do that then you can make any number of body parts.'

'That's right. That's right. We're freer to do this. With using stem cells we had the Pope frowning at us, we had numerous other bodies damning us to hell, but this? Well, it's seen as being more ethical.'

Hamish's phone beeped out its tune, *Ye Banks* ... 'Hello.'

'Hi, Hamish. I wanted to tell you that the first woman has come in and she's as happy as a princess.'

'Good one, Terri. And guess what Bertha's done?'

'I'll guess. From skin she's cloned a heart muscle.'

'No. Liver!'

'Superb! Congratulations! Must go.'

'Right. Bye.'

Bertha's glasses were down her nose and she was humming softly. She smiled.

'You've got this bonny braes song on your mobile. Groovy, eh?'

'Och! It's a laugh. I'll keep it a week, then go back to beeps.'

In the evening, when Rose was asleep, Hamish felt more relaxed than he had in years. He put on a CD of ballroom music, and knowing that Terri excelled in ballroom dancing, he invited her to dance. She loved this romantic intimacy which they had developed, but always expressed evocative surprise. 'Why, I'd love to, Hamish McLeod!'

Their cheeks pressed in a slow waltz. He spoke softly as he said, 'Would you come to Japan, with me? Take a two-week break?' He had been waiting for the right moment. The time when he could leave his work for two weeks, and visit the Fujiwaras again. Some time, even well into the future, he believed that family would welcome publicity. Kentaro could show the world that it was possible to produce a first rate violinist to order, as it were. Hamish was determined to keep seeing them, watch Hiro's progress.

The music changed dramatically to a cha-cha. Terri's slim and perfumed body inspired and lured Hamish into a vigorous response. They swung and dipped about their living room as if it were a large dance hall, and they, competitors in the international arena.

'I'd love to. And yes, this is a suitable time.' As always when the last dance ended, they had a spa, and went up to bed naked. First to peel an orange and eat it, accompanied by a glass of Chardonnay, laugh together and then to make passionate love.

The phone-call which Yuki took sent cold shivers down her spine. Why will Hamish not leave them alone? 'Of course I would like to meet your wife and Rose. Yes, please come at 8 o'clock this evening. I'll make sure that Kentaro joins us for dinner.'

'Who was that, Mummy?' Hiro was her watch-dog.

'A friend. He lives in Italy and is holidaying right here. He is bringing his wife and child to meet us.'

Yuki knew that Hiro would stay up, and would also decide when he would go to bed. In just this last week, Yuki felt that her young son was out of her control. She felt frightened. As soon as they returned from their music lesson, she had talked to him again about not answering with a line to complete a *haiku* when the teacher was asking someone else. She had said, 'Unless it is you who is having the lesson, you stay quiet, please. Do you hear me, Hiro?'

'But I can't. I know the answers and I'm going to say them.'

At the next lesson he had done just that, so Yuki, feeling very angry with him, suggested to the teacher that they would wait outside until lesson time in future. She wanted to discourage her son from answering for anyone else. Chiyo had offered a better idea. She would like to teach him in her schedule of advanced players, and he could listen to the girl prior to him if they came at 5 o'clock. That way, he would get some inspiration. It was working better this way, though she did not get a lesson herself. She would never get on to concertos at this rate, she inwardly confessed, with amusement.

It was a shock to Kentaro to learn that Hamish McLeod was bringing a new wife and his daughter Rose to dinner. Ichiro would drag himself away from his study and join them for the meal at the very last minute, but Yuki had said she wished that she could have Hiro in bed by seven. Out of the way! He did not like cancelling a lesson, but to support Yuki he did, and cycled home in time to tidy himself and await the visitors.

Nervous and tired but dressed for the occasion in black skirt and floral blouse, Yuki was ready. The house was cleaned and tidy. The doorbell sounded and she answered it, graciously bowing to Terri whom, she decided, was Italian aristocracy – tall, elegant, and well groomed. Yuki had brought out some Japanese slippers for each one of them including some in Rose's size. Rose said, 'They're pretty. *Arigato gozaimashita, Fujiwara san,*' with such poise that Yuki was rather taken aback.

'Please come in. Kentaro is waiting.'

Hiro came running out from his bedroom. 'Hello. Hello.' He stopped when he saw the strangers and, turning on his heels, he ran back to his room and slammed the door.

'Hiro,' his mother called. 'Come back.' And to the visitors she said, 'I'll go and get him in a minute. Please excuse his rudeness. He wasn't nice, was he, Rose?'

Kentaro, Hamish and Terri sat together in the lounge room and they conversed at once, in spite of the fact that Kentaro barely recognised the well-groomed person that Hamish had become. He kept casting his memory about to recall what he looked like when they met in Austria at the ceremony to dedicate the memorial. He had looked ill. This was a new Hamish.

Yuki had Rose on a stool beside her at the kitchen table where she was showing some photographs of the kindergarten which Hiro would attend as soon as there was a vacancy. 'It's made from Canadian cedar for the wonderful smell,' she said. 'Rose, come with me and we'll find Hiro shall we?'

They walked hand in hand to Hiro's room and found him playing with his trains as if no one else existed.

'Hiro, this is Rose and she's come all the way from Italy to see you.'

He made the sound of a train whistle and ignored his mother. 'Hiro,' she said going to the switch and turning it off. 'I want you to let Rose play too.'

He looked sulkily from the *shinkansen* he was about to put on the rails to a train standing idle at the station. 'She can have the number sixteen.'

'Thank you,' Yuki said. 'Now you be nice to Rose.' She smiled at the little girl.

'I'm sure you'll get along when I'm not here,' she said.

'But if you need me just come to the lounge again. OK?' To Hiro she said, 'Give your visitor a good time now. I'll call you when it's time for supper.'

When she joined the adults, Yuki heard the tail-end of a conversation about the extraordinarily beautiful tulips that had been grown in northern Italy in the spring. 'Artists and photographers have come in droves,' Terri said.

'And, tourists?'

'Oh, yes. I believe it's been impossible for everyone to be accommodated. But oh, well, that's the way it goes. They usually end up by going away from the main cities to the coast or further up the lake.'

Kentaro wanted to get on to the subject which he knew was the motivation for the visit, so he looked at Hamish and said, 'The world has come a long way towards acceptance of cloning in the past four years, wouldn't you agree?'

'Undoubtedly! There've been two enormous developments, and our Biotech Centre is responsible for one of them. There's the mapping of the human gene, and in our lab the use of a cell from skin to grow any body part required. That is major because it means that blood, heart muscles, livers, nerves, you name it – they can be produced from a cell of skin. The big step forward needless to say, is that we can change one cell into another and no longer have to rely on stem cells. We have knowledge we didn't dream about when you were in Italy. But, it's been a personal journey as well. I've managed to get beyond the small-mindedness of, for example, the Church of Scotland which had been so influential in my early life. Lost that crippling fear which, although I didn't tell you about was very real to me.'

Terri said, 'We were all afraid, I think.'

'Yeah, and all working behind closed doors. A lot still are I hasten to add.'

'Oh, yes,' said Terri, 'Even though many of the public want cloned babies, success is anything but guaranteed, so it's a huge concern in fact.'

'We've a long way to go, but I for one feel that we need to keep persisting with it. And many others seem to have reached a similar conclusion.'

Yuki wanted to know more on the publicity front. 'I haven't read of successfully created babies. How many have you made?'

The two visitors were not willing to answer outright. Hamish said, 'We're not going public with photos splashed about any more – for the sake of the children.'

Terri supported this view, and didn't want to reveal anything more.

'As a gynaecologist I have come to cloning from a different standpoint. So many men can't have children now. Pollution in the atmosphere, chemicals in food and the high life have caused so much sterility amongst men that couples are demanding that we clone a child for them. We can relieve their mental pain, it is beautiful to see. I love my work for that reason.'

Yuki took her cue from Terri. She spoke strongly. Kentaro was uneasy about the note of cynicism in his wife's voice. 'So we will not need men, the next generation can be all women?'

Attempting to temper Yuki's extreme opinion, Kentaro said, 'Terri is making a very good point.'

Rose burst into the room screaming, 'I don't like that boy, Mummy.'

'Rose. Come here please and tell me what the problem is.' Terri beckoned her daughter.

She sniffed and spluttered and shook a wrist. 'He's bossing me about. He twisted my hand.'

Kentaro left the room saying, 'Excuse me,' and went to see what Hiro had done.

'Hiro, you want to tell me what's been happening here?'

Hiro was lying face down on the floor watching a train pull away from the station. 'Nothing.'

Kentaro turned off the power switch and said, 'Hiro. Come here, please.' The child had pressed his face to the floor. He mumbled into the matting words that his father didn't want to hear: 'You can't boss me.'

'Come here right now.' He was sitting down and he slapped his knee hoping that Hiro would come without delay.

Instead, he got up from the floor, opened his violin case and played the opening phrase of *Sakura*. Kentaro was silenced. Overwhelmed. He had only heard the "ladder" games, and mostly missed out on listening to his practice because Yuki had taken responsibility for it. Besides had he not just got his real violin? He clapped his hands in applause for the child. Hiro was all smiles, very pleased with himself.

'Come and tell Rose you are sorry. Play your violin for her, and she will feel better.'

'I don't know what you mean.'

'Well, come and play, any way.'

Looking pleased with himself, Hiro followed his dad to the lounge with his violin in his hand. His father affected a smile.

'Hiro will say he's sorry and then play for us. I'm sure we'll all feel better when he's played.'

Yuki was about to say – 'But he can only play up and down the D string. We have to practise so that his fingers fall in the right place every time. Chiyo said …'

Hiro put his violin up, glanced at Rose, said, 'Sorry', then placed his bow on the A string, and played *Sakura* with very good intonation. Yuki was speechless. She patted Hiro and said, 'When did you learn that?'

Ichiro had come into the room after hearing the screaming. He was introduced to the visitors and acted as if he did not know Hamish. He answered for Hiro.

While he listened, Hamish found it difficult to reconcile this boy with the deep voice, with the boy whose finger he had taken skin from over four years ago.

'I taught him,' Ichiro said.

Everyone looked at Ichiro waiting for an explanation. 'Yes, in the morning when I was practising the piano. He asked me to play it with him and he seemed to already know it. Then we played a Chopin melody – one that Jiro …'

'Yes. Yes. Now we must have our meal. Please help me Ichiro, and please excuse me everyone.' With a little bow, Yuki left the room. Ichiro also.

Once they entered the kitchen, Yuki closed the *shoji* and said, 'Ichiro. What's this about Hiro knowing what Jiro knew?'

'It's true, Mum. He played three pieces like he knew them.

Folk songs and Chopin like I said.'

Yuki felt very uneasy. 'Please don't do that any more. Hiro and I have our lessons with Chiyo. She is our teacher and tells us what we must practise. He's not ready for those things yet.'

'He is ready. But if I can stop him, I will. Mum, why are those people here?'

'You get the table things together, and I'll tell you while I prepare the soup.'

He opened the drawer and started to count the spoons and chopsticks. He listened as carefully as he could but kept losing count. His mother was interrupting too, asking if he remembered Dr McLeod?

'Dr McLeod? Yes, of course I remember. I remember how sore my finger was.' He counted the chopsticks again and said, 'Did he tell you about my DNA? He was going to study my skin. He said so.'

'Oh, yes. But it's so long ago, I'd forget about that if I were you.'

During the meal, after the miso soup had been enjoyed, Yuki left the table to go to the kitchen. 'Excuse me,' she said. 'I'll get the rice.' Ichiro saw his moment.

'Dr McLeod, I can remember you. You took skin from my finger. It was very sore and I felt angry. The tests must have been important. What did they show? You were going to send me the picture of my gene pattern.'

Hamish didn't turn a hair. 'First, I'm sorry that your finger was sore. And I must apologise Ichiro. I forgot to send the print-out. I'm very sorry. About the tests, they showed that you have an exceptional gift. Will you play to us later please?'

Ichiro looked dissatisfied by the answer. 'But at school, our teacher said that you shouldn't have made my finger so sore, just to get my DNA.'

'Dr McLeod knew what he was doing,' Kentaro said.

'Ichiro, go and help your mother carry in the dishes.'

Ichiro turned at the door. 'I believe my teacher, Dr McLeod,' he said, and opened the screen and disappeared.

Kentaro looked directly at Hamish. 'Please forgive him. He's full of himself these days. He'll grow out of it.'

'So will you ever tell all that you know?' He had chosen his words carefully.

Kentaro glanced at the young children sitting side by side, and was happy to see that they had found something to do that was fun.

'I don't know. In fact I find that the hardest part. If he finds out, well, who knows what he will say or do.'

'Ever thought how much value to society it would be if they knew about Hiro, even on no-names terms?'

Just then Yuki, followed by Ichiro, carried in the trays of food and Ichiro placed the small dishes appropriately, saying the name of each condiment aloud. Yuki served each person with rice.

Terri asked Ichiro many questions about his school and music lessons, revealing an intimate knowledge of piano repertoire. Soon everyone was talking about their favourite topics and avoiding anything relating to Austria, Jiro or cloning. Yuki kept a strict eye on Hiro to make certain he continued to be kind to Rose. She thought reluctantly, it will be good when these people go. The chill which came with the phone call had not entirely left her.

Part Three
Chapter 5

'There is nothing, absolutely nothing I can do!'

Hamish, returned from his trip to Japan but twenty-four hours ago, was contacted by Gianfranco at two in the morning. Gianfranco was in the hospital office of the intensive care unit using his cell phone. Hamish could hear him pacing about. The saliva, too much for Giano's mouth – he could hear that too –'Think! For God's sake. Why have these three boys succumbed to a virus when everyone else has a mild dose?'

'Who told you about others?'

'The doctor. Mr Bonticelli. The very best in the whole of Italy. He doesn't know why my boys are so ill.'

'He's the specialist, Gianfranco. I'm merely the embryologist.'

'That scientist in Toronto. He fuckin' took out the Alzheimer's gene. Maybe you put something into my sons which made them soft! Sookies! I'll get you for this. If they die, there'll be repercussions for you. Got that?'

Hamish hung up. Gianfranco, too. 'Blast you. You fuckin' idiot!' he snarled into the floor, and spat over his shoulder.

'Mr Manganaro. Is there something I can do to help?' The young nurse had come from beside a bed, removed her mask and touched him on the shoulder as he peered through the glass wall of the isolation room. Giano was getting tired of telling the staff what they could do to help him. How very special his three sons were. He had pleaded with them all not to let the children die. The least experienced of the nurses had difficulty believing what he said. Thought he was "unstable!" But he knew the three youngsters were special, all right. He knew how little success he had had with women, yet could not see the reason for their shunning him. His mamma had told him repeatedly he was going to be popular with the girls, he was so handsome. Like his grandfather and great grandfather, a veritable Greek god. Never mind that his father had a squashed face and was hunted down by the police. His mother had convinced him, as he pondered his looks in the mirror when he reached adolescence, that it was her antecedents that mattered. He turned to the nurse with impatience and said, 'Those boys. They are very special. Do you know how I got them?'

'Triplets, born a minute or so apart I assume.'

'No. No. No. They are clones of me. Yes, they are me.' He thumped his chest for emphasis. 'Nurse you must not let them die.'

The nurse said, 'I'll get you a chair.'

She detoured to knock at the doctor's room. 'Doctor Franklin, I think Mr Manganaro is unwell.'

'What? Same symptoms as the boys?'

'No. Delirious, or deranged. He claims the boys are clones of him.'

'But they are. Didn't you read the notes?'

The nurse blushed deeply. 'Well, I missed that. Probably couldn't see the words for disbelief! Cloned? It's hard to take that in. So why are these three infants so ill? Is it because they're cloned?'

It had been admitted by the doctor in charge of the ward, to the Head Nurse, that he was completely baffled by the case. It was unknown for anyone to be in need of isolation when suffering from the simple virus that was affecting these children. They were waiting for the very likely occurrence that the father might get it too. However, if he were to present with extreme symptoms, they would be totally baffled.

'Let me know if he faints or vomits,' the doctor asked. 'Otherwise continue to keep a close eye on the boys.'

'I will. But there are three of us with them.'

'And so there should be.'

She hurried back with a chair for Mr Manganaro. He was

gone.

In the distance, a bell echoed through the dimly lit unit. Two reserve nurses threw off rugs which covered them, their sleep interrupted by beeps from their pagers. 'Male found lying near exit three. Bringing him up.' They looked at the panel of lights, and rushed to have the bed in ward three ready for the emergency admission.

'He was out cold,' the orderly said. 'Thought he might be dead. Then he stirred and vomited over my foot.'

'Any idea who he is?' The nurse was taking his pulse. The other removed his shoes now that he was stretched out on the bed. 'Here Jo, help us get him out of his clothes will you?' To the second orderly she said, 'Press that bell for the doctor please.'

'That's Mr Manganaro,' the doctor said, 'Father of the three little boys.' Emergency procedures were followed, tests taken and the staff nurse just arrived on duty was asked to ring the Manganaro household in case a domestic servant answered the call.

'And tell them what, sir?'

'Tell them that we suspect the same virus as his clones have.'

The nurse went white. 'Did you really say clones, doctor?'

'I did. His clones. Might as well get used to that term, Nurse.' He turned to her, and smiled. 'It's a shock when it comes to light the first time. Get yourself a drink before you phone. A few moments won't make any difference. We haven't the faintest idea how to treat the little guys. None at all.'

Hamish got on to the phone to Keith Robertson. 'I'm sorry to trouble you at this time of the morning but I hope you might be able to help me.'

Dr Robertson was not pleased to have his sleep interrupted. He swung his pyjama-clad legs out of bed and bent down to talk into his phone. His wife would murder him if she woke at three in the morning. When Hamish revealed concern about the three cloned boys, Robertson was enraged that he should have been so idiotic as to clone an egocentric man just because he fancied seeing himself go on living.

'You're jumping to conclusions,' Hamish countered.

'I'm not prepared to disclose my reason.'

'Completely understandable. For God's sake man, haven't you come to the only conclusion there is to come to? Clones are particularly susceptible to viruses! Isn't that one of the biggest knowns we have to face? I have no hesitation in saying that I will resist the cloning of anyone who suffers from narcissism.

'But you've cloned very successfully.'

'Look, I cloned for sound medical reasons. Nevertheless the risk is there. Whereas you have done it for the worst of all reasons.'

'That's your opinion.'

It proved impossible to discuss this case rationally with the half-asleep Dr Robertson who kept repeating his deduction that cloning weakened the immune system and would eventually create self-destructing wimps. Hamish attempted to make an overture by asking him if he would be at the geneticists conference in Manchester.

'Of course. I'm giving the keynote address.'

Hamish had been hoping to deliver a paper on his triple success but felt uneasy at the prospect now. Robertson would take all the glory. 'Great. I'll look forward to that then.'

Dr Robertson walked away from the bed and out on to the landing. 'I'd go back to sleep if I were you. But just one more thing. I give my address on the first morning. Be there. Goodnight.'

Part Three
Chapter 6

It was a beautiful morning in London, Ontario. Tom looked out his window to see the goldfinches energetically flicking seed as they ate hungrily at the bird feeder. On the fence, bronze grackles and blue jays preened themselves. They know there's a wedding today! He smiled at the thought. They are up. I am up! He had heard the chirping before he had found his own morning voice. He shouted, 'My dad marries Donna today.' Racing to his father's room he put his hand on his untied hair, and wondered if waking one's father on his wedding day was actually a fair thing to do. Deciding that it was not, he went to the kitchen to get some cereal and milk and ate it watching the television.

He was so engrossed that when Warren shouted 'This is my wedding day!' Tom jumped. He ran to his father.

'I'm in the ceremony too, don't forget. I nearly woke you up but didn't like to. You were dreaming about Donna. You had this ginormous smirk on your face.'

'Tom, you're teasing. But you're right. I have dreamt about Donna every day and every night since that summer camp in Banff.'

They had walked back to the kitchen. Tom put his bowl and spoon into the sink. He turned as his father was pouring out his corn crisps and said, 'Was I a pain then, Dad?'

'Oh, yes.' his father teased. 'A little terror actually. And prim as well – a really odd mixture.'

'How was I prim?'

'Donna will remember. When she asked you what you wanted to be called you said "Thomas."'

'Donna called me Thomas?'

'Of course.'

'What a dork!'

'No, prim.'

'So when do we get ready for the wedding?'

'At a quarter to nine. Good and early. Donna's going to arrive at the Story Book Garden Entrance at ten sharp. So she says. I want to be early. We leave here at ten past nine. Andreas too of course. He wants me to wake him if he's not already up at eight. You need to check that your violin's ready and you're ready to play. That's your job.'

It was still only 7.30 a.m., and yes, he would fill in the time somehow. Playing with Andreas for the wedding would be marvellous, and he would need to be ready with a big tone to match the big guy's. It was like there was too much happening to take it all in. It would be great to live in the city of London, real neat. But a new mom and new school, well it was going to be a lot of stuff. But no two ways about it, this was their second last day in Dorchester and it was the day of the wedding so he had to be ready to make heaps of changes – even to prepare for his first days at Fanshaw High – whether he liked it or not. Blow the honeymoon, though! He would rather his dad was not going away for a few days! But Andreas was going to help him. Good old Andreas.

Donna had spent the night at the Park Royal in London, and was in no hurry to get out of bed until she really had to. She did not want to mooch about trying to fill in time. She had made up her mind to ask for a wake-up call at twenty-five to nine and then there would be a feeling of rush and excitement which she claimed as her right. Her plan was to jog for fifteen minutes, then eat a light breakfast, take a shower and dress. Oh how she longed to wear the lovely dress that her aunty and uncle had paid for. Dear things. They had said, 'It's the least we can do. Just one thing. We want a big photo of you in the dress – with Warren of course.' Her aunty had proved to be very nostalgic about her own wedding over half a century ago. 'I won't say it was the happiest day of my life, but I'd have to say it was pretty near. And,' she added coyly, 'definitely matched by going to bed with your uncle for the first time.'

'Aunty, you're amazing.'

'No, it was Jack who was amazing. Oh, how happy I felt to be his wife. I just wished we'd been twenty and not forty.'

Donna looked long and hard at the soft gold-green dress that hung on an open door. She did not want to put it away in a closet that had been used by who knows how many smelly people? I do not want anyone else's odours to come anywhere near my dress. She smiled now at how beautiful the sheen underskirt looked beneath the soft layers of gold organza – not full, elegant. Warren will love it. He liked my Tchaikovsky dress. But this is something again. Story Book Gardens is the right setting if ever, and floating away in the boat will seem unreal – all of us and the reflections of daffodils along the bank. Oh, my! And on the dresser stood the bottle of French perfume ready and waiting for the big moment. It was Tom's gift and she had been touched by what he had said, 'It's French. You like that stuff, don't you?' She had smiled, almost laughed at the truth of it, then realised the care with which he had chosen it.

'I'm touched. You remembered from way back at that summer camp, didn't you?' A voice interrupted her thoughts, 'Ms Beauchamp, this is your wake-up call. Can you hear me?'

Donna turned her head towards the small gadget on her dresser and pressed the button.

'Yes. Thank you.' She put her feet to the floor. 'Yipee! I'm going to be married to Warren today. Today!' She had forgotten to turn the pager off. The woman at reception laughed with the man standing at the desk. He was laden down with a child in each arm. They heard a slight howl of embarrassment. Then silence. Very soon a young woman came bounding down the stairs dressed in a tracksuit, off to do a circuit of the hotel gardens. 'Good day,' she called.

They smiled and the man called, 'Have a very good day.'

'I will,' the young woman replied as the footman opened the door for her.

Bach and Vivaldi two-part works for violin. They would be perfect for this wedding. Andreas and Tom stood before the chapel and tuned their violins together. Dressed in black suits with red sashes about their middles, lemon fuchsia buttonholes on their lapels, they looked splendid. Tall and larger than life beside this fairy-tale chapel of diminutive proportions. They wanted to do a professional job. Only the best would be good enough for Donna's wedding. Warren gave Tom a reassuring smile before he went to meet his bride. They had asked the park attendant not to stop anyone joining in, even if only to listen to the music. They had invited only a few guests. All of them were on time. Andreas looked up from his music to see if Peter had brought Celia, and sure enough she was there looking very chic. Donna had said, 'I want all the music department there, even Peter.' She had long ago forgiven him for his hasty exit. Even told Warren it was the best thing that ever happened. 'You knew where you stood. So did I. And no, I shan't mind working with him. He has confidence in my ability. Or so he said when I met with the selection committee.' Andreas caught Miguel's attention as he cast a quick eye over the gathered group and smiled. Miguel raised a hand, smiled in acknowledgement, and excused himself from his wife to take advantage of this photo opportunity.

'I'll be delighted to attend the wedding. And why don't I take your photos?' Miguel had said to Warren who had made a point of asking him in person at his studio. 'By the way, I can't believe the difference in Andreas since you've befriended him.' He even looked grateful. 'What's the secret remedy?'

Warren did not want to get things out of proportion since he had looked forward to employing a student at some time in the future to help him with his child. But the staff had obviously been concerned about Andreas who had developed signs of stress ever since CT had died. He assured Miguel that Andreas had needed to talk, and he needed family. Not very different from most other people he knew, but particularly those who had moved away to study at some institute or other. Miguel admitted that instead of giving the student time for talking, they worked him hard to help him achieve his goal.

'Well, that's paid off too. He's a fine player and you've made sure he's achieved his doctorate. That's marvellous. He's playing at the wedding, you know, do you?'

'Oh, yes. And we know about Tom and what a good player he is!'

'Well, you'll get a chance to hear him on Saturday week.'

Tom's vibrato was a little too vigorous for the style of music. He knew he should not be using it much at all, but he was shaking all over. Between pieces he said to Andreas, 'I'm shaking like a leaf. I'm so excited.'

'I bet! You're doing just fine. They'll be here soon.' Andreas smiled down at his young companion.

And all too soon, there was the inevitable tooting of car horns making an enormous distraction in the park, announcing to all and sundry that a bridal party was arriving, but the violinists played on.

Warren walked out over the drawbridge to welcome his bride. The car pulled up before him, and the driver hopped out and opened the door. Warren had stopped dead at the sight of Donna, so stunned did he feel. 'Oh my God!' he exclaimed, and took a step to hug and kiss her on both cheeks. Donna checked her sheaf of spring flowers, laughed and said, 'I guess this is made to stand up to being pressed. Is everyone here?'

'Everyone.' Miguel and a friend of Donna's clicked their cameras to record the moment. The photographers stepped back, and the couple proceeded over the drawbridge and along the path. They linked hands and after walking a few more steps, the music reached their ears. Donna exclaimed, 'They sound great!' Warren squeezed her hand. 'You're trembling sweetheart, and yes, they're playing well.' The group of friends came towards them down the path a little then moved onto the grass to spontaneously form a guard of honour. Everyone was smiling and inwardly gasping at the exquisite beauty of the sun-lit gold-green apparition that glided through – accompanied by her handsome partner dressed in black tails, his light brown hair tied back but loosely falling at his neck. The celebrant came to the door of the chapel to greet them and led them straight in. The young men stopped playing and slipped inside to stand as close as they dared to the couple. The voice of the celebrant was strong, giving confidence to Warren and Donna, Tom and Andreas, carrying through the small chapel where as many as possible had taken up their places, and outside to the few who remained near the door.

'We are here today to unite Donna Jane Beauchamp and Warren Timothy Blackwell in marriage.' Donna felt reassured, and let go of Warren's hand. She clutched the dainty sheaf with both hands, trying to steady it. Real orange blossom tucked into the arrangement of spring flowers from the florist's nursery, the aroma was delicate and warm. I'm glad Aunty Beth told me I had to. The marriage proceeded, and the tremble in Donna's voice as she took her vows was balanced by the strength of Warren's reply. Rings were exchanged, and they were pronounced husband and wife. As they turned to the table where they were to sign the register, the violinists played the Strauss waltz. The signing done, the couple led the way outdoors. Everyone was relaxed, and inclined to dance right there in the park. Donna and Warren were showered with rose petals and they laughingly greeted their guests as the waltz continued.

The steamboat, adorned with gold ribbons and white balloons, awaited them at the new jetty below the parking lot. But before the couple preceded their guests to the river, Donna went to Tom as he put his violin away and said, 'Tom, thank you. You and Andreas made this a really special occasion.' She gave him a hug. Then she smiled at Andreas.

'Thanks. From my heart. Now come on board for the reception. Look for the captain with roses on his cap.'

'Not to mention the ribbons and balloons!' said Warren, turning to smile at them.

Andreas caught up with Warren. 'Sorry to hold you back, but I've got to tell you. I played here today without giving CT a thought.'

'I know,' said Warren. 'I could tell.'

'But could you tell I felt real sad about going away from you guys?'

They laughed. 'No, but I thought you might have been.'

'So, enough of this sadness, now. I'll take good care of Tom while you're honeycrooning.'

Warren gave a small chuckle at the new version. 'Of course. We wouldn't have asked you if we hadn't known you would.' He slackened his pace. 'Andreas, you can always look on our place as your second home you know.'

'By the time I've helped you move to your new place, and stayed with Tom for a week, it'll certainly be familiar. But seriously, I'll miss you guys very much. Yes, yours will be my second home all right. Thanks.'

Tom joined them, but Warren was keen to join Donna again. They kept pace and headed for the jetty. Andreas confided to Tom that it felt good that he had his doctorate and could go back to Europe. He felt ready to face whatever was waiting for him there, but he could not have done without him and his dad over the past year. Tom insisted that Andreas must keep in touch by email. In the next two weeks though, they would spend a lot of time together. Tom confided, too. He expressed his hopes that one day he could travel to Berlin to study with Andreas.

'You mean when I'm a professor at the *Internationale Musikhochschule* Berlin?'

'Why not?' They had now reached the jetty, and were back to reality. Donna and Warren had gone on board, and were only just visible as they moved about amongst their guests on the deck of this amazing steamboat which had been given a complete overhaul. Photographers almost out-numbered the guests. There was a splendid photo opportunity here, a wedding party boarding a vessel which had only been in operation one week. It was a double whammy!

All the guests had followed the bride and groom and were either looking for a seat or standing about chatting. The clicking and flashing continued. The guests were not only photographing this special event, but were taking the opportunity to capture images of the park from the water. The reflections of the new jetty being scrutinised by sight-seers were a picture in themselves, but there were sights for the artistically minded in the calm water, splashed with the yellow of daffodils, and trees in their spring softness. Further downstream, the party and guests would be invited to take their places at the table ready and waiting on the upper level. In the meantime the captain, with roses in his cap, was busy ushering everyone on board and making the most of every photo opportunity while keeping the press from actually getting on to the boat. 'Just one – yes, one of you may come.'

PART THREE
CHAPTER 7

Warren read over the manuscript Keith Robertson had given him. It gripped him.

Donna looked in. 'Warren.' He leaned into his desk, his pony-tail fell over one shoulder and his eyes stayed glued to the monitor. 'Good God!' he exclaimed and sat back and ran his hand through the dangling hair, then pressed 'send'.

'Warren.'

He looked round. 'How long have you been there?'

She hinted that he should make room for her to sit on his knee.

'I love you,' she said, her arms draped around his neck. 'I want to know when you're coming to bed?'

He drew her face to his, and kissed her lips lightly, then hungrily and pushed back his chair as she stood up to take his hand and run to their bedroom. She flung herself backwards on to the bed and he landed next to her, face down at the same time. With speed he whisked off her nightie. She said, 'Hey, hey! I've got to catch up,' and started with his sweatshirt.

Sitting down to breakfast together, Donna said, '1299 Kensington Avenue, London, Ontario. Nice isn't it?'

Warren paused with the spoon full of flakes doused with milk and said, 'What? The address or the house at the address?'

Donna had not begun to eat. She sat smugly looking around at the well-designed kitchen lit by early morning sun. She had been able to display her china pieces in a glassed space between two cupboards, and her Toby jugs had taken pride of place on an open shelf. Warren had asked her what it was about Toby jugs that appealed to her 'a fine-boned and sensitive modern woman'. She had laughed at his description of herself but said, 'There's something of the Toby in me! I'm surprised you didn't mention those facets of my personality.' And she had made him come up with comments like, 'You're perky no, gutsy, colourful and funny, no fun! Oh, and open to whatever.' That appealed to both of them, and when they had stopped laughing and hugging, Donna managed, 'OK, so there you have it. I'm open and funny.' Already she had a white-board covered in snapshots of wedding guests, taken by her friends. Her eyes rested a moment on the dresser, where stood the formal photos which had been Miguel's gift to them, of violinists Andreas and Tom looking giant-sized in front of the chapel, the bridal couple with the captain – all three looking ridiculously happy – and one of Donna and Warren showing the dress to advantage. 'It's home. Already. My violin likes it too. It's the height of the ceiling, the plaster walls. It makes it easy to prepare for a concert. I pretend.' Donna continued to eat.

'Warren, what were you reading at the monitor last night? You exclaimed! You did.'

'Keith's paper that he's giving in Manchester. It's the bi-annual forum for embryologists and geneticists. They tell about their marvellous achievements over the past two years, rather intense I believe. A bit like an auction or horse fair, each outdoing the other.' He reached for the coffee pot and filled in the details about Keith Robertson's keynote address. As always, Keith had emailed Warren a copy, so that while he was actually delivering it to his colleagues, it would be sold on street corners around the world and reported on TV, radio and internet. Between sips of coffee, he relayed a bit of the theme of the address, declaring it to be rather frightening stuff – about cloning putting the brakes on evolution. 'He reckons that's what vanity cloning does,' he said.

'Vanity cloning?'

'Yep. His word for cloning done for egocentric despots. As opposed to cloning for medical reasons.'

He stood to get ready for work. 'By the way, do you know

that Tom said the same thing about practising in the hallway as you? Andreas told him to do that to get a feeling of space!' He bent to kiss Donna on the lips.

'Oh, that lovely young man. I wonder how he is.'

'Me too. He said he'd email me but I'm still waiting. He really wanted the job of Associate Professor of Violin. I hope it's his.' He took the dishes to the kitchen.

'Probably it is and he's too busy to sit at a computer,' she called.

The *Internationale Musikhochschule Berlin* had made Andreas feel welcome. All the professors had gathered to welcome him to the staff. The Professor of Violin, Dr Anna Freese, shook his hand warmly and said, 'It's very good to have such a young person on the staff. You will inspire the students, Dr Bonnheimer.' Tea and coffee were served, and then it was off to the studios to begin the day's teaching. Andreas' first lesson involved hearing the most advanced violinist at the *Musikhochschule*, Johanna Shackleton, with her chosen accompanist Ichiro Fujiwara.

Part Three
Chapter 8

The moment that Hamish McLeod sat beside Keith Robertson in the taxi traveling from the Manchester airport to the Science Conference Centre, he knew he should never have phoned him. Neither should he have taken Robertson up on the offer of sharing the taxi. He could not get out of telling him that Giano's clones had died, yet he would much rather the news had been kept secret until after the conference. He felt trapped. Robertson turned to look into the eyes of his colleague, and exclaimed in a tone of voice which was a mixture of I told you so, and sarcastic commiseration for him and his team. His stare was penetrating. His breath foul. Hamish even wished that he had not come at all. This was one colleague who was not going to give him any credit for what he knew to be an amazing feat. If only the boys had not died. He looked from the window of the taxi at buildings going by, trying to convince himself that it could have been worse. Gianfranco was still very sick, too ill to come after him, to keep to his threat in person. For the time being he was alive. He would keep Gianfranco's illness to himself.

Warren's story was overshadowed in the media by "Three Cloned Boys Die from Virus Not Killing Others". It was splurged over all the prominent papers! And it was followed by a paragraph beginning, "Questions on the wisdom of human cloning will be raised at the biannual conference in Manchester, as this paper is released. For the full story see page two." Keith would be furious. He so much wanted his opinion as expressed in his keynote address to be front-page news. He had envisaged the headline, "Cloning Will Halt Human Evolution". Robertson was the scientist in the strongest position in the world to say this. He had achieved a huge leap for medicine. He alone had it right.

Through the sudden cancellation of a paper, Hamish was

invited to take the floor as first speaker at the afternoon session. The media story had influenced the choice of Dr Hamish McLeod over other speakers, who had much to contribute about the cloning of body parts, but nothing as monumental as cloning to produce a living human-being, let alone three. These children had, until two weeks ago, been happy, laughing toddlers cutting teeth and trying to run. The esteemed audience could barely hear the weak voice when Hamish began.

'Mr Chair, and fellow scientists.' Hamish panicked, felt foolish. He took a deep breath, cleared his throat, and cast an eye around the upturned faces. All eyes were on him. Waiting. His chin went up and his voice was strong. 'I am proud of what I have done. This morning, we listened with respect to our esteemed colleague, Dr Robertson, but he was theorizing. All talk. What was theoretically believed by us all – namely that a genetically uniform population could well be wiped out by a virus – is proven. Yes fellow geneticists, it is proven. Cloned children, weak immune systems! It was the last thing we wanted to learn by experience, but in spite of our expertise in the area of genetic reproduction, the children who were healthy, bonnie wee children two weeks ago, were unable to withstand a mild dose of influenza. And I mean a mild dose.'

He had turned things around, and was now in a strong position. He returned to his notes and recounted the details of the cloning of the three boys. It was difficult not to say how much he despised himself for doing it, or give a derogatory run-down on the narcissistic adult he cloned. Very difficult. But he stuck to his notes, kept emotion out of it.

The ovation was tumultuous. Hamish felt that this was his proudest moment. Colleagues were reputedly the pits when it came to assessment of one's work. Good at denigration, often subtle. But real, nevertheless. Now with their support, he need not be intimidated by Keith Robertson or anybody else. He had made a huge and historical leap in the field of genetics and it had been acknowledged. The New Biotec Centre would no doubt take the credit but he knew, and Mary had known, that most of the credit was due to his own research and his stubborn perseverance. If only he could have also told them the story of the amazing young Japanese child, alive and smarter than average. Hiro and Rose were his truly successful clonings.

Warren phoned Donna at MAAC. 'Sorry to interrupt a lesson sweetheart, but I'm off to Italy.'

'Why?'

'There's a story too big to miss. I'll fly to Milan and get to the Biotec Centre at Como as fast as. Sweetheart, explain to Tom please. My contact details are on my desk.'

'Phone me from Italy. Every day. And please! Please! Don't stay long. Love you.'

'Love you. Cheers.'

Warren rang from Italy just as Donna was getting into bed. 'Donna how are things? You all right?'

She was able to cope well, but conceded that Tom was an asset. But everyone she had spoken to that day had been full of the news of the three little boys. She was glad that Warren was on to the story, especially as his own, which relied on Keith Robertson's paper, barely got a look in after all that.

'Good and bad all at once but, the big question is, why didn't McLeod crow about his success when the kids were born?'

'And now they're dead.'

The gaggle of journalists who had gathered at the same Como hotel had learned a few of the facts – that the boys had been born to different mothers, none of whom was even remotely connected to the Italian. As to him, well it was all hearsay. He was semi-conscious in the isolation ward at the hospital with a complex number of ailments, most unrelated to the virus.

'I'm trying to piece the story together, but Hamish

McLeod, damn him, is back visiting old haunts in Scotland. I believe he'll be back late tomorrow. At best, I'll get to talk to him on Friday.'

Donna wanted to keep Warren talking, so asked him to guess who she had lunch with, and wanting him to know it was Peter, and that she was entirely over her infatuation with him and glad he had his partner back. And did he think she should grow her hair. And such other important trivia. He responded by suggesting she was jealous of his long hair and she retorted, 'That has nothing to do with it. I'm cold, that's why.'

'Grow it, then sweetheart. Yes. Have a change. Must go. Sleep well. Love to Tom. I'll call you about this time tomorrow.'

'Bye, my darling. Love you.'

'Love you too. *Ciao.*'

PART THREE
CHAPTER 9

'I will play. I will. I like playing *Czardas*. I won't stop.'

'But Mum told me I'm not to let you play what Jiro played. Go listen to your discs.'

'I will not. I will play *Czardas*.' Hiro stamped his foot and began to play. Ichiro was defeated yet again. He joined in with the piano accompaniment and hoped his mother was not awake yet.

'Again! Faster. You slowed me down.'

'No. I have to do my own practice. Truly. You go and do yours. You're supposed to play your finger exercises and folk songs. Go away.' He played three chromatic scales over the full range of the piano. Hiro stood entranced. He picked up his violin and found the chromatic sequence and played along, changing key with Ichiro who ignored him as best he could. He is a little wizard. And a dork.

Their mother came in with a small dish of rice to put at Jiro's shrine. 'Excuse me, Ichiro. Have you seen Hiro this morning? I can't find him. But his violin's not in his room, either.'

'I don't know, Mum,' Ichiro said. At the same time he made a face and pointed behind the piano. 'Have you looked in the hall cupboard? He sometimes hides from me there.'

Yuki placed the rice, and Ichiro slipped off the piano stool and sounded the gong. His mother lit the incense stick and they put their hands together to pray. Hiro rushed out of hiding. 'You've got to let me ding the gong.' He snatched it from Ichiro with a dark expression, and beat it hard. 'I hate Jiro,' he said.

Yuki looked askance at her three-year-old and growled at him for expressing such negativity about his dead brother. But it did not take her long to find out that it was because she had told Ichiro not to encourage him to play the music that Jiro used to. She had come to attend the shrine, so she turned to do what she needed, and when she had finished praying, invited Hiro to sound the gong. Together they went to have breakfast and, Yuki hoped, sort out a few of these problems. To her surprise Ichiro revealed the news that Hiro was playing Monte's *Czardas*. Her chopsticks dropped into her rice and she put a napkin to her mouth feeling alarm for what she had just heard.

'This guy is brilliant. I try to stop him but I can't,' confessed Ichiro.

Yuki was quiet for several minutes, looking at each of her sons – the teenager who was showing all signs of a strong and determined individual, as well as the need to shave away the fine hair from his upper lip, the occasional rash of pimples and self-loathing; and the little guy who was so fast, self-willed and clever, but so rude and insolent that he was making her feel totally inadequate, confused and hurt. All three returned to eating. When the rice was finished and they had their warm drinks, Yuki said softly, 'I want you to play *Czardas* for me now. Together.'

Hiro ran to the music room and checked his violin. Ichiro took his place at the piano and Yuki carried over the one chair to where she could see Hiro's face. She nodded to them to begin. Ichiro played the stirring introduction, and Hiro placed his bow for the G string. Once begun, the octave leap sent an orgasmic chill through her taut body, so perfect was it. She shook. The music unfolded deftly played, in tune, racing along or slow and calculating, as required. The short bow bounced for the staccato and spiccato. The small fingers hit the right spots for every note. Most sections were repeated as the music required, and the climax raced to the fortissimo final double note. Yuki beamed at one child, then the other, but could not speak. She replaced her chair against the wall.

'Mum. See what I mean?' Ichiro said.

'Yes, son. I see what you mean. I'll talk to your dad.' Little Hiro's lip was pouting. He was furious with his mother. 'You don't like me,' he muttered and stamped out of the room.

Yuki followed.

'Hiro. I do. I do. You are a wonderful violinist. You are. I love you.' He had gone to the hall cupboard to hide. She tried the door but it would not open. 'Your daddy will be so proud of you,' she said loudly at the closed door.

She rang the Institute. She must tell Kentaro. But his secretary reported that he was teaching and could not be contacted. So she had no choice but to tell him later. Now she had to take Hiro to kindergarten, relieved at least that she could escape him for the morning.

'It's time for kindergarten, Hiro. Come on out and get your jacket on. You're going to have fun today making kites. Remember?'

The door opened and Hiro raced past her to get his jacket and put on his shoes. He took his bag off the hook and said, 'Hurry up. You silly mummy. You slow coach.'

'I don't like you to speak to me like that. Say sorry, please.'

'No.'

'I think you should. Your daddy will have to be told.' She put on her shoes and said, 'Come on, now.'

He pushed past her and out the door.

When Hiro was finally asleep for the night, Yuki burst into tears. 'Kentaro, Hiro is a monster!'

Kentaro wanted to argue about her choice of words. He thought that cheeky might describe the child, but monster was extreme, something implied that suggested he was not entirely human. And of course, that reflected Yuki's deepest concern. The child was not normal where she was concerned. Lacked a soul, was unfeelingly destructive. But she still needed to tell her husband about how he had played Monte's *Czardas* with Ichiro. 'Even the harmonics! Brilliantly. I didn't know what to say.'

Kentaro's eyes widened. 'Who taught him?'

'He's learnt it – I realise now – from listening to the girl that Chiyo teaches before him. He's heard it once. But then he listens to the disc too.'

Kentaro was silent. A mix of pride and sadness. Bewilderment too. 'We wanted a violinist.' He smiled at her. 'This is incredible. Rather too wonderful.'

'It's not. Not when he is so rude with it. Honestly, I'd rather he were polite to me. My days are ruined.'

'But that is terrible. I must talk to him.'

'Please get him to play with Ichiro tomorrow. Hear *Czardas* for yourself. As well, see how he behaves.'

He could hear that Yuki was fed up. 'Pet, you are worn out. Let's go to bed together, tonight. I love you very much. Your life has to be better than just one big fight with your pre-schooler. Come on.'

He led her upstairs as if he had only just realised how easily she was hurt. He put the wall light on and said, 'Can you wait while I bathe? I am tired from teaching and sweaty too. I'll be very quick.'

Yuki spent the time brushing her hair and cleansing her face until she, too, felt relaxed. She found her red nightie and pantie set, smoothed out the lace and put them on. Kentaro joined her wearing his robe which he slid from his shoulders at the door and she saw how warm he was, and smelt his cleanliness.

'I love you,' she said with her arms outstretched.

'You are very wonderful, Yuki.' He picked her up as they hugged, and lay her on the bed.

'Rough me up,' she whispered, and he pulled her panties down with his teeth, and kissed her body where they had been and went on kissing her as he travelled up to find her mouth. His fingers began to take the same route, but lingered to play. All the while they kissed passionately and roughly, she pushing her fingers to and fro through his thick hair, and he, getting harder and harder. She, moist and ready. She let him enter her, and they climaxed again and again.

As they lay still, and beside each other in the bed, Yuki

asked, 'Is Hiro going to be all right?' He reassured her while feeling a sense of dismay and doubt himself. He was used to clever children, but not one who was too advanced for his own good.

'Please don't let him be a monster. I'll feel so guilty.'

He was furious that she had used that word again. It had become personal. He turned to her, raised himself up on an elbow, and said, 'My pet. A monster? My son a monster?'

'He's not your son, Kentaro.'

Suddenly he slapped her face. 'Don't ever say that again. Go to sleep. And you keep saying it over and over until you believe it – Kentaro is his father. Kentaro is his father.'

She turned away from him and cried to herself – and I am Enola Gay.

Part Three
Chapter 10

Donna sped home. Tom was to leave school about five o'clock when the chamber music group finished, and she would be home at much the same time. She zapped the garage door with the remote and it rolled out of sight. Tom bounded down the steps from the house as she parked. He had come to grab her bag from her. She marvelled at his exuberance. It made her feel old. That was one of the things that having a son of eleven did for her! But he continued to heap her with help by cooking a pasta dish for tea, saying that his hands were so frozen from throwing snowballs that he needed to be near hot things. Then when he offered to go without the usual practice with her, she said with exaggerated knowing, 'I'll be happy to leave my violin in its case tonight. Thanks. You'll work on your own then?'

'No, I want to keep the house quiet for you.'

She laughed. 'Cunning little monkey.'

When Warren returned from Italy, she was already in bed reading. She heard his steps in the hall, and excited at having him back, went to sit with him for a bit. They hugged and kissed in the hallway.

'My sweetheart, you look tired,' he said to her.

'I am,' she said. 'But let's have a warm drink, and talk before I go back to bed. I want to know all about the hot one.'

Beside her on the settee which had once belonged only to Donna, Warren began. 'It's an absolutely ghastly story actually. For the first time in my career, I felt as if I'd visited hell for a time. Not because of any crime but the whole scenario of three children cloned and dead. Their parent, I hardly know how to express that, their 'original' is lying in a coma. We were herded into the foyer at the Biotech Centre and talked to by this short-sighted woman called Bertha. She was the last person to deal with media. An awkward body to say the least. But apart from some words from an Italian man of dubious character, Roberto someone or other, she was the only one prepared to talk to us. We all felt like the unclean for a time there.' He took a drink, then put an arm about Donna. 'When Hamish McLeod came back, he wanted to talk to us. The tune changed. He told us that he had proved to the world that the supposition about halting human development by cloning a race of look-alikes was correct. "Humanity could be wiped off the face of the earth," he said. As he talked his cheeks got ruddier and his eyes brighter! He's a big man – a regular Scotsman with a ginger beard – and is even more handsome than publicity showed him up to be four years ago. God, he was mighty pleased with his visit to England and Scotland. Must have been given a hero's welcome or something. One could hear the braying of the pipes in his voice.' They laughed together.

'That much of a Scotsman, is he?'

'I would think that when he wants to be, he is. But I have to say he dresses like an Italian! Whatever that means. Stylish, I guess.'

'So it really is a dreadful story. Didn't anyone feel sad about the children?'

'I asked Hamish about that. It was a bit daunting, really. I said, "You are telling us that the human cost of these children means nothing more than that your supposition is proven?" Hamish looked a lot taken aback. But then he recovered. He said "There has to be some cost. These children paid the price. Yes. But therein is the dreadful challenge with which this generation of geneticists is faced. We're only just developing gene maps and the confidence to clone humans. It's early days. Inevitably we're going to run risks, even make foolish mistakes."'

'"Three young mistakes? And no one mourns?" I asked him. "Of course people have mourned," he snapped. I persisted. "So now you stop cloning humans. Is that the result?"'

'"Of course not!" he said, then added, "We'll go on learning and develop better techniques and more reliable results. We'll clone for medical reasons. Do the kind of work Keith Robertson has done in the area of Alzheimer's, for example. So you are saying – " Oh, darling, I'm boring you.'

'No. Just tell me that last bit.'

'I said, "So you are saying that Keith Robertson's cloning efforts are all right?" That ruffled him. "I am saying that embryologists agree that there can be sound medical reasons for cloning but cloning for self-idolisation is not acceptable." And then I really stuffed it up by saying, "A fine line there, isn't it?" That's when he walked out on me. Now I write my story. And you go to bed, eh, hon?'

Donna sighed and said, 'I think that cloning business sounds so cold. Sterile. I think a baby should be conceived in love. You know, choosing one's partner, courting, mating – all that stuff – it's too much fun. Warren, we want a baby don't we?' She snuggled up a bit and kissed him on the cheek.

He studied her face a moment then smiled broadly. 'We most certainly do.'

'Well, how about you come to bed for a few minutes. Then write your story?'

He got up, pulled her to her feet 'A few minutes! One go and we'll have our baby. Easy, eh?'

'Fun!'

Part Three
Chapter 11

Angry that he could not get any sense about Giano's condition from Mr Bonticelli by phone, Hamish was shouting into thin air. But Terri was trying to calm him down by telling him that he should not expect to have a medical report, which under normal conditions is given to close family only, handed to him on a plate. She told him he was getting upset over nothing, but could go and talk again with Bonticelli since he was the doctor in charge in this case too, and had told him about the boys' deaths.

Hamish strode toward the isolation unit. He knew the rules, so announced his arrival and removed his overcoat and beret and donned a gown and facemask. Before going to Giano's bedside, he knocked on the door of the doctor's room. No answer. So! He was not going to waste any more time and entered Giano's room without hesitation. The nurse looked up, and recognising him, said, '*Buongiorno*, Dr McLeod.'

'*Buongiorno*, Nurse. How is Giano? Is there really no change?'

'Oh, yes. There is. He is a lot better and is asleep just now.'

Hamish didn't know if he was pleased or not.

'So why is he still in isolation?'

'He is paying for privacy. And there are other reasons.'

'Such as?'

'That is confidential, Dr McLeod.'

'I see. So when will he be well enough to go home?'

'We can't tell, but soon probably.'

He felt he could hear the rattle of money in the nurse's words.

'Right, then. I'm off.'

'Any message for my patient when he wakes?'

'Tell him I called please. And give him this.'

He had felt that it was the least he could do, to give him a duplicate of the letter of resignation he had given to Roberto. Silently he hoped that Giano would sleep a long time. At least until they got out of the country. Accepting a post back in Scotland had been easy. He had earned a reputation for cloning. And he had living proof of how perfect, in every way, the result could be. Rose was perfect. Four years old and doing what all four-year-olds do – pestering her parents with questions about everything and everyone, wanting to do everything for herself, and beginning to read and write. It would seem that she had in no way been affected by her mother's tragic death. Accepting Terri as her new mother had been total – arms and heart wide to Terri's love for her. Hamish's heart was warmed by her childish innocence.

Home from the hospital, Hamish helped Terri to pack their belongings. With Rose at kindergarten they had a clear run. What to do with Mary's things had now to be faced. He wanted to keep only a few mementos for Rose, and sought Terri's advice. 'If you were Rose, what would you like to have from your mother?'

'Oh, just some photos. Yes, I'd want to know what she looked like more than anything. And one or two little things. Maybe a hairbrush, a favourite picture, something she had made like a crocheted mat. But Mary did tatting, I think. So yes, a tatted dressing table set. That would probably be all. Is that any help?'

'Yes, a great help. And then maybe we should keep one or two things from her babyhood – her first dress, a shawl and a knitted pram set. Her aunt had knitted those things especially for her. I'll keep them too. He put all of the keepsakes into the quilted bag that had once held Mary's tatting, and packed it in his large case into which would go his personal things.

At the Biotech Centre, a message from Giano was given to

Hamish by his secretary as he joined other staff in the common room for a farewell party. He read it quickly and felt shocked. "*Dottore* McLeod, I shall always hold you personally responsible for the death of the three boys. You will pay. Be sure about that. Gianfranco."

Hamish stood before the gathered scientists and Roberto, and listened to farewell speeches with sweat trickling down his back and arms. His mouth went dry as he spoke, because he knew that, however many fine words were expressed, this was no idle threat and would not go away.

Bertha made the speech on behalf of the department: 'We have learned much from you, Hamish. We have risen from ignorance to knowledge because of your willingness to teach us, and we are very sorry to lose you. It has not been an easy road for any of us, but it has been especially hard, and at times heart-breakingly sad for you. Because of you we can go on. We have our production line set up and thriving. That took courage and tenacity. You taught us to believe in ourselves, so that hardly a day goes by without several requests for body parts. And more!' She was getting into deep water here, went red, and added, 'Medical science has taken a giant leap forward because of research led by you. And it's too bad to lose you at this, the crossroads of stem research, especially as we're losing you to Scotland.' She looked boldly at him and said, 'Hamish are you sure you're not going there to solve their huge foot and mouth problem?' Everyone laughed. She was pleased with herself, and raising her glass and her voice, said, 'And lest I be accused of suffering from the dreaded disease myself ...' her smile and shaking bosom could only just be contained while she waited for the groan to subside. 'Colleagues, Roberto Cammarata, I ask you to fill your glasses and drink to the amazing, the wonderful, the clever Dr Hamish McLeod.'

Roberto took Hamish aside and said, 'You would get Giano's message?'

Hamish looked into the crooked face before him for signs

of complicity with Giano. What he saw was greed, imprinted on every feature. He was not certain that he saw agreement with Giano.

'You have supported me and my research in a way which has been the envy of my colleagues around the world. And you have not pushed me to do any cloning that I did not want to do. For that, I thank you Roberto.'

Roberto surprised him. He squeezed his hand and said, 'Take care Hamish McLeod. And take care of that little girl of yours. And by the way, now this will please you, I'm marrying a lovely Italian woman. We hope to have our own children, and since she is already pregnant by me, it is pretty well certain.' His face almost looked pleasant.

Hamish was stunned. The relief he felt, that Roberto would not be after him to clone him, was like a going-away present of unexceeded value. 'Congratulations! Roberto. And to your fiancée. *Buona fortuna*! *Ciao*. Such good news. *Mi scusi*.' And he went to join Bill and share his staggering news.

It was dark when the plane circled at Gatwick. Snow had crystallized on the windows and took out any view of lights that they could have expected. 'If only we didn't have to make this transfer,' said Terri as she helped Rose into her coat. 'You're tired already, aren't you, darling?'

Rose's cheeks were pink with excitement but her voice was small as she said, 'Where's Aunty Janice?'

'Not here, darling. We've got a bit of a walk through the airport then a bus ride to a smaller plane which takes us to Edinburgh. Then we'll see Aunty Janice.' She hurriedly pulled down their two packs. She smiled at Hamish as much as to say nearly there, and helped Rose into her pack. 'We'd best keep moving now.' Terri followed the scramble of passengers along the aisle as Hamish lifted Rose up in his arms and followed closely behind. She glanced back whenever there was a hold-up, and smiled reassuringly at them both. Once, when stalled because of baggage being retrieved from overhead storage by a short man standing on a seat, she said to Hamish, 'Departure gate five for flight connections.'

'OK. I heard it.'

The sound from the television in the lounge area of gate five was turned up very high and they found seats as far from the speakers as possible. 'Daddy, why aren't we in Edinburgh now?'

So it was that Hamish spun out the story of how aeroplanes were what was best if you had a long journey to make, and that sometimes you had to take not one plane but two or more, with a wait in between. And sometimes take a bus or taxi ride to get to the next plane. Quite a lot of the waiting time was filled in, but waiting in an airport can be as tiring as the journey itself. So since everyone was tired and thirsty, they went to the café, and Rose was chuffed at being allowed to choose a fizzy drink. Between swallows she pestered about the journey.

'It's not a straight run to get to Edinburgh, is it?' he laughed. 'Four short flights of steps to go, then on to the bus that winds about quite some, then another plane journey to Edinburgh and Aunty Janice.'

Janice stood at the place where she said she would be, in front of the car rental, thoughtlessly muffled up so that even Hamish looked right past her. But when she caught sight of Rose with her parents, she threw back her hood and ran to hug the child. 'But you're a big girlee you are!' Rose was uncertain. It had been a long time. Almost four years. She cringed and held Terri's hand tightly. Hamish interrupted, smiling with joy at introducing his new wife to his sister. 'Janice, this is Terri.' The women hugged, and Janice turned back to talk to Rose as they walked together toward the exit.

'You don't remember me? That's all right, Rose.' She smiled at her, and addressed the adults. 'All right now. Come along and I'll get my car and take you home. You'll all be weary of travelling.'

PART THREE
CHAPTER 12

Ichiro stood beside Hiro's bed tweaking his ear and saying, 'Wake up. Wake up.' Then, when his little brother opened his eyes he changed to, 'Get up. Quick! Dress warm and be quiet. Dad's gone to work but Mum's still asleep.'

There was barely any daylight in the room, so Ichiro put on the main light, and at the piano played the A for Hiro to tune to. It did not take long. The little fellow acted like he had been tuning a violin for years. 'Right, so we're going to play the *Spring Sonata*. All ready?'

'*Hai.*'

The theme rippled along and Ichiro felt that it could have been Jiro playing. The same keeping together of the smooth sixteenth notes that he had worked so hard to achieve, was there as if gifted to them. At the close of the movement Ichiro said, 'You're smart. You can play hard pieces without learning them. Let's play that movement again.'

'*Hai.*'

Ichiro was disobeying his mother but had this uncanny impression that his brother was back, and he goaded him on. After the first movement, Hiro told Ichiro that he had not learnt the second movement yet because Akiko, who had a lesson before him, had not played it. But that was not the only way to learn it and Hiro knew as well as he did that he could listen to the recording made by Jiro and Ichiro anyway.

'Well you make sure you hear it soon. I want to play it all with you. All, do you hear me?'

'*Hai!*'

'Does Chiyo know you can play *Czardas?* Or the first movement of the *Spring Sonata?*'

'Course not. I told you she gets me to play baby stuff.'

Ichiro hopped off the stool. He gave his little brother a hug and said, 'You can go back to bed now. Go on and I'll do my practice.'

While Hiro and his mother observed Akiko playing the first movement of the *Spring Sonata* in her next lesson, Chiyo felt distracted by the intent look on Hiro's face and the movement of his fingers in the air. She turned away so that she could not see him. Yuki wondered what prompted the teacher to ask her student to move so she could stand with her back to the observing families. She put a hand around Hiro's back to hold him still in case that was the problem. Hiro said, 'Don't', very loudly and Yuki's embarrassment coloured her cheeks and she said, '*Gomen nasai*, Chiyo *sensei*.'

Twenty minutes went by with lots of repetitions of phrases from the first movement, and Hiro began to fidget. His teacher looked at him and said, 'Not long now, Hiro.' He slid from his chair to stamp a foot for the third time as he said, 'I want to hear the other movements. I know that one.'

Yuki looked uncomfortable, and cupped Hiro's chin to make him look at her when she said, 'Please say sorry for interrupting.'

Chiyo came over to them. 'Mrs Fujiwara, is it true that Hiro can play the first movement?'

'I don't know.'

'It's true. Ichiro and I played it this morning.'

Chiyo looked at the mother and smiled. 'So Hiro can play it to me soon.' She turned to Akiko and said, 'Now let me hear the scherzo and trio, Akiko.'

Akiko began it more slowly than the given tempo and Chiyo went to her and at a break in the music said, '*Tempo!*' The music came in a strongly syncopated rhythm and Hiro sat enthralled until he got the idea, then his small body kicked and clapped to the half beats. When it ended, he and Yuki clapped vociferously and Akiko bowed to them, smiling with pleasure.

'I want the next one too. That was short.'

Chiyo said, 'No, time's up. It's your turn in a minute.' She talked with Akiko about what she was to practise and then they bowed to each other and Akiko packed her things away and left the room.

'We'll leave the adagio for when he's older, Fujiwara *san*. But now it's Hiro's turn.'

He was all smiles. 'I want to play with Ichiro.'

'But Ichiro's at school,' said Yuki and Chiyo together. They laughed.

'I could put on the recording of Ichiro and Jiro and let him play along,' suggested Chiyo. 'So long as …'

'That will be all right,' said Yuki with a nod of acknowledgement that it gave her both joy and sadness to hear recordings of the twins. 'I want you to hear Hiro. It's time you knew what he has been getting up to with Ichiro's influence. *Czardas* too.'

'Oh, really?' The look on Chiyo's face expressed something akin to both fear and delight. She watched intrigued as Hiro got his violin and bow ready to play. He tuned, then stood in playing position. Impatiently he said, 'Ready!'

With a little shake of her head as if to bring her back into the moment, Chiyo walked to the CD player, selected the disc, checked that Hiro was still ready and pressed play.

Yuki walked to the end of the room to sit again.

The afternoon sun played on the face of the child and the tops of his flying fingers, the golden violin, and the cheek, hair and throat of the teacher. Through her eyes she tried to interpret this strange phenomenon. Hiro, soon to be four, playing advanced music as if he had practised it for years, keeping up with the recording by his brothers. Chiyo's expression was unfathomable. She kept swallowing. Yuki could see that. Was it tears? Fear? Happiness? She did not know. She herself was anguished. Very puzzled that the child cloned from his big brother's cells was way ahead of his years. What did this mean? The music was muffled by her thoughts, her head pounded out the worst of them. Little

Boy! She'd carried a Little Boy!

At the end of the first movement, Chiyo walked to the player to turn it off.

'No. No.' Hiro shrieked.

'Well, the scherzo then.' The music continued, relentless in its syncopated rhythm. Hiro joined in at the first repeat, and played until the movement was finished. Then he put his violin down and said, 'Was I all right?'

'I can't believe you did that. I can't,' Chiyo said.

Hiro's lip went down and he ran, and shouted out, 'I did. I did.' And he buried his head in his mother's lap and sobbed.

His mother took his violin and bow from his tightly gripped fingers and stroked his hair. 'You did. You did. You were wonderful.'

'Hiro, you played very well.' His teacher stood near and pleaded with Hiro to listen to her. 'I'll tell you what we will do. We will learn all the pieces you want to learn. I will let you.'

The tear-stained face lifted off his mother's knee. 'I want to. I want to.'

'You shall then. I will talk to your mummy and daddy and we will work out what you can learn.' She took his hand and took him to her chair. She sat, and their eyes met.

'Listen, Hiro.' His small hand rested on her knee as he concentrated hard. 'I shall write in your notebook now, that you are to listen to all the movements of the *Spring Sonata*. And play as many as you want to. Does that make you happy?'

'Yes.' He ran calling to his mother, 'We have to listen to all the movements. Chiyo *sensei* said so.'

'Very well. We must listen, then.'

'And, when can I play *Czardas?*' He had turned back to his teacher.

'I'm not sure, Hiro. Perhaps your mummy can tell me when.' She directed her comment to Yuki. 'I'd like the two boys to play together, either here or at your place. Whichever suits.'

'So what can I learn next then, Mum?'

'Chiyo *sensei*, your dad, and I will make a plan.'

A knock on the door heralded the arrival of the next pupil. Chiyo asked Hiro to get his violin and bow, and stand in rest position. She picked up hers and they bowed, each to the other. The lesson was finished. The sun vanished and Chiyo turned on the lights. 'Hello, Daisuke, your lesson now please.'

Rushing into the house to tell his big brother his news, Hiro started shouting as soon as he opened the door. He scuffed off his shoes as he yelled, 'Ichiro, Ichiro, I can learn any piece I want.'

Ichiro came out of his room from pre-occupation with homework. Hardly thinking what was said, he walked towards Hiro saying, 'What?'

'I said, I'm allowed to play any piece I want.'

'Oh, so how come?'

'Chiyo heard me play the *Spring Sonata*. Two movements.'

'Two? The first and second?'

'No. The first and third. Akiko played the third one and I learned it.'

'Is this right, Mum?'

Yuki had taken off her shoes and jacket and was watching her two boys. 'That's right. He played the two movements very well.'

Hiro stamped a foot. 'I want to make the plan. I have to choose.' And he rushed inside to the pile of CDs and put on the Bach *Concerto in a Moll*.' He sat on the small stool near the speakers to listen, and did not move until it was finished.

Yuki caught up with him. Standing in the doorway, she thought – he's a pre-schooler, yet he sits enthralled. She waited for him to move; to show signs of boredom. There were none. As she turned to leave the room, her foot caught a chair leg and crashed the chair against the wall. Hiro got up from his stool and started to hit her as she righted the chair. He didn't stop. Again and again he hit her, crying, 'You silly woman. You made me stop listening.'

Yuki called to Ichiro. He came fast, saw what was happening, and grabbed his brother around the chest.

'Hiro. Stop that!' He held him so he couldn't hit his mother. He saw that Yuki was crying. 'You say sorry to Mum. You mustn't hit people. I'll tell dad on you.'

The child scowled. 'You tell dad and I'll smash the piano.'

Yuki looked askance at Hiro. 'You're being a monster.'

Hiro looked pleased with himself. 'I am a monster.'

'Thank you Ichiro,' Yuki said. 'You needn't tell dad, but I will.' She turned to leave the room for the kitchen. 'I must make dinner now.'

Hiro gave her a push from behind. Yuki cried out with fright.

'And I'll tell him about that, too.'

Hiro went back to the CD player with the scowl still puckering his face and put the concerto on at the beginning again. His mother kept clear of him and remained in the kitchen.

After an uncomfortable dinner when everyone was quieter than usual, Kentaro asked Ichiro how his day had gone. He then learned something of what had happened between Hiro and Yuki, and was horrified. It did not compensate for the great news that Hiro had been told by his teacher that he could choose his pieces from now on.

'Hiro, what did you do?'

'Nothing. Nothing.'

So Yuki had to say how he had hit her hard, again and again so that she cried, and Ichiro had come to her aid. Kentaro lifted up the boy and carried him kicking and screaming through to his bedroom, slowing only to catch the door with his foot and close it behind them. And it was half an hour later that he came from the bedroom, alone.

'The child's asleep now. Yuki, I am sorry that you have

had such a rough day.'
　'I tell you Kentaro, that child is a monster.'

Part Three
Chapter 13

Hamish and his family had been in Kirkliston at Janice's for one day, and Hamish could only think of Mary – his Scottish lassie. Before anything else – house hunting, buying a car, everything that seemed necessary to their new life – Hamish ached to go back to the Firth of Forth and Queensferry South where Mary had drowned. It was just something he had to do. Again. And alone. As soon as Rose was down for an afternoon nap and Terri beside her asleep with jet lag, he wrote a note saying he would be back for the evening meal. Terri would know what he was doing; in fact she had said that he must deal with his grief once and for all or he would become a cot-case himself. Now was as good a time as any.

It was a short drive from Kirkliston, and within twenty minutes Hamish had parked his car across the road from Hawes Inn on the banks of the Forth. At the same moment as his key stopped swinging in the lock, he gave way to the feeling that had dogged him for weeks – the desire to disappear out of sight. He let his body droop into the space of the seat. Drop, drop away to Mary, to his love, away from the sights and smells of the lab. He was tired of keeping a brave face.

The weariness he felt now took him to places he had not known existed. Where was Mary? Why did she leave him? In one moment she seemed close, as if breathing hot into his beard, in another it was as if he could see her on this very place, playing like a child with her child – being a playmate to Trish, the lively, brightest little girl one could ever wish for. Dressed in look-alike yellow tee shirts with the Firth bridges on their backs, they would hunt for a stone, a leaf, a pirate's lost jewel, anything to keep them occupied while he sat reading the last chapter of one or other of his scientific journals. Then they would go together into the inn and have a meal or just a drink. Maybe if he turned his head she would be there beside him, laughing at him, about to say, 'Hamish, love, what's bothering you?' He felt pains like no other pains he had ever felt. And they were right through his body. A limpness that was not physical, but like wet concrete, beginning in his mind, reflecting light from a watery sun, a little dry, a little wet, not stinging, but hurting until it soaked his bones. He wondered if others who had lost a dear person to suicide shared his black trauma, his pain, his overwhelming times of panic and desperation. And worst of all, his guilt. He should have been more attentive to Mary's needs, been less in the lab and more with her. In anger he grabbed at the steering wheel and shook it, and himself. On and on. Then he shouted and thumped the wheel in rhythm with his words: 'She was ill! Mary, my darling Mary was ill! Very, very ... out of her mind ill – and we couldna' see it! Me, me, me where was I? ... At work. Posing for the cameras! Taking all the credit for God's sake! Smiling for the bloody news of the world ... cloning more babies – Mafia look-a-likes!' He hoped Mary's God was hearing this because it was his confession. He needed to be rid of his guilt – shout it from his bones, his heart, his head. Needed to give voice to the words imprinted on his soul in lead type ever since she had died. He shouted them again and again and again until he felt the force of their conviction diminish, die away. Then he cried, slumped as far as he could, and he kept on crying until he thought he had fainted away. All the sensations of being alive were no longer present.

Gradually, gradually, he connected with a finger, then a hand, the other hand. He curled his toes to press his shoe. One foot then another. A sigh convinced him that he was still a living being. The blurred figures of his watch assured him that a lot of time had passed and yes, he was still alive.

He looked to see if anyone was staring at him. Assured that he was alone, he pulled himself together enough to start the engine. In that point of ignition, that first movement of the car in response to his actions, his mind and body seemed less hindered than before. He felt puzzlement and embarrassment at what had just happened. Yet knew that it had to, or he too, would have taken his life. He backed away from the wall that separated him from the Firth of Forth, and turned to drive the cobbled road to retrace in part, the route of the funeral cortege.

Mary used to come here alone. She sometimes said that the cobbled road was the reason why she kept returning to Queensferry South. She could see Queen Margaret – the figure she had created together with a little history and a lot of fantasy – riding side-saddle along the road to attend worship in the stone church, or distribute food to the hungry. She could hear the clip-clopping of the horse's hooves and the echo of shouting voices bouncing between the mud, stone and timber of the buildings. As he drove slowly, Hamish felt a new closeness to Mary. A closeness which was almost companionable. He smiled a little and wanted to say, 'And Mary, where do you think you're going to spend this Christmas, lassie?' It had been their joke. Their way of coping with the frequent change of environment since they married.

He did not go up to the church, but along the dirt road to the yard of the slipway where boats settled themselves for their next period at sea. He returned a friendly wave from two men painting the underside of a boat and he began to feel glad he had come. Maybe by the time the afternoon was over, he would have done what Terri had said he must do as soon as they got to Scotland, and before he started a new job. That was to drown the spectre of the ghost once and for all. When she had realised the irony in what she had said as encouragement, she had countered, 'Oh, sorry. I put that badly.' And she kissed him and said, 'You know what I mean.'

He stopped his car just short of the slipway. It was dry and hard on the stones, and he got out of the car and walked about, very much aware that a stream of cars was crossing over both bridges in silent succession high above him. There was a certain mix of peace and unrest in his mind. How could she have walked straight out into this cold, grey water? The question kept surfacing as he looked and listened. The only reply his mind would yield was what the doctor had said: "She believed she was Queen Margaret. She talked about a book of the Gospels she said she kept close to her heart. She said she was afraid it might get lost. I asked her to show it to me but she said, 'No, but I'll tell you about it,' and, without stopping she described the figures of the four evangelists and how they were adorned with gold and that every capital letter was gilded. The thing that struck me most was that she seemed afraid she might lose it. I know that story a little – it's part of the history of Scotland, after all. I knew that this precious copy of the gospels, adorned with jewels and gold, was inadvertently dropped and lost in a river. But I also knew that it had been found. I can only assume that, on that dreadful day that Mary walked into the Firth, she was looking for it."

Hamish bent to pick up a few stones to throw – to contact the water that Mary had braved. As he threw them he no longer felt anger. Each grey stone spun away from him carrying his pain and his love ... to the depths, to that place ... And then his imagination started to play havoc. If only I could have her exhumed. I could have a new Mary. The thought engulfed him for a minute. He spun some more stones ... and then hung his head in shame. What a thought!

Amongst the stones at his feet was something that caught his eye. At first, it looked like a tiny wooden cross. On closer examination, it was an ebony cross – probably the end part of rosary beads. He fingered it and remembered Mary's devotion to Mother Mary and felt stunned by his find. He turned the small black cross over and over pondering the dichotomy in her religious life. She would often laugh about that and say, "Born into a dogmatic Presbyterian home yet very much a Catholic in my heart. I could have been a nun if I hadn't fallen for you Hamish, love." He put the cross in his pocket. I'll look after this. It could well have been Mary's.

He had not actually enjoyed his contact with the Catholic Church but had not doubted that it was the place to farewell his darling from. Yet, there had been a price. The priest's words had pierced his heart on that day. "Dr McLeod, be assured that your wife is forgiven." Forgiven? For what! Being ill. Stupid bastard, not fit to minister the sacraments. He spun noisily on the stones. It was time to get back to Hawes Inn and meet with Jeannie.

As soon as he opened the door to the pub, he experienced a warm feeling. He had been there several times with Mary and Janice and other students, but that was a long time ago. For a moment he stood adjusting to the light. There was a warm surge of history, merriment and drama; a collage of paper money slapped on to the fascia above the bar; voices, past and present; the smell of frothing lager; and a flame ghosting from the hearth. He looked for Jeannie and saw no one that could be her so took a seat to the left of the doorway. On being handed a menu, he said, 'Thanks. I'll wait for my friend.'

There was stuff to read. He busied himself with the brochure, then the framed poster on the wall. The association of Robert Louis Stevenson with the place fascinated him again. He remembered how one of his student friends, and Mary in particular, had been keen on anything historical or literary and laughed merrily at the way Robert Louis Stevenson had put it in *Kidnapped*: "And presently we were set down at a table in the front room of the Hawes Inn and both eating and drinking with a good appetite." He smiled as he remembered those good times. He was stimulated enough to want to eat a hearty meal for old times sake. He picked up the pamphlet again and read the menu.

'You must be Hamish.' A tall dark woman was smiling down at him, looking into his eyes as if she had known him a long time. 'Mary told me all about you, even to the colour of your beard.'

'Jeannie?' he said, getting up, smiling. 'Thank you for coming. Shall we – well look at that fire now. Shall we go nearer?' As they moved along the bar to the table adjacent to the hearth, Jeannie began to unclip the sling in which she carried her baby.

'How old is he?'

'She. I've called her Mary. She's just six weeks.'

'Can I help you?' He said it as he pulled the chair out for her but he was barely coping. The closeness to a young mother with her small baby was almost more than he could stand today. Why did she have to call her Mary? Mary, it was all too much.

'Now what will you drink? How about something to eat?' He must carry through with this. After all, he had invited her to meet him because she was a friend till the last. He needed to hear her story. 'I'm going for a clootie dumpling if that helps.' He managed a smile.

'Why not. With tea, thanks Hamish.'

Jeannie placed her sleeping child in the corner a bit away from the heat of the fire while Hamish gave the order, then went to the bar to collect the drinks.

'It wouldn't be a pint if it weren't frothing to the top,' he laughed as he sat down.

'Thanks. They make good tea here too, and I know from experience, the dumplings will be here before we can say Jack Robinson.'

He looked about for the baby.

'Where's baby Mary?'

'There, in the corner.'

He looked at the baby-seat, and could only just see a small face enveloped by a pixie hood. 'Fast asleep.' He took a drink and wiped his mouth. 'Jeannie …'

'Excuse me. Here we are now.' The clooties were placed with care by the young man in black with a number one haircut. His skin glowed with health and he smiled as he spoke. 'Anything else, then?'

Hamish looked at Jeannie. She spoke for them. 'No, thanks.' Then, after some time eating, looked hard at Hamish and said, 'I should have heard what your Mary said that day.' Tears filled her eyes; she sniffed. 'I'm sorry, Hamish. Really sorry.'

'Sorry?'

'Yes. The day that Mary died we met by chance, really. That is, met outside here in the car park. I invited her to have a meal. She said she wouldn't eat, that she was fasting, but that she'd stay a wee while for a chat. I have to say there was something really different about her that day.'

'Fasting! That had to mean she was copying her idol – Margaret, the very pious Queen who frequented this area. Before Easter and Christmas, she'd fast for a long time. I had to stop Mary from copying her. Oh, poor woman, she was in a bad way.'

Jeannie took a last scoop of the dumpling in her spoon, and savoured it. The exquisite cape gooseberry which had decorated her dumpling was still sitting on the side of her plate. He held his up and said, 'The paper-crisp leaves on this thing, aren't they incredible? And – well – I've kept mine till the last, too.' He put the yellow fruit into his mouth and relished the taste of it.

'Jeannie,' his voice quavered. 'What do you mean? There was something different?'

'Well, I knew she'd been really ill. But for the weeks when we met here quite regularly to mainly talk babies – my little boy's in a nursery school today – she was fun to be with. Great fun. She talked quite openly about her illness, saying that when she was really ill she was convinced she was Queen Margaret! She'd laugh at herself over this. Then she'd say, "But I never remember being the Queen, Dr Palgrave tells me." I loved Mary's manner, she was such a warm, sparkling woman when she was well. And she was the greatest teacher. Children followed her around in the playground, carried her bags, and all that stuff that kids do if they like someone.' Her brown eyes were burdened. 'I didn't feel happy being with Mary that day. The baby was with your sister and several times she said she'd be all right. In one moment I thought she said royal baby, as if there was a retinue of staff to care for her. She drank quite a lot of red wine and kind of muttered as if she were praying, even had a little black cross that she held in one hand all the time. Then she rather hurried away saying something about looking for a precious book and I called out "Drive carefully, Mary," and she didn't answer. Why I didn't follow her or call for the ambulance or something, I'll never know. What I do know is that my wee Trevor was bawling and needed feeding so I became preoccupied.' Her hand went to her breast in an unconscious movement. Her breasts were full, even now. She looked down at her baby who was beginning to gurgle. 'Have I been of any help?'

'Yes. A lot of help. Thank you.'

'Well if you don't mind, I must feed wee Mary now.'

'Of course, of course.' He glanced at his watch. 'And I must get back to my family. But one thing. I believe I found that very cross on the stones along near the slipway. Here, it's this one.' He brought it from his pocket.

Jeannie gasped a little. 'If it is then that's amazing!' She smiled broadly, eyes brimming with tears. 'I do hope that was it because you now have a very special link with Mary on that day.'

They stood up and Hamish picked the cradle and child from the floor and handed them to Jeannie. 'A lovely name you've chosen,' he braved as he touched the little one's cheek. Her dark eyes looked through him. 'There's a lovely wee lass there Jeannie, thank you for being Mary's friend. You just must not take any blame. Never. Do ye hear me, lass? My Mary was beyond help just then. Look after yourself and maybe we'll meet again.'

'My hands are full but, here ...' and she kissed him on the cheek. 'If ever you want to talk ... oh, please grab my card from the small pocket of my bag. I'm here for you.'

'Thanks,' he said waving the card. 'I'll remember. And, you remember what I said.'

'I will.' Her smile followed him to the door then she turned to enter the family room.

Terri and Rose were up and looking at photo albums when Hamish returned. Terri kissed him, and he picked up Rose when she ran to him and held her tight.

'We've been looking at photos of her and her mummy,' Terri said. 'Baby photos.'

'Daddy, where did Mummy go?'

He whispered because that's all the voice he could manage. 'To heaven, sweetheart.'

Rose knew about heaven. She did not need to ask any more. Not just now anyway. Hamish knew she would ask the same question many times in the future just as she had for the past three years. It's the sky house that God built for people who die. That's what she knew.

'Terri, your mother's in heaven too isn't she?'

'Oh, yes.'

'So she and my mummy will be good friends. Like you and Aunty Janice.'

Janice came into the room just as Rose said that and she smiled at all of them. Only Rose was smiling at her. Terri had noticed Hamish's voice, and had gone to give him the hug he so craved. He left the room lest Rose should see his tears.

Terri followed. 'Hamish, are you going to find Scotland too full of memories?'

'Och, I'm a bit ashamed of myself. Just now it's damned evocative.' He gave a shot at a smile. 'Tomorrow I'll be better. I've had a really helpful time today. I think I've put the ghost to rest.' It seemed funny. They laughed. At first it was more of a titter then it became a joke to share and they laughed and hugged and laughed again, and hand in hand went to join Rose and Janice. 'And we must go house hunting, school hunting, the lot. We need a home for the three of us. Ours.'

'And Aunty Janice!' rebuked Rose.

'Of course, of course! What say we look for the right school for you Rose, then a house nearby that has plenty of room for all of us.'

'I think so,' Terri said. 'That's the right order.'

Breakfast was under way and all four were back to normal, or so it appeared. Janice was in charge offering too much food, and Terri only wanted coffee and a crumpet. Hamish felt obliged to eat the fruit and cereal, and the scrambled egg, which Janice insisted they must have in order to make good decisions about all these things.

'Right, so we'll study your directory, Janice, unless you can advise us.'

'I know a good bit about schools here, and there's no doubt that St Miriam's, just around the corner from Polwarth Parish church, has by far the best reputation. I wouldn't go past it.'

Hamish smiled at her assurance. 'Up the hill isn't it? And a residential area. I know it.'

'A long way from the Kings BioGen Building for you?'

'It's nothing – maybe twenty minutes on a bad day.'

'In that case, we'll ring St Miriam's and see if we can visit.'

Terri swallowed the last of her coffee and said to Janice, 'That was very good. Thank you.'

'And she's an expert on coffee is Terri.' Hamish looked proudly at his wife. 'You'll want to set up a practice, too. We'll take a look at what specialists are already in the city centre. It's easy for me, my mind is made up for me, but housing? Well, it may be hard to get a city place.'

'Contact an agent. As soon as we've sussed out the school we'll see an agent and find out what's offering.'

Rose had been listening. Eating crumpets piled high with jam, and listening. 'I want to go to the school Aunty Janice says'. Then she turned to her father with a surprise question.

'Daddy, you speak funny. Aunty Janice doesn't.'

The adults laughed, and then felt sorry for Rose who needed a serious answer.

'It's simple. I'm seven years older than Aunty Janice. I was born in Aberdeen and went to school there, and she was brought up in Edinburgh. Here they speak English. In Aberdeen we spoke a Scottish dialect – funny as you call it. But my speech is a bit of both, so you're right, I speak funny.'

Janice smiled concurrence and began to clear away. 'You'll be wanting to get on the road, then.'

Part Three
Chapter 14

'Please Daddy, I want to learn *Ave Maria*.'
'But it needs feeling. Expression.'
'I don't know what you mean.'

Kentaro checked the tuning of his violin. 'Now, you must listen. I will play the piece to you and then you can play it as I played it.'

Hiro knew he had no choice but to listen. It was not good that Chiyo said she would not teach him when he turned eight. He knew that none of the other teachers at the Institute would either. His father did not have the heart to ask them why. Knew that all of them could teach advanced students, but he just didn't want to hear them say, 'Because your son's a little terror, that's why.' So Kentaro was teaching him and not enjoying it. Hiro sat on the small stool and listened as his father overdid the soulful expression to see if he could convey to his son the meaning of feeling. But when the young boy played again, it was as if he had not heard his father. He presented as having no idea what feeling was, let alone finer nuances of tone. Kentaro's heart was sore. This child could not touch Jiro in expressing the music. Jiro had soul in his playing. Any future teacher would have to be able to help him play with expression. No easy task.

Ichiro lay in his hard bed at the top of the building, his bed lamp shining across his face, going over things in his mind. In his hand was a drooped book on the history of music but it held nothing of interest to him. It was three weeks since he had left Japan, but the sense persisted that his parents were glad that he had been accepted for the *Internationale Musikhochschule Berlin* not just for his own sake, but to get him out of their hair now that life with Hiro had become so difficult. The change of living conditions made little difference to how he felt about himself and his brother's existence.

He had tried to concentrate on music and on reading the prescribed texts – had really tried. At home in Japan, he had often read till midnight while listening to tapes of rock music lent him by his friends, and felt smart that his parents never guessed that he was reading books on embryology which he had borrowed from the library, nor that he was listening to rock or rap for that matter. Now in his bed-sit at the *Musikhochschule* he was supposed to be concentrating on classical music, but the conviction he had as a result of his reading – the conviction that he had been violated by three adults in cahoots – dogged his footsteps every minute of his day and night. Puzzlement over Hiro's origins acted like an optometrist's lens. It kept slipping between him and the score he was reading. It coloured everything he looked at; distorted his view of things.

The first biological glimpse of his relationship to Hiro had come in his last year at high school. It had been in the lesson in the bio-tech class on DNA and the make-up of living layers of skin. His finger had felt sore again, trying to tell him something. He felt mad. Yes, he would go mad if he did not get rid of the stupid idea that Hiro might have been cloned from his skin. The semi-darkness was unbearable. He snapped on his room light and threw the book at the wall as he slid out of bed to pace around. The question he felt he must ask his parents was forming in his mind. But how on earth could he ask his parents if a cell of his was used to clone his little brother then grown in his mother's womb? He bent over the wash basin in his bed-sit and splashed his face. Watched the water run down the drain and wished, for all the world, that it was that easy to be rid of a terrifying thought.

Much as he loved his young brother, he had become a catastrophic pain in the arse. A pain he so much wanted to leave behind him when he came to Berlin. The piano score that he was currently learning lay open on his desk. He fingered it fondly. Chopin's *Fantasie-Impromptu*. It demanded more of him than he was giving. Oh how he cursed the whole idea that Hiro had been cloned. It could break him. Unless he could quell it. *'Dame desu. Dame desu!'* He exclaimed in anger.

He knew his parents found Hiro a problem. He stopped to remember that last occasion when he and Hiro had given a recital together.

> His mother had sat in the front row because she had wanted to keep an eye on things. Ichiro thought she would have been happier upstairs where she would have looked down on them, not up at them. It was a strain. But she had insisted. She could slip out easily if she was needed back stage.
>
> The final piece in this farewell recital was with his young brother – the last movement of Cesar Frank's Sonata in A. It left Ichiro feeling exhausted, if not Hiro. The clapping was noisy as both boys smiled and bowed, and then the stamping of students took over as they called for Ichiro to play a last solo. 'Ichiro, Ichiro,' they shouted. Hiro left the stage and his mother slipped out, knowing that he would be in a rage. She could only stand and wait in the side room, horrified at the behaviour of her eight-year-old son who stamped and cried. She felt that this was her worst experience ever, and was relieved when Ichiro and his father appeared again.
>
> 'What on earth is going on here?' Kentaro said. 'Get yourself together Hiro, and go back on to the stage for the presentation of flowers.'
>
> Hiro pushed past Ichiro and together they faced the cheering audience. Ichiro did his best to smile, even took his brother's damp hand in his as they bowed to acknowledge the applause. Many people filed on to the stage to

give them bunches of flowers, and some cried at the thought of having to let Ichiro go off to Berlin. His parents were proud of him, had few qualms about letting him go. It would be the appropriate thing for Ichiro. His talent would blossom. No doubt about that.

As Ichiro packed his bags next day, he overheard his father and his mother in a shouting match. His mother cried, 'Hiro is too much for me. He spoils everything. Everything. Did you see his pouting lips hanging over the bunches of beautiful flowers?'

'I was ashamed.' His father's tone changed. 'I have an idea. Why don't we ask someone like Donna Beauchamp to teach him?'

'But she's in Canada.'

'Yes. You can be free to take him to her. It could do you both good.'

Yuki was quiet. Ichiro waited to hear her answer. He had to listen well for she spoke quietly now. 'Yes. I'll take him to Donna. She's a good teacher, and very sensible.'

Part Three
Chapter 15

In order to get a conversation with her husband, Donna chatted to him while he did some filing. She swiveled back and forth on the chair.

'I reckon this is the appropriate time for Tom to take lessons from Andreas.'

'What, at the *Musikhochschule Berlin* ?'

'Yes.'

'Why now?'

Donna had mulled over this one. She was beginning to think that, while she loved having Tom about, for his own good he must be given wings, something special for himself. Especially after junior arrived, or he would feel obliged to help too often. But she had begun to see that the birth must be a sheltered time for the three of them, most particularly. Warren would understand that, but would Tom? That was the challenge.

She started to search for email. 'Hey, hey.' Her eyes were glued to the screen. She pressed print. 'Hey, look at this.' She wanted to pass the copy to Warren.

'No, you tell me. I'm busy.' He had a bundle of photographs in his hand, and his filing case was open.

'OK. Kentaro and Yuki Fujiwara want me to teach their eight-year-old son, Hiro. They say he's brilliant, but hard to handle. They think I might be able to help him.'

'Help him what? Behave? Be modest? Courteous?'

She did not know exactly what would be expected of her, but she told Warren that for sure, they were not going to offer them board. It was imperative that if she was to teach Hiro, she must keep a professional distance.

Warren laughed. 'Last time you let down your guard, you fell in up to your neck!' He winked at her and she laughed. 'Something like that.'

'So when will they come?'

'If I say yes, they'll come just as soon as passports and visas are sorted. In other words as soon as possible.'

'And you'll say yes?'

Donna had left Japan thinking – if ever I can return the love of these people even a little, I will.

She had wanted to learn the art of calligraphy for one thing, and Yuki had spent hours rubbing the *sumi* stick for her so that she could practise with the brush, and waste no time on making ink. It was often an evening activity, and Yuki would have her in their home so that the twins would be cared for. On a cold night, when they sat together at the *kotatsu*, Donna felt the peacefulness and cheerfulness that came with the sharing of warmth. She felt that she was the fortunate one when Yuki would break from the *kotatsu* and go to fetch tea. But her turn to leave was inevitable. She had to get back to her landlady, her bed.

In the moments it took to roll up her tools in the bamboo mat, then get back into her snow gear, she had a sense of finality, a time to prepare her for her bike ride along the path where the snow had been cleared earlier in the day and was still safe.

'I couldn't not say yes. They were very good to me when I lived in Japan. Spent so much time with me – helping me with my playing. And calligraphy, not to mention Japanese.'

'Of course! You know their language so I guess that'll be one reason why they've asked you.'

'I guess.'

'And of course your reputation as a great teacher.' He was goading her.

'Of course,' she countered. 'And I do know what Fuji expects from his students.'

'So it's Fuji now, is it?'

'No. We always talked about him like that in Japan.'

Warren was concerned that Donna was taking on too much – a baby due so soon, and only twenty-two months after their first. Yet he did not want to sow negative thoughts and decided that Donna knew herself best anyway. He knew that he would have to be more available to help, and they discussed the merits of Tom's going to Berlin now, rather than delaying his opportunity because of the baby. They agreed that they must encourage him to think about himself. The baby would still need lots of holding and pushing when he got back.

Almost the second that Donna arrived back from teaching, Tom swung into the hallway and dumped his pack, took in her flurried appearance, and said, 'Hi! You OK?'

She laughed a little. 'Yes. Still in one piece! Guess, what?'

'Well, it can't be that I have a baby sister,' he teased. 'No, what else could be good news?' He closed the door and they walked to the living room together.

'How would you like to go to Berlin for a stint with Andreas?'

Tom stood in the middle of the room. His mouth wide open. His eyes, enormous.

'But I'll miss the baby. And school. I can't just walk out on my studies!'

'Your holidays? You won't miss school if we can manage it! Depends on when Andreas can take you.'

'OK. So I can handle that.' His eyes clouded a bit. 'Does Dad mind?'

She looked serious. 'He minds, but will let you go for a bit – just a short bit. And we still haven't asked Andreas about it. How about we suggest your going as soon as possible. See if he has room on his time-table.'

He laughed and said, 'And in his apartment.'

He dumped his schoolbag and kissed her on both cheeks. 'Well, I won't say no. Thank you, Donna. Thank you. I feel like a drink. Would you like tea?'

'Yes, thanks.'

Tom clattered about making tea and putting a milkshake on to whirr for a bit, and when the tea was ready he carried a tray to her. She told him about the letter from Japan. He looked impressed. 'Shit! Coming from Japan to take lessons with you! Are you that famous?'

'Nothing like that. It just so happens that arts and music have this marvellous programme going whereby parents and students of music can watch the teacher behind one-way glass. I want to spread the Fujiwara method and my remedial skills as widely as I can. They've probably heard about that. But of course I've known them a long time and they know I speak their language. It's hard teaching your own kid' – she made a wry face at Tom – 'and Hiro needs another teacher. That will be me. I'm planning on saying yes.'

He collected his milkshake from the bench and came back.

'Dad told me what a pain I was. Do you agree?' He sat down and faced her.

'Not at all. You've actually been the exception. After all we're not flesh and blood. That makes a difference!'

His eyes were smiling in answer as he continued to drink his milkshake. He finished with a deliberate noise. Laughed mischievously and said, 'I might have been OK then, but I'm a pain now.'

'Oh, yes. That's for real! Tom, stay a minute. I want you to know a bit more about the Fujiwaras before you go off to your room.' He sat on the humpty nearer her and she told him about the tragedy, and the sadness of losing one twin in Austria. She passed on what she had heard of Ichiro's early reaction – how he did not want to play the piano for a while. 'But now he's excelled himself. He's won a scholarship to study – guess where?'

'At the *Musikhochschule Berlin*? Oh, good one. Perhaps he can accompany me. Oh wow, what a small world! You in Japan, and now Ichiro and me in Berlin!'

'It is! So that's why you need to know that sad, sad story. Ichiro will need all the friends he can make.'

Part Four

Does the soul bear the Child?
Or the Child bear the soul?
What if there is no soul?
Is the Being a monster?

Part Four
Chapter 1

Terri tried desperately to get in touch with Hamish. Did he ever turn off his cell phone? So why, now? She tried his office but the minder wanted her to leave a message. 'For God's sake, that too!' She rang the woman who cleaned for her. 'Doreen, sorry about this. I'm at the school. Rose is missing. The principal tells me that the relief teacher said an Italian man had come for her, said he was a relative. Even though the teacher had said no she lost sight of him, then couldn't find Rose. She's been trying ever since to contact me! I can't reach Hamish. Please get hold of him and tell him to go home. I'm worried out of my mind.'

'Of course. And you ring the police.'

Just as Terri had her finger poised to dial, her mobile rang. 'Hello.'

A voice, a muffled, ugly voice said, 'I've got Rose. Don't contact the police but tell *Dottore* McLeod that if he wants Rose back, he will have to promise to clone Giano. Again! And this time the boys will not die. They will be immune to disease! And they will be tall and intelligent!' His voice had risen.

'Giano? You are Giano? Where are you? You are the lowest of the low. How can Dr McLeod guarantee anything?' She used the language they had for keeping the public at bay.

'Besides, he has a contract and a schedule to research animal health. You're not included! Or are you?' She was putting Rose at risk.

'But of course Dr McLeod must speak for himself. Where can he reach you?'

'He must come to the café at the south end of BioGen buildings at six o'clock. I will wait in my car. He should stand on the corner.'

'I'll tell him. And for God's sake have Rose there safe and

sound.'

'It's over to *Dottore* McLeod.'

She must try to intercept Hamish. Still there was no answer! Damn! If he is ploughing through the traffic on Princes Street at grid-lock hour he will be ages. She pulled out into the traffic – five minutes and she would be home if she were lucky.

As she entered their lounge she heard his car and ran back to greet him. His question hit first.

'Is Rose home?'

'No. So Doreen told you. Thank God there's still time.'

'Time for what?'

'Be calm. Listen. It was Giano snatched Rose from school. He posed as my brother. But he's asked to meet you at 6 o'clock.'

'Gianfranco? Here in Edinburgh? Why? Where?'

'At the south end of BioGen. Outside the café.'

'But …'

'Well, you didn't answer! I couldn't tell you!'

He started for the door.

'He said you must promise to clone him again. This time so that they will not get sick.'

'They? Oh, my God! But I must go.'

'I'm coming.' She grabbed a jacket as they went together down the steps to the car. Hamish did a fast U-turn and sped back along the route he had just come.

'I'm glad you're coming, Terri.'

'I'd rather run actually. Run well away from this Giano. Uh! I never trusted that man.'

They had had a quick run so far and were on the intersection with Princes Street. Hamish had his eyes on the lights. 'Rose's teacher. Is she stupid or something?' Green. He joined the through-traffic and was relieved to be with the flow.

'The class teacher isn't, but she was away! The relief probably doesn't know the kids so well.'

'I guess!' He had a chance to swerve past a slowing bus and gain some speed. 'But there's something important, exciting I wanted to tell you when I got home today! Some really big news! BioGen Science are going to start openly cloning babies! I'm to lead the team.'

'It was coming! It had to come. The world's ready. I see frustrated families every single day. Impotent men crying like hurt children.'

'If only Giano hadn't been so stupid as to turn on these dirty tricks. We could have put him on the list. Decently!'

At the road to the bridge they turned away and pulled in near the café. 'There he is. Hurry.' She looked all about for Rose. 'I can't see Rose. But go, I'll park the car somewhere.' He stopped alongside a parked car, and with the engine running hurtled out almost getting run over. 'Walk slowly,' she hissed. Her words were swallowed by traffic. She saw the men shake hands.

'Giano, where's Rose?'

'Take your time. She's in my friend's car. He is caring for her very well.' His hair was greased to a slick curve above his forehead. The scar on the once-smashed nose showed purple, bridged by the black lenses of his glasses. Hamish felt ill.

'So what do you want from me, Giano? Say it as fast as you can.'

'Aspetti! Aspetti!' Come. We cannot talk here. I must ask you to join me in my car. We will talk where and when I choose.'

'But what about Rose?'

'She will be close by. Don't you worry.'

'Terri is parking the car.'

'Well that's too bad. We did not say we wanted to see her. Before you think of anyone else, give me your mobile.'

Hamish reacted. 'Good God, man! When did you join the Mafia?' But the hand was proffered and he reluctantly handed his phone over.

'Now,' he pointed from his shoulders to a black Mercedes, 'Get in there *Dottore* McLeod.'

Hamish looked about hoping to see Terri. Should he run or scream? Get help? But there was no time, no choice. Nothing but doing as he was commanded. Rose, the poor wee girl. He could not afford to put his darling Rose in jeopardy. He slowly walked the few steps to the car and had to get into the back seat, where he sat confronted by an extremely unpleasant looking man who spread over the remaining two seats. He felt repulsed. Giano drove away at speed, weaving in and out of the busy evening traffic. Hamish hoped they would be caught, but he knew Giano was too cunning to lay himself open to that. He simply drove at the maximum. Hamish tried to look back to see if a car carrying Rose was behind them. All he could see were lights and not faces. It would soon be dark. If only he could get a message to Terri.

Terri walked briskly the two blocks to the café expecting to see Hamish and Giano having coffee and plying Rose with her favourite cookies. The atmosphere was smoky and convivial. She had to move about to see the faces, and nodded to the BioGen staff whom she recognised a little – Jamie, the assistant; Paula Johns, office manager; Alex Kerr, who did lab research, deep in conversation with another woman. It was useless. Hamish was not there. She went outside and waited on the corner in the growing darkness feeling sick and cold. Should she ring the police? But Giano had warned her and she would be stupid not to take notice of Giano. She was familiar with the ways of the mafia. She had been brought up in the south. It scared her. I must keep calm. Go home and wait? Yes, wait. She could be sure Hamish would phone her. Yes, he will call me. She walked, almost ran back to the car and swung into the heavy traffic.

Once they were out of the stream of cars heading away from the city, Hamish leaned towards the driver. 'Giano,' he said.

'What is it you want?'

Giano spat, *'Aspetti!* I cannot talk in the car. I have to remember where to go.'

Hamish knew very well that they must be heading towards the airport. He knew the streets. Then finally, the high-class hotel where they turned in. A car followed close behind. In it would be Rose, perhaps. No, perhaps was not strong enough. It had to be Rose. His precious darling. Both cars arrived in tandem at the well-lit archway to the hotel. The doors to the second one remained closed. Hamish was hurried inside to the elevator, closely shadowed by the big fellow. Giano had a card and used it on the third floor. As soon as Hamish was inside the large, well-appointed suite of rooms Giano said, 'We can talk now.' He indicated a chair that would have been inviting under better circumstances. The big fellow stood at the door with a dead-pan face, hands behind his back, thick jaw stuck forward.

Giano poured whisky and handed Hamish a small goblet. He made pretence at conviviality. Hamish sipped with difficulty, his throat gagged. His lips were numb. Yet he must talk.

'You recovered from your illness then, Giano?'

'I did. But it took a long time. They found all kinds of things wrong with me – everything from my heart to my kidneys. Now two years later, I've never felt better. But the boys! They were weaklings, *signore*. Weak specimens.' His voice was loud, unpleasantly thick and rasping. He gesticulated with his whole arms in a mixture of pleading and desperation. 'All three boys died. Died of a little bit of a sneezy wheezy cold. You got it wrong, *Dottore*. I am giving you a second chance.'

For the first time in Hamish's company, Giano took off his black glasses. He did it with such close attention to Hamish's reaction, that he knew this was part of the persuasive moves planned by him.

Hamish was repelled by his ugliness, but kept on looking.

Was the disfigurement – that obvious cause of childhood trauma and youthful doubt and despair – trying to escape Giano? His lips and cheek twisted towards an ear as he pleaded with Hamish to give it a second go. He cried and held his hands to his head. Throwing up his loose arms in a gesture of despair, he got up from his chair and stomped about repeatedly calling out, 'Another chance! *Dottore!* I give you another chance!'

Eventually he became quiet, sat opposite Hamish, and sipped his drink.

Hamish spoke quietly. 'Why is it so important to you to be cloned at all?'

Giano's head was down, he looked a tragic figure.

'I wasn't fuckin' born like this. I was five – a little, good looking kid five years old when my old man beat me up.' He looked up at Hamish. 'My own daddy. A drinking, violent man who lost control and took to me with a carving knife because I spilt my soup on the table-cloth. On Mamma's white table-cloth. That made him mad as hell. He lashed and slashed until my screaming Mamma and my brother pulled him over backwards on to the floor. Mamma sat on him and Marco got our neighbour and the ambulance and the police. But it was too late for me. I was one fuckin' terrible mess.' He stood up and looked down on Hamish and thumped his chest. 'I want me back again! The nice-looking me that never had a dog's chance.' He poured another whisky and fell back into his chair.

'No woman wants me.' His voice was thick with pain and tears. I'll never have children – not lucky like Roberto. He's got two good kids. Did you know?'

Hamish smiled and acknowledged the news. 'Great! But why three of you?'

'Three it is. They can be mates. And three is what I learned in my catholic school. The Holy Trinity.' He crossed his heart. Hamish didn't want to argue with that one.

This could well become increasingly typical of people in

the future, diseased and damaged by violence both human and ecological, contaminated, impotent, disfigured, wanting to give the unblemished self the chance of a life. He was fully aware that his department would have to set their priorities, or there would be no end to the requests.

And nothing could kill this man's persistence, his dream.

'Genetics are now more advanced. Right?'

'Right.'

'And you can make babies to order. Right?'

Hamish knew what he was getting at. The gene map had been completed for four years now; he had full knowledge of it. 'Giano, there are still many issues to be faced. It will take time.'

'Such as?'

'The ethics of producing babies to order for any old reason. We don't know how much one can alter a child's inherent make-up without causing imbalance! There are many, many issues that will only be revealed in time. We will be experimenting for years yet – experimenting and learning – it will go on forever.'

'Terri did not tell you?'

'She told me. But boys immune to disease, tall and intelligent! No promises!' Hamish put down his glass, and looked sharply at Giano. 'I am not responsible for the diseases that befall humans. We have new and more virulent strains with every generation. There is absolutely no guarantee against diseases we know nothing about. We can inoculate against many of the known but we cannot see what is in store in the future.'

Giano did not sit for long. He was into his third drink, getting up and down, moving about, re-filling his glass, and pacing around. Hamish felt unnerved just keeping his eyes on the man. And he knew that what he was about to say was the crucial point, and that Giano would not like it.

'Clones are actually weaker than children conceived in the natural way. If we clone several generations, one from the other, all resistance to disease will lessen. There is no way we can beat future germs at their own game. Beside it is four years now since I cloned you. Four years! I've lost my touch.'

'But you can and you must clone me. Three of me. Three!' He shouted roughly, 'I gave you fame. You owe it to me. Got that? You owe me.'

'I ... Yes, you did a great deal for me. Perhaps –'

'That Canadian guy Robertson, he made certain that the clone would not have Alzheimer's. You can do something, surely.'

'Oh yes, I can almost certainly do something all right. But why not get the Italian geneticist Marcos to clone you? He is openly doing it. Give your boys Italian mothers? Why not?'

Giano's face was purple. 'The Italian! He has created imbeciles. All the stories are horror stories. They are being hushed up. No, you are the only one. The best.'

For Roses's sake he would concede. He sat forward in his chair.

'Yes, Rose is perfect. Raif's son is marvellous. You're right. Robertson sussed it out and so can I. Yes, I'll do it.'

For a moment Giano's eyes lit up. He stopped in front of Hamish who remained seated and looked down on him. 'If you do not achieve what I want, *Dottore*, you will die. Do you understand?'

'Giano, drop the Mafia tactics will you?'

Giano beckoned to the big fellow. 'Fetch the document, Trudo. *Dottore* McLeod will sign to show that he means it.'

Alarm bells rang when he read the document. Not only was he to agree to cloning him three times within six months, but he had to guarantee the health of the individuals. What was he to do? He knew that if he dithered he could be seen as unsure of himself. He might as well agree – the boys may well live to be a hundred. He signed.

At that moment a door opened and Rose was brought in. She was pale. Her eyes were large with fear. It took her a moment to register who was who in this strange room, and what was happening.

When her dad said, 'Rose, darling Rose. Are you all right? We can go home now,' she tore her hand from the man she was with, and ran to her father almost knocking him down by flinging herself into his arms. She sobbed into his shoulder as he said to Giano, 'We shall keep this secret. I will work on the detail and expect a visit from you. Be at my lab at four o'clock tomorrow. Now call me a cab. Or are you going to offer to take us home?' He whispered to Rose, 'You're heavy, pet.' Gently, he lowered her to the floor and held her hand. Tight.

Giano returned his phone to him. 'Ring Terri. Tell her you will be dropped off at the corner where we met.'

Terri answered too quickly. Her voice was loud and sharp. 'Yes?'

'It's me, darling. And I have Rose. Meet us at the same café corner. Whoever gets there first. Bye.'

Part Four
Chapter 2

Andreas looked at his list and checked the names of those who were to have the first lesson of the day with him. Fujiwara had a familiar ring to it. That's it! The method that Tom was learning by, and which Peter taught us about. He will be a son. If this were so, Ichiro would be an exceptional sixteen, maybe seventeen-year-old. He looked forward to working with him, had seen him around and knew that his new image attracted a lot of attention. But then so what! Each and every one of the students was distinctive.

When Ichiro came in with the violinist Johanna, Andreas was tempted to mention his dad, and then thought better of it. Ichiro was there in his own right as a promising pianist. *'Hallo, guten Tag, Johanna.* Hello, Ichiro, nice to meet you both. English is all right, isn't it? I'm Andreas.' The lesson had got off to a pleasant start, and within moments, the two musicians were positioned to play Brahms Concerto in D. Andreas nodded, and sat down ready to enjoy every moment.

He was enthralled at the excellence of both musicians. Johanna was especially convincing. Some pointers about cohesion between accompanist and soloist were all he could think of, and he emphasised the need for the pianist to be very sensitive to the mood and nuance of the soloist. He played sixteen bars of the slow movement, along with Ichiro, to illustrate his point. The young people caught on fast, playing those same bars of music superbly.

Nevertheless, Ichiro returned to his room after the two hours were up feeling despondent. If only he was not so damned tired. He had to close his eyes during a lot of the slow movement in order to concentrate. Not that that was a problem, because he knew it so well, but he would have liked to have glanced more often at the beautiful girl he was accompanying, if nothing else.

This lack of concentration was one of the reasons why his parents had insisted on his applying for a place at the conservatoire. They were becoming aggravated by the influence Ichiro was having over Hiro. Besides, Ichiro must develop his own ability and should not be in constant league with his young brother, egging him on to play hard pieces. They suspected that, in the seclusion of the music room, where Jiro looked down upon them, Ichiro pushed Hiro. Even though Ichiro had shouted at them, 'Don't you realise, he's trying to win?'

'Win over who?'

'Me. He wants to be like me. Let alone Jiro!'

'Surely not. Hiro is himself a brilliant child. He doesn't need to compete with anyone!' His father had said that, but his parents agreed. Ichiro had it wrong. He was pushing his young brother. They decided he needed a change of teacher, environment, everything. He threatened to shave his head, hang a chain about his neck. Play in a band. Be like his mates, have posters in his room. That had not deterred them.

Now, away from home and in a new environment, he was meant to be feeling cool. He was not. He still could not sleep properly. Even with his shaven head, contact lenses and adornments, he was no different and he knew why. Ever since Hamish McLeod had visited them, he had felt ill at ease and begun to have nightmares where Hamish stood over him with a scalpel in his hand, threatening to take off a finger. He would wake up in a cold sweat, and was increasingly anxious. And then one day as he was careering around, on and off the pavement on his bike with two friends, his hooked-on mini disc pounding hip hop through his earphones, he suddenly saw that he had a kindred spirit in the band TOS! He could see the dripping blood, hear the pain. He wanted to see the Scottish scientist dead. Anyone who did not keep his word deserved to be killed. Yes, Hamish McLeod deserved to die!

He did not have a piano class till the afternoon so he decided to put his stuff around the room to make it a bit more like home. He had to admit he did not feel at home. The crazy accents everyone spoke English with, for one thing. On top of that, the noise of twenty pianos and goodness knows how many strings and woodwinds all practising at the same time. If you went down any one of six corridors, this barrage of sound came at you, changing every three steps or so. And you had to book a room for practise wherever you could. Too bad for him, he was second to last down one corridor and next to a loud cello.

The one really good thing was that he had a bed-sit room with big windows and he could look down on to the sports complex and trees in the park, as well as see across the roofs of buildings, ancient and solid-looking, to the Kaiser Wilhelm Memorial Church with its jagged war-torn steeple. He liked being high up. Home had been on level land with one-and-a-half storeys. Here, he whizzed up in the lift or took the stairs to the third floor and two more steps to his room at the very top. Already, he had put his laptop on his desk and his brand new multi-media player on the table beside his bed. He selected *Out of my Flesh* and played it loudly. On the wall he put up the one poster he had bought at the airport – the adored shaven head, chain, and earring with the words that really spoke to him: "Run in My sandals/Blister your toes …" Mum and dad would go berserk if they saw me with this, he thought. Let alone the hip-hop!

But he was on his own now, and would do exactly as he liked. He studied the family photograph and thought – We didn't hate each other did we? Young Hiro was a dork of the worst order. Plays like he is crazy and it works.

The photograph he had brought with him of himself and Jiro in Galtür stood alongside the family photograph. Then he took a bit of time to consider the likeness between himself, Jiro and Hiro. We are spitting images of each other! Why had I not seen that. Even the glasses. I have heard that foreigners reckon all Japanese look alike, but we do not. This is uncanny. Hiro, Jiro and me – peas in a pod. Clones! A chill went down his back, he felt sick. Was sure of it now. Absolutely no doubt. Yet he did not want to believe it. They wouldn't. I must not think about it. My parents are supposed to be decent people. They are decent people. And Hamish McLeod? Oh, no. It now fell into place, the reason for the nightmares and his absorbing hatred of the geneticist. That is why we went to Italy. Oh, my God, my God! I always knew.

He threw himself on to his bed and cried until he fell into a deep sleep.

An hour later, he woke up with a start, remembering what had happened and what he had been doing. He must do some more unpacking. Make himself busy. He opened a cupboard and looked towards the bag he had pulled from under his bed, and thought this is the place for all that stuff. Japanese food in packets – enough to keep him going until a parcel of more between-meals nibbles arrived from his mother. That was the thing he had dreaded most – having to eat German food! But how was he going to beat the smell? He knew that his room would soon be stinking of noodles and crisps. He would buy air-freshener, that is what he would do.

There was a tentative knock on his door. Ichiro zapped his multi-media player into silence and opened the door to Johanna and felt awkward. 'Hello. Please come in.' He could hear his mother's voice, her way of welcoming people with politeness. He had never asked a girl to his place ever, and here he was with one in his study-come bedroom. But Johanna was not shy.

'You play the Brahms like it's easy, Ichiro.'

'It is.' He did not want to sound overly smart so he added, 'It took a lot of work.'

'I bet. By the way, I thought you might like to listen to this.' She held out a mini disc. Know it?' The TOS poster caught her eye. She gulped. 'You like that stuff? I didn't know, wouldn't have guessed. Maybe ...'

'Oh, it's personal. I'm not into drugs or anything, it's that I sometimes feel marginalized – like Tiny Smithers.'

'Can I be mega personal?'

'I guess.'

'You look a bit like him – shaven head, chain.'

Ichiro wished that this moment was not so embarrassing. 'Yeah. I copied him I dare to say!' He wanted to get away from this stuff, talk about her. He looked at the title – *Tom Petty and the Heartbreakers Echo,* and the title of the first song, *Room at the Top.* His face lit up and he laughed as Johanna laughed with him. 'I have to say it looks weirdly appropriate! Why don't you sit down on the bed, and I'll put it on.' And then he realized – 'Stupid me, my mini disc player, it's still packed away. Can you please wait while I find it?' Half of him disappeared under the bed, and after some rummaging around in two different boxes, he wriggled backward and stood up with a red face. They both laughed as he extracted the cord and plugged it in. The bag still stood in the middle of the floor, so as he pressed play, he said, 'I want to pack this food away. You take the chair, and I'll get this stuff into the cupboard while we listen. OK?'

It took the best part of a quarter-of-an-hour to pack the dried food on to shelves neatly enough for his liking. The syncopation in the songs kept him moving – at times he swung about as well – and he had to acknowledge to himself that he had seldom enjoyed himself so much. Occasionally he glanced at Johanna and felt overwhelmed by her presence. She looked so lovely, the clearest ever blue eyes set in neatly formed features, and long fair hair tied up to both sit on top and fall around her face as well. She had been brought up in New Zealand, but her mother was German. She had told him that when they had been introduced on his second day there.

'Like it?' Johanna asked.

'Yes. I do.' And because it was ingrained in him to do so, he gave a slight bow. 'Very much.'

'Well then, why don't you keep it for a couple of days?'

'I'd like to. Thank you.'

And suddenly she was gone, and he was left to hear the next songs himself. The first was *Free girl now*. He thought, rather coyly, that maybe she was a bit shy to share the next song in his company.

In bed at midnight, after two hours of tossing and turning and going crazy in his head, in the room adorned with meaningful images, at the top of a foreign conservatoire, Ichiro Fujiwara, son of a famous and decent man and his charming wife, came to the realisation that he was unfit to continue as a musician and as a human being. He felt the force of desire for a girl for the first time ever. His mind and his body were out of control. Every possible emotional problem encountered by the human race was suddenly his. He was in despair. From the moment he had looked at his family photographs of three boys staring out as if they were each other, he knew that his life was unredeemable. He had been ill-used by Dr Hamish McLeod. Betrayed by his parents. Violated. He was bad. Totally corrupted. He could not become good on earth. It was too late for that, he would have to look for safety in another place. He got out of bed, studied the darkness which covered everything, and used his memory of the intricate layout beneath him to imagine the trees, the sports complex, the swimming pool, the streets and buildings at the heart of Berlin. That broken-down tower, it was clear. There was a flare of light in the distance which turned the church to gold and sharply defined the war-damaged tower. He knew exactly what he was to do.

Part Four
Chapter 3

'I don't know what to do for Luke, he's too wide awake for this time of night,' Donna said to Warren who also looked tired.

'Hand him to me, darling. I'll push him up and down the hallway. I've got a lot of thinking to do and the movement will help.' Donna handed the grizzling boy to his daddy, and the child swung around and reached for her again, almost falling from his daddy's arms. 'My golly, he's strong! I nearly dropped him.'

'Come on Luke, I'm going to push you in your stroller.' Luke became quieter but fought sleep. Once tucked up and on the move, he stopped simpering and sucked a corner of the cuddly rug while keeping his eyes open. Warren kept pushing. Each time he passed the doorway to the living room, he caught sight of his pregnant wife sitting listening to music through earphones. She was a picture. The light from the window to the right of her created an aura about her blond hair, now shoulder length. It curved over the orange-clad length of her and poured into the pages of the score she was holding. He felt deeply, profoundly happy, yet mildly guilty that he had let her have a second child so soon. His mind sharpened. He did some intensive thinking and shaped the story he would write. Robertson was making history again. This time, not happily.

The little girl, whose birth had done so much for genetic history, was now showing signs of retarded growth. At seven she was still as small as when she had been five. Would she grow any more? Was her growth only temporarily stunted? Did this have anything or nothing to do with the protection she was given against Alzheimer's? Her parents were considering taking Dr Robertson to court. Did they have a case? Warren considered the facts of the case as he knew them. Indeed, he needed to be careful that he give only details which would not influence any court hearing. It was brave of the parents to tell the world that their daughter was, in fact, the child cloned by Robertson over seven years ago.

Luke's eyes were closed but Warren decided to keep the stroller moving a little while longer to be certain that he was asleep and would stay that way when transferred to his cot. His heart went out to the parents of little Louisa. Perhaps, now that he had considered the whole issue, he would see if the parents would give him an interview on how it felt to be part of history. Yes, he would call Don and Jianne Maynard and see if they would tell their story. He lifted Luke from his stroller and kept him swinging a little until he was in the cot and then rocked his body some more. Less and less. And yes, he did not stir. Warren tiptoed from the room and his step became normal as he reached Donna. She looked up, took off her earphones and smiled.

'Thanks, honey. I was tired out.'

He bent to kiss her and said, 'Can you get an early night? You've earned it. You taught three hours and,' he gently laid a hand over her bulge, 'carried this one around all day.'

She got up from her chair and curved her spine backwards with her hand splayed over her hip. It had been a tough day, but she would wait for Tom. He was not out often, but recently had become as crazy about the computer as his friend Johnny. He would be back at ten, brought home by Johnny's mum. That would not be too bad. Warren had been a bit doubtful about this new activity, but Donna had reminded him that it was the interactive learning of the future, and Tom was fortunate that he had a friend with some of the latest programmes.

'Games, I suspect. OK. I'm anxious to get the Maynard's case sorted so I'll try and see them tonight.'

After arranging to visit the Maynards in forty-five minutes, Warren sat at his desk and formulated the questions he would put to them. And now that he was sitting in their lounge, looking into their eager faces, he was glad of his preparation. He addressed his first question to Jianne.

'How many family members have Alzheimer's disease?'

'Five.'

'Is it only the females?'

'Yes.'

'Have you, Jianne, any evidence that you will get it? Been tested? Or are you fearful because it's likely, given family history?'

Jianne came up with her considered answer. 'I hate admitting this, but I have tested positive, yes. I even half told you when you took those photos after Louisa was born. Remember?'

'Yes. Yes.' When he had been at his monitor thinking of questions, Warren had decided against asking, 'Has the cloning of Louisa been worth it?' If ever Louisa read reports, and well she might, it would break her heart if her parents said no to that. He continued to address the mother.

'Louisa is a beautiful child. You must be more than glad that she will never get Alzheimer's. Do you think that you will encourage others in your position to take the same course of action? Especially now that Dr Robertson has perfected his technique?'

This question brought forth a torrent of anger from both parents. They had already made up their minds that his technique was totally undeveloped and inadequate for what he claimed he could do. He should not have used them as guinea pigs. Absolutely not! They had suffered most awfully since Louisa stopped growing. It had become a living nightmare. Day and night it haunted them. They are taking Dr Robertson to court to settle their concern once and for all. For a while no one said anything, and Warren decided on letting one of them break the silence.

It was Don. Suddenly he said, 'OK. If his lack of experience in cloning is proved not to be the reason for Louisa's retarded growth, and if Dr Robertson has now perfected the technique, then not only has he given us a wonderful gift but he has benefited the whole of humanity. And in regard to the principle of cloning, to which we've given a great deal of thought, then we are convinced it is the way of the future. My experience proves it.' Tears caught in the young man's throat. He coughed a bit before he carried on. 'You see, I cannot produce a child. My sperm count has been so weak that it might as well have been nil. The struggle we went through to conceive was terrible.' And now he let his emotions overwhelm him. Unashamedly, he cried. After a time when both his wife and Warren sat waiting in limbo, he said, 'You can tell my story if you want. More and more men are losing their sperm to pollution of all kinds. It's sad. In fact it's a bloody catastrophe.' He stood up. 'Yes, tell my story to the world's media. There will be millions of us men in the same plight. In fact, you can put my photo in and all, if you wish. I mean, look at me. I'm told I'm a clone of Tom Hanks. He's a blimmin star! If good looks count, I should be virile. Fathering a child every year. And I can't have a bloody one. Not one.' He sat down. Warren thought he looked washed out. After a moment he bucked up and said, 'I'm beginning to feel relieved that I've said all that.' He looked directly at Warren. 'Tell me mate, have you got any kids?'

Warren brought a photograph from his pocket. 'That's my big boy holding my young son by my second wife. We waited almost four years for the baby. But he's a great wee fellow.'

Jianne's eyes shone. 'Oh, you must feel really happy about that. Congratulations on those fine children. No, truly.' She showed it to her husband. 'Did you see them, lovie?'

He acknowledged his wife again now that he'd had his say. 'We'd have liked some boys, wouldn't we?'

Warren stood up, ready to leave. 'I'll be reporting the trial.'

Together they said, 'Oh, that's great!' Jianne continued, 'We feel we can trust you to handle it well.'

'Thanks for that. I'll certainly do my best – especially for

Louisa's sake. You know, her future and so on. The press can be vicious. I'm aware of that. So of course, there's no way I can stop some other journos from being stupid and insensitive. You must think about that too before you take Dr Robertson to court.'

'Warren, guess what?' Donna got up from sitting listening to music to greet Warren with an email letter in her hand.
'So?'
'Andreas insists that Tom come now. Later, he'll be too busy.'
'Have you told Tom?'
'Yes, I did. I rang him at his friends, and he's OK. He knows there's time enough to help with the baby later, and now is his moment to learn from Andreas. He can accept that!'

Part Four
Chapter 4

Terri checked the time. 'Hamish, I have to go. Get up, sluggard. Rose is at school.'

Hamish blinked his eyes. Registered who was talking. Saw the light of day through the window west of their bed and said, 'Shit!' as he dashed to take a shower and dress.

Gulping coffee he set out for work as fast as the streets, now cleared of snow, allowed. This could be the day!

The semi-furtive business of cloning his first two babies in Italy was no longer relevant. He was now doing all the things he wanted – would never need to lie, keep certain tasks for himself alone, or refuse to discuss his views on cloning with anyone. Best of all, he did not need to work alone at night in the lab. That is, except for Giano's babies. He would clear that one, then start doing it with the team and all above-board. Giano, who had returned to Italy, contacted him every third day, and Hamish dreaded admitting that this time the fertilisation was not happening. He would inject their every conversation with words of hope he did not feel.

'I'm wanting to use my new technique. We talked about it once. Even laughed about it. Dividing an embryo into three. It still requires patience. I am confident it will be all go any day now.' He felt two-faced. He was in fact, holding the new method in abeyance in case the old did not work. He finished every conversation by saying, 'I must go, now. It could be tonight!'

Running up the steps into the BioGen science building was about the sum total of his exercise for the day. He hung up his snow jacket in the outer cloakroom, and donned his white coat without more than a nod to others who were doing much the same. Except that an assistant stopped him and said, 'I have a problem in wording the announcement that we're going public. I need help, Dr McLeod. Can you give me some of your time?'

'When?'

'Now?' The young woman looked eager.

'No. No. Not first thing. Sorry. Say, er, at three this afternoon?'

Her face fell. 'But …'

'Sorry. I will see you at three.' He pushed past and almost ran to make up lost time in getting to his lab and the heat-controlled chambers. Two of the eggs had taken. Yipee! He would work quickly to have them implanted by Terri. On his cell phone he pressed her code. 'Terri. Good news about two.'

'Only two?'

'That's right. Two. We'll get a third soon, I'm sure of it now.'

'Right. Then bring the embryos to my rooms. I'll have the women there as soon as can be arranged.'

Hamish carefully placed the eggs into the carry-bag designed for safe transportation of embryos at the right temperature. Och, this has to be a good day.

He rushed past Jamie with barely a nod, and he heard him say, 'I can't believe I'm seeing Hamish McLeod in such a hurry.' He called, 'Have a good day, Hamish.'

Hamish ignored him knowing that he deserved all he got. After all, he used to behave much more civilly. Jamie was more than a student, he was a colleague. 'Get these blasted eggs into wombs and I will be myself again,' he thought.

He drove the short distance to Terri's rooms and he felt good when he saw her smile. It had been a tough two months. And as if Hamish didn't have enough to deal with, an old concern was resurfacing. A personal resolve he had made after that conversation with Ichiro in Japan, when the lad had told him what his science teacher had said about the collection of DNA samples – and that was, to tell him the exact origin of Hiro. He was feeling an increasing need to get the truth off his chest. It probably mattered more to the young man than it did even to his parents, especially now that he was nearing adulthood. He would find out his address, in case he had left home, and see him in person. Sense his readiness to know the truth.

Terri was ready and excited. He watched with admiration as she dealt with the embryos, and left her surgery before he committed any professional indiscretion. He had his own work to do, and there was snow in the air, which gave him added incentive to get work done before he literally got snowed in.

At night, he aimed to get home at his usual time for dinner. A light fall of snow had made the roads annoyingly slow again. He had to take care and was delayed by some eight minutes. Rose ran to the garage when she heard the car and said, 'Daddy, I'm organising my birthday party all myself.'

'Very good, Rose. Am I invited?'

Rose took his hand and said, 'Nine years since I was born. You were there weren't you? So you have to come to every one of my birthdays.'

Rose had touched the centre of his being. He put down his bags and gave his daughter a long hug. Her slight frame, the long and curly hair which fell about her shoulders and back, impacted on him. He felt more himself again. Human. He had become something other than his true self. The hard shell which coated his senses was cracked open.

'So tell me when your party is and I'll be there.'

'It will be a Saturday and I'm inviting ten friends.'

'And that's because you're turning nine or because that's all the friends you have?'

She laughed. 'You're funny, Daddy. Another friend can't come so I didn't invite her.'

'And what do you want from Terri and me?'

'A bike. I told Terri.'

'Oh, I see. I'll talk to Terri, then.'

Hamish made the dreaded call to Giano from his bedroom. He had missed his call at work by turning off his phone at three, so had to call him back whether he liked it or not. Giano wasn't satisfied. 'Two? Only two?'

'Soon, I believe there will be a third. I will let you know as soon as the third has taken. Please be patient. It is the essence of my work.'

'And three is what I want. You make sure it's three I get, Hamish.'

After the meal, Hamish promised to help Rose with some science homework. It took an hour, but when Rose was getting ready for bed, Hamish said to Terri, 'She's a good, clear thinker, that wee lass.'

'Yes. I'm impressed. Her teachers are too, by what I gather from my brief chats at the classroom door.'

Rose came back dressed in her long nightie and dressing gown. Hamish thought she looked beautiful and said so.

'Daddy, you're biased! You should see my friends. I'm really old-fashioned with my long hair. Tina has this very short cut that she zizzes to stand it up.' She'd mimed as she spoke, and they all laughed. 'I want to get my hair cut too.'

'And zizz it?'

'Yes! I do!'

'Well Terri, we can arrange that, can we?'

'You mean me?' Terri was in a good mood. 'Of course. And now it's to bed, Rose. Goodnight.' She hugged her tight, then Rose hugged her daddy and ran off to bed. 'Thanks for helping me tonight, Dad.'

'This is a pleasant change.' Hamish poured drinks – a gin and tonic for them both.

'Yes, we're more relaxed than we've been for a long while.'

'How about we dance, sweetheart?'

'Oh, I've lost the habit. I was about to settle down with a book. No, I could do with that. Let's dance.'

Hamish put on a waltz. 'Terri, may I have the pleasure of this dance?'

'Why yes, you may.' She hurried to take another sip before putting down her glass and stepping out. They were happy.

It had been almost three months since they had danced and gone to bed together. He felt her tension go as he held her to himself. Whispered in her ear words which only she would understand. She let her dark head rest against his shoulder and gave way to the slow beat of the waltz. They would dance for the next hour, and finish with the *cha cha*.

Just as they ended with an exaggerated flourish and a wild shout, the phone rang. It was Gianfranco. 'I forgot to say that I will be coming to visit at the beginning of February. I must meet the three women who are carrying my boys then. It is important to me that I know them and want to make sure that they are well remunerated.'

'All right. So let us know when you will be here.'

'I will. Goodnight.'

'Goodnight.'

Hamish snapped off his phone. 'I could do without his pestering me. That guy makes me nervous.' They made their way upstairs. In bed, his laughing was charged with nervousness. Terri tried to distract him. 'Can you peel an orange without breaking the skin? I'll race you, starting now ...'

'You know I cannot. I can clone babies. Well, some anyway. But I cannot peel ... not this one. Bother! It's messy.' He put the oozing orange back on the saucer and hopped from the bed to wash his hands. He came back and said, 'There's something else I am really good at though, and that is peeling clothes.' He stripped off and slipped into bed. She put a warm dry hand on his thigh, and at the same time reached to put her half-eaten orange on the bedside table. They snuggled down. 'You'll just see. I can get your nightie off in the twinkling of an eye.'

'Can you now?' And their laughter was no longer fraught by tension.

They slept soundly and woke with the alarm. As they dressed, Terri said, 'It's good to be back to normal. Don't let that scoundrel come between us again. This last three months have been awful.'

'It's not over yet, I'm afraid. Not until the third egg is fertilised!' He ran a comb through his hair and thought, Mary would be telling me to get a trim, she would. 'And why it has not fertilised is anybody's guess.'

'Except that just anybody wouldn't have a hope of guessing. I must hurry. I have a string of appointments today quite apart from keeping Rose in mind. Ever since that awful day I've made sure of getting to her classroom before the bell.'

'I'm grateful.' He kissed her and said, 'I'll fix breakfast.'

'Thanks. There's new coffee on the bench.'

Part Four
Chapter 5

'Our baby could be two weeks early, Warren!'

He was a bit concerned because he understood it was best to be full-term.

'If there's something I can do to help you get to term, tell me won't you. You are OK, aren't you?'

'Yes, I'm fine. We might have got our dates wrong! Maths and all that!'

He laughed. 'Let's sit down. I'm stuffed after being in court all day.'

'The Maynard case?' She sat with him and put an arm across his shoulders.

'Tell me exactly what they've taken Robertson to court for.'

The day had got off to a slow start in the courtroom, mainly because the judge had skidded on an icy road and had to wait for a tow. When they did get started the prosecution claimed that Robertson was inexperienced, and had no right to lead the Maynards to believe that he could clone a human, let alone achieve genetic modification. This amounted to pronouncements of inexperience and incompetence. When the doctor was called to tell the court the details of Jianne's family, she quietly sobbed, and that had been a distraction. He showed the judge photographs of all the family, and talked about the incidence of Alzheimer's in the women, but emphasised in no uncertain terms that every family member, as far back as the five generations they knew about, was of normal stature. Warren had watched Jianne's reaction in particular. He sensed that for her, it was like being pinned to the wall as a numbered exhibit. Once she had her sobbing under control she held the floor in place with her eyes, her usually glowing skin a ghastly grey.

Warren told Donna some of this and her response showed concern for the child, Louisa. Warren affirmed her concerns.

'Yes, I worry about her. All those people who filled the court have intimate knowledge of her background and will always recognise her. I was feeling sorry for her when I heard the family doctor giving his evidence. He suspects that she will remain a little person, the first in her family. It kind of points to the incompetence of Robertson. He'll cop it if that's what comes out, eventually.'

'By the way, I read the article you'd written on Don Maynard and his impotence. It was good. Not to say that the photo didn't help. A spitting image of Tom Hanks for sure!'

Warren laughed as he stood up. 'He knows he is! It's a good likeness. Now, about you. Are you equal to getting supper, sweetheart?'

'Yes. Sure. But first I must pick up Luke from the nursery. I'll have supper ready at about six-thirty.'

'Great.' He gave her a kiss and headed to the basement.

A week had gone by since Tom had left for Berlin. The day was different without him – his violin, his chatter and company at meals as much as anything. Donna thought of him now as she drove to pick up Luke. She had to take him home to a quiet house. Warren in his office made no difference to household noise. Tom did.

'Hello, darling,' she said, when he ran into her arms, and gave the extra swing of his little body which helped Donna lift him up high before carrying him to the car. It always made her laugh at how he did that. She said, 'Wave goodbye to Danielle and Tim. Bye now. See you tomorrow.'

When he sat down to supper, Warren said, 'There's a brief note from Tom. Shall I read it to you?'

Donna knew that Warren needed to read Tom's words many times. He missed him so much. 'Sure. Thanks.'

'"Hi Donna, Dad and Luke. I'll give you the bad news first. I thought my violin playing was pretty good until I heard all the guys here. They're all geniuses. Andreas tells me I will make it, too, given time. But I'm in for some mighty hard work. The good news is that Ichiro is a wow pianist and will play Svendsen's *Romance* with me at my first lunch-hour recital. Well, not mine only. All the class will play items, and it's just internal – no one from the public. The food is great. Andreas is just as much a pal as ever. Love you. I miss Luke. And the Tobys. Cheers, Tom."'

'Thanks. He sounds OK. By the way, Yuki actually phoned me at work. She said that she and Hiro are stopping off to see Ichiro on their way here, so they'll be delayed by a few days. They'd like to have a first lesson a week later.' Warren and she had agreed that they would not let Hiro's lessons put her under any extra pressure. If they came a week late, they might not get a lesson for a few weeks, but that would be their problem.

'Good. It's great she can see Ichiro. I hope she says hi to Tom, too.'

The Ichiro that came down the last segment of the stairs to the foyer of the halls of residence towards Yuki and Hiro looked like a Buddhist monk toYuki. She was surprised to see such a person in this place, but not fazed, because that bare head was a familiar part of her schemata. Except that as he got nearer, he spoke and called, 'Mother, you have come!' His arms came out to her; he smiled. 'You don't recognise me?'

'Is it? Oh, of course! Ichiro. My son, my son. No I didn't see you – the light from the window in the stairwell – it gave you a halo.' She laughed; he laughed. The ice was broken.

He was pleased about two things. The first one he had debated over ever since he knew his mother was visiting, and then decided to take the poster down and not openly arouse her over TOS. The second thing that pleased him was that his mother was wearing the fur coat which he thought made her look so glamorous. As for his young brother Hiro, he looked small and pale in his warm navy jacket and plaid muffler, tired from his journey. Ichiro did not need to look at the label to know that the scarf was his Burberry one. 'Sorry

I couldn't meet your plane,' he said, hugging his little brother. When he pulled up again, he put a hand on Hiro's shoulder and asked, 'How's your playing, Hiro?'

'Good. I'm on to Mozart now.' It was as if he didn't know his brother, yet when Ichiro, knowing this was how it was for the little guy, hummed a fragment of *Czardas*, it all came to him. He put his violin case down on the stair and threw himself at his brother and hugged him so tightly that they, and their mother, all cried. Laughed and cried. 'I miss you too much.' Hiro whispered. 'You were my best teacher ever!'

'I miss you too. Let's go to my room,' said Ichiro who was fighting to cope with his emotions. Guilt was the most invasive. He did not want to upset his mother but he knew that if he did not get the truth today he would break into bits.

'There's a lift right here. Mum, let me take your case.'

As they zoomed up the three floors, Ichiro said to Hiro, 'What? You playing Mozart concertos?'

'*Rondo*. Soon, I'll do the concertos.'

'Good man!' They had stopped at the second floor. 'Not yet. I'm right at the top of this building. Do you want to see my view?'

'*Hai!*'

As they left the lift, Ichiro said, 'I have a surprise for you, Hiro.' To his mother he said, 'Mum, you know Donna of course. Well her stepson, Tom, is here for a few weeks. Tom offered to let Hiro sit in on his violin lesson. It starts in twenty minutes. Tom's waiting in my room.'

'Should I be there too?'

'No, Mum. I want you all to myself. Hiro'll be fine.' To Hiro he said, 'You'll sit and listen without being cheeky, won't you?'

Even before Ichiro opened the door to his room, they could hear Tom's scales rising and falling in roller-coaster shapes. When the door opened, Tom stopped playing, and said, '*Konnichi wa!*'

'*Konnichi wa*, Tom!' Yuki was smiling.

So this is Ichiro's mother. She's beautiful. 'Hiro, hello.'

'Hello, Tom. I'm coming to your lesson.'

'So Ichiro's told you, eh?'

'Yep.'

Tom packed up his instrument and bow, and said, 'Ready? Come on then.'

'Just a moment. I have to see Ichiro's view!'

Ichiro led him to the window. 'See, I'm right at the top here. Look over there. All the sports facilities, a gym, an Olympic-sized swimming pool. And can you see that broken spire in the distance – looking golden in the sun? That's the famous Kaiser Wilhelm Memorial Church!'

'*Nani?*'

'Never mind. But it's the city over there. There's everything. But you can see more later, Hiro. Better go with Tom.'

'*Daijobu*' he said, and off he went.

'See you later, Hiro,' said his mother.

'Well son, you're looking pale,' Yuki said, when alone with Ichiro.

'Yes, Mum. I can't sleep. But you must sit down. Come and sit on my chair and I'll sit on my bed.'

'Thanks, darling.' Yuki knew that Ichiro's heart was heavy. She could only guess why, and felt more frightened than she had ever felt. She hoped she was wrong.

'Are you working too hard, son?'

'No. That's not it. I can't work at all. It's probably crazy Mum, but I keep worrying about …' He stopped. Sat on his hands, swung his legs, and his toes scraped over the floor.

'Worrying? What about?'

'I can't bear to say it, Mum.'

Yuki stood up, and walked to sit beside him on the bed. 'Please tell me.'

'Well, you know how my finger was scraped by that Hamish in Italy?'

'Of course. It's not still sore is it?'

He was crying. The tears fell heavily to his knees. 'No. No.'

'Well then?' She gave him a tissue from her purse. 'Here, wipe your eyes.'

He turned his head away and dabbed his eyes and cheeks. 'It's Hiro. You see, I know that babies can be cloned using someone else's cell – all that stuff – well I thought that maybe Hiro was cloned using my skin cell, and …' He sniffed and blew his nose.

Yuki felt nauseated. Why do I have to go through this alone? Kentaro should be here. How can I tell my boy the truth? It is too hard for me. It will kill us yet.

Yuki spoke softly, haltingly. 'Well yes, Hiro was … well he … your father's idea. Not mine. But I had to bear the child.' Now she was crying, and Ichiro felt angry. Angry at his father and angry at his mother. He stood up and looked down on his mother.

'So I am Hiro's father? Whatever. Surrogate? That will do. Aren't I? Aren't I? Look at me, Mum. Am I Hiro's surrogate father?'

'I'm not sure. That doesn't seem right. It's much more noble than that, Ichiro.'

'Noble?' he shouted. 'Noble? I wasn't asked. I didn't give my permission, did I?'

Yuki got up and tried to hug him. He shoved her away. She trembled and cried loudly.

'Mum, be quiet. Someone may hear you. Just tell me. Am I his father? Father to that little boy you call a monster? I've heard you. And who's the mother? Can't you see it? I know about incest too. So we are the parents, you and I. Oh …' He fell on to his bed and buried his head and wept so that his whole body shook.

Yuki looked about for help not knowing what to do. She could not touch him or speak to him. She would just have to sit and wait.

After half an hour, Tom and Hiro burst into the room. Yuki had splashed her face. She tried to be cheerful as she said, 'You're back, then.' She felt quite faint.

Ichiro got up from the bed, grabbed his music satchel and dashed out of the room without a word.

Tom and Hiro were dismayed. Silenced. 'What has happened?' Tom managed to say after a few moments.

Yuki could not put the truth into words no matter how much she might have wanted to.

'He's a troubled young man', was what she said. 'Tom, please excuse us. Is there someone in authority I can speak to?' She looked at her watch. 'Yet, there's barely time for anything. We must get back to the hotel. Hiro, come please.' She smiled weakly. 'Tom, thank you for letting Hiro listen to your lesson. We'll come back tomorrow. Ichiro will be more cheerful by then. Please, please, can you keep an eye on him for me? I'm to see the Director tomorrow, anyway. Please tell Ichiro I'm coming back. We want to hear him play, don't we, Hiro?'

'Yes I'll do that,' Tom said, 'but Mrs Fujiwara, excuse me, but you look very faint. Can I help?'

'Thank you, Tom. Ichiro is the one you must help. Please. He has had a shock.'

Part Four
Chapter 6

The courtroom was silent. Everyone stood waiting for the judge on day seven of the trial. Professor Keith Robertson was to speak in his own defence and many eyes were focused on him since there was no other diversion. He was wearing a dark pin-striped suit that must have been a recent purchase. In fact it had been made for him, so short was he. He did not like to have a suit that had been tucked and sewn until it was small enough to hang well. The circlet of hair around his bald pate was carefully trimmed and brushed. His face was expressionless but those nearest him were aware of his attempt at slow, rather noisy deep breathing to steady himself. He had failed to trim the hair in his nostrils for some time.

Don and Jianne looked comfortably confident that Robertson would not have a case that was worth making. The evidence from doctors and their own lawyer had been totally in their favour. They had almost lost sight of the fact that Louisa was the sad little figure at the centre of all this because the media had treated them like millennium heroes, people who have been prepared to test the science of cloning. Warren need not have worried about adverse reporting. His colleagues had shown a high degree of sensitivity that he almost found hard to match. And that went for television and radio too.

'Please rise.' Everyone rose as one body, except that as she stood, a journalist somehow managed to knock her laptop to the floor with a terrible clatter. She bent to pick it up and when everyone was seated, she sat down, embarrassed and eager to check the screen to make sure she had not lost any of the notes she had accumulated.

'Silence in the court.'

Dr Robertson was called forward and asked to swear to

tell the truth. There was no problem with that. He wanted to tell the truth. As he saw it.

'I have a double doctorate – in biology and in embryology. For my work in the elimination of Alzheimer's disease, I have been nominated for the Packman Prize for 2009.' He put up a hand to smooth his hair, a gesture which made some people smile. Dr Robertson mistook their animation for acclamation, and he almost smiled as he continued: 'I began my experiments in cloning by working with mice. I worked long and hard over a period of fifteen years to perfect my technique. In regard to cloning humans there had to be a first. Mr and Mrs Maynard pleaded with me to clone a child for them.'

He glanced at the couple then went on, 'Mr Maynard has gone public about the reason why he wanted a cloned child. The reason was totally compelling. Sterility.' He paused, and waited for this to impact upon the judge and jury, the lawyers, the journalists and the public. It was, as he said, a totally compelling reason for wanting a cloned child.

At the end of the day, the courtroom was quickly vacated. People did not stand around in groups as they had at the lunch-hour break. Daylight would soon give way to a black and snowy night. People wanted to get home. Warren had parked his car in his designated park close to the court, and he was in it and away without a word to anyone. He had talked to the Maynards at lunch-time and they spoke of their disbelief at the pride of the man. For the first time since they had met him, they realised that they had become a statistic. 'I feel dehumanised,' said Jianne with tears in her eyes.

Toward supper time, Donna was wanting to lie down, so uncomfortable was she on her feet. She wished that Tom were here to play with Luke who seemed to be particularly scratchy. She put on the CD of the piece that Hiro had most recently learned in Japan, the Mozart Rondo in D, then thought it was not the best choice. Little Luke was jiggling around with excitement and she wanted him to quieten down. This had been one of Tom's favourite pieces to learn and she thought of him now. Dear Tom, he wrote of his concern about Ichiro, saying, "He's as moody as", and Donna could tell from her meeting with Yuki that she was worried about him. Poor Ichiro.

She herself could do without negativity as she neared her revised due date. Yesterday and today she had coped with false labour pains as she taught her students, but was very uncomfortable. 'So Luke, what am I going to give you for supper?' She reached into a cupboard and brought out a jar of junior rice and fruit. 'This will do nicely. Come on, little fellow, you sit in your high-chair. Here, have this crusket while I warm your supper.' He willingly let his mummy sit him down, but kept on jiggling, and he grabbed the crusket as she made the high-chair secure. 'Daddy will be home soon.'

Warren came in ten minutes later and said, 'How are you, sweethearts?' He kissed Luke's chubby cheeks and turned to Donna for her answer.

'My tummy goes into these tight spasms – and I'm craving rest.'

He put down his satchel and said, 'Right then. This is where I take over. Luke, daddy's going to feed you now.'

Donna kissed his cheek and said, 'You're a honey. I'll sit down right here.'

'Lie down, why don't you?'

'No. I want to be here with you. I'll sit here and wait. You can tell me how the court case went.'

As he spooned Luke's supper into his mouth, he said, 'Well, as a matter of fact, I think the Maynards are now feeling that they'd rather hide than be in the public eye.'

'Oh?'

'Robertson did his own pleading and he made them feel like numbers in a chain of events. But all the same, no-one who's anybody believes that they will lose. It was his first human cloning and he could well have made a mistake. After all, a mouse is a mouse and a human a human!'

Donna laughed. 'Gosh, you're into the heavy stuff now aren't you?'

Warren laughed with her and Luke made a big noise with his spoon and chuckled too.

Part Four
Chapter 7

'Andreas, what's wrong with Ichiro?'

Andreas was cooking up a quick meal for Tom and himself before they went out to a concert by visiting cellist, Deidrich Mann. He did not look up but said, 'Is there something wrong with Ichiro?'

'Well, ever since his mother visited he's been slamming around, or if he's not slamming he's so quiet and withdrawn he gives you the creeps. He'll give a one-word answer if you're lucky. I reckon his mother upset him.'

'Thanks. I'll see if the Director knows anything. It doesn't sound good.'

Tom and Ichiro were to play at the lunch-hour recital a week away and Tom was getting overly anxious. He asked Ichiro if he would have two practices with him during the week.

Ichiro was in a practice studio and Tom had interrupted. 'Why?' he snapped.

'Just so I feel really good at the recital.'

'Child's play.'

'Not for me, it's not.'

'Please get out. I'm practising – trying to learn two Chopin preludes and a Brahms sonata. And six accompaniments. I can't spare time for you.'

'Ichiro!'

'Go on. Get out.'

Andreas asked the Director if there was anything that he knew about Ichiro which would account for his mood.

'Yes. His mother spoke to me in confidence a week ago. I feel sick about what she told me, but all I can say is we must all look out for Ichiro and see that he is as OK as possible. I'm quite at sea as to what more we can do.'

'All right. Fair enough. I'll keep an eye on him.' Andreas

was due to teach for the rest of the afternoon but determined to look in on Ichiro in the evening.

Ichiro heard the knock on his door. He did not care to answer. He only wanted to hide, to talk to Jiro.

> Our parents deserve to be shot. How could Dad be so stupid as to try and replace you? Jiro, Jiro, why did you go away? I miss you. You and me we were like one person. Jiro … I loved you with all my heart …

The pain he felt when he learned of Jiro's death by the avalanche came back to him and it was as if Jiro was there with him now.

> You didn't go away down the river, did you, Jiro? The priest made out you did. My parents believed you did, but you didn't, did you? He thought of the people along the river bank, and the candles alight in the river! It was beautiful, magical. I heard the swish of the water, saw the reflections shimmer and you, you stayed with me. But, Jiro, isn't it time for you to leave this mean world where adults think they can replace you with a monster? I would be better off with you … I know what I can do … we will be together, always. Always. Yes, Jiro, that's a promise.

He turned over and slept for ten hours.

PART FOUR
CHAPTER 8

Yuki and Donna hugged, as big a hug as Donna's bulge allowed. Yuki's eyes spilled tears, while Donna's were filled by happiness.

'I'm so glad you saw Tom. He'll be full of himself now having met the wife and son of the famous Fujiwara *sensei*.'

'No. No. He was so good to Hiro that I couldn't thank him enough for taking him to his lesson.'

Donna did not know the reason for the tears. Prying seemed inappropriate now, since they were there to have Hiro's first lesson. The child was waiting in the side room so that his mother could explain why she and her husband asked her to teach him.

'Please sit down Yuki, here, and tell me why you've come.'

Yuki sat down quickly. 'It's difficult to say it, but Hiro is the most brilliant student Kentaro has known, but his behaviour is odd. He is a little monster with me, yet that is not a musical problem. It is that he seems to have no feeling. He plays like a robot! Yes, a mechanical thing, not a feeling person.'

'So, I think I'm hearing you say that you want me to teach him how to play expressively. Is that it?'

'That's exactly it. You see, Jiro played with extraordinary expression. People were always moved by his playing. Young though he was.'

'Hiro's eight isn't he?'

'Nearly nine. He is old enough.'

'Well, you understand that you are asking a lot of me.' She put a hand over her unborn baby and said, 'This little one is going to interrupt lessons, for one. But to help a child put feeling into his playing is not something I've been asked to do, ever. Usually it just happens as they get older. But you are here.' She smiled warmly. 'You were so good to me in Japan I shall certainly do my very best for you. Do you want to ask Hiro to come in now and play for me? That's the first thing, I want him to play a piece.'

Yuki hurried to the door and entered the side room. 'Hiro?' She looked about her at the easy chairs and coffee table adorned by a bunch of unseasonable flowers, and turned back to Donna. 'He's gone. Where might he have gone?' She giggled now, out of embarrassment more than anything.

'I can't imagine. Unless … unless he's gone down the hall, and followed the sounds of music in the recital hall. Possibly. Come along and we'll see.'

Not only was Hiro in the concert hall, he was on the stage playing the Mozart Concerto in D that he'd heard his father play. Donna sat at the centre of the hall and whispered to Yuki to sit with her and listen. 'Now I know what you mean,' she whispered. 'He's brilliant.'

Hiro stood as if performing to an audience in the body of the hall. He was oblivious of people sitting watching, and played on, listening only to himself. He made a slip over a wide leap up the E string, stamped a foot and muttered *'Dame desu'*, and played it again with impeccable intonation. Donna and Yuki smiled at each other, then continued to listen in amazement.

Just before the end of the first movement, Hiro stopped playing and rushed to the back of the stage. Donna moved as quickly as she could to catch up with him in the dressing room where he would have left his case. Yuki ran lightly to follow when she realised what was happening. The women reached the dressing room together. Hiro was in tears. His mother went to him first and said, 'What's the matter?'

'I don't like this place. The echoes in the hall sounded weird.' Yuki looked to Donna for guidance.

'I know why, Hiro.' The child looked up at her with disgust on his tear-stained face.

'The hall's empty, that's why.'

'I don't like it.'

She tried a different tack. 'Your playing sounded wonderful from the middle of the hall. You are a very good violinist.'

'I know,' he said, matter-of-factly. 'I want to play what Tom was playing.'

Donna smiled. After all, Tom was now sixteen and Hiro not yet nine. How can she tell him he has to work hard at all kinds of things first?

'I've got lots of recordings in my studio. If you and mummy come with me now, I'll put some on for you and you can choose which piece you'd like to learn first. Come on, now.'

'Me, too?' Yuki said.

As Donna said, 'Yes, of course,' Hiro was saying, 'No. No. No. Tom's mother didn't go to his lesson.'

The women conferred for a minute and Yuki said, 'Right-oh, Hiro, I'm going shopping. I will see you in the foyer here in forty minutes.' Yuki knew it was almost impossible to get to and from the shops in that time. Instead, Yuki would wander around the campus and find a café.

'You're having a birthday soon, Hiro,' said Donna as she opened her studio.

'Yep, and I'm going to get a very big surprise because Ichiro told me.'

'Oh, my goodness. That is exciting. Now put your violin on that shelf there and come and listen to my discs. I've got three to play you and you can choose which one you'd like to learn.' She made sure that he was comfortable on an adult-sized chair by placing a cushion behind his back, and pressed play. She had selected three soulful pieces from the violin repertoire and Hiro sat enraptured. As the amplitude of Paradisi's *Sicilienne* increased so did the intensity in Hiro's dark eyes. He became lost in the music and made no comments as the pieces changed.

After the recordings stopped, Hiro said, 'I want to play *Leibeslied* first.'

'Right, we've got half an hour left so we can have a lesson. Just let me tune my violin then we'll tune together.'

The nasal tones of Donna's violin fascinated Hiro. He said, 'Your violin's different from mine!'

'Yes, mine's French. Yours was probably made in Japan was it?'

'No. It was made for Jiro in Italy.'

'Oh, how special.'

'I don't think so. I deserve the best because I'm good. Jiro was too.'

'Well then, let's start our lesson properly with a bow. *Onegaishimasu*' she said, as they bowed to each other.

'Let's play a tone study. How about the Japanese folk song *Sakura*, that your daddy likes?'

'I don't want to play a study. I want to play *Liebeslied*. Now.'

Donna felt defeated. She could do without this stroppiness especially as her womb was tightening again. 'I'll get the music, then.' She opened her filing cabinet, and was thumbing through when Hiro began to play. She turned to listen, then knew he had no need of music and sat down on the chair after throwing the cushion to the floor. I cannot believe this. But as the piece progressed she understood his parent's concern. Absolutely rigid timing and no soul. No soul at all. How can she explain to this child what it means to play with expression when he has no innate sense of it?

Part Four
Chapter 9

There was nothing more that Hamish could do to get a third egg to fertilise. Nothing. In fact Terri thought that he might need two more. One of the implanted embryos was only just hanging on to life. His surrogate mother was having to lie down in order that she did not mis-carry. When Hamish heard that from Terri, he was alarmed.

He danced with his wife in the evening for the sake of keeping up a brave front, but he could not get it off his mind. As soon as the orange-eating frivolity was finished he said, 'I have to talk, Terri. I'm going crazy with worry.'

'What about?'

'Oh, you know how it is. Whatever you do, don't lose that child. It's getting to be as much as my life's worth. If Giano tells me one more time that I should remember his terms, I'll have to lie my way out of this mess. Get one of your unmarried mothers who's likely to want to be rid of her baby to pretend her child is a clone of Giano. Make any sense?'

'What, pay her to keep quiet? And what if the baby's a girl? No Hamish. Look, my darling. Stick at it. Any day now you'll have your third one and I'll make sure the second one doesn't miscarry. Anyway, Rose needs a cheerful daddy at her party, not a kill-joy. You look worn out and very untidy. How about taking a little time out to get yourself back together?

'I can't. Not yet. I haven't any time. He'll be here any day now, wanting to meet his three women. Offer them big money. Make sure they will keep their mouths shut. I have to get out of bed at four and be in the lab by five. Hopefully, it will be as you say, the third will have fertilised and the second baby will stay in his mother's womb.'

'Going to sleep, then? Not going to play a bed game?'

'Terri, I'm sorry, if I thought I could do it, I would. Just haven't got the energy.'

'And you haven't had the energy for three months. It's becoming a long three months.'

'We did. Once. Just let me get these three boys on the way and I'll be a new person.' He kissed her, a quick smack of his lips, and fell asleep before she could remonstrate.

I wish I could fall asleep so easily, she thought, as she turned out the light.

Two more days to Roses' ninth birthday. Hamish was back on the road with very little traffic about. Pitch dark except for lights along the road, the odd vehicle. He thought of Rose and how bonny she was. Oh, that Mary could be the one to collect her at the school gate. I wonder how the Fujiwara boy, Hiro, is? He'll soon turn nine, too. If only I could tell the world about him. Why should I not? It must surely break, some time. Enthusiasm infused his being for a moment and he felt good. Successful. But the moment he turned into the grounds of BioGen Science, he felt depressed again. He let himself in at the main entrance and turned on only the essential lights. He ran along the corridor to his lab and locked the door behind him. He knew that the night security officer would want to stop him for a chat if he gave him half a chance. Most of them thought him somewhat mad to be working at such an hour.

His lab was eerie with only a night light on. He walked past the racks of test tubes, abandoned microscopes and jars of chemicals, to the temperature controlled areas where tissue was stored. He put on the lights and looked closely at the dish, his heart racing. A pulse beat at his temples. It's worked! It's worked! With eyes half-closed, he looked again to see if he could still define what he was seeing as an embryo. Yes. Yes. He looked about him as if that might help him to bring Terri to his side. He wanted to make up to her, play bed games again and again. Three embryos now a possibility. He would ring Terri as soon as he could, without getting her out of bed. Yet it was the great news they had both wanted. He would take the day off once the implanting was done, tidy himself up. Be the life and soul of Rose's party.

Terri rang him from the hospital even before she knew his news. 'Hamish. Bad news, honey.'

'No, it can't be. You can't do this to me. You cannot, you cannot. And I have good news for you, but what's the use?'

'Oh, well done. I said …'

'But he wants three. Terri what will I do? I have the feeling that he'll kill me. I do really. He's obsessed by three. Must be superstitious or something.'

'No, just an egomaniac. Twisted, that's what. You shouldn't let him get to you.'

'Maybe not! But he does.'

'I must go. Now that I'm at the hospital, Doreen will get Rose to school, and I'll do my rounds early. You get that embryo to me as soon as you can.'

In spite of the set-back Hamish had received, he had made an effort to be home for Rose's birthday celebration. The party was not for another hour, but he found Rose dressed and excited.

'Rose, you look beautiful. That new dress is your best colour, isn't it?'

'I quite like this bright blue, but we did try to get a purple one. That's my favourite colour.' She turned to show her daddy the back of the dress. 'See, it's got flowers on the buttons. But the buttons are only make-believe.' She faced her daddy again, smiling up at him. 'There's a hidden zip. Crafty, eh?'

'Very. And, let me say how good your hair is, zizzed and all.' He laughed and gave her a hug.

'I love you, daddy.'

'And I love you. By the way, would you like your present now?'

'Course! Please.'

He looked at her dress and thought – not suitable for where we're going. 'Rose, this involves a wee trip down the road. Could you change to jeans just for now? I'll tell mummy that we're going while you get changed, OK?'

'Mummy's icing the cake.'

'OK.'

As they travelled through the city, along her daddy's usual route to work, Rose kept asking questions about all manner of things, but finally insisted on guessing what her present was. 'I had to change my clothes so is it a hamster?'

'No. But you're getting close.' He pulled the car up outside the veterinary hospital. 'See? Look where we are, eh? The animal hospital.'

'You work over the road.'

'That's right. And I've become friends with the vets. They want to meet you. Come on.'

'But I want to meet my present!'

'Both. Give us a wee minute and you will!'

A tall man in a white half-coat beamed at them from behind the counter. 'So this is Rose. Hello and happy birthday.' Jamie turned and called out, 'Monica, come and meet young Rose.'

A young woman, whose black hair just had to have been zizzed, appeared with a cat in her arms. 'Hello, Rose.'

'Hello. Is that my cat?'

Monica laughed. 'No, this little cat is sick and rather frightened. Your pet is healthy. Just didn't get picked up by his owner, that's why we can give him to you.'

Rose looked about her. Hamish said to Monica, 'Maybe, we'd better introduce them, then!'

Monica said, 'Sure', and took them through a door and into a corridor with a bank of cages on either side. 'Come past these special care animals to the healthy ones. By the way, where do you guys live?'

'On West Bryson, near Harrison and the two parks,' said Hamish.

'Perfect.'

'This way, Rose,' Monica said, smiling. 'You'll see him in

half a moment. Then you'll have to think of a name. Look for a cage with "Rose" on it.'

The healthy animals were full of life – some meowing, some barking, some snuffling. The atmosphere felt strange to Rose, even a little scary when animals shot furtive glances at her. She did not care for the smell. A guinea pig? No. She peered into each cage. If a friendly animal looked out at her, she talked to it. 'Hello, puss cat. Hello, little puppy. You're nice, aren't you?'

The small cages were replaced by roomier ones, some with bigger and busier animals in them. 'Rose'. There's my name. Here it is. A puppy.' A shiny black puppy looked at them through dark, questioning eyes. 'Daddy, is this little scamp really for me?'

'It is. And many happy returns to you both.'

She put her arms about her daddy and hugged him.

'It's a labrador,' he said.

'And he's pure black. Is Blackie all right?' she asked, excitedly.

'You can call him whatever you like. Blackie is good.'

Part Four
Chapter 10

Warren stood wiping his brow and drying his tears. Donna had asked him to call her aunty and uncle with the joyous news of their daughter's birth. He had waited, at least until her uncle would be up. As soon as the call connected, he handed the phone to Donna. 'Uncle JJ, it's Donna. I have great news for you. We have a daughter and she's beautiful.'

'Congratulations. Both of you. Don't tell me her weight – I'm still no good at kilogrammes, but is she bonny?'

'She is. She's healthy and strong and Warren reckons she looks like me!'

'Oh, my! Donna, can you wait? I'll get your aunty.'

'Of course.'

'Hang on then.'

In a few moments he was back. His voice had changed. He sounded upset. 'Donna lass. I can't wake her. I'll leave her be.'

'That's all right, Uncle. Tell her when she wakes. Bye now.'

'Bye.'

'Warren, I have this awful feeling that Aunty Beth's not just asleep and I reckon Uncle JJ knew that. He sounded as if he was in shock. I want you to call him again, say in an hour, and see if everything's all right. Will you, please?'

'Of course. Now, who else shall I call?'

'First, Luke, then Tom. You won't believe this but I've written out announcement cards, addressed them and all, but the word daughter has to be added. That's all. I'll fill them in today and then you can post them for me.' She lay back on her pillow. 'I'm tired, but tell me, you did take the photos didn't you?'

'All except me holding Anna.' He laughed. 'That's a bit tricky though it can be done! Yes, but when you're feeling strong, I'd like some of me with her.'

'Of course, sweetheart. Come here.' She threw her arms about him, smelt his smell and felt so happy she cried. 'You were so wonderful. Thank you.'

'No, thank you. You did all the work and you were brilliant. Perfect. Both of you.' He pulled away gently and peeped into the crib beside the bed, bent to kiss the chubby cheek of the baby they were calling Anna, then said, 'I'll go and take a shower, and get back home while you take a sleep.'

'Fine. But you will ring Uncle JJ, won't you?'

'Yes. And I'll develop these photos and send one or two good ones on email to our net-working friends.'

'Oh, great. Yes, of course.'

As he traced his way back along the corridors, he thought that a community such as a maternity hospital which was just coming to life on a spring morning, must be one of the loveliest places on earth. Bunches of perfumed spring flowers were being delivered to wards. He saw flashes of yellow daffodils, and smelt the whiff of them as they were carried past, and he felt a quickening of his spirit, the relief and the joy of having helped to usher in his little daughter. The best thing I have done since Luke. He would buy some flowers before he did anything else.

When he returned to see Donna he had Luke with him, and the flowers.

'What a lovely sight. Luke, come to Mummy.' He sat on his mother's lap where she sat in the wicker chair. Warren pulled a stool out from under the bed, and said, 'How are you, sweetheart?'

'Mostly good. And all the better for your being here. Tell me Warren, Aunty Beth's dead, isn't she?'

'I hoped to avoid telling you, but yes.'

Donna was quiet. Kissed Luke some more. Blinked as she took in the bouquet of spring flowers, jasmine the dominant perfume, then said, 'I so much wanted her to know.'

'I thought so,' he said.

In the conservatoire, amongst all these young adults, Tom simply had to share his news of a baby sister with someone. He ran to catch Ichiro in his room before he left. 'Hi, Ichiro.'

'Hi. I'm just off to my lesson, you know.'

'Yes, I know. But I wanted to tell you my good news. I have a baby sister.'

'Sounds good.' He stopped piling music into his satchel and looked at Tom. 'Ask your parents where she came from.' He found a book he was looking for and put it into his satchel and was heading out the door. 'Close my door for me, please.'

'Ichiro! That was a terrible thing to say.' He pulled the door to. Ichiro was already out of sight.

Hiro could not have a lesson with Donna for a week, but Yuki and he visited her at home two days after the birth. Yuki had dressed in the colours she loved best, a soft wine with a touch of lime in a trimming around the organza jacket. She looked beautiful. Her jaunty haircut suited her round face. Hiro insisted on dressing no differently from usual and wore a fresh white shirt and navy pants with his school socks and shoes. Donna was overjoyed to see them.

'How lovely of you to come. I'll take you to peep at Anna. I've just got her to sleep.' Yuki took two parcels from her bag and laughingly said, 'I hope that these are OK.'

'Oh, you shouldn't have. I'll open them first.' There were ever so many baby things – toiletries, small jackets and booties, and in the second parcel, the mini disc of music that her husband had prepared for babies.

Donna held up the small disc and said, 'I didn't have one for Luke. Just played him lots of Haydn! This will be perfect for Anna, and Luke'll love it too. Thank you Yuki. And Hiro. Did you help choose some of these things?'

'Nope! Donna, will you give me a birthday present?'

'My word. Yes. It's soon, isn't it?'

'Next Friday. I'll be nine.'

'Hiro,' Yuki said, 'You don't ask people for presents. It's rude.'

'Well, I know that Ichiro is giving me something special. He said so.'

'Did he, now?'

Donna smiled at both Yuki and Hiro. 'Birthdays are wonderful, aren't they? So, now to see the baby.' She led the way by opening the door for them.

Hiro pushed past his mother and said, 'I bet she's in your bedroom, Donna.'

'She is, too. But please be very quiet.'

'Why?'

'I want to keep her asleep. She was a bit restless last night.'

Part Four
Chapter 11

Don Maynard and Jianne Maynard sat stunned by the verdict.

'Not guilty.' They glanced at the rotund and smiling figure of Dr Keith Robertson, and Jianne burst into tears. She bit her lower lip and put a hand into his. They would accept the verdict, they had agreed on that. They had neither the energy nor the resources to fight on.

'Jianne, Don, are you able to come now? Your car is waiting.' Their neighbour had promised to get a car to pick them up and hurry them away no matter what the verdict. He led them out of the courtroom, and was so tall and strong that people were intimidated. No-one, barring two journalists, tried to communicate with them. He even answered for them, 'No comment,' he repeated, as he forced a path through the crowd.

Warren reported the verdict. "Dr Robertson Found Not Guilty of Carelessness in Cloning Case."

It was a triumph for genetic engineering. Warren felt genuinely happy for Keith Robertson. He had, in fact, anticipated the outcome and had prepared his article ahead. It had not been difficult. A packed courtroom, the terrible silence, the clipped words of the verdict, the tears of Dr Robertson. He had got it right, and sent his story down the line within moments of the verdict.

Dr Robertson called him later in the day, just as he was driving home after viewing an exhibition on spring gardens he was to write up. 'Keith, here. What did you think?'

Warren laughed a little, still in an electric state of mind at his daughter's birth.

'I'm really glad it turned out in your favour, Keith. I'm sorry for the Maynards of course, but I had to agree with the judge that no evidence was proven against you. The fact that

Louisa is a dwarf seems to have been unavoidable.'

'Quite. And this is where science now has the chance to step in and say in future, given time and the chance to prove ourselves, embryologists will be able to detect and alter the gene that has caused the retarded growth. In that regard it is a triumph. I can go on. Got a lot of life ahead of me yet.'

Warren could see him. Puffed chest, brisk walk, black suit and satchel. Yes, he would make it big-time again. He sat back and smiled, thinking, 'Bit tinny for me that I get to write his stories.' Donna and Anna came to mind as he pulled into his garage. He would get inside as fast as he could and see what he could do to help. Running up the steps he called, 'I'm home, sweetheart.' At the same moment, a courier arrived at the front door. Warren received the two oddly-shaped parcels addressed to Donna, then decided to hide them under the stairs. 'Coming.'

Donna greeted him, baby in her arms. 'Good to see you, love.'

'Tired?'

'Well, yes. But not because of Anna so much as trying to get a gift sorted for Hiro. It's his birthday and I've got two days to decide. I looked around shops and couldn't make up my mind.'

'How are you coping about your aunty?'

'Need you ask? I think you've got something there. Her funeral was today and I should have been there for Uncle JJ. I'm mad at myself.'

'Hey, no. You were probably not quite ready for walking the streets let alone flying to New Brunswick for a funeral. Give yourself a break.'

'I suppose.'

He reached out to take Anna and hugged her to his chest as he kissed her cheeks. 'Oh, isn't she a darling. I'd swear she wriggled when I kissed her. And look at that thumb! Already her comforter.' He walked her about for a minute. 'Look, she's asleep. I'll put her down, right?'

'Oh, please do.'

He came rushing back and said, 'And now I have two big surprises for you.' He was smiling as he carried in the strange-looking parcels.

She was taken aback. 'Parcels!'

'A courier came.' He read the addresses 'From New Brunswick. For you.'

'Oh, no! Uncle JJ had time to think of me?'

'Well, open them and see what he says.'

After some frantic moments of unwrapping the first parcel, the black clock ticked on regardless of its new place on the dresser. Donna was crying. 'I love that clock.'

'And the note? What does it say?'

Donna was overcome. She snivelled and read, "Sometimes, Donna, something seems to nag until it's done. I've had the strongest urge to send you both the clock and this plant. I think I know why, but can't say it. If I am right, then all I can say is, look after them for me and us, we want you to have them, we love you so much. Aunty Beth."

Warren held her in his arms while she cried out her sadness.

After some time, and still snivelling, Donna carefully unwrapped the second parcel thinking, it cannot be! Not the wax flower plant! 'Not Aunty's pot plant that's never flowered!' Warren took away the paper and stuffed it and the heavy cardboard into the recycling bin while she stood the heavy plant on the table.

Warren tenderly lifted one of the branches, just to cheer it up a little, and then said, 'Donna. Come here. Look.'

She shouted for joy, spinning around the room. 'It's a flower! The first in fifty years! A waxen flower.' She returned to peer at it and said quietly, 'It has to be Aunty Beth's doing!'

Warren laughed. Donna laughed, 'Oh, the wicked lady. She had to die before it would flower!'

Keith Robertson was back in his lab, dreaming up new possibilities for assisting medical science. His lawyer had informed him that the Maynards would not be contesting the verdict. They had enough on their plate trying to cope with the hundreds of letters they had received in response to Warren's article on Don's sterility. That seemed to have caused a tsunami of a reaction and actually worked in Dr Robertson's favour.

'You'll be inundated with requests from hundreds, maybe thousands of couples asking for cloned babies. The Maynards have actually done you a favour,' he had said.

Part Four
Chapter 12

The puppy yapped at his heels the minute he was out of the car and raced with him as if party to the good news that another egg had fertilised. Hamish dumped his satchel and called to Terri.

'Good news. Good news. Where are you?'

He found both Terri and Rose in the kitchen preparing dinner. Rose dropped a peeler and took a flying jump at her father almost knocking him over. The puppy got under his feet, and he almost fell across Terri as he kissed her.

'Did I hear you say you've got another one?'

'Yes. Three little boys on the way – or nearly. It's over to you, now.'

'Daddy. What three little boys?'

'Tell her, Hamish. She'll read it in the papers before long. Tell her now.'

Hamish felt horrified at where his excitement had led him. 'About the boys, you mean?'

'Oh, the other too, if you think you should.'

'What other, Daddy?'

Looking down into the beautiful face of his daughter, Hamish was painfully reminded of her likeness to Trish at nine years of age. Rose was growing fast, her shoulders were broad, her limbs long and gangly. She had blue eyes that sparkled when she was happy, and became dusky when she was morose or angry. Her hair could have come from Trish's head, it was the same rich auburn and thick, even when zizzed! Oh, that Mary were here to put it into the context of love.

How they had loved Trish. How they wanted Rose. She was loved in the womb. Loved as if conceived by their loving. Did she have to know now? At nine years of age?

'Rose, there is something you should know,' Hamish said.

'You are unique. Very special.'

The child stood still, her puppy in her arms also quiet, waiting.

'Rose, at my work in the lab, I do a very special kind of science. It's what we call genetic shaping of children or cloning.'

'I know about Dolly. I've heard you talk about Dolly and now my teacher told us. Scots are proud, I think.'

'Well, as a matter of fact, I was at Dolly's birth. But now, I can create people.'

'That's scary, Dad.'

'It is and it isn't.' He hesitated, but knew it was now or at what could be a totally inappropriate moment in the future. 'Rose, what if I said that you'd been cloned?'

She looked disbelieving. Her eyes were dusky. In them Hamish saw the firth where Mary drowned. He felt afraid. 'You don't believe me?'

'Are you God?' she asked. Blackie jumped from her arms and whined at the door.

'Daddy. Are you God?' she said, going to the door to open it for Blackie. Then she came back and confronted her parents.

'Darling, it's what you learn at school and church isn't it?' Terri said.

'Yes. Our teacher says, "God made people in his own image." We say that every Friday in my class.'

Hamish didn't know what to say. 'Yes, that's what Christians believe.'

'Are you a Christian, Dad? I am.' Rose seemed taller than before. She flicked her head. 'Are you?'

'Yes. I am.'

'But you said you can create people. Only God makes people.'

'I'll say this one thing. I believe we can help God. We can assist God in the wonderful work of creation. But …' He looked at Terri in desperation, and said, 'But you've cooked dinner, I think. Shouldn't we eat now before it's spoiled?'

Rose was furious. 'Are you being God? Answer me!'

'No, I'm not being God.'

'Well, I thought I was Mummy's and your baby. Look at my hair. Now I'm confused. I don't have cloned friends. That's creepy. Anyway, Dolly grew old too fast. What will happen to me? Cloned! I can't believe you. I didn't want to start my life in a stupid laboratory. I don't want to know anything more. You're lying. You're not God. And you only want to eat your dinner. Well, I'm never going to eat with you again!' She stormed out of the room.

Terri followed her. 'I'll talk to her, try and explain some of it,' she called back to him.

Eventually, and without eating her meal, Rose fell asleep in her bed. Terri encouraged Hamish to take time to think things through and in the meantime, to relax, to dance.

'I'm in no mood to dance, Terri. I feel sick at heart. How in the name of heaven can I convince Rose that being cloned is OK with God?'

'I did my best, but she's not too convinced. And I do have moments when I ask that same question. Is it OK with God? Really?'

They sat facing each other. 'I didn't know. But I do know that it's not OK with God that we've let the world get so mucked up that men are impotent! And think of Giano and the violence which his father – his father, of all people – used to smash his child's face about. That's not all right, is it?'

Terri nodded in acquiescence, and put on a CD to play very quietly. 'Come, let's have a glass of wine and talk for a while. Then, when Janice is here, we'll do what we have to do to get the third little boy on the way.'

'Aren't you convinced?'

She sat down beside him with her glass in her hand. 'I can support cloning for medical reasons, including impotence, but as I've said before Giano is an egocentric maniac. I loath him and I almost loath myself for being the one to implant his clones, even though I detest the person his father must have been.'

Hamish stretched his legs and puckered his face as if disgusted with himself. He took a quick swig of wine and pursed his lips. Terri ran both her hands from his forehead up over his head to his shoulders, and let them rest there. 'Upset, aren't you?'

'Not just upset. Actually, loath would be a mild way of saying how I feel about myself. I can empathise with Lady MacBeth. My hands are covered in blood. And no amount of washing them will make any difference.' He got up and paced around. The puppy was crying because it was shut in the laundry and lonely. 'Damn that puppy. It's all set for another howling match by the sound of it.'

'Ignore him. We're training him and I promised Rose I'd leave him!'

He stopped at the window and looked through the curtains, then seeing the stars, he opened the curtains so that Terri could see the sky. 'Remember that saying, "God's in his heaven, and all is right with the world?" That was my mother's version of it anyway.'

'Yes. I know it. Difficult isn't it? Playing at being God.'

Suddenly he snapped the curtains closed again. 'When I look at Rose, I feel grateful to God. That is my reaction. When I see Giano, I think that I am confronting the Devil himself. That's the difference.' He sat beside Terri again. 'Honey, I need to tell you something.' He put an arm around her shoulders and drew her close. Felt her warmth. She, his. She planted a kiss on his cheek.

'When we first came here, it would have been so easy then to have asked for Mary to be exhumed. I was overwhelmed by the desire to clone her. And in cloning her, bring her back from the dead. I'm glad I got distracted.' He laughed and Terri smiled at him, almost laughing, too. At him. 'Just imagine a wife coming back as your child. Wiping her bottom, putting her to the breast. All of that. It becomes ludicrous, doesn't it?' They laughed hysterically together at the thought.

'That was a near miss. That was. How could I have been so stupid?'

'You've had so much pleasure from Rose, you got carried away by your own skill. Easily done. Just carried away. But remember, Trish was dead. And don't forget the other really successful one. You cloned Hiro from his brother, didn't you?'

'Och, Terri. You've reminded me. I need to get in touch with Ichiro Fujiwara. Yeah! Tomorrow. I'll get an email address or something and find a way to talk to him.'

'Sounds important.'

'It is. But it'll be news he'll want to hear. Why, he'll be about eighteen, a good age to learn the truth.'

'Do you feel you've got cloning under your belt? Done it often enough to be confident in the future?'

'Oh no. And I often worry that you and I persuaded Bertha and her team to help us answer those calls for babies. I know you felt good about the impotent men, but who knows where Bertha and her team are taking it now. All hushed up, to boot. I'll never forget the way she blushed as she gave her farewell speech to me. Almost put her foot in it, she did.' He squirmed and guffawed at the memory of Bertha's shaking bosom. He stood up and stretched. 'We can't get out of this one though. Let's give Janice a call and tell her we need her here sooner rather than later. Maybe she can stay a couple of days to help us through. We've got a job to do – for the sake of staying alive.'

'Then, it's on to cloning people in a big way, and with the sanction of your board.'

'It scares me, Terri. Even though it'll be sanctioned. Thousands of requests will have come in within hours of the announcement. Thank God I've got a good team. They're brilliant in fact!'

Part Four
Chapter 13

'Happy birthday, Hiro.' It was six o'clock in the morning, and Hiro scrambled about in his mother's bedroom looking for a parcel. She woke to the sound of cupboard doors banging. 'Hiro, Hiro. What are you doing?'

'I'm looking for my presents.' His mother felt a chill go through her. Such a self-centred child! If only Kentaro could see him now! She sat up and brought out a parcel from inside her bed. 'Happy birthday, Hiro. Come and get your present.'

He stamped his bare feet to her side of the bed after slamming a drawer shut. 'Only one?'

'Open it.'

He tore away the paper and grabbed at the thing inside the parcel. Yuki had talked it over with Kentaro and he'd suggested a multimedia-card player. She'd bought a good one.

'A stupid little card and ear-phones!'

'Hiro, don't you remember Ichiro's flash multimedia-card that had earphones and a camera to play and record? The one that he could send us photos through his laptop?'

'What – these earphones?'

'And the rest.' She had already transferred all the music recordings he needed for his lessons with Donna. 'Put them on. Then I'll show you how to select any piece of music you want. Just name it.'

His eyes lit up. 'The Mendelssohn.' Yuki showed him which tiny buttons to press, what to adjust. When the music began to play he said, 'It's coolest, Mum!'

Then he suddenly pulled off his earphones and said, 'Where's my special present from Ichiro? He told me I'd get it.'

'I don't know. Maybe it'll come by courier today. It's very

early, yet.'

'It'd better come!' he said as he left the room.

The Director gave Andreas and Ichiro's piano teacher, Rupert Freese, permission to search Ichiro's room. While they were doing that, the security guards of the conservatoire were told to search the conservatoire and the boarding establishment for Ichiro, then anywhere else they could think of.

He had said he would be in the concert hall at 9 a.m. sharp. The violinists Johanna, Tom and Reuben, and oboist, Juanita, whom he was to accompany, were there waiting. When he did not answer the loud knocking and banging on his door, Andreas had reported to the group that Ichiro was not in his room.

'I mean, I almost broke his door down, and he still didn't answer.'

'Andreas,' Rupert Freese had said, 'We'll get permission to break the lock on his door.'

The Director called a security guard to break into Ichiro's room and gave his staff permission to search it.

'Rather a mess,' commented Andreas, picking up used clothing off the floor and putting it into the basket provided. 'Did his mother pick up after him?' Tiny Smithers dominated the room. Andreas drew in a big breath and studied the poster, reading the words. He gasped, '*Mein Gott*! It could almost be Ichiro himself!'

Then he noticed that the monitor was blipping to announce an email message awaiting Ichiro. Andreas took a moment to see if Ichiro had left a message, but no, it was just that a message had been sent to him from a Dr Hamish McLeod. It could wait.

Rupert asked Andreas, 'Do you read Japanese?' There were three addressed envelopes with Japanese characters, as well as names and addresses mostly in English. They stood on the desk propped against a photo of Ichiro and his brother. But for the sharp pencils placed ready to annotate his manuscripts, the rest of the desk was clear.

'No, but that seems ominous, doesn't it?'

'I reckon! He's been so moody lately. At every lesson in the past two weeks he's stopped in the middle of a piece as if his memory has failed him. I tried to ask him what the problem was, but he muttered something like, "It's not my problem. It's my parents." Then he's got his music down, read it, and picked up where he left off. I didn't get the chance to ask him what he meant.'

'OK. So I'll take these letters to the Director, and do you think that maybe either you or a student could play the accompaniments for all those guys who are waiting in the hall? The recital has to go ahead without Ichiro, maybe.'

Andreas arrived at the Director's office just as the phone rang. He watched the Director's expression change from expectant to appalled. 'Oh, no! *Mein Gott*, no! I'll be there as quickly as I can.' He shook his head as if wanting to be rid of the news he had just heard. 'Andreas, this is terrible.'

'Sir?'

'It can't be true. An Asian youth, shaved head, neck chain and earring, has been found face down in the – Heaven forbid – in the swimming pool. The security guards want me to be there. Please come with me.'

Ichiro lay on a mat at the side of the pool. Security and police stood near, making notes. A police photographer used his flash to get several photographs.

Andreas felt faint in the warm, damp atmosphere of the pool. He looked at the body lying on the wet concrete, and felt the colour drain from his face. His vision blurred, and he was unsteady on his feet. He nodded, muttering, 'Ichiro, Ichiro. Yes, yes, Ichiro. It's Ichiro Fujiwara. But why? Why?' He bent down as if to hear the young man's heart, and sobbed in anguish. Images of Miguel, Donna and Warren, the people he had loved and had made life worthwhile for him in his time of despair, crowded his mind. Why? Why? Why did I not learn? If Ichiro could have talked to me, he may not have died. He felt the wetness of Ichiro's tee shirt mingle with the tears on his face. He stood and wiped them with a towel handed to him by the pool attendant. Then, a touch on the shoulder from the Director imparted some measure of reassurance, and he went to sit on a nearby bench where he put his head between his knees and waited. The Director looked down at the peaceful face of the youth, and noted that the usually smartly dressed student wore only jeans and a tee shirt with the monogram in large letters, 'Run in My Sandals'. They were soaking wet. Would have been heavy in the pool. 'This is a terrible tragedy. Yes, it is Ichiro Fujiwara, I'm very sad to say.'

Police lifted the body on to a stretcher and covered it completely, before taking it out of the pool complex to a waiting van, and Andreas and the Director returned to the office to do whatever was necessary. To his secretary who awaited them, the Director said, 'Please get a drink of strong tea for Andreas. I'll have one too.' Then when that was attended to, he requested that Satumi, the Japanese student bassoonist, be told what had happened and invited to translate what was on the envelopes.

Satumi joined them. She was pale and tearful. They offered her tea and she sat and sipped the warm drink and kept wiping her eyes. Once she had recovered a little, the Director showed her the envelopes.

'We need to know what Ichiro has written, please, Satumi. The names are clear enough but as you see there are notes as well.'

Before writing anything down, Satumi picked up the addressed envelopes one by one and said, 'This one is to his parents, Dr Kentaro and Mrs Fujiwara, care of Donna Beauchamp, 1299 Kensington Avenue, London, Ontario, and this one is to a Dr Hamish McLeod. And sorry, there's no proper address, just a note that he once was in Como, Italy but he might have moved.' Satumi sniffed, and blinked away some tears. 'This last one is for his young brother Hiro, also at

Donna Beauchamp's address, and there's some Kanji that says, "To go with the birthday present."'

The Director thanked Satumi and offered her some more tea. 'Stay a while and recover from the shock you've had. I will put a call through to Dr Fujiwara at once. He speaks English I believe, but I'll call you if I have a problem with translation if that's all right.' He walked through to a neighbouring room to deal with imparting the sad news alone.

When Yuki got a call from Kentaro, she was still in bed. She barely recognised his faltering voice, and could not believe what he was saying. 'Yuki my pet, I have just heard terrible … terrible … news from Berlin. About Ichiro – Ichiro's … dead.'

'Ichiro? Kentaro, don't, don't, don't …' Her voice got louder with every anguished cry. 'Don't', she screamed. Then sobbed out the words, 'What … happened?'

His voice was like the sting of his hand on her cheek: 'Yuki, listen to me! Are you listening?'

'Yes,' she said, faintly.

'Good. They think he, oh Yuki, they think … that … he drowned himself.' She heard him breathe deeply to gain self-control. She could barely stay the distance, but his voice came again, more clearly, 'He's left what the Director thinks are … are suicide notes. One to you and me, one to Hamish McLeod and one to Hiro. I'm coming, coming to be with you and Hiro. But listen carefully. The JAL ConFlight to Frankfurt is cancelled. Such a nuisance, but they have another to Heathrow leaving tonight. You and Hiro must fly up to Toronto then Canada ConFlight will get you to Heathrow. We'll pick up a JAL ConFlight together for Berlin. Can you do that, Yuki? Oh, dear pet. This is so very terrible.'

'Of course, we can do that. I want to get moving all ready!'

'And I nearly forgot. It's Hiro's birthday. Did he … did he like our present?'

'Yes.' She was already impatient to pack. Do something.

She wanted to get to Berlin, see Ichiro for herself. 'Hiro and I will leave for the UK today, if at all possible.'

'Right. Tell you what, I'll book a room at the Renaissance Hotel. It's close enough to Heathrow – there's a shuttle – Hotel Hopper they call it if I remember right. Renaissance. I'll be there before you.'

'We'll fly to Berlin soon after we get there, won't we?'

'As soon as we possibly can. I'll have all the reservations made. Yuki, be brave. Please be brave.'

She lay down on her bed and cried out her disbelief. Called, 'Ichiro, Ichiro, why, why, why?' That his sudden death was somehow the special gift to Hiro, came to her like the thrust of a sword through her chest. 'Oh, no! No!' she screamed, doubling over with pain.

'Mum, what's wrong?'

She sat up slowly. Took a long time to dry her eyes. Then she said, 'Come and listen to me, Hiro. Daddy has just rung to tell me and you something very, very sad.' She blew her nose and wiped her eyes some more.

'What, Mummy?'

'He said that Ichiro is dead.'

'Oh, Mummy.' He threw his arms about her neck and whispered, 'I came to tell you that.' He let her go, studied her face. She looked long and hard at her son. Blinked her eyes in amazement. Wiped them again. The child that stood before her was calm. All the anger that had clouded his face almost since the day he was born, was gone. For a moment she wanted to say, Jiro? My darling Jiro? What is it? Instead, she ran her fingers around his face and said, 'Hiro, what are you saying?'

'Mummy, I knew that Ichiro had died. He came into my room to tell me. He said, 'Happy birthday.'

'Into your room? But he is …'

'He said that he had to go away to be with Jiro.'

'With Jiro?'

'And they will help me.'

Yuki was near to fainting, yet there was a feeling of strange excitement flooding through her, keeping her buoyant and hopeful. 'Hiro. Please play your violin to me. Play me some sad music. Play the Mendelssohn slow movement, please.'

The young boy ran to get his violin, and came back with it in one hand and his bow in the other. He was smiling and happy. He stood as far from the bed as he could, framed in the doorway. Yuki fell back on to her pillow and closed her eyes.

The strong, poignant melody came with an unbelievable serenity; the breeze rippled through the trees. She was back in Matsumoto, walking through the castle grounds, pink blossom fluttering to the lawn below. She felt the loss of spring as the heat of a summer sun warmed her face. Then with her head held high, she mounted the worn wooden steps of the castle to look from the highest window and open wide her arms to the day. And to the new season that would warm her heart, and melt her sadness.

Part Four
Chapter 14

'Two letters?'

'Yes, I received a hand-written letter to-day from Ichiro, and a voice-mail message that told me what Ichiro had done after writing the letter. It had been re-addressed. I can barely tell you, it is so terrible.' Hamish had struggled through the evening meal and kept a brave face for the sake of Rose. Now, alone with himself, and before his wife the truth confronted him. He had to face it.

'Well?' Terri had already undressed. The oranges were there on the bed-side table but his life had been sapped, his cheeks were drained of colour. He sat fully clothed on the side of the bed and took out the letter and looked at it. On to the page fell unchecked tears. Quietly Terri said, 'Tell me Hamish, tell me.'

'Och! I have been so stupid. The poor lad.'

'Well, can you go and see him. You sent an e-message, didn't you?'

'Too late. It was too late. It didn't reach him.' He looked straight at his wife for the first time in this conversation, and said, 'Ichiro killed himself.'

Terri gasped. 'But what has that got to do with you?'

Hamish began to pace around the bedroom, his voice coming in short bursts. 'Ichiro was a thinker. DNA from his finger to find out why he was so clever? Bullshit! And he knew it. I did not like myself for deceiving him. Anything but. Ichiro was sensitive and smart. His parents and I, all of us together, he had us sussed. We stole from him. Took away his choice. Used him. Raped him of his integrity!' He sat hard down on the bed again and looked into the distressed eyes of his wife. 'Why could I not see it? I didn't stop long enough, that's why. In my heart I knew, but kept avoiding the issue. I was too busy courting fame. Can you see me? On the steps of the birthing unit after Rose was born? Pleased with myself – smiling for all those cameras. I was it. It!' He put his hands to his head, covering his eyes. 'What a record. Mary gone. The three little boys. All dead. Giano's high hopes dashed – his self-esteem trashed yet again. No wonder he threatened me. I deserved to die. Not Ichiro. He was so endowed with talent, a beautiful young man.'

Terri got out of bed and went to him. She held him strongly about his shoulders.

'You were responding to human need. You never intended to hurt, only to heal. As you said to Rose, you were co-creating with God.' She could say nothing more. Hamish too, was silent, unmoving. They were together like this for some time, then Hamish slid down on to his knees and knelt beside the bed, his head in his hands.

'I need to think this through with God, Terri,' she heard him say.